GOODNIGHT, SINNERS

Sinner's Empire Book 3

NIKITA SLATER

AUTHOR'S NOTE

Dear readers,

Thank you for purchasing Goodnight, Sinners. This is the third and final book in the Sinner's Empire trilogy, following Sin of Silence and A Silent Reckoning. If you haven't read the first two books, you will want to go back and start with them before continuing with Goodnight, Sinners. Each book must be read in order for the full reading experience.

Goodnight, Sinners immediately follows the events of A Silent Reckoning. This book will continue the pattern of the first two bookss, with all sign language conversation taking place in italics. This book is a work of fiction and while some aspects will seem realistic, this book was written from the author's imagination. I am not an expert in sign language, medicine, mercenary work, mafia, geography, or any other subject written into the book. I do research the subjects and themes within my books and try to write as realistically as possible, but this book should not be taken as an accurate representation on any of the above subjects. Having said that, it is important to me, as an author, to shed light on experiences that are not necessarily mainstream in romance writing. I hope that you enjoy my diverse characters and the situations I thrust them into.

Please note, some of the scenes in this book contains elements of PTSD and panic attacks, which can be distressing for some readers. Please read with caution. I hope you enjoy Goodnight, Sinners, the third book in my Sinner's Empire Series.

Thank you,
Nikita Slater

CHAPTER ONE

An explosion shook the building.

Though they'd fought their own personal battle, the war still raged on the floors below them.

Shaun tried to blink the dust away, then realized it was catching in her eyelashes. Drywall, plaster and pulverized stone were floating in the air, coating everything around them.

"Jozef," she croaked, rubbing her eyes. "We have to go."

He was sitting next to his uncle's body, a look of shell-shocked despair on his face.

He looked at her, and for a moment she doubted he recognized her.

"We have to go," she urged again.

He shook his head and a cloud of dust lifted from his hair. His expression hardened as he gave a quick, decisive nod. He pushed to his feet and signed at her as he strode to her side.

She blinked again, trying to clear her vision enough to see what he was saying.

"No," she said, moving away from his reaching hands. "I'm not going back into the safe room again."

He growled and moved toward her, his intent clear.

"I'm going with you," she said stubbornly. "I've worked in battle zones. You have to trust that I can do this. I know how to stay out of the way and let the soldiers work. I just want to help."

When he still looked indecisive, she snapped, "My mother could be bleeding out on the floor somewhere in this building. You're taking me with you."

He gave a curt nod and signed, *you stay behind me and listen to every word I say.*

"Yes, I will."

Jozef grabbed a bulletproof vest from a hidden cubby behind the TV and thrust it over Shaun's head, securing the straps against her sides. It felt strangely heavy, but it also gave her a feeling of security.

When he released her, Shaun rushed to grab the First Aid kit they kept in the washroom. It was fully equipped with everything a field medic might need. It would be good enough until they could transfer the injured to a hospital.

She threw on a sweater, zipping it up the front and wincing as the wound on her wrist gave a jolt of pain. It was strange to think that Dasha had attacked her a few hours earlier. Considering everything that had happened, it felt like days or weeks.

She strode back into the living room in time to see Jozef strap a truly astonishing amount of weaponry to his body.

"Is that a rocket launcher?" she asked when he slung a huge pipe-looking object across his back.

He nodded grimly and reached for her hand, dragging her forward.

You stay behind me and if I tell you to run, you run. You find the nearest safe room and lock yourself inside, understand?

Nodding, her serious gaze met his.

She read agony there, but he was doing his best to bury it.

Touching his cheek, she tipped her face up to press her lips against his.

He wrapped an arm around her waist and dragged her in for an earth-shattering kiss that lasted only seconds.

"I love you," she whispered, before he set her away from him.

He nodded in return, pulling his gun and holding it low at his side.

They'd barely cleared the apartment door when they found their first victim, the guard Jozef had stationed outside the door. At a glance Shaun knew he was dead. His bullet wounds had stopped bleeding and his eyes were open and glassy.

Still, she dropped to her knee beside him and checked his pulse. She shook her head, stood and took Jozef's proffered hand. They took off down the hall again, jogging while Jozef covered them.

She knew Jozef should have both hands free in case they were attacked, but the warm reassuring squeeze of his hand against hers kept her sane as they searched the building. They came across two more bodies before they made their way to her mother's apartment.

Shaun stood back, tears in her eyes and heart in her throat as Jozef went ahead of her and did a first sweep. He glanced back to where she was standing in the doorway and jerked his head toward the bedroom.

Shoving clothes aside, they reached for the back of the closet. Jozef punched the code into the safe room door panel. When the door opened, Shaun let out a cry of relief and launched herself past Jozef, wrapping her arms around her mother's neck before Fatima fully knew what was happening.

"Oh, my baby!" she exclaimed, gripping Shaun tightly. "Thank god, you're okay. I've been going crazy in here wondering what's been happening. I can't hear a damn thing."

Shaun swiped at tears and glanced back at Jozef, who jerked his head toward the door, showing he was impatient to leave. She understood. He would want to check on his men and the club, round up any last attackers.

"Mom, we have to go," Shaun said gently, unwinding her mother's arms.

"No, you absolutely do not have to go," Fatima snapped, standing to her full not-so-impressive height. "Or if you insist, then I'll be going with you."

"No, mom," Shaun protested, trying not to sound impatient.

Jozef stepped between them and gently took Fatima's face in his hands, then leaned down to kiss her cheek. When he let go, he made sure she was watching when he signed, *you must stay here and stay safe.*

"But my daughter," she protested, waving her hand at Shaun.

She has battle experience. She knows how to provide medical care in combat situations. We're looking for survivors. I promise, I won't let anything happen to her.

She stared at him hard before finally nodding. "You better keep that promise."

They left the room, Shaun's parting words as they closed the door, "We'll be back for you soon."

Jozef locked the door, gripped Shaun's hand and pulled her from the apartment, scouting the hallway before waving her forward. She cringed as she heard gunfire coming from the floor below them.

They checked each apartment, Jozef kicking in two of the doors that were locked. They were all empty except for one.

"Oh my god!" Shaun exclaimed, hand over her mouth.

The door was partially blocked, and they discovered why when Jozef gave the door an extra hard shove.

A dead woman lay face-down on the floor. The back of

her head was such a mess of blood and bone that Shaun didn't bother to check for a pulse.

Jozef rolled her over, and another shock revealed the woman as Giselle, a frequent customer of the club below and the woman who had pined after Jozef. Shaun felt a wave of pity for the woman, erasing any negative feelings she'd had toward Giselle's jealous, petty nature. She'd been too young, too vivacious to die this horribly on the floor of an apartment.

Jozef frowned down at her and glanced around, as if trying to figure out what'd happened. He strode toward the back of the apartment, seconds later making a sound of alarm that had Shaun hurtling toward him.

"Halil," she said softly as she looked around the side of the kitchen island.

The young man was laying sprawled out on the floor, still as death, his eyes closed. There was a small, almost perfect hole in the middle of his forehead, as though his attacker had the opportunity to take aim. His skin was pink, which had Shaun dropping to her knees beside him and checking for a pulse. It was thready, nearly gone.

She looked up at Jozef, a wealth of concern in her eyes. "He's still alive, but he'll die soon if he doesn't get help."

Jozef looked torn, then frustrated. Finally, he jerked his head in a shake. *No*, he signed, *we have to leave him. We have to secure the building.*

"I'll stay with him," she said quickly.

You stay with me. A dead man can't keep you safe.

"But he's not dead!"

He reached down, took her arm and jerked her to her feet. He pulled her over Halil's body and toward the door. Shaun glanced back, tears forming in her eyes. He wouldn't live long, maybe a few more minutes. It was gut-wrenching to leave the young man behind to die alone on the floor after he'd survived a gun battle.

When they reached the stairwell, they took the stairs two at a time, Jozef flying down, his gun raised to eye level and his shoulders hunched. She supposed he was making himself a smaller target and protecting his core as he moved quickly. Shaun ran after him, gripping the railing so she wouldn't fall as she tried to keep up with him.

It wasn't until they reached Jozef's offices that they ran into resistance. One of Krystoff's men was pinned by the elevator, taking fire from an unknown opponent. He was firing back, but it was clear he wasn't hitting anything. The man didn't see them as they came out of the stairwell.

Jozef strode up to the man and just as he turned to see who was behind him, Jozef put a bullet in his head.

Shaun tried to swallow her shocked scream, but a garbled shout slipped from her lips.

Jozef swung an icy gaze toward her, his expression impatient. He wouldn't stand for her judgment when she'd insisted on coming with him.

"I'm fine," she said, rushing to his side. She avoided looking down at the man. There wasn't any point in checking him for a pulse. Jozef was an excellent shot.

Shaun went to step past Jozef, but he blocked her, pushing her back. He reached out and knocked loudly on the wall leading to the main part of the offices. His fist hit the wall in a booming pattern. Morse code, she suspected.

"'Bout fucking time you got here," came an answering shout.

Shaun recognized Havel's deep voice and when her gaze met Jozef's he nodded. They carefully made their way through the maze of desks until they found Jozef's second-in-command.

"Shit," Shaun breathed out, clutching her med kit.

Havel's big body was leaned back against the door to a cage with one arm propped in his lap and a gun clutched in his other. Blood poured from a wound on his shoulder, thick and steady. The pulse point in his throat was beating a rapid tattoo.

Shaun dropped next to him and immediately set about unzipping her medical kit.

"Good thing we kept you alive, eh doc?"

Shaun's head snapped up as she looked at him in disbelief but catching the humour in his eyes realized he was joking with her.

She took a handful of gauze and pressed it against the wound hard enough to make him flinch. "You might not think so by the time I'm done with you."

He barked his laughter, then coughed. She didn't like the gurgling sound he made.

Jozef kept one eye on the hallway as he signed, *I thought you were wearing a vest.*

"Asshole got a lucky shot," Havel grunted. "It went in under my arm. Think it's lodged against a rib somewhere."

I have to secure the club.

"Go." Havel waved his gun. "I'll be fine."

Jozef reached for Shaun, but she lurched back and stared up at Jozef.

He pressed his lips together and shook his head. *You promised you would stay with me. You promised you would listen to every word I say. I'm telling you to move your ass now.*

She signed back, *if I leave, he could die. He doesn't have the strength to keep enough pressure on the bandage.*

"I'm plenty strong, doc," Havel argued, proving his point by flipping his gun into the air, sending it end-over-end before catching it and pointing it.

Shaun couldn't help herself, she laughed, shaking her head.

She quickly sobered. "Please go without me. I'll be safer here than in the club anyway."

Jozef looked torn until Havel said, "I'll take care of her, bro. You know I will."

Finally, Jozef nodded and without a backward glance, ran down the hall.

Havel swiveled his head toward her, his eyes taking on a terrifying glassy sheen. "Now tell me what you wouldn't tell him."

Shaun stood and removed her sweater, exposing her bulletproof vest. She glanced around and, spotting a desk lamp, flipped the 'on' switch and dragged it over to Havel, propping it up beside him so the light shone down at the carpet. Reaching into the medical kit, she pulled out a bottle of disinfectant, and used it to wash her hands and arms, then pulled on a pair of gloves.

"We have to remove your shirt and vest and lay you down," she said briskly, reaching for him.

He grabbed her fingers. "Tell me."

She looked him in the eye and said, "The bullet nicked an artery. You only have a few minutes before you lose consciousness and maybe five more before you die. I have to stop the bleeding."

"Fuck me." He sounded dazed.

"Shirt, now," she snapped, pulling her fingers from his.

She grabbed the scissors from the medical kit and began cutting his shirt away. He grunted in pain but twisted his body to help her, his hand firmly over the wound, keeping pressure on it. It wasn't enough, she could already see blood seeping through the gauze.

She hooked her fingers in the heavy bulletproof vest, releasing the sides and then dragging it over his head.

She helped him lay down, positioning the lamp so it shone directly on the wound.

His eyes rolled up to meet hers as she used the disinfectant on the blade and clamps she'd dug out of the med kit. "If I pass out, you take this gun," he waved it in the air between them, "And you fucking kill anyone who comes down that hall. You understand."

She smiled at him. "If you keep being so nice to me, I'll start to think you like me."

He shouted in pain, then grit his teeth, as she peeled the bandage back and set to work with her scalpel, making the hole large enough that she could manoeuvre inside the wound.

It took her seconds to find the bleeder and a few more seconds to clamp it. By the time she'd finished, her patient had slipped from consciousness, likely a result of blood loss and pain.

She reached across his prone body and picked up the gun which had landed next to him on the now bloody carpet. She lifted it in one hand and pointed it toward the hallway, her other hand on his neck, keeping tabs on the steady rhythmic beat of his heart.

CHAPTER TWO

Two weeks later

Jozef took a deep breath, closing his eyes for a second, pushing his emotions into a tidy box to set aside for the foreseeable future. He wasn't ready for this day. Hadn't been ready a week ago when he made arrangements and definitely wasn't ready now. What he wanted didn't matter. His life had been one of duty up to this point, and his duties had only increased with the death of his uncle.

Jozef strode around the limousine. Before he could open Shaun's door, she opened it herself. He thrust a hand toward her, squeezing her slim fingers tighter than normal in his annoyance. He'd told her to stay put until he had a moment to assess their surroundings. Shaun's thoughts had been so scattered since the night of the attack, he doubted she remembered what he told her.

He didn't blame her. His thoughts might have been scattered as well over the past few weeks, except he'd had to show fortitude as he managed damage control in his club, took over the entire Koba organization and took his place as a top Vor within the Bratva.

In the two weeks following Krystoff's death, Jozef had done more for his reputation, holdings and standing within the Bratva, than he'd done in the past several years. Everything hinged on the death of his uncle.

He involuntarily squeezed Shaun's fingers too hard again, and she looked at him. There was no censure in her eyes, only shock and grief. The same look that had been there since that night in their apartment when everything had gone to hell. The look hadn't abated and Jozef didn't have time to deal with it.

His fiancé was traumatized once more, and he didn't have time to be there for her. The situation made him want to howl at the unfairness, but he had to hold his shit together. Not only were people depending on him, but a loss of control at this crucial point would be very dangerous.

The Bratva would replace him in a heartbeat if they thought he couldn't manage the Koba organization, Prague, and the surrounding territories.

"Are you okay?" Shaun whispered, her gaze roving over his face and down his body. "You look great."

For a split second there was a sparkle to her golden eyes. It released the tight knot in his chest. This was one reason he loved Shaun. She was intuitive, knew what to say, and could look past her own trauma to help others.

Jozef gave her a grim smile and tilted his head toward her. He released her hand so he could sign, *I would love to say the same, but truthfully, I despise that colour on you. You are too beautiful to wear black. You should be draped in colour.*

Her lips tilted up. Not quite a smile, but the closest thing she'd managed in two weeks. She signed back, *that's the sweetest insult I've ever received.*

Jozef chuckled and gathered her against his chest, kissing her lips. He held her tightly, holding her head to his, her chest to his, her hips to his. He loved feeling her body against his. It grounded him while chaos surrounded them.

She was wearing black heels, a slim fitting black dress and a knee-length black coat. She was bundled for the cool December weather, but looked sophisticated and beautiful. Her heels made her almost the same height as Jozef.

He stepped away from her and linked their hands, guiding Shaun forward. Havel fell into step behind them, while the rest of Jozef's men followed. Havel had talked to Shaun in the vehicle about what to expect. Jozef wasn't worried, Shaun was the epitome of grace and poise. She did well under pressure, despite her panic attacks, which had returned.

"Shaun, Jozef." Fatima joined them from a separate escort.

The night of the attack, Terek had made the life-saving decision to hustle her into her panic room rather than try to sneak her out of the building. As a result, Fatima hadn't seen even a moment's action. Jozef had given the man a sizeable bonus for saving the life of his mother-in-law.

Fatima was dressed in black as well, her somber golden eyes searching Jozef's face. He wasn't sure what she was looking for, but something in her expression softened and she gave him a weak smile.

Fatima took Shaun's other hand.

Jozef followed the path through the cemetery until he reached his family plot. The Koba mausoleum was in a secluded part of the cemetery, surrounded by trees. The grass was cut short around the large stone, white-washed building, and there were flowers in the holders by the door.

Most of those invited to attend had already arrived. Jozef nodded at Klaus, an old friend to both Krystoff and Jozef. His gaze was unyielding, angry. He might understand the transfer of power and how it came about, but he wasn't happy with the situation. Jozef would have to schedule a meeting.

Jozef's gaze followed the line of men, his gaze meeting

Alexei Ivanov's. Jozef schooled his features so as not to give away his surprise at seeing a senior member of the Russian Bratva at his uncle's funeral. Of course, Krystoff had been connected, and so now was Jozef, but the Bratva rarely traveled into unsettled situations.

Standing next to Alexei was Yuri Antonovich, gatekeeper to the Bratva. The man acted as both a Vory and a secretary. He was cold-blooded and brutal. He would kill his own mother if it meant getting ahead. If he made Jozef's accession within the Bratva difficult, Jozef could have a rocky few years ahead of him.

Yuri's steady gaze met Jozef's and, after a prolonged moment where neither man looked away, Yuri finally nodded his head. Jozef returned the nod. Yuri turned to his man and said something. The two were standing a short distance away. Jozef couldn't hear them, but he would bet his newly acquired fortune Yuri was asking his man to arrange a meeting.

Havel pulled the door of the mausoleum open for the immediate family to pass through. The rest of the mourners would remain outside until the family had finished.

Jozef stopped for a moment to pay his respects to his parents, whose names were etched onto two marble plaques and set in the wall: Analise Koba and Gregor Koba.

Shaun squeezed his arm and stood quietly beside him, her gaze on the beautifully carved marble.

Jozef moved past his parents' plaques to stand next to his uncle's urn. It was large, almost the size of one of his aunt's great vases, made of white marble and inlaid with gold. It was resting on top of a white stone pedestal and would remain until after the ceremony when they would place it in the wall with the plaque affixed afterward.

The service was short and standard, without fanfare. Though top mob bosses often had lavish funerals with many mourners, it wasn't in Krystoff's nature to seek the extra attention. He had been a reserved man.

Without Aunt Dasha, Leeza or Saskia in attendance, it hadn't seemed right to give Krystoff more than a basic ceremony. Jozef hadn't wanted to plan anything for the man he'd killed, but he'd had to do something. Show his respect.

It wasn't uncommon for the mantle of a mafia family to pass down to the heir through bloodshed. It didn't make taking over an organization from someone Jozef loved any easier.

He'd had no luck in locating any of his female family members. He had to admit that they were craftier than he'd given them credit for. His job had always been to protect them; he hadn't spent enough time with them as individuals to see their strengths.

He believed, given reports from the hospital, that Leeza had rescued her mother before fleeing the city. It hammered one more nail in her coffin. Had Leeza been willing to simply disappear, Jozef might have let her go. Told the Bratva she'd been quietly executed and buried in a forest somewhere. Now that he was certain she was aiding the woman responsible for the downfall of the Koba organization, Jozef would have no choice but to put her down. Swiftly and without mercy.

It grieved him that the cousins he'd grown up with, that he'd spent a lifetime protecting, were now his targets, but he would do what was necessary. He would do his duty.

He had no plans to kill Saskia, but he needed her located and brought back into the fold. She was a loose cannon on the outside. She was highly intelligent, but she was also erratic and unpredictable.

Shaun slid her arm through his and looked at him expectantly.

Jozef blinked and glanced around. The service had

finished, and the mausoleum was opened to the other mourners.

Jozef accepted the well wishes of those gathered as they filed through. Shaun spoke soft words of condolences, while Jozef shook hands. Finally, once everyone left, Jozef took a moment to say one last goodbye to the man who had been a father to him. He allowed himself to feel everything he'd been holding in for two weeks. The grief was nearly overwhelming.

Shaun clasped his hand tightly as he blinked back tears. Together they turned and left the cemetery, following the procession back to the mansion for a brief reception.

Dasha waited until the cemetery was empty. Jozef's men were stationed all over the grounds in anticipation of either her or the girls showing up. Dasha wasn't stupid enough to actually attend her husband's funeral, but she couldn't leave without saying goodbye.

She waited until evening fell, then wound her way through the trees until she had the Koba mausoleum in her line of sight.

It was a risk. Jozef might still be on the lookout for her. She didn't care. She would rather court death than leave without one last word with her husband. She rushed down the hill and through the doors of the mausoleum, slamming them shut behind her.

Dasha walked slowly to the plaque on the wall that had her husband's name etched into it. She touched it with her fingertips, tracing each beloved letter. It seemed impossible that two weeks ago he was living, breathing, making love to her. Now he was ash.

She banged her fist on the plaque, wishing she'd thought to bring a chisel or something to pry it off the wall. She wanted Krystoff's ashes. They belonged to her, not to the cold, dark box that held them hostage.

She turned her back to the wall, pressing herself against the cold marble before sliding to the ground in a heap. Her arm twinged painfully in its sling beneath her jacket.

For the first time since learning of Krystoff's death, she allowed the tears to fall. They rained freely down her face, dripping onto her chest. She didn't know how long she sat and cried for, but it surprised her.

She didn't cry. Ever.

She'd spent years hating this man until the day she realized she didn't. She'd fallen in love with her mobster husband, but Dasha hadn't realized quite how much she loved him and depended on him until now. Her life had been a series of events that were out of her control. In order to regain that control, she'd learned the art of manipulation, which often meant putting her feelings on the back burner as she fought her way to the top.

She'd loved Jozef's parents.

Gregor Koba had been just like Krystoff. Big, bearded, jovial, but also chillingly brutal. Annalise Koba had been beautiful. Like Jozef, she'd been tall, slim, graceful. And like the rest of the family, she had also been brutal.

Dasha hadn't known if they were plotting against the Koba patriarch, but she wasn't willing to wait and find out. She'd preemptively done what her husband hadn't been able to do. She'd eliminated the potential threat to their organization.

All for nothing. The organization had fallen into the hands of the son, despite all of Dasha's machinations. She should've eliminated the child when she'd had the chance, but when she stood over him, gripping the knife that should have ended his life, she'd been unable to bring herself to do more than destroy his voice. He'd retaliated by pulling the knife out and stabbing the man who'd been holding him, killing her accomplice.

"You should have been stronger," she sobbed to her dead husband. "You should have taken care of the boy for me. You were weak, and you allowed your heart to get in the way of what you knew you had to do. Now we're all dead."

....

CHAPTER THREE

....

S haun hated everything about the mansion. It had never been her favourite place, but today, the heavy opulence made her want to scream. Then again, everything made her want to scream. She was barely keeping her shit together, and the only reason she appeared to be calm was because she knew Jozef needed her to project a united front for the guests.

She understood the importance of the occasion, the funeral and the reception. They were living in a volatile and dangerous situation. Until Jozef brought his uncle's organization completely under his control, the threat of enemies could and would haunt them.

When he'd told her of the importance of the funeral, Shaun had decided she could pull her shit together until they got home. She could do it for Jozef. He was the one who'd experienced the loss of his family, not her. Yet, it hit her like a ton of bricks and settled on her shoulders as a colossal weight.

Jozef had moved them into the Koba estate the day following Krystoff's death. She'd balked, but he'd insisted it was the only thing they could do. He had to project a front of complete control. He was expected to take the seat of power along with all the Koba assets.

He'd stripped the master suite and had their bed brought in. It turned Shaun's stomach that she was sleeping in the same room where Krystoff and Dasha had slept only days earlier. Nightmares plagued Shaun, keeping her awake at night and turning her into a zombie during the day.

It wasn't like when she worked an extra-long shift at the hospital. She understood long hours. She hated them, but she was prepared to put them in when she was working.

But the nightmares... they sapped her strength and stole her ability to concentrate. She wanted to be strong, to engage, to be there for Jozef when he needed her most.

Instead, she watched helplessly as her topsy-turvy life became even more unrecognizable. She might have broken down completely, if not for Jozef's constant vigilance. Despite having an enormous weight dropped on him, he spent nearly every waking moment with Shaun, his beautiful eyes concerned as they searched her for answers. He kept her close at all times, including during business meetings. She sat with him in Krystoff's study while a procession of men came and went, reporting, begging for a job, begging for their lives.

It was a rare glimpse into Jozef's mafia dealings, and it both fascinated and frightened her. At first, she'd listen closely, waiting for Jozef's contacts to leave before asking Jozef the questions that piled up in her head. She'd always imagined mafia to be so sinister and had seen a lot to confirm these thoughts over the past few years. Yet, the inner day-to-day workings were very much like a business and Jozef was proving himself, at least in her eyes, to be a master businessman.

After a few days, the conversations became repetitive.

She'd stopped listening, instead choosing to pick up a book and curl into a chair by the fire.

When he finished his meetings, Jozef would take her hand and lead her to the private dining room to eat. She hadn't known that room existed until Jozef showed her. She'd always eaten with the family in the formal dining room.

The smaller room was set off the kitchen, making it easier for the staff to bring their meals. It had become Jozef's habit to eat off Shaun's plate before allowing her to eat. He said until they found his aunt, there was still a risk for Shaun.

Shaun couldn't move without a contingent of armed men shadowing her steps. After Dasha's attack in the restaurant, Shaun appreciated the vigilance. She couldn't close her eyes without reliving those moments, both in the bathroom and in the car, when Karl, her bodyguard, had died. Then, later, the apartment, the bodies, her inability to save them all, knowing that her fiancé had been responsible for killing some of them.

Shaun went daily to visit her mother, who'd decided not to move to the mansion. Shaun wanted her mother close but understood why Fatima would want her own space. As much as she loved her daughter, she was an independent woman.

Fatima had taken Karl's death particularly badly. She'd insisted on handling all funeral arrangements, which Jozef had been happy to give up, after handing off a list of guests who would want to attend the wake. It was a pitifully short list; Karl's sister, a few friends and Jozef's men. Karl was well-liked, but his entire life had revolved around the Koba family. He had lived and breathed their security until the day he died in the line of duty.

The painful memory of Karl's small but warm funeral brought fresh tears to Shaun's eyes. She hadn't known him well, but he'd been kind to her and she respected him.

"You okay?"

Shaun looked over as Havel stopped next to her.

Havel had warmed to her considerably after she'd patched his wound on the floor of the Guard Dog Securities office. He'd woken up minutes before Jozef had come back to collect Shaun. Havel had taken the gun from her and taken over protecting both of them. Neither had told Jozef about those few moments when Havel had been unconscious. Shaun didn't think Jozef would blame his second-in-command, but it seemed important to Havel to be in control of himself at all times.

After Jozef had come back, he'd asked her to go with him to the club where more of his men were injured. Jozef shadowed her every step as she worked on those in need. Two more of Jozef's men had been shot, one wound serious, the other superficial. She worked on the seriously wounded man first, then moved on to the wounded who weren't Jozef's men. Jozef stood over her with a gun trained on the men as she worked to patch them up.

It was like being in a war zone again, and many of the images she saw that day were seared into her memory. They featured heavily in her nightmares.

She shook the memories away and turned to Havel, who was looking down at her with concern. He was wearing a black suit and tie, his arm sitting in a sling. He hadn't been wearing it earlier when they'd been in the graveyard. He'd said he didn't want his movement obstructed if he had to act quickly.

"I'm okay," she told him.

It was a lie, and they both knew it. Havel didn't call her out for it, though. He nodded and continued to stand sentinel next to her until Jozef could make his way back to her. Havel wasn't okay either. He hovered around her and Jozef and looked haunted, even though he tried to suppress the emotions.

It helped to have him near. It was like having Karl again.

She felt less lonely, less lost in a world she didn't understand. A world that swallowed people up and either turned them into killers or captives.

Which was she now? Killer or captive?

The air seemed to go out of the room and Shaun searched desperately for Jozef. He was standing with the two Bratva men Havel had pointed out to her. He was nodding his head, but his face was unreadable. She couldn't tell if he was happy, sad, angry.

She hated when Jozef became blank to her.

A cold sweat broke out across her body. She shivered and wrapped her arms around herself. It didn't help. The squeezing in her chest continued, suffocating her until she thought she would scream.

A warm hand touched her back, causing her to jump. She looked at Havel, unable to hide her vulnerability. She hated him seeing her this way. He'd been the one who'd wanted her to die all those months ago when they first met. He had rightfully pointed out that she didn't belong in their world, and now here she was, proving his point.

"Breathe," he told her.

She nodded, unable to speak, and turned her mind to her breathing exercises. As she sucked in air through her nose, releasing it through her mouth, she practiced her therapist's mental exercises. She pictured a filing cabinet in her mind. Reaching in, she opened a file and carefully placed her fear and all the terrible memories inside. She closed the file and replaced it in the cabinet. She closed the drawer and locked it, sealing her fear away. It wouldn't stay there forever. She would pull it out and examine it when she was ready to deal with the trauma surrounding the emotion, but for now, anxiety and fear wouldn't serve her well.

When Jozef approached, the two Bratva men following him, Shaun was breathing normally again and able to give him a tight smile. Havel's hand fell away from her back before Jozef could see him touching her. It was an innocent touch. Shaun knew Havel had no designs on her, but Jozef didn't like any of his men touching her unless there was a good reason.

Jozef took her hand and lifted it to his lips, kissing her fingers, before letting go.

Come with me, he signed, then added, *both of you*, looking at Havel. *We have a meeting to attend.*

"I'll say goodbye to my mother first." Shaun held her breath as she realized she should have made it a question instead of a comment. Havel and Jozef had warned her she needed to play submissive around the men of the Bratva.

Of course, Jozef signed. *I'll go with you.*

They left the two men with Havel and made their way toward Fatima, who was sitting on the couch with a woman who was sobbing. Shaun didn't recognize the woman, but she seemed genuinely distraught by Krystoff's death. Judging by the size of the reception, Krystoff had been a well-liked, well-respected man.

Fatima was handing the woman a tissue, looking up as Jozef and Shaun arrived by her side.

"Shaun, Jozef, this is Cece Mountbatten. She had gone to school with Krystoff and kept in touch with him over the years."

"I'm so sorry for your loss," Shaun said, reaching a hand out to the woman.

Cece narrowed her eyes and slid along the couch, further away from Shaun. "You," she said scathingly. "This is all your fault. I talked to Dasha a few months ago. I know everything."

Jozef was quick to tuck Shaun against his side and drop his hand beneath his jacket where his holster lay. He narrowed his eyes at the woman, silently telling her to back off.

"Where is your aunt?" she asked Jozef. "Did you have her killed too?"

Jozef's body tightened, but Shaun was quicker. She took a step in front of Jozef.

"You'll want to control yourself, Ms. Mountbatten." Shaun's voice was chilly. "If you knew Dasha and Krystoff the way you say, then you know that this is the wrong room and the wrong group of people to throw accusations around."

Shaun lifted her gaze to the two Bratva men and the woman followed her line of sight. It was clear she either knew who they were or understood the implication behind Shaun's words.

Fatima pushed herself off the couch and stood to Jozef's other side. "You are welcome to mourn, but you won't be insulting this family while you're enjoying their hospitality."

"I..." she stared at the trio in front of her. "My apologies, I'm simply distraught over what happened. If you'll excuse me."

The woman stood and quickly left the room.

Once she was gone, Shaun deflated. Defending Jozef had come easily to her, but the energy it took after so many sleepless nights was almost more than she could handle.

"Do you think she's going to be a problem?" Fatima asked anxiously. "I saw her crying and thought no one should have to cry alone. I shouldn't have spoken to her."

Jozef shook his head. *You should speak with whoever you want. C-E-C-E won't be a problem. She knew my aunt and uncle a long time ago, but she has no power to make a nuisance of herself now.*

"We're going to a meeting," Shaun told her mother, remembering the reason they'd come over. "Will you be alright alone?"

"If you don't need me anymore, I think I'll go home." She hugged each of them and waved to her new bodyguard, heading toward the man.

"Thank you for assigning someone to her. I think it helps her feel more secure." Shaun watched her mother talk to her bodyguard, smiling at something he said.

Her safety means as much to me as yours, Jozef signed. *Come, it's time for us to find out what the Russians have to say to me.*

CHAPTER FOUR

You'll translate, Jozef told Shaun, leading the procession into his study and closing the door. He took Shaun's arm and led her to the seat she liked in front of the fireplace.

She sank gratefully into the plush leather armchair, wishing she could kick her shoes off and rub her feet. It had been a long day for heels, but she chose them knowing there would be powerful men at the funeral and reception. She felt better, more powerful, with more height. She couldn't afford to look weak around these people, couldn't afford to make Jozef look weak. He'd been preparing her for weeks so she would understand what was at stake. It wasn't just his livelihood, but their lives as well.

Jozef didn't invite the others to sit, so the group of men remained standing. Shaun nearly stood as well, wanting to be on equal footing, but resisted the urge. Jozef placed her in the chair for a reason. She wouldn't question his decision. Not in front of these men, anyway.

While Jozef poured drinks, Shaun studied the two newcomers.

One was named Alexei Ivanov. Jozef had told her the man

was there to assess the level of organization surrounding the Kobas. If it looked like Jozef had the situation well in hand, then he would keep the power he had seized for himself. Alexei could make Jozef's life difficult if he took a less than stellar report back to the rest of the Bratva.

The man wore a beautifully tailored suit. He was tall and robust. He looked to be around fifty, but it was difficult to tell. She looked him over with a professional eye. He'd had work done. Facelift, cheek surgery, chin surgery, lip surgery. She wondered if cosmetic surgery was common to the oligarchs of Russia or if this one was vain.

Shaun glanced away, realizing her bias toward these criminals could be a problem if she continued down the path of her current thoughts. She didn't think cosmetic surgery was inherently wrong. She'd seen gastric bypass surgeries give patients a new lease on life and something as simple as a Botox injection give patients the self-esteem they needed to face the world again.

But there was something about Alexei that rubbed her the wrong way. She just knew he chose his surgeries with the same whim he used to choose his next meal.

She glanced at the other man, Yuri Antonovich. She was curious about him. Both Havel and Jozef had warned her to keep her distance. Neither explained why, but she suspected it had something to do with the cold, slimy eyes slithering down her body and resting on her crossed legs.

She held his stare for several uncomfortable seconds. The heat rose in Shaun's cheeks and she was about to move, just to break his intense look, when Jozef stepped in between them, breaking Yuri's line of sight.

Shaun sighed her relief and accepted the glass of red wine Jozef handed her.

Jozef stood next to Shaun's chair, his hand sliding across the back. He didn't touch her, but his presence warmed the room and chased away any lingering panic she'd been feeling earlier.

"Let's get started," Alexei said, glancing around, probably for a chair. When he failed to come up with one, he leaned his hip against Jozef's desk.

Jozef dipped his head in a nod and straightened. He positioned himself so the men could see him and so Shaun could too for translation. She didn't understand why he wanted her to translate instead of Havel, but she suspected it was so Jozef could project a united front to the Bratva. She was to be his bride and would occupy an important role in his life and organization.

There is nothing to discuss. I will not relinquish my title or holdings to the Bratva. You will recognize my right to ownership, or you will declare war with the Czech Republic.

It was everything Shaun could do not to gape at Jozef. Then it was everything she could do not to question him in front of these men. He'd assured her that these two men spoke for the Bratva and could bury the Koba organization if they judged against Jozef. Did he really want to start off so aggressively?

Apparently, he did.

Shaun dutifully translated.

Alexei laughed. A chilling, disdainful laugh that gave Shaun goosebumps.

"You speak boldly for someone of your position. You are new to the title of Vor, yet you challenge those who are well established. I'm not sure if you are incredibly smart or stupid, but I will warn you to go more carefully with this conversation."

Shaun agreed with Alexei.

Jozef didn't.

You will recognize my claim, or you will leave. If you choose the second option, the next time we meet you will die by my hand.

Alexei straightened from the desk and glared at Jozef. "You shouldn't make threats you could come to regret. The power of the Koba organization may be behind you, but you are in disarray. You couldn't organize a coup if you wanted to, and you certainly couldn't bring it to Moscow."

Are you so sure of that? Do you want to risk everything on that assumption? We are a powerful family with a powerful nation behind us. We have allies in Poland, Ukraine, and beyond who will not hesitate to side with me. Some who are tired of living under the thumb of the Bratva would welcome a war.

Shaun bowed her head as she translated, not wanting to meet the eyes of Alexei as she said the words.

She felt a slight tug on the back of her head and realized Jozef was lightly pulling her hair. He wanted her to project a calm and professional front. They'd already talked about this.

Shaun took a deep breath and straightened her spine, lifting her chin. She didn't meet Alexei's gaze, but she feigned the calm arrogance Jozef always seemed to project with such ease.

"You would make an enemy of Moscow?" Alexei asked incredulously.

"Enough." This came from Yuri, who calmly interjected into the conversation. "Jozef is not threatening. I have known this young man since he was a child, he does not threaten. He will follow through on everything he says, even if it kills him. Am I correct?"

Jozef didn't respond, and Shaun supposed he didn't need to. His actions spoke louder than words. He'd made a name for himself as a mobster and a mercenary.

"We were sent here to welcome you to the Bratva and negotiate terms, not threaten the empire you have rightfully claimed," Yuri continued. He was calm and measured, but there was a coldness to him that Shaun suspected seeped into every aspect of his life. She wondered if she was looking at a true sociopath.

Then let's negotiate, Jozef signed while Shaun spoke for him.

"Twenty-five percent and you will attend all Bratva meetings for five years until we are sure of your loyalty."

Jozef barked his laughter but quickly sobered. *Eight percent and I will attend the annual meetings only.*

Shaun realized Jozef wanted these men to think he intended to treat the Bratva cavalierly, but in reality, she knew he had great respect for the institution and was looking forward to joining the ranks of the Vory. She wondered why he was playing hard to get.

"You will pay twenty percent and you will attend the next five meetings, then annually."

Havel and Alexei stood silently, watching while Jozef and Yuri negotiated. The percentages confused Shaun. She didn't understand what exactly they were negotiating. Her confusion must've shown on her face, because when she glanced up, Havel began signing to her, quickly and out of sight of Alexei and Yuri.

They're negotiating for a portion of Jozef's fortune. He will relinquish the amount they agree on, then he will pay that same percentage of his yearly earnings.

Shaun discreetly nodded and sent Havel a quick smile while she continued to translate. It helped to understand what the men were negotiating for. She didn't know how much money Jozef had inherited from Krystoff, but she suspected it was quite a lot.

Ten percent and annual meetings.

It was Yuri's turn. "Fifteen percent and one visit to Moscow in the next few months, then annual meetings after that."

Twelve percent, Jozef signed.

Yuri's gaze settled on Shaun's face as he thought about it.

Then he nodded, his head bobbing up and down in an exaggerated motion. "Fine, twelve percent and you bring your lovely fiancé to the palace when you visit. You can explain your marriage plans to the council."

Jozef growled, but Shaun reached out to take his hand, squeezing it. He looked down at her. His eyes were glittering with anger. She was the only thing that could set him off like a firework. It didn't matter what anyone said to him, he was always the picture of calm unless she came into the discussion.

Shaun turned a smile on their guest. "I would love to visit Russia. It's always been on my list of places to visit."

Yuri's gaze continued to linger. "You must allow me to show you around the Kremlin while your... fiancé is busy."

Shaun shivered but kept the smile plastered to her face. "Of course, that would be lovely."

Tension vibrated through Jozef and Shaun gripped his hand harder to keep him from flying across the room and strangling the Bratva's secretary. She didn't know what the man was playing at, but she suspected he was deliberately trying to provoke a reaction.

Havel must have sensed the same intention because he stepped forward and said in a jovial voice, "Come, we must celebrate the success of this negotiation with Vodka. We have the best here, imported from your homeland."

CHAPTER FIVE

The soft glow of the lamp caressed Shaun's features, giving her an ethereal appearance. Jozef had been watching her for hours, occasionally picking up a nearby book and reading while she slept. He wouldn't sleep himself until she woke.

Her enormous orange cat, Fitzy, was curled on top of the blankets against the inside of her knees. He was relaxed but alert, his eyes open and shining in the lamplight as he waited. He knew what was coming as well as Jozef did.

Shaun had been experiencing nightmares every night since the attack on the club. Like clockwork, her body would jerk beneath the covers, then she would cry out, until finally she was thrashing and screaming for help.

Jozef stayed awake so he could bring her out of her nightmare before it reached that point. He knew he wasn't getting enough sleep and that it could make his thinking sloppy when he couldn't take a single misstep, but he refused to allow Shaun to suffer. Not even for a few extra seconds.

Watching over her had become an obsession. He watched her constantly through cameras as she drifted restlessly through the mansion. He watched her while she ate and slept. Watched as she tried to navigate a mansion filled with staff. He clocked her every move and worked to help her when she hit an obstacle. She didn't know it, but he'd fired a maid who'd gotten impatient with her and a gardener for snapping at her when she stepped off the stone path winding through the garden.

He knew it would be a long time before Shaun could consider the mansion home, and he would do whatever it took to make her feel more comfortable. If he could, he would burn it to the ground and start over, but the estate was too important to the Koba organization. It was a symbolic seat of power.

Given their past, it amazed Jozef that Shaun wanted to try to make things work with him. But she'd been clear. She was with him willingly now, and she wanted to work on their relationship. It was a far cry from a year earlier when she couldn't see a clear path for their love. It'd taken a lot of sacrifice on her part to get to where they were now.

Jozef owed Shaun everything. She might've been the catalyst that ultimately pulled his family apart, but she also helped him see the reality of his existence. His family had valued him when it was convenient. They'd used him to further their own gains. He'd been the guard dog rather than the loved son he'd always longed to be.

Without Shaun, he wouldn't have questioned Krystoff's orders. He wouldn't have wondered what'd happened to his parents, instead continuing to believe the old story of revenge killing. He still didn't know the whole truth, but now he knew to look past the half-truths and lies.

Before Shaun, his existence had been simple. He'd been a weapon; point and shoot. Now, he was master of his own destiny.

A sigh escaped her lips and he straightened in his chair.

The nightmare was coming. It always started this way, quiet and soft, like a pleasant dream. He'd asked her about it once, but she'd shaken her head and cuddled into his chest so they couldn't sign.

Normally, he would've insisted she talk to him, but he didn't want to push her to the breaking point. She was fragile, vulnerable, and too easily broken. He shoved a hand through his hair and leaned forward in his seat, elbows on his knees as he watched her face.

He wished he could take her away. Give her a few days of peace without the constant pressures of a new and massive household, a mafia empire, and a fiancé with too many demands on his time to give her what she needed. It was a bad time for a vacation, though. The worst. The Bratva, his enemies, his allies, they were watching his every move; waiting for the moment he fucked up so they could pounce. Jozef wouldn't give up his position without a war, which meant he needed to be present, every step he made carefully choreographed.

Then an idea struck him. A very stupid one that he nearly rejected out of hand. He knew a place he could take her. A place he needed to visit anyway. Two days wasn't much. They could get there without anyone on the estate knowing until they were already gone.

Shaun would love it. The area was peaceful.

He shook his head. No, too risky.

A moan slipped from her, and she tried to lift her arm. The blanket trapped it. He carefully lifted the blanket, and she flung her arm out, nearly hitting him. He smiled grimly and gently took her proffered limb, caressing the silky smooth ebony skin.

Fitzy stood, stretched and walked to the end of the bed where he could watch over his mistress from a safe distance.

Shaun's brow wrinkled as though a fly were buzzing

around her head. Except this one was on the inside. Slowly her frown melted into an expression of panic and she opened her mouth to scream.

It was time.

Jozef climbed onto the bed with her, gathering her against his chest. He wrapped one hand around her head and held it against his chest so she could hear his heartbeat as she woke up. It seemed to help calm her.

Shaun was a heavy sleeper, which made waking her up more difficult. Jozef had learned to let her come out of it mostly on her own, with a little help. He would be there to comfort her when she woke up completely.

Her cries grew progressively louder, shattering his heart with each one. It was at these moments that his guilt became nearly overwhelming. He could have left her behind, left her to continue a life of her choosing, rather than dragging her into a family drama that would lead to this moment. To the breakdown of a tough, beautiful and talented woman.

Her cries grew in crescendo until she was screaming, her mouth opening and closing, tears pouring down her cheeks, her eyelids screwed up in terror. He tipped her against his chest and pressed her face to his shirt, allowing her to soak it with her tears.

Finally, he coaxed her awake. He tilted her head, looking down at her as her eyes fluttered open, revealing her bright tear-flooded golden eyes. She blinked up at him until recognition registered in her expression. She gasped and tried to sit up, pushing away from him.

He'd tried to hold her down before, force her to accept his help, but he'd quickly learned that if he held on to her while she was waking from a nightmare, she would become panicked and start thrashing.

She shoved away from him and sat up on the side of the bed, taking big gasping breaths.

Jozef picked up the glass of water he'd refilled after sitting down to watch her. She reached for it and took thirsty gulps until she was calmer.

"I'm sorry," she whispered, handing the glass back.

Once she'd realized they were falling into a pattern, she'd gotten used to accepting his help. She didn't like it though. Didn't like the idea that she was keeping him up, though he'd assured her he was up with work anyway. She always apologized for her night terrors, and it alternately pissed him off and made him want to try harder to protect her.

Once she was fully awake, he pulled her against his chest and she collapsed gratefully against him. He buried his nose in her hair, which was warm from her heavy sleep. It smelled like her special brand of shampoo and the orange blossom body spray she used.

As she lay shuddering and breathing against him, he made the decision. They were going to do it; they were going to take off for a few days. It was a stupid plan and a terrible decision, but he couldn't think of anything else. They needed to get away from the mansion, away from the memories, they needed to sort themselves out and then come back stronger.

After Shaun calmed down, he set her away from him and looked her over. He used the edge of his thumb to wipe away the tears that lingered.

She gave him a shaky smile and signed, *thank you.*

She'd been using sign language when it was just the two of them, especially at night when she woke up from her nightmare. It wrapped them in a special bubble of silence together.

You're still having nightmares.

She nodded, then shrugged. *My counselor says it's normal after a trauma.*

A trauma that I'm responsible for.

She reached for his face, cupping his cheeks. She slowly and deliberately shook her head, then dropped her hands to sign, *you are not responsible for the actions of your family. You did nothing to provoke them. They made the choice to attack us, and they bear all the responsibility.*

Jozef smiled grimly and lifted her hand to kiss the fingers. He didn't argue with her, he couldn't. She was so sure she was right and she needed his support, not his reality. The truth was, he was completely responsible.

Mafia families handled their own. While an individual could bear responsibility for his or her own actions, the head of the family bore the most responsibility. When Dasha attacked Shaun at the restaurant, it was up to Krystoff to respond to her infraction. Krystoff had made the choice to attack Jozef and had died in the attack, making Jozef head of the family. Jozef now bore responsibility for everything that'd happened.

Shaun lived in a world of black and white fairness. Either a thing was fair or it was not. Jozef didn't have the luxury of living in her world.

I want to take you away for a few days. We'll go to a cabin in the woods. No bodyguards, no worries.

Her face lit up and when she signed back, her words were so jumbled it took him a moment to realize what she was saying. *Really? Can we really? What about security? What about your enemies?*

Jozef chuckled and squeezed the tips of her fingers as her hand flew past him while she was wildly signing.

Leave it to me. We'll slip away before anyone can notice. I'll let H-A-V-E-L know once we're on the road.

Is it dangerous? she asked, but the excitement remained bright in her eyes.

Jozef thought about it. He had an ulterior motive for taking her away. He'd needed to visit this cabin for a while but had put it off. Was now really the right time for this meeting? He shouldn't be taking Shaun with him, but she needed to get away, and he needed to make the trip.

Her excitement tipped him over the edge and he shook his head. *It's not dangerous, but even if it were, I'd be there to protect you.*

She grinned at him. *Can we go now?*

Jozef was about to tell her no, then he thought about it. Why not? If they decided to go and then just went, his people would be none the wiser until they were well away from the area. Leaving in the darkness of night with no one knowing was the safest way to go.

He grinned back at her. *Let's do it.*

Her eyes widened and she threw her arms around his neck, squeezing. His heart jumped at the contact and he hesitated for a second before wrapping his arms around her and hugging her back.

They hadn't had sex in weeks. Not since the attack. Jozef had been busy with work and Shaun was too traumatized. Or so he assumed. He didn't want to push her and hadn't initiated any sexual contact. Shaun hadn't either.

He was feeling the strain, though. When she was near, or when her scent lingered around him, he would get an uncomfortable erection that didn't go away until he either took a cold shower or thought about something deeply unsexy for a prolonged period of time.

Maybe some time away from the mansion could reboot their sex life too.

Shaun shoved away from Jozef and headed to her closet. "What should I bring?"

When she looked back at him, he signed, *bring warm clothes, enough for two or three days. We'll be deep in the woods. We'll need to hike part of the way in.*

She grinned and nodded, before going into the closet and coming out with a suitcase that was much bigger than what

Jozef had imagined she would need. He watched in amusement as she filled it with every unnecessary thing she would never need in the place he was taking her. He barked with laughter when she folded an evening gown into the case.

She laughed as well, but defended herself, "What if we go out for a fancy dinner? You bought me a closet full of clothes and I plan on using them."

CHAPTER SIX

They snuck out of the mansion like two teenagers creeping around under the cover of darkness. Jozef carried their bags down to his Bugatti and packed them in the trunk, then came back for Shaun. She giggled when a night guard was passing through the halls and Jozef shoved her into an alcove, his hand over her mouth.

Of course, the guard saw them. He moved along quickly though, his expression blank. It wasn't up to him to have an opinion about what Shaun and Jozef got up to. If their kink was creeping around the mansion and making out in alcoves, that was nobody's business but theirs.

Jozef held a finger up to her lips. Shaun crossed her eyes and licked his finger.

Jozef chuckled and pulled her out of the darkened corner. Together they ran down the stairs and headed for the garage. There was another night guard who looked startled when they streaked by him.

"Mr. Koba, Dr. Patterson!" he called after them. "Do you need assistance?"

Shaun spoke for both of them. "No, thanks!" she yelled

over her shoulder. "We're just checking on something. No need to come with us. Have a great night!"

Jozef whisked her into the garage before the guard could say anything else. Shaun was laughing hysterically by the time they were buckled into their seats. He revved the engine like a racecar driver as the garage door lifted, then shot forward as soon as he could, taking the curves of the driveway with a roar of his engine.

They approached the guardhouse at the gate. Jozef gave his men a sign that he wanted the gates opened. They tried to talk to him, but he refused to open the window, making the sign again. Finally, they had no choice but to open the gate.

As they raced toward the highway, stars and streets streaking past them, Shaun let out a whoop of joy. "Freedom!"

Jozef grinned at her and floored the Bugatti when they reached the highway.

"We need music," she announced, reaching for the stereo.

Before she could choose a track, the mechanical voice of an incoming text came through the speaker.

Where the fuck do you think you're going? The text belonged to Havel.

Shaun slapped a hand over her mouth to cover her laughter. Poor Havel. Since Shaun had come into Jozef's life, Havel's had become dramatically more difficult.

Jozef reached out to text back, but Shaun slapped his hand away. "I'll do it, you keep your hands on the wheel."

She typed into the dash, **we're fine. Going on vacation for a few days. No need to come after us.**

Tell Jozef to turn around now. We need to talk before you take this so-called vacation.

Shaun and Jozef both laughed and Jozef shook his head. Havel had quickly deduced he was talking to Shaun. She supposed everyone had a particular texting style but was impressed with Havel's ability to tell who was texting him in the middle of the night when he'd likely been woken from a sound sleep.

Shaun texted: **Take care of yourself. We'll be back soon!**

She blocked any more text messages from coming through, chose a playlist from Jozef's phone that seemed fitting for a road trip and relaxed into her seat.

Just leaving the mansion and grounds lifted her spirits enormously. She finally felt good about something. She would call her mother in the morning and explain, in case anyone mentioned Shaun and Jozef's wild escape to her. Shaun knew her mother would understand and probably encourage them.

Shaun and Jozef had known each other for a year and a half, yet they hadn't established any kind of normal. It was time to take back their lives, even if it was only for a few days.

After a few hours, Shaun fell asleep, curled on her side on her reclined seat. She'd offered to drive, but Jozef had given her a horrified look that eloquently spoke to his thoughts of her driving his precious Bugatti.

"I'm an excellent driver!" She'd laughingly protested.

He'd given her another skeptical look and refocused on the road.

Shaun had taken his dismissal as permission to sleep, so she'd made herself as comfortable as possible and snatched a few hours of sleep. When she woke, she felt oddly refreshed, a feeling she hadn't had since the night Krystoff died.

She blinked and covered her face with her hands to escape the bright sun pouring in through the windows. Sitting up slowly, she lowered her hands, looking around in confusion. She remembered their wild ride through the night, racing up the highway, and she remembered texting Havel.

The car was stopped, and Jozef was nowhere in sight.

Panic swelled in her chest, but she forced it back, taking several deep breaths.

"He wouldn't leave you alone," she mumbled to herself, scanning the area through the windshield.

They were in a large parking lot with a sprinkling of other vehicles. Next to the parking lot was a highway where cars were flying past. There was a building with a large sign announcing washrooms and food. Jozef must've gone inside.

Shaun had to pee and the longer she waited, the more urgent her situation became. She chewed on her lip and pondered her dilemma, finally deciding that Jozef would figure out where she went.

She jumped out of the car, slammed the door shut and ran for the washrooms. She finished quickly, wanting to get back to the car before Jozef noticed she was missing. Flushing the toilet, she opened the stall door and let out a startled scream.

Jozef was standing on the other side, his arms crossed over his chest, his brow lowered in a thunderous frown. His eyes scanned her from head to foot, then he jerked his head in a nod toward the door.

"I have to wash my hands."

He waited impatiently for her to clean up. She splashed water on her face and did what she could for her hair before accompanying him back to the car. As they walked across the lot, he made his displeasure at her disappearance clear.

You don't leave my sight when we are on the road, understood? His signs were sharp and jerky.

Shaun responded, contorting her face in a frown to emphasize her own signs. *You were the one who left my sight. What did you expect me to do, pee in the car?*

He looked so horrified by the idea that Shaun had to stifle a laugh. *I expected you to wait for me,* he signed. *I didn't think you would wake up. You sleep like the dead. You were safe in a locked, bullet-proof car, but I can't take care of you if I don't know where you are.*

A shiver ran through her. It was too soon to be mentioning the dead. It stole some of the warmth from their day.

Noticing her change in mood, Jozef stopped next to the car and pulled her against his chest, running his hands down her back, tracing her spine until her shivers of fear turned to shivers of pleasure. He gave her a lingering kiss.

It will get easier. The nightmares will stop and you will move past this.

"How do you know?" she whispered.

Because it happened to me. I used to get nightmares from the things that I saw and the things that I did. It will always stay with you, but you'll learn how to handle the worst and move on.

She licked her lips and nodded, though she didn't entirely agree with him. They were two different people, with two very different upbringings. Violence had been a peripheral in her life until she met Jozef, whereas he'd been immersed in a violent mafia world his entire life. As a child, his brain would have been formed by the world around him, making him better able to cope. Some of his coping mechanisms weren't exactly healthy, though. Their argument was case in point. Jozef couldn't allow Shaun out of his sight because he feared something would happen to her. That level of constant anxiety wasn't good for a person.

She turned to open her door, but Jozef grabbed her arm and pulled her back around.

Please don't leave my sight again, he signed. *I will do a better job of caring for your needs, but I have to know that you'll be where I left you.* Catching her frown, he shook his head. *I'm not trying to lock you away from the world. I'm worried about your safety. I would feel the same for anyone I loved. I feel the same for my cousins.*

His face twisted in grief as he mentioned his family. They

hadn't talked about Leeza or Saskia since the attack. Both women had escaped the fallout and were in the wind.

Shaun was fairly certain Jozef was searching for them, but they'd avoided speaking of the two women. Shaun wasn't sure she wanted to know what he had planned. If he told her he had to kill his cousins, Shaun didn't know what she would do. Actually, that wasn't true. She knew she wouldn't be able to stay with him if he targeted two innocent women. And because she knew that about herself, she buried her head in the sand. For a few weeks, anyway. Once they returned from their trip, they would have a conversation.

Shaun nodded in response to Jozef's plea and signed, *I'll do my best to keep you informed of my movements. You need to be patient, though. This is all still relatively new to me. Back home, I could come and go as I pleased.*

Jozef leaned over to kiss her. It was a peck, the slight pressure of his lips against hers, but it sent a zing of pleasure through her. He reached around Shaun and opened her door.

She sank into her seat and then gasped as the smell hit her.

"Eggs!" she exclaimed and reached for the containers on Jozef's seat. She was tearing into them before he opened his own door and climbed into the car with her.

"I hope this is all for me, because I'm not sharing," she joked as he reached for the food and she held it away from him.

He tickled her ribs and she nearly dropped the food, but he deftly grabbed it before it hit the console.

She watched in admiration as he opened the packages and began splitting the food in two, giving her a bigger portion than she could eat, despite her insistence that she was hungry enough to eat it all by herself.

There was something extra sexy about a man who looked like Jozef, with his rippling muscles and plethora of tattoos as he did something as domestic as preparing food. Shaun smiled, the feeling of joy rising in her and spreading warmth.

She accepted the paper plate of food he handed to her and immediately started devouring the delicious eggs, smoked sausage, fresh fruit, cheese and jam filled pastries. Shaun surprised herself by eating everything on her plate. When she finished, a small burp escaped her.

Jozef laughed and took her plate, dropping a quick kiss on her lips. He got rid of their garbage and started the car, turning it back onto the highway.

CHAPTER SEVEN

Shaun soon realized that they were heading toward Poland. Her excitement grew with each passing hour. Jozef had told her they were going some place secluded, so she knew it wouldn't be near any major cities. Though she would've loved to check out Warsaw. Perhaps another time.

They continued to drive for another three hours, crossing the border into Poland. With each passing kilometre, the weight that had settled on Shaun's shoulders the past few weeks, lifted. She felt truly free for the first time in weeks. No, months!

She perked up as Jozef took the vehicle through a thickly wooded area, finally turning onto an unpaved road. He parked the Bugatti next to another car.

As Jozef climbed out of their vehicle, he approached the other one with a frown. He looked around and then leaned over to stare through the windows. Shaun joined him, slipping her hand into his.

"What's wrong?" she asked anxiously.

When Jozef looked at her, his face revealed nothing, though she could feel tension thrumming through him. He shook his head, and she knew he was about to lie to her and tell her nothing was wrong.

"Don't you dare," she said sharply. "I know you well enough to know when you're concerned. Spill it, mister."

His face creased in surprise, then he laughed.

Mister? He signed.

She shrugged. "We don't really have pet names for each other like dear, sweetheart, whatever."

He nodded thoughtfully. *My family called me the dog.*

She wrinkled her nose and signed back, *I don't like that nickname; it sounds so derogatory. You aren't a pet, you're a person, and you deserve to be treated that way.*

He stared at her and she saw the softening in his eyes that showed he liked what she said to him.

Don't change the subject, she signed, though her lips curved in a smile. *Tell me what's going on.*

He sighed heavily and ran a hand through his hair, ruffling it. *I don't know, just a feeling.* He swept the area with his arm. *There's only one home in this area, buried deep in the woods. The caretaker doesn't have a car, which means he must have a visitor.*

Shaun nodded, but asked, "Could it be a hiker?"

He looked skeptical. *Maybe, but we have to assume there's someone at the cabin who doesn't belong. We need to proceed with caution.*

Jozef glanced around the small clearing with the two cars as if looking for something. Then she realized he was searching for a place to stash her while he checked out the cabin.

"Absolutely not," she said sharply. "I'm going with you." He shook his head, but she talked over his objection. "I'm not trying to be difficult, Jozef, but I can't be alone here. I *will* have a panic attack. I won't be able to help it."

She let him hear some of the fear and frustration in her voice. She hated that she couldn't control the panic that swelled up inside her regularly. It made her feel so helpless, so out of control.

Jozef curved a hand against her cheek before dropping it to sign. *I won't leave you, I promise.*

"Thank you," she whispered, blinking back the tears that had leapt to her eyes when she thought he would insist on leaving her alone.

When she was looking at him again, he signed, *we need to leave our stuff so my hands are free. I can come back for it. You'll have to walk behind me. Stay tight to my left side and slightly behind.*

"Okay," she said, her heart pumping in fear. "Should I... should I be worried?"

He shook his head emphatically. *No, this is probably nothing. I'm being cautious.*

Shaun suspected he was just saying that to make her feel better, but it worked. She trusted him. If he thought there was really a threat, he would bundle her back into the Bugatti and get her out of there.

Together they made their way through the forest. The walk to the cabin took about half an hour and by the time they could see it, nestled among towering maple trees, the sun was high overhead, shining across the area.

Jozef moved silently through the forest, while Shaun probably made way more noise than she should have. She couldn't help herself. She'd never been outdoorsy, hated camping, and hadn't actively practiced stealth guerilla tactics while moving through a forest the way she suspected Jozef had.

When they sighted the cabin, Jozef stopped her. He made them stand silent and mostly unmoving while he surveilled the area. They stood that way for about fifteen minutes before he deemed it safe enough to approach the cabin.

As they made their way down the path, the gate to a high fence opened and an elderly man stepped through. Though

Jozef reached beneath his jacket for his gun, Shaun sensed that he wasn't alarmed by the older man.

The man didn't seem surprised to see them.

"Jozef Koba, it's good to see you again."

The words seemed sincere, and some of the tension left Shaun as Jozef's hand fell away from the butt of his pistol.

Jozef reached for Shaun and pulled her forward, signing, *I need you to translate, V-A-S-I-L-I-Y doesn't understand sign language.*

Leeza crouched in the bushes on a rise overlooking her father's cottage. Her heart was beating faster than a rabbit's after being caught in a snare. Kristoph struggled in her arms and pushed against her shoulder.

"Want down, mama," he whined.

She loosened her grip but didn't set him on his feet. Instead, she leaned back so she could see his face. Good, no signs of fear. Their frantic flight from the cottage hadn't frightened him.

"Shhh, baby," she whispered. "We must continue our game of pretend. The bad guys are after us and we have to slip through the forest as quiet as we can. Are you going to be our mission commander, or do I need to take charge?"

He grinned at her, his gaze lingering over her shoulder. He rarely made eye contact. "Mission commander!"

"Okay, then you'll have to be very quiet. We need to go find our ride and get out of here before we're caught. You're the boss, Commander. Which way do we go?"

He pointed in the opposite direction of where they needed to go, so Leeza stood and spun on the spot until they were both dizzy and Kristoph was giggling. She wanted to shush him, but she held her admonishment in. They were far enough from the cabin that she was certain Jozef couldn't hear them. Luckily, he had Shaun in tow and was unlikely to come after them immediately. He wouldn't want to leave his fiancé alone with Vasiliy, though Leeza's father wouldn't touch a hair on her head.

If Jozef brought men with him, that would be a different story. They would easily track Leeza and Kristoph. She hadn't seen any of his guard when he pulled up next to her car in the clearing. Thank god Vasiliy had cameras and motion sensors all over the area.

They'd been about to settle down for a cup of tea while Kristoph played with his grandfather's dolls, but the perimeter alert had gone off. When they checked the cameras, they found Jozef and Shaun bent over Leeza's getaway car.

Leeza hadn't wanted to leave her father behind, had tried to insist he come with her and Kristoph. Vasiliy had been equally stubborn, insisting that he would stay to distract Jozef so she could get away. If Leeza hadn't had Kristoph, she would've dragged Vasiliy out by his ears.

Instead, she'd been forced to leave him behind. She'd frantically stuffed their things into a backpack and rushed through the tunnel, to her father's workshop and out through the trapdoor.

Now they were running through the forest in the opposite direction of her car. She would have to leave it behind. Jozef knew what it looked like now. If he had it fingerprinted or tested for DNA, she was fucked. He would connect the dots and realize his cousin, the one he was already gunning for, was also the elusive Phantom. The woman who'd been shadowing his footsteps for years. Learning and waiting until the time was right to seize her own empire and rule her own slice of the underworld.

CHAPTER EIGHT

"On the contrary," the older man interrupted, speaking English with a heavy accent. "I've been learning sign language, though I am not fluent yet." He turned to Shaun and reached a hand out to her. "Dr. Patterson, I've heard so much about you. It's truly a pleasure to make your acquaintance."

Shaun felt instantly at ease, taking Vasiliy's hand and squeezing, before letting go.

Jozef stepped between them, his expression fierce as he demanded. *Who is visiting you?*

Vasiliy stared at Jozef for a moment, as if debating his words, then he admitted, "My daughter."

Jozef's expression became truly terrifying. Shaun took a step back so he wouldn't hit her with his rapid signs. *Tell me where she is.*

Vasiliy shook his head. "She left the moment we realized you were headed here."

Jozef snarled and grabbed Vasiliy, shoving him backwards into the fence behind him.

"Jozef!" Shaun grabbed his arm. "Stop it."

To his credit, Vasiliy did nothing to defend himself. Some of his calm must have penetrated Jozef's anger, because gradually he loosened his hold on Vasiliy and his expression cleared. He let the older man go and stepped back.

"What's going on?" Shaun asked, a waver in her voice. "Why did we come here if you were just going to threaten this man who I assume is to be our host?"

Jozef turned to her, remorse bright in his eyes. *I'm sorry,* he signed, then pointed at Vasiliy. *His daughter is a danger to us. I shouldn't have brought you here. We should go.*

Shaun sensed that if she weren't there, Jozef would already be running through the forest, tracking Vasiliy's daughter.

"Of course she's not a danger to you," Vasiliy interrupted them, allowing some annoyance to leak into his voice. "If she wanted either of you dead, you'd be dead. Instead, she's avoided crossing paths with you."

Because she knows I'll kill her when I get my hands on her, Jozef countered.

"Stop threatening him," Shaun snapped at Jozef, losing her patience. "You brought me here for a reason. Right now, the only person who's acting threatening is you. Enough violence, Jozef. For once, can't we try to solve a problem without pulling a gun?"

Jozef stared at her, then his lips twitched, and she knew he was amused by her. She jutted her chin out and glared.

"Come inside," Vasiliy interrupted them. "I have a pot of hot tea steeping. I was going to share it with my daughter, but she had to leave in rather a hurry."

There was amusement in Vasiliy's voice, but Shaun also heard the longing for his child. She almost wished they hadn't interrupted the small family. She was curious about why Jozef had brought her to the secluded cabin with the strange man, so she followed him, throwing Jozef a warning look over her shoulder.

When they entered the house, Shaun was pleasantly surprised to find cozily furnished rooms filled with books, paintings and little wooden dolls.

She stared her fill as Vasiliy led them into the kitchen where a teapot was indeed steaming on the counter. After setting out three teacups on a tray, a small pitcher of milk and a jar with honey, he added several cookies to the tray and led them back through to the living room.

The furniture was an interesting hodgepodge of chairs and a small couch. All were draped in handmade quilts and padded with pillows. Shaun sat on the small couch and Jozef crammed himself in next to her, his bulk making the squeeze somewhat difficult, while Vasiliy sat opposite them in a rocking chair.

"I hadn't thought to see you again, Jozef," Vasiliy said bluntly.

Shaun swung her gaze to Jozef, who signed, *I hadn't thought to come here again, but you invited me last time we saw each other, and I needed somewhere quiet to bring Shaun.*

Vasiliy's smile was bright with genuine warmth. "It pleases me that you thought of my humble home. I'm happy to have you here for as long as you'd like to stay. I rarely get company around here."

Shaun returned his smile, then asked, "How do you and Jozef know each other?"

Though the smile faded from Vasiliy's face, the sparkle in his eyes remained. He reminded Shaun of a mall Santa. Perpetually happy, jovial and kind. Of course, she had no idea if he really was kind, she'd only known him a few minutes, but she sensed a friendly spirit. Which is why she was shocked by Vasiliy's next statement.

"Jozef was sent here to kill me."

Her mouth fell open and her gaze swung toward Jozef. His expression was carefully blank, but he nodded at Shaun, agreeing with Vasiliy.

"Krystoff Koba believed I was involved in his kidnapping," Vasiliy continued. "He sent Jozef to extract an explanation and to put me in the ground."

Shaun was a little surprised at Vasiliy's admission. Then she remembered his lack of fear when Jozef attacked him.

"Did you kidnap Krystoff?"

Vasiliy shook his head. "No, it was my daughter."

Ah, that explained why Jozef was so hot to get his hands on the daughter.

"And who is your daughter?" she asked.

Vasiliy flashed her a grin. "Now isn't that the million-dollar question."

Jozef turned to Shaun, catching her attention. *She calls herself the P-H-A-N-T-O-M. She's been a thorn in my side for a few years now, scooping minor jobs out from under me, but the kidnapping was the catalyst to finally hunting her down.*

Shaun was getting the picture. "You came here looking for the Phantom and discovered Vasiliy instead."

Jozef nodded. *We thought they were the same person, but I quickly realized V-A-S-I-L-I-Y had nothing to do with my uncle's abduction.*

"Is that why you chose not to kill him?"

Jozef nodded, then thought about it and shook his head, then signed, *I don't know. I just couldn't.*

Shaun's heart squeezed in sympathy at Jozef's confession. He'd met her shortly before he'd been ordered by Krystoff to kill Vasiliy. He hadn't wanted to kill her either, hadn't been able to bring himself to pull the trigger. Perhaps the Koba guard dog had already started questioning his uncle's orders prior to meeting Shaun.

"You didn't kill him because he didn't deserve to die," she said knowingly.

Both Jozef and Vasiliy laughed out loud while Shaun looked bewildered.

It was Vasiliy who told her the truth of who he was. "My dear, I was a Vor until about five years ago. I ran the Stanovich crime syndicate out of Kiev until I retired and moved here."

Shaun's mouth formed an 'o' as she tried to picture the pleasant, round man sitting across from her as one of the fearsome mobsters Karl had described to her when he taught her the word Vory. She didn't know what to say.

Vasiliy sensed her discomfort and attempted to put her at ease.

"I was never very good at it," he admitted. "Didn't have the stomach for the job, unlike the Kobas. As I weakened in my resolve to remain at the top of the Bratva food chain, Krystoff sliced up my territory one piece at a time and seized it for his organization."

There was no bitterness to Vasiliy's words. He was simply describing events.

"You were married to Dasha's sister, weren't you?" Though Shaun framed it as a question, she already knew the answer.

Vasiliy dipped his head in a nod. "Still am."

He must have seen Shaun's next question, because he answered before she could form the words. "My wife remained in Kiev. Though much of her family is now dead, she wasn't willing to leave the life behind." At Shaun's questioning look, he added, "The mafia life. Like her sister, she was never one for the simple life. She enjoys the money, glamour, prestige... not that we have much of that left. Between my retirement and our son's playboy reputation, the family name is in shambles."

"I'm sorry," Shaun murmured, glancing sideways at Jozef.

His own gaze was scornful. He didn't understand Vasiliy's choices. Didn't condone them. As far as Jozef was concerned, a man showed strength, he kept his family and organization in order. He didn't abandon them on a whim. Vory didn't retire.

Yet, Jozef had left Vasiliy alive. She suspected he did it because he wanted to understand how a man could walk away from the life he was born to without a single regret. And it certainly seemed like Vasiliy had no regrets about living off the grid, in his own little slice of paradise, unknown to the outside world. Unknown to the mafia world.

Shaun's admiration for Jozef grew. He was a good man, even if he couldn't see it.

The three talked well into the evening until the shadows crept through the windows, blanketing them in cozy darkness. It was Vasiliy who called a halt to their discussion by standing and stretching.

"I assume you will spend the night?" Vasiliy asked. At Jozef's nod, he continued, "I will show you to your room then and give you a change of sheets. My daughter and... my daughter has been staying in there for a few weeks. You will want to freshen the room while I prepare our supper."

Shaun stood as well, her back protesting at being in one position for hours. The time had passed quickly and pleasantly.

"Thank you," she said, following Vasiliy down a hallway. "We appreciate your accommodating us last minute. I'm sorry we interrupted your time with your daughter."

Jozef put his hand on Shaun's arm, stopping her. She glanced back. Jozef moved past her, pushing her behind him, his hand snaking beneath his jacket as they traversed the length of the cabin. He still didn't trust Vasiliy not to lead them into a trap.

She supposed his cautious nature had helped keep him

alive over the years, but it saddened her that he couldn't relax and breathe without the constant fear of attack. She hoped that a few days spent with Vasiliy would help him learn to relax and trust someone.

Her heart ached as she realized he had trusted someone. And that someone had tried to kill him a few weeks ago.

CHAPTER NINE

Once they were alone in the bedroom, Jozef began pacing and signing.

It might be stupid to stay here. Maybe we should go.

It was weird for Jozef to be indecisive. It took Shaun a moment to realize he wasn't indecisive for himself, but for her. He didn't want a decision he made to put her in danger. A laughable idea since his existence put her in danger, but she appreciated his hesitance anyway. She reached to take his hand. He let her pull him in for a loose hug. She wrapped her arms around his waist and held him.

"I trust you, and if you're willing to stay here, then a part of you trusts Vasiliy. I trust that part of you, Jozef." She tipped her face up to kiss his jaw. "We came here for a reason. Go with your gut on this one."

He didn't smile, but his eyes softened to a deep blue velvet and he kissed her. He didn't use his tongue, but rested his mouth against hers for a few seconds, whisper soft. Though it wasn't an erotic kiss, it still made Shaun's heart leap with anticipation.

He nodded, as if coming to a decision, and gently pushed her away, reaching for the sheets Vasiliy set out for them.

Shaun's lips quirked in amusement as it became clear Jozef had never changed a bed in his life. In the mansion, he had servants to make up the beds, and in their apartment, Shaun had always been the one to rise last and had made the bed for them.

She giggled and took the fitted sheet from him, showing him how to tuck the corners around the edges of the mattress. He watched in fascination, then put the same amount of focus into making up the bed as he would in cleaning and assembling his gun.

He frowned at the bed once they finished. It looked sloppy.

Shaun tossed herself onto the mattress and patted the blanket beside her. Jozef pulled his jacket off, then, with some hesitation, unbuckled his holster and pulled it off too. He settled onto the mattress next to Shaun, easing her head under his arm.

It was a small bed, meant for one, but Shaun appreciated its coziness. She loved touching Jozef, breathing him in, holding him close. He was her anchor and she needed him close.

Even the few hours they'd spent with Vasiliy had done what weeks of counselling had not. Shaun felt relaxed. She felt more confident and able to deal with life. She was grateful to Jozef for bringing her here, though he himself wasn't entirely sure he'd made the right decision.

They lay together until Shaun fell asleep, her head pillowed on Jozef's outstretched arm. She woke to Jozef gently shaking her. She looked up at him sleepily where he sat on the bed next to her hip.

Time for supper, he signed.

Vasiliy must've knocked on the door. She dragged herself

up and stretched, feeling more energized than she had in weeks.

No nightmares, Jozef told her as she pushed herself off the bed.

She tried to determine if any bad dreams had interrupted her nap, but she didn't think so.

She caught Jozef's hand and pulled him to the door. "Let's go. Something smells delicious and I'm starving."

***

Later, after a satisfying meal of homemade Borscht with sour cream and biscuits, Jozef and Shaun were tucked away in their bedroom once more. Shaun had fallen quickly asleep, while Jozef sat on the edge of the bed with his phone.

Vasiliy's daughter was here before we arrived. After you set up a perimeter, make sure someone tracks her path out of the woods. Given how elusive she's been, I doubt you'll be able to capture her. Try anyway.

Jozef sent the text to Havel, who had finally caught up to them. Jozef hadn't been particularly careful in covering their tracks, so he wasn't surprised when Havel showed up with a handful of men, insisting on providing security for the cottage. Jozef agreed under the strict condition that Shaun not find out the team was out there. Which meant they would have to sleep, eat and piss in the woods.

His men were used to harsher conditions. He wasn't worried.

An hour later, he got a text from Havel. He'd been expecting a check-in once they followed the Phantom's trail through the forest. What he wasn't expecting was the contents of the message.

The daughter wasn't alone. There was a small set of

footprints with hers, heading south, away from the vehicles. The second set of prints weren't deep. Probably a child.

Jozef leaned forward, elbows on his thighs, and frowned at his phone. He wasn't surprised that Vasiliy had kept the existence of a child from him. But something was bothering him, niggling at his consciousness. Like a puzzle with only one piece missing before it was solved.

It was time to have a discussion with Vasiliy. No more insistences that he couldn't tell Jozef who his daughter was. No more calm assurances that he didn't care if he lived or died as long as she was safe. Jozef needed the information, if only to keep his budding empire safe. He needed to know that the Phantom wouldn't come after him, and indirectly, Shaun.

He stood, careful not to bounce the bed as he moved and then glanced down at his fiancé. Soon to be wife. He was done waiting. He didn't want to force her decision, but he wasn't going to change his mind.

She wanted to be sure of him, of their lives together. He'd been giving her time for her own peace of mind, but it was time to take the step she seemed so reluctant to take with him. He needed to know that she was tied to him in every possible way. Spiritually, physically, mentally and legally.

He made his way silently from the room, grateful that Shaun slept heavily. He worried she would have a nightmare while he was gone, but he didn't have a choice. If things got ugly with Vasiliy, he absolutely didn't want her witnessing it.

He made his way noiselessly down the hall to Vasiliy's bedroom. As Jozef suspected, it was empty. He'd done some reconnaissance around the cabin, before settling down with Shaun for the night. His host hadn't been in the cabin when they'd retired.

Jozef made his way to the bookshelf in Vasiliy's office. It

was already standing open. An invitation? Jozef entered the long passageway that led away from the cabin, into an underground bunker that contained Vasiliy's workroom. As he neared the workroom, he realized Vasiliy had left the workroom door open as well. The strains of a Spanish opera reached down the corridor.

Sure enough, the door was wide open, an invitation to Jozef.

As Jozef stepped through the doorway, the smell of turpentine hit his nose. Vasiliy, who was sitting on a stool and leaning over a doll, said, "I was expecting you."

It was an eerie reminder of the first time they'd met – in that very workroom. Only that time Havel had been there, Vasiliy hadn't known sign language, and Jozef had been on a mission to kill the older man.

"Pull up a seat," Vasiliy invited, waving a hand toward the other side of the table where a stool was tucked neatly under the table. Vasiliy leaned back, holding a paintbrush aloft as he stared down at the doll he was working on.

Jozef hesitated, glanced back at the door, then pulled the stool out and sat down. He arranged his body so he could face both the door and Vasiliy. It made him uncomfortable to have the trapdoor leading into the forest at his back, but he had to compromise something and he assumed the trapdoor was firmly latched.

When Vasiliy was looking at him, Jozef signed, *who is your daughter?*

Vasiliy smiled slightly. "I believe we've had this conversation, Jozef. And it has led us to an impasse."

The impasse will end tonight, Jozef assured him. *I don't want to hurt you, but I need the information and I don't have the luxury of time anymore. I have an empire to build. I need to know who my enemies are, and who are my allies.*

Vasiliy nodded thoughtfully and carefully set his brush

aside. He leaned back in his stool and studied Jozef. "Alright, I will tell you." When Jozef lifted his hands to sign, Vasiliy interrupted him. "You'll have to patient though. I won't give you a direct answer, I will simply give you a piece of the puzzle. It's up to you to figure out where it fits."

Jozef growled his frustration but didn't argue. Vasiliy's words were eerily similar to his own thoughts of a few minutes before. He was here, with Vasiliy, and he had nowhere else to go. He could work on his patience, while at the same time hopefully get the answers he needed.

Proceed.

Vasiliy remained silent for a minute, as though gathering his thoughts, then nodded decisively, finally allowing his gaze to fall on Jozef.

"I knew your father... well, actually, both of your parents." He paused, waiting for Jozef to absorb the shock. And it was a shock. Of all the directions he thought this conversation could take, he hadn't expected his parents to be the subject. Luckily, he'd had years of practice schooling his features and didn't give his surprise away.

Vasiliy gave him a knowing look, indicating he could read Jozef's thoughts. It was tempting to kill the man just to get Vasiliy out of his damn head.

"Your father worked as liaison to your uncle. He ran the street crews and travelled between cities meeting with Krystoff's contacts when he couldn't go himself."

Jozef signed that he already knew this.

"Back then I did business often with your uncle, though I met more often with your father." He paused again, his faded eyes on Jozef. "Gregor was a tough man, but he was also fair. After several meetings, we established a friendship, along with an alliance. This is how I know it was your uncle, or someone in his inner circle, who killed your father."

Jozef's hand came down on the table hard, causing the

doll to jump. Vasiliy frowned and lifted her from the table, setting it carefully on the bench behind him before refocusing on Jozef.

You will not throw out accusations without proof, Jozef signed, adding a snarl for emphasis.

Vasiliy shrugged. "Of course, I have no proof. You will have to take my word. And I would appreciate if you withheld your threats until I've finished. I've been waiting years to tell you this story, and I'd rather not keep it to myself anymore. Too much responsibility for a retiree."

Spit it out then, Jozef signed.

"Your legendary patience is slipping, Mr. Koba," Vasiliy said chidingly. "You must maintain your cool. Especially with the jackals who'll be circling your newfound empire. You've spent years building your reputation, don't damage it now."

Jozef heard the words, felt the words, but couldn't contain his anger. Vasiliy was correct. He'd spent a lifetime learning how to become thoughtful, measured, patient. Like a jungle cat, he didn't strike until he was sure of his kill. Only the events of the past few weeks had rattled him to the core. He was no longer certain of who he was, where his place was, or where he really wanted to be. Perhaps that was what drew him to Vasiliy and his little cottage. He knew Vasiliy had answers to questions he didn't even know to ask.

He took a calming breath and nodded at Vasiliy to continue, before signing, *I won't interrupt again. Please say what you wish without fear of retaliation.*

"Good... now where was I?" Vasiliy trailed off. "Your father came to visit me often and we bonded over cigars and vodka." At Jozef's look, Vasiliy chuckled. "Yes, we were your stereotypical tough guys. We had the world at our fingertips, or at least I did. As you know, your father was the younger son of a powerful mafia family, and while he'd been raised understanding that he would follow in Krystoff's footsteps, it wasn't enough for him. He wanted what his brother refused to share. He wanted equal power and equal placement in the family hierarchy and he wanted his son to eventually take up the Koba mantle."

Jozef couldn't hide his shock this time. He'd been five when his parents died. He didn't remember them well, but what he did remember was pleasant. The smell of his mother's skin, her soft voice, his father's boisterous laugh and jovial temperament.

He couldn't picture his father plotting to take over his uncle's empire. It made sense, though. A part of him had always wondered if his uncle had killed his parents. He hadn't wanted to believe that the man who raised him was also responsible for his status as an orphan. But knowing his father was planning an attack made Krystoff's actions more understandable. If that was indeed what had happened.

Vasiliy confirmed Jozef's thoughts. "Your father carefully plotted to overthrow his brother. He didn't want to take the entire Koba organization for himself, just what he considered his fair piece. Though I understood his disgruntlement with his placement, I tried to talk him out of his plans. The longer he thought about it, the firmer he became. His plan was solid too. He had many people working the streets of Prague, all loyal to him. He was going to use them to take the estate in a bloodless coup. Or so he hoped. His plan might have been successful, except Krystoff found out."

Jozef swallowed hard, trying to stifle the long-buried emotions rising in his chest. Images were flooding his brain, distracting him, making it harder to keep a straight face. Images of his parents lying dead on the floor, riddled with bullets. His mother's beautiful brown eyes, frozen open for eternity, forever burned in Jozef's brain.

Did you tell my uncle about my father's plan?

"No. Though I didn't agree with Gregor, I wouldn't have

put him in danger." Vasiliy's answer was immediate and heart-felt. "I believe my wife, Vasha," he said her name with such disgust there was no missing the hatred he harboured for his wife, "must've overheard one of our meetings and told her sister. She confessed after your father was killed, and I realized there was only one source the information could've come from. I nearly killed her in my rage."

And you're positive it was my uncle who killed my parents? Though the story made sense, explained a lot of things, he had trouble believing his uncle had caused such damage to his family. Now, it was too late to ask Krystoff what had really happened all those years ago.

Jozef touched the scar on his throat, tracing the ridges with his fingers. He rarely thought of his lack of voice. No point. He was mute and that wouldn't change. But once again, burning rage threatened to consume him as he thought about the destruction to his family and his voice.

Vasiliy's gaze softened as he watched Jozef.

"Who else would leave a child witness alive?" Vasiliy asked softly. "Only someone who cared. Who couldn't bring themselves to do more than make sure you never spoke your story?"

Jozef shrugged. *It was overkill. I remember little from that night. Never have.*

"I'm sorry that happened to you, Jozef. You didn't deserve it then, and you don't deserve it now. You should have grown up knowing your parents. Knowing the strength of your father and the love of your mother. You should have your voice."

Jozef glanced away from Vasiliy, pain blossoming in his chest. It was the first real emotional reaction he'd had to the deaths of his parents since he was a child. It was the first time he really felt their loss. Then, Vasiliy was the first person to really talk to him about them.

Vasiliy changed the subject, giving Jozef time to collect himself and regain his ability to sort through the plethora of information Vasiliy was giving him with a cool head.

"It was shortly after that I became better acquainted with your aunt and uncle." He cleared his throat. "There's no straightforward way to say this, and I'm not one to sugar-coat things. It was at this time that your aunt and I had a brief affair. She was grieving for your parents and knew that I'd been friends with Gregor. I think being together gave us both a place to shelter during the storm of change that came after their deaths. When I found out she'd tried to kill my wife while the two were still living at home, I broke off the affair."

Jozef stared at Vasiliy. An affair? He hadn't seen that coming.

What does this have to do with me? Jozef signed, then he stopped as he realized where Vasiliy was headed. The conversation had started with Vasiliy's daughter, had wound its way to Jozef's parents, and then landed on an affair with Dasha.

Motherfucker.

There was a child from the union with my aunt, wasn't there? Jozef asked.

Vasiliy nodded, watching Jozef expectantly, without adding more to his story. He didn't need to. Jozef could do the math on his own.

To be sure he was correct, Jozef signed, *L-E-E-Z-A is your daughter?*

"Yes," Vasiliy confirmed, then waited as Jozef reached the next conclusion.

Leeza was the Phantom.

CHAPTER TEN

Jozef was stunned by the news that Leeza was not only Vasiliy's biological daughter, but she was also the elusive Phantom. The more he thought about it, the more sense it made. Leeza had become secretive over the years. She used to be outgoing, caring, fun. But since her marriage she'd become withdrawn, impatient, unfeeling.

Jozef stared at Vasiliy.

He had to make some decisions and Vasiliy wouldn't like any of them.

Why did you tell me this? Jozef asked.

He almost wished Vasiliy had kept the information to himself. Though Jozef had ordered his cousin's death, it didn't sit well with him. When Leeza escaped with her son, Jozef had been relieved. He could let her go; let her live her life somewhere else, away from the mafia world they grew up in.

Now, Jozef was faced with a much worse scenario. Leeza had been building her own empire, her own army over the years, using her biological father's resources. Jozef couldn't allow her to live. She was more of a threat to him than ever.

Vasiliy watched Jozef work through his thoughts and

emotions. When Jozef finally looked him in the eye, Vasiliy spoke, but instead of answering Jozef's question, he asked one of his own. "Why did you come here?"

Jozef wanted to rage at Vasiliy, demand his answers, kill him on the spot. His upbringing, his training, was clashing with the man he'd become in the past year, outside of the Koba influence. It confused him, made him feel off-balance. His legendary calm, his ability to assess all situations and see a way through was failing him. Everything was murky when it should be clear. He felt lost, felt like a failure.

He couldn't keep Shaun happy. Had traumatized her yet again with his family and his way of life.

Why had he come to Vasiliy?

Their last meeting should have been the last time they saw each other. Jozef had spared Vasiliy's life, and in return the old man was supposed to remain in hiding, away from the politics and power of the Bratva influence.

Vasiliy had done his part. The only thing he was guilty of was omitting the truth of who his daughter was.

Finally, after a few minutes of introspection, Jozef told Vasiliy the truth. *You got out. You forged a life away from the mafia, the life you were born into.*

Vasiliy watched Jozef, his expression sad. Jozef could've hated Vasiliy if he'd looked at him with pity or knowing arrogance. Instead, he looked at Jozef with compassion. A compassion he sorely needed.

"This life destroys our children, Jozef," Vasiliy said heavily. "They're raised with the privileges of the mafia, but it's not a happy life. All the power and money in the world won't buy what you're missing. You've just taken on an enormous burden by taking over the Koba holdings. You need allies, the right kind, to have your back."

Jozef nodded his agreement. He'd been raised to become the family guard dog. The position had held pride and power, but it hadn't fulfilled him. He'd created his own team, a brotherhood, in search of whatever elusive thing he'd been missing. While his men were like family, they never quite filled in the missing piece. Not until he met Shaun.

As if reading Jozef's mind, Vasiliy said, "She loves you, the same as your family did. The difference is, she also cares about you. She loves you deeply, not because of what you do, but in spite of it."

Jozef's heart was pounding and his eyes burned. He should hate Vasiliy, the failed mobster who was lecturing him on what he needed in life, but he knew better. This was why he had come. He needed to see another way to live, make some decisions.

Jozef stood and looked steadily at Vasiliy before signing, *thank you for being so forthcoming, as well as accommodating my wife and myself. We appreciate your hospitality. I will take all that you have told me into consideration before making any decisions about your daughter.*

Without waiting for a reply from Vasiliy, Jozef strode away from the other man, through the makeshift tunnel and back into the house. He slipped quietly into the bedroom and sat on the bed next to Shaun.

He looked down at her face, which was bathed in the moonlight pushing its way through the crack in the curtain. She looked peaceful, much more so than she had since their lives exploded all around them. Her mouth was open slightly and she was breathing heavily, one arm flung over her head while the other was curled against her neck.

Jozef wanted to give her the world, because she deserved the world, but what kind of world did she want to live in? What kind of world was best for her?

Jozef curled on his side on top of the blanket, facing her so he could watch her as he drifted into sleep. For the first time in a long time, he fell asleep with his back to the door.

They stayed with Vasiliy for two-and-a-half days. Jozef had only intended to stay for one, but the peace Shaun was finding in spending time in the cottage, the woods and with Vasiliy was worth the extra days. She slept without nightmares, heartily ate whatever food Vasiliy put in front of her, and smiled more than Jozef had seen her smile in months.

The time spent with Vasiliy was good for Jozef as well. Though Jozef knew he had to get back, that the Bratva were watching him carefully, waiting for him to misstep, he couldn't bring himself to regret their impromptu vacation. The problems of his new empire melted away and he was able to spend time in his own head without the clutter of a lifetime of responsibility.

It was their last day with Vasiliy. They would walk out of the woods in a few hours, timing their departure with the setting of the sun. They would have daylight until they reached their car and made their way back to the highway. Jozef would have to drive through the night, while Shaun slept in the passenger seat, but it was worth giving her as much time as he could in the peaceful setting.

She was on her hands and knees next to Vasiliy, pulling weeds from his small garden with a trowel. It was winter, and the air was chill, but Shaun was determined to spend as much time outdoors as she could. Once they finished clearing the patch they were working on, Vasiliy would insist on filling Shaun with cider and cookies until she was warm and pleasantly stuffed.

Vasiliy laughed loudly at whatever Shaun had said to him, and she grinned at him. She was telling him an anecdote about her mother's garden in Montreal. Something about Fitzy chasing a squirrel through it and breaking every sunflower stem as his chubby body smacked them on the way by.

She glanced over her shoulder at Jozef, her dark eyes dancing. His lips quirked and he winked at her. She looked startled and laughed. He supposed it was the first time she was seeing him so carefree.

After they shared cider and snacks with Vasiliy, it was time to go. Shaun hugged the older man tightly, murmuring her thanks to him for his hospitality. He patted her back and told her to come back any time, with or without Jozef.

Jozef didn't comment. There was no chance Shaun would travel anywhere without him, let alone through a forest to meet a retired mobster.

Jozef was startled when Vasiliy reached out to grip his shoulders, then pulled him in for a hug. He stood with his arms dangling at his sides as Vasiliy held him.

Outside of Shaun, it was rare for anyone to touch Jozef. The embrace was uncomfortable, but not terrible. Finally, he lifted his arms and thumped Vasiliy's back before stepping quickly away.

Before Jozef could fully extricate himself from the hug, Vasiliy took him by the shoulder and said seriously, "You will find your path, son. You're a strong man. Your parents would be proud."

Jozef nodded and glanced away, catching Shaun's gaze. She took his hand and squeezed.

They left Vasiliy and the cottage behind and made their way back through the woods. The setting sun lit the surrounding forest, turning the bed of leaves beneath their feet into an array of bright yellows, greens and reds. Shaun reached down to pick up an oak tree leaf and held it against her nose, inhaling.

When they reached the car, they discovered a gift sitting

in the passenger seat. Jozef frowned. The car had been locked and the area was crawling with his men.

The car also had an alarm that would send an alert to his phone if it'd been broken into. Whoever left the small gift-wrapped package had used keys to get inside; Jozef's keys.

It had to be Vasiliy.

Jozef unlocked the Buggati and reached inside, picking up the package.

"What's that?" Shaun asked curiously, peeking over Jozef's shoulder.

He shook his head.

The old man was enigmatic. Caring, but crafty. Whatever Jozef was holding was a message. The placement had been carefully orchestrated to show Jozef that Vasiliy might seem innocuous, but the retired mobster still had some tricks up his sleeve.

"Is it safe to open?"

Though it saddened him that because of his lifestyle Shaun had to think in terms of what was safe and what was not, he was proud of her for asking instead of simply reacting to a gift.

He thought about it and then nodded, handing the package to her. The placement of the package was a some-what sinister message to Jozef, but if Vasiliy had wanted to hurt them, he'd had two-and-a-half days to do it.

Shaun tore the wrapping paper, revealing a wooden box, about a foot long and half a foot wide. Jozef suspected he knew what was inside, and Shaun's sharp intake of breath, along with her exclamation, "It's so beautiful!" told him he was correct.

Jozef looked down at the open box. Nestled in a bed of red velvet was a doll. It was rounded with the traditional shape of Russian nesting dolls. The body was painted in a red and white dress with brown clog shoes. Its face was a deep mahogany with lighter brown circles painted on the cheeks. It had beautiful chocolate brown eyes. The curly hair was created with short black swirls, outlined in white to make them seem almost real.

Despite the doll being a caricature, it looked remarkably similar to Shaun.

She set the wooden box down on the hood of the Bugatti.

Jozef wondered if Havel was watching them. He would be appalled that Shaun was using the hood of Jozef's high-end car as a table. Jozef didn't care. He'd buy a new one if she scratched it. He'd rather buy a thousand cars than say anything to wipe the expression of wonder from her face as she lifted the top from the first nesting doll to reveal the one beneath.

Shaun laughed out loud and pointed at the face. The second doll looked very much like the first, but this one was wearing a dress of blue instead of red, and one of its eyes was closed in a mischievous wink.

Shaun lifted the next doll, revealing the last one. Both eyes were half lowered, and it was wearing a white lab coat. Shaun laughed when she noticed a stethoscope around the doll's neck and hugged it to her chest.

It was worth it. Bringing Shaun to Poland was worth leaving his post for a few days. If he was being honest with himself, Jozef had to admit he was more relaxed too, refreshed, and determined to make their new life work in a way he despaired of a few days earlier.

CHAPTER ELEVEN

"You can't take off like that."

Jozef stared across his desk at his second-in-command.

The moment Jozef was back in the mansion, Havel hunted him down and insisted on a meeting. Though he'd kept his distance while they were in Poland, he'd been furious at Jozef's impromptu vacation.

Jozef understood. They were in the middle of a takeover, the Bratva were breathing down their necks, the Koba women were in the wind, probably scattered across Europe looking for allies. Jozef had abandoned his responsibilities to give Shaun some time away from the pressures surrounding them and the grim reality of living in the mansion again.

"We need to talk about this," Havel snapped when Jozef failed to react to his demand. "I can't protect you if you go off on your own. Our enemies could've been sitting at the gate, waiting for you to emerge without your usual entourage. Hell, you didn't even try to cover your tracks into Poland. We were on your tail almost the entire way. The only reason we didn't catch up right away is that damn Bugatti is faster than anything else we have."

Jozef let out a growling laugh. When Shaun had fallen asleep, he'd let the car fly, opening it up to its full potential as it ate up the highway.

Instead of addressing Havel's concerns, Jozef signed, *my cousin is the Phantom.*

Jozef watched Havel's face closely. Havel was loyal to a fault. He was the one person besides Shaun that Jozef would rely on without a second thought. But Havel loved Jozef's cousin with an unrequited longing that could twist his loyalties. Jozef knew, because he loved Shaun the same way. Though she returned his love, Jozef knew she didn't feel the obsessive pull he did. If she asked him to kill Havel, Jozef wouldn't hesitate to pull the trigger. Of course, part of the reason he loved Shaun was because she would never ask him to do such a thing.

Jozef knew he was fucked up inside. Accepted it in the way he accepted the mafia life as his only course of existence. It was the same for Havel. They were mafia through and through. They were brothers, but they were also twisted.

If Havel loved as deeply as Jozef, then their friendship and partnership could be in jeopardy. It was why Jozef was being blunt with his second-in-command and watching the other man's reactions closely.

Though Havel had stood by when Jozef ordered Leeza's death a few weeks earlier, Jozef had felt the other man's resistance, his pain. It was the same thing Jozef had felt when he'd put a gun to Shaun's head. The pull between worlds. To kill the woman he loved or to let her live.

"It makes sense," Havel said, his face still in the same hard lines they'd been in when he confronted Jozef. "Saskia has been a sneaky thorn in the side of this family for years. She must've started young, though. The first rumours we had that the Phantom was active started a few years ago. She would've been around fifteen."

Jozef was amused at Havel's assumption. He hadn't thought of Saskia, but the brat certainly had the potential to cause the havoc the Phantom had caused in the Koba family.

Jozef shook his head. *Not S-A-S-K-I-A.*

Havel stared at him. "Impossible."

Jozef stared back, giving Havel time to absorb the new information. It took Havel about as long as it had taken Jozef to connect the dots. Leeza's withdrawal, her secretive nature, her trips to the gun range. Her shopping getaways that failed to produce the expected purchases.

"I don't understand," Havel said, his voice low. "I thought I knew her."

Jozef thought Havel was talking to himself rather than Jozef, but he caught Havel's attention and began signing, telling the other man everything, including Leeza's parentage.

The two men discussed the recent development at length, piecing together the story until they thought they came up with the complete picture.

"Why do you think she kidnapped Krystoff?" Havel asked.

It's only a guess until we can get our hands on her, but I think it was for two reasons: to see if she could infiltrate the family with her newfound resources, and for revenge.

"Revenge?"

Jozef nodded. *My uncle pushed her into a marriage she hated. We all thought her withdrawal was from a bad marriage, but I now believe it was so she could build her new empire.*

"She was always smarter than we gave her credit for," Havel murmured, still looking like he'd been struck with a bat.

Jozef couldn't disagree. Leeza had been the quiet, obedient one. She didn't get in trouble like her sister. As a result, she was often overlooked, left to her own devices. Even as a child.

Jozef remembered back to the day he accompanied her on a trip to the gun range and discovered she could easily out-shoot any man on the property. When Jozef had commented, she'd laughed it off and said she'd played too many video games with Saskia as a child. Jozef knew better now.

Havel asked the million-dollar question. "What are you going to do?"

Jozef made a decision that he'd been contemplating since discovering who Leeza really was. He couldn't leave her to run loose. She was too dangerous now, and she carried the genes of her mother. Dasha had shown how the intelligent women of their family could go wrong. It would be a deadly mistake to underestimate Dasha's daughter.

You can have her, Jozef signed.

Havel stared at him in disbelief. "Come again?"

I will give her to you in marriage, if you want her.

Jozef observed his friend, watching his face for signs of rejection. Rather than immediately shutting down Jozef's idea, he nodded his head slowly.

"Yes, I'll take her."

Jozef felt immense relief at Havel's acceptance. He hadn't wanted to put his cousin down. He'd grown up with her, protected her, even played with her when she was small. It had gutted him to order her death a few weeks earlier. This moment felt like redemption for that decision. He didn't have to kill a beautiful, intelligent, and resourceful woman. He would put a leash on her and hand her over to his best friend.

Ensure her widowhood before you take her in marriage.

"Not a problem," Havel said easily, a gleam in his eyes as he thought about taking out Leeza's abusive husband.

Closeted in the office, they discussed every aspect of

their new enterprise, taking on the Koba organization. It wasn't something Jozef had wanted or prepared for. He'd been happy making a success of Guard Dog Securities, and now the ground beneath his feet had shifted again. He was happy to have a staunch ally and friend in Havel, who understood everything Jozef was dealing with and supported him.

The two men agreed that Guard Dog Securities would run as is, though Havel would replace Jozef as lead on the missions. Jozef was needed at home. He would organize their people in the city and throughout the Czech Republic, then make moves to take Ukraine, since Vasiliy had left a leadership vacuum that had yet to be filled by a powerful organization.

It was while they were discussing Jozef's upcoming responsibilities that Havel finally spoke his mind.

"It's time to take your head out of your ass and look around," Havel said in his usual blunt manner. "Appear strong if you wish to keep everything that has fallen to you. You cannot question yourself, or your place, or the Bratva will step in."

Jozef narrowed his eyes at his second-in-command but didn't shut him down. This was why Jozef was an effective leader. He listened to what his men had to say, particularly Havel, whether they were imparting good information or bad information. As long as they had something valid to say, he would listen.

When Havel was confident he could speak freely, he continued, "The Bratva are watching your every move. If for a second they think you've blinked, they will strip you of everything, kill everyone loyal to you and absorb your holdings."

Jozef nodded slowly. *The trip to P-O-L-A-N-D was stupid.*

"Very," Havel agreed.

Jozef didn't bother to justify his actions. Though the trip

had been a bad idea from a business perspective, he didn't regret it.

Shaun had been happy. For a few days, she'd relaxed, smiled, laughed and shared herself. Jozef would lay the world at her feet for a few smiles. He'd known he needed to stay at the mansion, while also knowing she needed to get away. He'd made her the priority. He always would. And he would never justify that decision to Havel or anyone else.

When Havel finished saying his piece, Jozef held a hand up to get his attention. *I will not allow our Russian brothers to take what is rightfully mine. If they try, I will bring them down. They will underestimate me to their detriment.*

Havel flashed him a grin. "That's what I want to hear."

Jozef grunted. *Don't bring this up again. My decisions are my own. While I understand they will affect you and the others, know that any decisions I make will be with the weight of the organization on my shoulders. I will not fail you or anyone else.*

Havel dipped his head in a nod, his eyes dancing with excitement. He was looking forward to rebuilding the Koba organization, modelled after Jozef's philosophies and work ethic. This was a new dawn on an old family.

While Jozef had been born and raised as mafia royalty, Havel had grown up in the trenches. They'd formed a close bond, but their outlooks were different. While Jozef saw his climb to the top as a responsibility, and sometimes a burden, Havel relished every step of the way. He was the true mobster of the two of them.

Before they wrapped up their meeting, Jozef tasked Havel with one more thing, on top of his already enormous workload.

I want you to fill the empty position in our team with a new member. Jozef tossed a file at Havel.

Havel raised an eyebrow and picked up the file, flipping it open. It was unusual for Jozef to fill their empty positions himself. Havel was used to being the voice of the business, while Jozef stayed behind the scenes orchestrating their missions. The two men and their entire team worked as a well-oiled machine, but they were down men.

Then there was Jozef. While he intended to continue running missions with his men, he wouldn't always be available. If there was a scheduling conflict, his place was as boss of the Koba organization, not lead on an elite mercenary unit. He would need an alternate.

Flipping through the file, Havel started laughing. "You can't be serious."

Jozef stared at him without speaking.

Havel sobered quickly. "A woman."

Jozef nodded.

Havel was the more likely of the two to underestimate a woman. Jozef had spent more than a year either with Shaun or studying her. He knew better than to underestimate the power and determination a woman could hold.

As Havel thought about it, he began to nod. "Yeah, okay, I see the advantages, but this particular woman?"

She's qualified.

"She'll get us all killed," Havel countered.

Jozef grinned. *Maybe, but the battle will be fun. Find her, recruit her. Let me worry about the rest.*

CHAPTER TWELVE

Shaun took Jozef's hand as he helped her from the SUV. She gazed up the side of Jozef's building, squinting at the top floor, where she'd lived only a few weeks earlier.

Havel, Cooper, Terek and Nikolay surrounded them.

Jozef touched her back, urging her inside. He didn't like it when she lingered on the street. Both of them had become somewhat infamous since the funeral. They'd been gossiped about in the society pages, speculated about and spied on. Out of the corner of her eye, Shaun spotted two men with cameras coming toward them.

Jozef had assured her the interest would die down soon. Mobsters didn't like the limelight. Or at least, not Jozef. He fully intended to lead a boring life until the attention faded away. He'd told her they were targets of the local paparazzi because Jozef had inherited his uncle's massive fortune and was engaged to the doctor who was kidnapped out of Ukraine.

Somehow Jozef had kept the attack out of the newspapers. They could only speculate on the death of Krystoff

Koba, though the rumour was that Jozef had killed him for his fortune. Jozef ignored the gossip, though Shaun wondered if it bothered him. It wasn't far from the truth, but Jozef's reason for killing his uncle was complicated.

They walked into the club together. It was 10:00 AM and empty.

"It looks so different in the light of day," Shaun murmured.

Much of the destruction had been cleaned up, though there were work crews rebuilding the sections that had been shot up or destroyed. Sawdust filtered through the air, giving the club a pleasant scent. It felt strange standing exactly where a storm of men and bullets had come through.

Shaun shuddered at the memory and continued walking.

Jozef planned on working with Guard Dog Securities for the day. He was amalgamating several of his uncle's holdings into his business. A complicated process that would take months of work.

When they reached the security floor, Jozef turned to Shaun, trapping her in the corner of the elevator. He lifted her chin and stared down at her, his gorgeous blue eyes speaking to her.

She kissed him. "I know," she whispered for him alone. "Stay with my mother, don't leave the building and listen to Cooper."

He nodded, his eyes softening.

"I'll be good, I promise."

He wrapped an arm around her back and held her close, pressing a lingering kiss to her lips and stealing her breath. Her chest filled with warmth and she slid her arms around his neck, anchoring herself against him.

They ignored the men standing in the elevator with them, stopping the metal doors from sliding shut and pretending they weren't there.

Finally, Jozef set Shaun away from him and stepped out of the elevator. He pointed at Cooper and signed, *defend her with your life.*

Always, Cooper signed back.

Jozef strode away and the doors closed.

Shaun sighed happily.

"So, do you have a wedding date yet?" Cooper asked as the elevator dinged on the fourth floor.

"Not really," Shaun admitted.

"What's the hesitation. You're obviously in love with the guy."

"What makes you think I'm the one hesitating?"

He gave her a look. "We both know it's not Jozef dragging his feet. If you gave him the word go, he'd have you in a chapel so fast your head would spin."

"Okay, fine. But I'm not dragging my feet, not really. There's too much for us to settle before I'll feel really ready to commit myself."

He gave her a skeptical look as he escorted her from the elevator. He shuffled Shaun to the side as he knocked on Fatima's door.

"Let yourself in," Fatima called, and Cooper opened the door.

"Lady, I think you can consider yourself committed. No way is that man letting you go."

"Why does it always have to sound so kidnappy?" Shaun complained, reaching out to hug her mother. "Mom, you need to keep your door locked."

"I knew you were on your way up." She pointed to her TV screen, which showed the building's cameras. "Havel gave me the channel for the security feed."

Cooper and Shaun stood in front of the TV, watching the workers as they moved through the building.

"That one likes to take his shirt off when he gets hot."

Fatima tapped the screen over a black and white figure who was talking to someone. He wore a tool belt that rode low on his hips. "I think he's the supervisor. He likes to boss the other ones around."

Shaun slapped a hand over her mouth to keep from laughing out loud while Cooper grinned.

The trio made their way to the top floor, to Shaun and Jozef's apartment. It was Shaun's first visit since the attack.

Cooper swept the apartment before allowing the two women inside.

She was nervous, but as she glanced around, she realized most of the broken furniture and other debris had been removed and there were no traces of death that she could see or smell. She felt... glad to be home. Sunlight filled the room from the two walls of windows.

"It feels small," she murmured.

"Well, you have a mansion now," Fatima said with a laugh. "This place is tiny in comparison."

Shaun ran her hand over the shiny chrome finish of a brand-new fridge. Her gaze dropped to the floor.

Krystoff would have died right where she was standing. His body had been destroyed. At a glance, she'd known he couldn't recover from his injuries. He'd died in pain, but he hadn't been alone. Jozef had sat beside him, holding his hand.

Shaun didn't notice her breathing becoming more erratic until she looked up and found herself surrounded by her mother and Cooper, both standing too close. She took a step back and waved them away.

"I'm fine, just a flashback."

Cooper nodded knowingly and gave her the space she desired, taking his place by the door. Fatima continued to look concerned.

"Mom, I'm fine, really." Shaun shook off the lingering

sadness and panic and moved out of the kitchen. "Let's decide what we want to do with the place. Jozef says we can use it as a weekend home when we want to get away from the mansion."

Fatima laughed. "So you have a mansion for weekdays and a luxury apartment for weekends. Life is going to be difficult for you."

Shaun forced a smile, but she had trouble sharing her mother's humour. The tradeoff for luxury living wasn't always worth it and there were days when she longed for the simple life Vasiliy led. Of course, she knew that kind of living would eventually drive her crazy too. It took a special person to hole up in the woods all alone, with his nearest neighbours a three-hour hike away.

"Will you be working here?" Fatima asked, looking around speculatively.

"I hope to," Shaun admitted. "I'm going to at least continue my research."

"Well, since it's usually just the two of you, I think you should buy a smaller table and put in an office against these windows. You'll get plenty of light and you can watch the city below while you work."

Shaun moved to stand beside her mother. "I love that idea. Maybe I'll ask the interior decorator to use brighter colours in here. Something that will really light up when the sun hits it."

"And for your second bedroom, you should consider a nursery."

The words were spoken so casually that Shaun almost missed them. "A nursery?" she sputtered and laughed at the same time. "Don't you think that's a little premature?"

Fatima looked at her. "You've been with Jozef for a while —"

"Off and on," Shaun cut in.

"I think you can consider yourself 'on ' from now on. Are you actively trying to stop a baby from happening? You're still young and you're healthy. Eventually one will come along if you two are doing what I assume you're doing."

Shaun laughed so hard she had to cover her mouth while Cooper bit his lip and stared at the ceiling.

Fatima gave her an annoyed look. "You know where babies come from, right?"

"Okay, I get it!" Shaun said, still laughing. "I could get pregnant."

"Well, you need to think about where you're going to put the baby, both in the mansion and in your weekend apartment."

"We don't exactly live a safe life," Shaun pointed out, sobering. "We're standing in an apartment that was shot to pieces. It doesn't seem quite right to bring a baby into the mix."

Fatima shook her head. "This is your life now, and you've accepted that. There are plenty of places in this world that we wouldn't consider safe, but babies are born every day. It's the cycle of life."

"I'm not sure the cycle of life should happen within the mafia," Shaun admitted, though the thought of a baby growing inside her, created by her and Jozef, was incredibly tempting. "I'm not sure if I'm ready."

"Well, you better figure it out. Babies have a way of happening when their parents don't take steps to stop them."

Shaun really didn't want to talk to her mother about birth control. She was almost thirty-six. They'd had 'the talk' about twenty years ago and it had been just as cringe-worthy then as this conversation was now.

"I'll think about a nursery, but not right now. For now,

we'll leave the spare room empty and concentrate on the main living area and bedroom."

Leaving the subject of babies behind, they continued to come up with design ideas until Jozef came looking for Shaun to take her back home.

CHAPTER THIRTEEN

S haun was busy clipping the dead roses and leaves from a bush in the rose garden when Atlas announced a visitor.

"There is a Dr. Elisa Černý here to see Dr. Patterson. I've put her in the formal sitting room."

Without waiting for a response, Atlas turned on his heel and left.

Shaun could only assume he was slithering back to whatever hole he spent his time in when he wasn't springing visitors on Shaun. He disapproved of her, and nothing she said or did seemed to change his attitude. She supposed he didn't see her as the proper rich lady of the household.

Jozef had hired him for his size and the air of deadliness swirling about him. Shaun believed he could back that air up. He certainly moved faster than he looked.

She sat back on her heels and dusted her hands on the thighs of her jeans before climbing to her feet. Shading her eyes, she looked out across the rose garden.

She wasn't sure exactly what she was trying to accomplish. She'd always been too busy with her work at the hospital to create and maintain a garden, but something drove her to take care of this one. To keep it alive and thriving, as if it could bring back the memory of the man who had spent so many hours tending it.

She did it for Jozef. He'd considered tearing it out as it was a constant reminder of his uncle, but she'd asked him to keep it. Maybe one day it would bring him more pleasure than pain.

She looked down at herself and thought about changing into something more presentable than a pair of dusty jeans and a dirt-streaked sweater. She'd left her coat and knit hat on the path when she'd gotten too hot from digging.

It was winter, but the roses were perennial and would come back in the Spring. She was tidying them while she had the chance. Jozef had told her it was unusual not to have snow on the ground at this time of year, but that it would come soon. The thought of snow made her miss home.

When she was a child, her father used to take her to the ice festival in Montreal, where they would tour the ice sculptures and play in the ice castle. She'd continued the tradition, even after her father's passing. It helped keep his memory alive. Perhaps, one day, she would convince Jozef to visit Canada in the winter and experience the unique beauty of the snowy landscape.

She made her way from the garden, into the dining room and through to the formal sitting room, a five-minute walk that gave her enough time to straighten her clothes and smooth a hand over her hair.

Shaun had never heard of their guest, Dr. Elisa Černý.

She paused for a second in the doorway of the sitting room, observing the woman. Not mafia, Shaun decided. Dr. Černý was sitting on the edge of a plush couch, her legs neatly tucked beneath her, her hands in her lap, fidgeting with a folder.

"Hello," Shaun greeted the other woman in halting Czech,

stepping into the room. "Dr. Černý, I'm Dr. Shaun Patterson."

The other woman stood and extended her hand, smiling. Relief was palpable on her face. Shaun suspected she was nervous about visiting a known mafia stronghold.

"I'm fluent in English."

Shaun was relieved to make the switch. She was slowly learning both Czech and Russian, but she found them difficult to get a handle on.

Shaun was intrigued by the other doctor. She'd overcome her natural fear of a potentially dangerous place, inhabited by dangerous people, to speak to Shaun. She looked to be in her mid to late fifties. She had sharp blue eyes and thin lips. Her blond hair was pinned back away from her face and her nails were short and unpainted. She wore chic but practical clothes.

Shaun would bet her newly acquired mansion the woman was a surgeon.

"Thank you so much for seeing me. Please, call me Elisa."

Shaun waved her hand back toward the couch that Elisa had just vacated. "Please sit down, I'll ring for coffee. Or would you prefer tea?"

Elisa shook her head. "Neither, thank you. I can't stay long."

"Are you on shift?" Shaun asked bluntly.

Elisa smiled and confirmed Shaun's suspicions about her. "Yes, it's a one-hour round trip to get out here, so I'll have to hurry back. I have surgery this afternoon."

"Then you're here for a reason, rather than a social visit."

"Both, actually." Elisa looked down at the file in her lap, but instead of opening it, she scanned Shaun from head to toe. "We met you last year. I was covering emergency for a colleague when you were brought in. I had the privilege of working on you after the poisoning."

Shaun stared at the woman, trying to place her, but she couldn't. She shook her head, but before she could speak, Elisa continued, "You were unconscious, and it was a fluke that I was in emergency that night. I'm usually in neurology. By the time you woke up, I had moved back to my department. I'd intended to drop by your room to introduce myself, but you'd already been moved and surrounded with enough security to make an airport blush."

Shaun sorted through her memories of that week spent in the Prague hospital. Between the hospital staff, security and the local police, she'd been constantly surrounded by people determined to keep her safe.

"Thank you," Shaun said, meaning it. She reached out to take Elisa's hand and, when the other woman gave it to her, squeezed it with feeling. "You saved my life."

Elisa nodded, her eyes serious. "When you were taken from Luhansk, it rocked all of us. Any of us could have been you. I've had friends and colleagues transfer to Ukraine to relieve the hospitals and clinics on the front lines."

The two women stared at each other for a moment, silently sharing in the hazards of their mutual profession. Though their jobs weren't inherently dangerous, every day they dealt with loss, life-altering decisions, unpredictable patients, grieving families.

"What brings you here today?" Shaun finally asked, her gaze dropping to the file clutched in Elisa's hands.

Elisa glanced down. "A patient," she admitted. "I want a second opinion on treatment. The tumour is complex, and you're well known for unorthodox methods that can increase survivability."

"You don't have any colleagues in neuro to bounce ideas off?" Shaun asked, intrigued. She desperately wanted to see the images in the file, to delve into a case once again. But surgeons were notoriously competitive.

"Sadly, no," Elisa admitted. "I have several excellent surgical nurses on my staff and a general surgeon who is only beginning to specialize in neurology. When I need another opinion, I often connect with colleagues in Moscow and Warsaw."

"And they weren't available today?" Shaun asked with a raised brow.

Elisa's lips thinned as Shaun forced her to explain herself. Finally, she shrugged, "You're one of the best in the world. Your theories and essays have elevated neurosurgery, and you've barely started your career. It's a rare opportunity to have you in my city, at my fingertips. I won't waste such an opportunity on an over-inflated ego. Better to make friends and learn from you."

Shaun stared at the other woman shrewdly, suspecting there was more to her story, but Shaun decided she'd pushed enough.

She held out a hand. "Let me see."

Elisa gave her the file and sat silently while Shaun looked over the images and read the patient's history. She picked out the glioblastoma right away. It took her less than a minute to understand what Elisa was doing in her sitting room.

"This is inoperable," Shaun said, handing the file back.

Elisa sighed heavily and took the file. "I know."

"Then why are you operating?"

Elisa looked down at her clasped hands and seemed to gather her thoughts before speaking. "The patient is high status. He knows that the tumour is inoperable, but he's insisting on surgery anyway. The hospital director is backing the surgery." She opened the file and pulled out an image, turning it toward Shaun, who leaned forward in her seat. She pointed at the shadow, then drew her finger to the left of the skull. "I will enter here, using laser tech, and manoeuvre around this section here." She tapped the photo again. "I will cut here and here, then pull the sections through. I figure the patient has a ten percent chance of survival."

"Five," Shaun said, studying the image. "Which is why we call them inoperable. He'll have another six months to a year if you leave it."

"He knows, and he still wants the surgery."

"Who is he?" Shaun asked, still studying the image. She was feeling the pull of a surgery. Even if it wasn't hers, she could live vicariously through Elisa for a few moments.

"Can't say. It's classified."

Shaun nodded. She'd had those patients before. Either celebrities or politicians. She guessed the patient was high up in the government since the hospital director was stepping in with an order for his staff, despite their clear opposition to the surgery.

Shaun kept her expression neutral as Elisa carefully watched her. Shaun knew exactly how Elisa was feeling, because she felt the same thing when presented with a challenging surgery.

"His chances would be closer to fifteen percent if you took lead on this surgery," Elisa said bluntly.

Shaun had suspected that this was the reason Elisa had shown up on her doorstep, on the Koba doorstep, despite her better instincts. She needed a skilled surgeon with a reputation for operating on the inoperable, and one had dropped into her lap.

"Twenty," Shaun admitted, snatching the file from Elisa and settling back into her chair to look it over more thoroughly.

"Is that a yes?" Elisa said, trying to suppress the excitement in her voice.

"No," Shaun said without looking up.

"Oh." Elisa was disappointed. "Well, I would appreciate any advice you can give me."

"It wasn't a no either."

The two women talked over the images for the better part of an hour, neither noticing when the maid slipped into the room to leave a tea service tray.

Finally, Shaun handed the file back to her guest and stared thoughtfully into nothing, murmuring, "When is the surgery?"

"Next week."

One week to convince Jozef.

Shaun stood and waited for Elisa to realize she was being dismissed. Elisa smiled wryly and reached for her purse, slinging it over her shoulder. "Thank you for your time, Dr. Patterson." She reached into the outside pocket of her purse and retrieved a card. "Please call."

Shaun nodded. "I'll let you know my decision in a few days."

"Thank you."

Shaun stood on the doorstep, watching as Dr. Elisa Černý drove her Prius up the winding driveway and out of sight. The moment the doctor had left the property, Shaun let out a whoop of joy.

A surgery!

Grinning, she slipped past a startled Atlas and ran up the stairs to her room to prepare her argument for Jozef. He was going to let her do the surgery. She wasn't going to take no for an answer.

CHAPTER FOURTEEN

S haun didn't see Jozef again until late that evening. He'd skipped supper and sent a servant to tell Shaun not to wait up for him. She'd been disappointed. Even though the mansion was huge, it wasn't so big that Jozef couldn't come find her and tell her himself when he was going to miss a meal.

She was tempted to go find him, assuming he was closeted in the study, but decided against a confrontation. They could work on his manners any time, but complex, exciting surgeries definitely did not happen every day. She needed him in a good mood if she was going to convince him to let her do the surgery.

In preparation, she pulled out the notes Jozef had copied while he was in prison. It still boggled her mind that he'd read everything she ever wrote. He was insane. But also very romantic, which she couldn't fault. She was getting used to his intensity.

When he finally entered their suite of rooms, it was clear he was expecting her to be in bed. He walked right past her, heading for the bedroom.

"Hello," she said softly from the couch.

To his credit, he didn't immediately reach for his gun, which was a common move when someone startled him. He was always so vigilant, it was rare that she startled him anyway. But in his own suite he wasn't expecting to be attacked.

Shaun was sitting in the shadows, still thinking about the surgery, planning her strategy and looking forward to working with Elisa. She knew she was getting ahead of herself, that Jozef would likely nix the surgery. She also knew that she wouldn't let him.

She felt for Jozef. He was rebuilding his uncle's mafia organization, restructuring and reorganizing. It was a big job. Havel had told her that the Bratva were breathing down Jozef's neck when he'd confronted her after their trip to Poland, insisting she never lure Jozef into doing that again. She had assured Havel that she would do and say what she pleased with Jozef. Then she'd told him that Poland hadn't been her idea. Hell, she was ashamed to admit, she hadn't even known Poland was a neighbouring country. Shaun had since pulled up Google Maps on her laptop and studied the part of the world she was now living in.

The gist of Havel's argument was that Jozef was busy and important, and she needed to give him breathing room. Havel had pointed out that Shaun was a distraction to Jozef. One that could get him killed. Shaun had taken his point, though she hated the way Havel delivered it. They'd known each other for a year and a half. Wasn't it time for Jozef's second-in-command to warm up to her?

She thought he'd softened after she patched up his wound and watched over him until he recovered enough to protect both of them. What more could she do to prove her loyalty? She was starting to believe he was unpleasant to everyone, not just her.

Regardless, she would do as Havel suggested and make sure she wasn't an added stressor in Jozef's life while he was managing a massive takeover. Her resolve lasted two days.

Because she was about to draw her line in the sand.

She couldn't allow Jozef to dictate her entire life. She had to tell him how her future would take shape, rather than allow him to shape it for her.

Or these were the things she told herself as she prepared her argument to convince Jozef to let her do the surgery.

"Can we talk?" she asked.

Jozef stepped into the lamplight surrounding the couch.

N-O, he signed.

Shaun frowned. "No, we can't talk."

He shook his head and looked pointedly at her hands, before signing, *we can talk any time you want. I was saying N-O to the surgery your guest proposed today.*

Shaun gaped at him, then shook her head. "I'm firing Atlas at the first opportunity."

No, you're not. He has 20 years of experience with the FSB and has worked with European intelligence. He stays.

At her blank look, he added, *Federal Security Service of the Russian Federation.*

I'm doing the surgery, she signed back.

He walked slowly toward her, his signs careful and measured. *It's too dangerous.*

Shaun pushed herself out of her chair and stood, holding his gaze. *I'm not a reckless person. I can take care of myself.*

You don't understand how easy it would be to get to you in a hospital.

She narrowed her eyes at him. *Maybe you don't understand how hard it is to get onto a surgical ward in a hospital.*

He shook his head in exasperation. *Like the one I took you from in M-O-N-T-R-E-A-L?*

Shaun crossed her arms over her chest. "You can't keep me locked up forever."

Jozef took the last step separating them and brushed his finger down her cheek. A shiver ran down her spine, though she tried to suppress it. She was taking a stand, not melting over her gorgeous fiancé.

I can keep you locked up forever, he signed, but before she could argue, he added, *I won't. I know it will hurt you and I refuse to do anything that will cause you harm, mental or physical.*

She softened and almost capitulated, but she really wanted to do the surgery. She lived for the knife and this surgery, after taking such a long break, felt like a toy in front of a toddler, just out of reach.

"I know you won't hurt me," she whispered. "You never really have, not deliberately."

He took her hand and placed it against his heart before signing over top of her arm, *I would rather die.*

She smiled. "Dramatic, but also romantic."

He leaned over and gently took her lips in a kiss so sweet Shaun's heart ached and her head swam. His love for her was an aphrodisiac. It was everything every woman wanted. It should be enough for her.

But it wasn't.

She needed more in her life than love. She needed purpose, she needed a challenge, and she needed to help people. It was her calling, had been for a long time, and she wasn't willing to give it up.

Since coming to Prague for the second time, she'd done nothing but compromise. It was time to take a stand and tell Jozef that she could love him, keep herself safe and do the work that she loved.

"I'm doing the surgery," she said the moment he released her lips.

He growled, probably at her stubborn tenacity, and

swooped in for a kiss much fiercer than the last. He stole her breath as he plunged his tongue into her mouth, forcing her own back. Gripping her head with his long fingers, he slid them into her hair and anchored her for his passionate kiss.

Shaun was helpless against his onslaught, but so caught up in the moment she didn't care. Heat flooded through her, sending her heart soaring as the butterflies in her belly went crazy.

He broke the kiss long enough to sweep her up into his arms. She squeaked in protest, but he was already striding toward their bedroom. She kissed his neck, sliding her arms around his shoulders and clutching him.

They hadn't had sex since before the night Dasha had attacked Shaun. She'd needed time to recover from her injuries, which still sometimes ached. Jozef had needed time to process the destruction of his family and the new world now laid at his feet.

Despite the distractions around them, the heat was always present. Shaun's heart pattered like crazy whenever Jozef was near, and she could see the near-constant erection he tried to hide when his men were around. It was heady knowing he reacted to her so strongly.

She felt the same.

He dropped them both onto the soft covers of their bed, his mouth finding hers and searing her with such heat that she moaned out loud. He swallowed the sound and thrust his tongue past her teeth, his kiss as aggressive as the rest of him.

When he broke the kiss, he took her wrist, the one that'd been injured, gently in his hand and brought it to his lips for a heartbreakingly light kiss. He looked at her, his bottomless blue eyes speaking eloquently.

She nodded and whispered, "I'm okay. I want this."

He didn't need more consent than that. He was on his feet and tearing her leggings away in seconds. Shaun laughed as he flipped her over onto her belly, gripped her panties and dragged everything down, including her socks.

This was Jozef, and this was why she loved him. He was intense, dangerous and serious, but he was also fun and funny. She loved that she could both predict what he would do, but also never knew what was happening. It was like living in a dream, floating from one moment to the next. She never could have imagined two years ago that this would be where her life would lead. Into the arms of a gangster who could kill as easily as he made love.

It was a terrifying thought, but not one that would stop her from enjoying the love she found in his arms.

He flipped her onto her back, straddled her and reached for the hem of her shirt. He dragged it up her body but stopped when it caught on her face. She couldn't see him, but suddenly she felt his lips on hers, wetting the soft cotton of the T-shirt as he devoured her.

It should have been a silly moment, probably looked silly, but it was so hot it sent streaks of pleasure zinging straight through her, from her head and neck, down to her puckered nipples and into her now very wet pussy.

Her arms were over her head, also trapped in the T-shirt. She was helpless in his grip but trusted him completely. She thrust her hips up against him. Rather than stopping to undress, he reached between them. She heard the zing of a zipper lowering and her heart hammered in response, her mouth watering as she pictured his thick, veined cock.

She gasped when he rocked himself against her hips, forcing her legs wider, before thrusting inside. Her head flooded with the sensation and she felt dizzy, breathless.

He didn't give her a chance to catch her breath but began pumping into her, his thick cock filling her to the hilt while he leaned over to kiss her through the shirt. She was helpless, at his mercy, and loving every second.

She didn't understand how they could have the chemistry they did, except that her pheromones were hard-wired to recognize his and zero in on them when there was so much as a whiff in the air. As a doctor, she tried to logic out their connection, but she kept coming back to the same thing; their souls recognized each other, even when they weren't on the same page.

Her lack of sight and inability to take a deep breath drove her higher and higher. Shaun was a sexual woman and enjoyed meeting her partners halfway, if not more than halfway. She'd always been one to climb on top and take herself to orgasm. But with Jozef it was different. He controlled her, moved her, treated her like a precious doll as he fucked her senseless.

The few times he allowed her to take control, he never let her take over completely. She always had an awareness that her moment of power could and would end.

He was physically stronger and could overpower her easily, but he chose his moments carefully. It was a strange thing to love, but she did. She loved how easily he wielded his strength. Loved that he was careful and measured, despite knowing he could have the upper hand.

He could easily tie her down and force her to stay home. Keep her locked up in their suite, but he wouldn't. And that was how she knew she would do the surgery. He wouldn't stop her because he couldn't bring himself to.

Did it make her a terrible person that she would use his desire for her to get what she wanted? Maybe. But no more terrible than a man who wielded control over entire countries through terror and brute force.

As he surged into her, she felt herself flying over the edge. Her orgasm was both intense and beautiful. It was sweet and painful. It was everything that was Shaun and Jozef.

He tore the shirt from her head as she screamed, the orgasm tearing through her in a rampage of flowing blood, hormones and racing pulse. She tried to gasp for air, but then his mouth was on hers and he was stealing her breath once more, sending her orgasm higher as she fought to breathe.

His cock grew inside her and his hips jerked against hers, before he bottomed out, filling her completely, then flooding her. When he lifted his head, spots swam in her vision. She blinked them away and stared up at him.

His expression was both triumphant and resigned. He was going to let her do the surgery.

CHAPTER FIFTEEN

Jozef's capitulation wasn't as easy as Shaun thought it would be. She should have known better. There was a reason Jozef was master of his slice of the underworld. He was an expert chess player and negotiator.

The next day, after an incredible night, where Jozef woke her repeatedly to fuck her into oblivion, Jozef called Shaun into his office. She felt a little like a schoolgirl being called to task by a parent or teacher. It was a strange feeling considering her years of education and work experience. But that was what Jozef did to her. He made her feel deliciously off-balance and a little unsure, while still building up her confidence.

When she arrived and knocked on the door, it was opened by Atlas, who nodded coldly at her and slipped past. She glanced after their boulder of a butler and then entered Jozef's office.

His face looked like it was carved from stone, but she wasn't worried. That was his usual expression when he was working. As soon as his eyes landed on her, his face softened. The implacable lines around his mouth and eyes smoothed, and his eyes shone with the love that was ever present around her.

She walked around the side of his desk and, as he pushed his chair back to make room, dropped into his lap. She pecked him on the lips and smoothed his hair behind his ear. He needed a haircut.

She wondered who cut his hair. A barber? Were they brought in or did he go to a shop? Or maybe he did it himself. Though she didn't think so, since his hair was always neatly layered and tidily buzzed around the neck.

"You wanted to see me?" she murmured.

He nodded and lifted her off his lap, setting her on his feet. He stood, his body brushing against hers.

Shaun's gaze drifted down him, taking in the glory of Jozef in a perfectly fitted business suit. He wore it informally, which made him even sexier. His jacket had been removed and his rich wine-coloured dress shirt was unbuttoned at the throat where his tattoos were most prominent, and the sleeves rolled up his muscular forearms.

He took Shaun's hand and led her back around the desk to the two chairs by the fireplace, which had a cozy fire snapping and flickering, casting shadows over the furniture.

Jozef hesitated, before waving his hand at the chair, indicating she should sit down. She sank into the chair as he dropped into his own. Some of the happiness he'd felt at seeing her drained from his expression.

She tapped his knee to bring his gaze back to her and signed, *please, tell me what's wrong.*

He stared at her, and she saw the struggle behind his deep blue gaze. Finally, he nodded. *This is where I sat with my uncle. We passed many pleasant hours here, discussing family and business. I...* he paused, as if searching for words, then signed, *I miss him.*

Shaun's throat felt tight, and she had to fight the urge to

apologize once more. She felt the weight of her responsibility toward the destruction of his family. Yet, she also knew that she wasn't to blame for their decisions. Dasha had made the decision to attack Shaun and Krystoff had made the decision to strike out at Jozef without discussion, without giving Jozef the chance to negotiate a cease-fire. Krystoff had defended his wife, while Jozef had defended Shaun.

She leaned over to touch his hand, which was resting on his thigh. *You have every right to feel sad and to miss your uncle. What happened was tragic and unnecessary. It's okay to cherish your memories of a man you loved.*

I killed him, Jozef countered.

You were defending yourself, your building and everyone inside. Just because you were the one to end his life, doesn't mean you don't get to mourn for him. Life is complicated and messy, no matter what we do to keep it in order. His decision to attack you and your decision to defend yourself doesn't take away from a lifetime of knowing him as a father figure. If the memories are too painful, then you can redo the office, get rid of the furniture. If the memories keep him alive for you and give you strength, then don't touch any of it.

Jozef blinked rapidly but nodded his head. He squeezed her hand, then signed, *I am grateful to have you.*

She laughed, and signed back, *you have me because you weren't going to take no for an answer.*

He looked back at her seriously, *no, I won't.*

It wasn't lost on Shaun that he'd switched from past tense to present. He wouldn't let her go back then, and he wouldn't let her go now.

They stared at each other and Jozef's gaze hardened, became purposeful, and she knew the balance of power had shifted once more. Being with Jozef was like standing on quicksand. One moment he was a normal, loving boyfriend, the next a terrifying mob boss who held her life in his hands.

Of course, he was one and the same, and she'd be lying if she said his shifting personality wasn't deeply sexy to her.

She licked her lips. "You're going to let me do the surgery, aren't you?"

She purposefully used spoken language, rather than sign language, as it made her feel more in control of the moment. Especially since she knew she was talking to the mob boss, not the guy who'd made love to her all night long, giving her the delicious ache she felt throughout her body.

He nodded. *Yes, but there are conditions.*

"What conditions?"

I will have a face-to-face discussion with the hospital director. He must allow my men access to every part of the hospital you will work in so we can keep you secure while you're distracted with your work.

Shaun felt some horror as she pictured the nightmare of logistics involved in securing an entire surgical ward. There were so many elements involved: sanitization, staffing, patients. None of it would be easy, but she could tell by looking at Jozef that he wasn't willing to budge on this condition.

She nodded. "Alright, talk to him. If he refuses, then I won't be doing the surgery."

I'm not trying to punish you, or stop you from doing your job, but I won't compromise with your safety.

She smiled and signed, *I know. You would never deliberately hurt me; mentally or physically.*

She used the same words he'd used the night before, and she could see the pleasure lighting his eyes.

I will make sure he doesn't say no, Jozef signed, his face twisting with purpose. *You can look forward to your surgery and let me take care of security.*

Shaun's heart ached with love for the man sitting across from her. She loved that he was using facial cues along with hand signals. When they first met, his face was carved of stone, even while he was signing. An unusual thing for someone who was nonverbal. Body language, hand signs and facial expressions went hand-in-hand with transmitting intent as well as language. But Jozef had lived a brutal life and hadn't incorporated facial expressions into his language. During their time together, he'd naturally fallen into it, and used facial cues often when they were together.

Thank you, this means a lot to me, she signed back.

He nodded, then said, *I have another condition.*

She tilted her head, waiting.

We set a wedding date.

Shaun's heart sank and she moved back in her chair, physically distancing from him.

You don't want to marry me? He frowned.

"It's not that." She sighed heavily. "I'm disappointed that you've made this part of a negotiation about my career. The two things are separate and shouldn't be part of the same discussion. You don't have to coerce me into marriage."

Then marry me tomorrow.

"No," she said automatically, shaking her head.

Then our wedding becomes part of this negotiation. He shoved a frustrated hand through his hair, before continuing. *I don't understand your reticence.*

Shaun turned her gaze to the fireplace because she hated seeing the disappointment on his face. "When we met, it was under extreme circumstances and I was forced into an engagement. Then, six months ago, you came to Canada and kidnapped me again, forcing me to move to a part of the world that I would never have considered home. With your actions, you sent not only my life into a spiral but also my mother's. Though we've found common ground, and I can't argue that there is love between us, I'm also not ready to tie my life to yours irrevocably. Not without sorting through our issues."

Yet, you wear my mother's ring. His gaze dropped to the lovely ring she almost never took off. *Willingly and with the knowledge that one day we will be married.*

She stared back at him, then signed, *I wear this ring with the understanding that there is enough love between us that we can sort through our differences before leaping into what could turn into a disaster of a marriage.* At his fierce frown, she held up a hand. *Not that I think our marriage will be a disaster, but we still have some major differences that need to be worked through before I'm willing to take the next step with you.*

He looked thoughtful as he considered her words, and she thought for a moment she'd convinced him. Then he signed, *no, I don't agree. We plan this wedding now. I'm done waiting. I have compromised on your surgery, now you will compromise on this.*

Frustration rose in Shaun. "You're forcing me to choose between a career I love and a wedding I'm not sure I want? You're holding this surgery hostage, Jozef, and that's not fair. This isn't a compromise."

He shook his head, *no, you're wrong about the surgery.*

"But you won't let me do the surgery unless I set a wedding date!" she exclaimed.

Is that what I said?

She opened her mouth, then closed it, thinking over what he'd actually told her. "You said the wedding date was part of our negotiations."

And so it is, he signed, pushing out of his chair, and standing. *As in, this wedding is non-negotiable. I also told you to look forward to your surgery, regardless of what else is happening in our lives. You will be in that room with your doctor friend, and you will get to conduct your surgery.*

Shaun was confused. "Then I don't have to plan a wedding?"

Jozef leaned over and took her arms in a gentle grip, lifting her from her chair. He kissed her lips, then set her away. *Yes, you most definitely have to plan the wedding. I've set the date.*

"What?" she exclaimed.

You have two weeks.

She gasped. "Jozef, no. We need to talk about this."

He pushed her toward the office door, opened it, and shoved her out into the path of a startled Cooper, who'd taken up post outside the door while waiting for Shaun's meeting to finish.

We'll talk later, but the wedding goes forward. I've waited a year and a half. I'm not waiting a minute longer.

She chewed her lip, then blurted out, "But I can do the surgery, regardless of my consent for the wedding?"

He flashed her a grin, then slammed the door in her face.

"You're a jackass!" she yelled through the door, before turning to walk into Cooper, who gripped her arms and set her away from him.

She glared at him. "Come on, we have work to do. I need to get my hands on every piece of research I left behind in Montreal. While we're waiting for it to get here, we can catalogue the furniture and paintings in this mausoleum of a mansion and decide what goes into storage."

The grin dropped from his face and she felt better.

CHAPTER SIXTEEN

"Saskia!"

Seconds after she heard her name, Saskia was enveloped in a tight hug. After a few seconds, she wrapped her arms around Madison and hugged her back. It had been three years since she'd seen her best school friend, but time fell away as the two reconnected.

"Let me look at you." Madison pushed Saskia back and looked her over from head to foot, clucking her tongue. "You've lost weight, you have rings under your eyes, and you look stressed as all fuck."

Saskia grinned, feeling herself relax for the first time in weeks. She'd taken a circuitous route to get herself into London. She'd had to go through Germany and Belgium, then France, using the fake IDs she'd commissioned after starting university.

"It could be worse," she said, her voice husky. "I could look a lot more dead."

Madison shook her head. "Don't even joke about that. When my dad heard rumours that your family was under attack and you were missing, I was frantic." Madison blinked rapidly. "I'm so sorry about your dad, he was a sweet man."

Saskia sucked in a deep breath as pain sliced through her. She'd suspected her father's fate but hadn't known for sure. She'd had to lie low, purposely cutting herself off from the outside world. She told herself it was because she hadn't wanted anyone to trace her movements, but in reality, she could have easily found out about her father. It was likely splashed all over European news.

She hadn't wanted to know how bad it was. She didn't think her heart could take it if any of her family members had died, and she'd been right. The news of her father gutted her. She started crying and couldn't stop.

Madison didn't say another word, gathering Saskia into her arms and rocking her on the city bench where they'd agreed to meet.

Saskia wasn't exactly sure why she was crying. She hadn't been close to her father, not in years. He was a mobster, and she was a family accessory. Decorative until she made an advantageous marriage, then the decoration of another mafia family.

Yet, her heart shattered at the news that Krystoff was dead. Her brain flooded with everything she would miss about him. She remembered the way he smelled as she sat on his lap when she was a child. A combination of tobacco, vodka, and crackling fireplace. He wasn't a good man, but he was the rock in the Koba family. He was her father, now he was gone, and she would never speak to him again.

She was glad she'd told him she loved him the last time she'd talked to him.

Saskia pushed away from her friend and wiped her face on her sleeve. "Have you... have you heard anything about my mom?"

Madison sighed, rubbing Saskia's back as she tried to

bring her tears under control. "No, nothing. She went missing from the Prague hospital the night your father died, and there hasn't been any news since. My father has been making inquiries on your behalf, hoping to find her safe and bring her over here."

Saskia wasn't surprised. Madison's father, Lord Alexander Grayson, was a significant part of the London underground. He would have his fingers in every part of the European mafia scene. Lord Grayson adored his daughter and would keep tabs on the Koba family for Madison's sake.

"Will you let me know if you hear anything?" Saskia asked, sniffling.

"Of course," Madison assured her. "I'll do you one better though. You'll stay with me while you're here, so you can get your news directly from the horse's mouth."

Saskia smiled weakly. "I appreciate that, Maddy, but it's like I told you when I phoned, I can't stay with you. I'm certain my cousin is looking for me, and I don't know if his intentions are good or murderous. I refuse to put you and your family in danger."

"Nonsense." Madison used her motherly voice, a voice she used often during their high school years, despite being single, gorgeous and a major part of the London party scene.

"There's no way I'm going to let you put yourself in danger for me. I can take care of myself," Saskia insisted.

"I'm sure you can," Madison said briskly. "But you aren't going to. We're doing this together. We'll lie low and we'll work out a plan for your future. I'm not letting you go anywhere until I know you're perfectly safe and happy."

Saskia let out a watery laugh. "Happy."

Madison wrapped her arm around Saskia and squeezed. "It'll be okay. I promise."

"It hasn't been okay in a long time," Saskia murmured,

laying her head on her friend's shoulder. "I don't even know what okay feels like."

"We'll get there, sweetie." Madison looked up as a car with tinted windows pulled up to the curb. "Our ride is here."

"Maddy..."

Madison shook her head. "You're coming with me. My dad has set up a safe-house for us. We'll stay there until he's able to either negotiate with your cousin or get you a new identity that can't be traced."

"Jozef has a long reach." Pain sliced through her as she thought of her cousin and the possibility that he might be gunning for her. She hated the mafia with a passion. In what other world would a beloved cousin, almost a brother, have to make such a terrible decision?

"Ours is just as long over here. He won't be able to reach you, I promise."

It was so tempting to allow Madison and Lord Grayson take care of her. In some ways she was much older than her years, having grown up in a demanding family, but she was also still a nineteen-year-old girl. She wanted to rest, to stop having to make decisions on the run, to let someone else take over for a while.

"Okay," she whispered, fear surging through her. Fear of the unknown, fear of putting her friend and her family in danger. "Let's go."

Together they climbed into the town car Lord Grayson had sent and sped through the streets of London toward an unknown safe-house.

They arrived less than an hour later.

Saskia's lips twitched as she climbed out of the town car and stared up at the magnificent towering glass skyscraper. The glass had a green tint that shone with sparkling newness as the sun hit it.

"This is lying low?" Saskia shook her head. "I was clearly not doing it right."

She thought of the tiny basement suite in Lichtenstein she'd rented through Airbnb using one of her fake ID's. Or the leaky hovel she'd spent four days in outside of Paris. That place had been a few hundred years old and likely never renovated.

Madison grinned. "A safe-house doesn't need to be disgusting. Trust me, we'll be safe here. This place belongs to a friend of my dad's so it can't be traced back to my family."

As they walked through the bright penthouse suite, filled with light, tasteful art and modern decor, Saskia wondered about the person who owned the place. What did his regular home look like if this was his spare?

She laughed out loud as she inspected the pool. "Yeah, I think I can lie low here."

The two women spent the rest of the afternoon getting reacquainted. They gossiped about old school friends, ordered sushi from one of Madison's favourite restaurants and made themselves at home.

Madison chose the master suite on the main floor while Saskia chose the loft bedroom. As she set her backpack down on the queen-sized bed, she looked around in awe. Huge skylights filled the room with light, casting soft shadows across the fluffy white duvet. Warmth caressed her skin, softening the brittleness of the last couple of weeks. The loft was huge, the furniture sleek, the ambiance modern, all of which appealed to her.

Unable to resist, Saskia let the lure of luxury lead her into the soft covers of the bed. She was still wearing her travel clothes, but she didn't care. Being surrounded by safety for the first time in weeks was a lullaby to her anxious brain.

She fell asleep almost instantly and slept heavily until something woke her up.

Saskia blinked into the gloom, trying to remember where she was as her exhausted brain played catch up. The shadows had shifted as the day progressed.

She yawned widely and glanced at the skylight over her bed. It was now dark out. She'd lost most of the day to sleep. She flipped the blankets back and shifted to the edge of the bed. That's when her brain registered what had woken her.

Voices.

She heard an indistinct murmur from the floor below hers. Since the loft was open, she could creep close to the stairs leading down and hear what was being said.

"Let me talk to her first." Saskia glanced down to see Madison talking to her father. She was about to interrupt them, when Madison said, "I don't want her to hate me. I can make her understand."

Lord Grayson, a tall, grey-haired man, snorted. "You think she'll understand that you've betrayed her for a luxury trip to New York with your boyfriend? No, Maddy, she's dangerous. Better to let me handle this. We'll have her removed quietly and sent back to her family."

Saskia didn't have time to process the betrayal of one of her closest friends. The moment Lord Grayson finished his sentence, she flew back into the bedroom, scooped up her backpack and frantically looked for an exit.

There was nothing in the bedroom, and of course the windows were sealed shut since they were on the top floor of a high-rise.

She ran down the carpeted hallway as Madison and her father continued to argue. Finally, she found a door with an exit sign over it. The alarm would go off once she pushed the door open, but it wasn't a problem. She just had to be smart and run as fast as she could.

She pulled her pack off her shoulder and dug through the contents until she came up with a can of pepper spray. She secured the backpack and took a deep breath. Holding the pepper spray in front of her, she shoved the door open and flung herself onto the landing of a stairwell.

Unfortunately, she flung herself into the arms of a very startled security guard. She lifted the spray and let loose on the man, searing his eyes with the noxious concoction. The spray drifted back toward her, so she squinted her eyes and slid past the screaming man.

Sadly, he wasn't the only security personnel in the stairwell to the penthouse. There were two more men behind him, and though the first man was leaning against the wall coughing, his eyes streaming, his compatriots were in perfect control. They grabbed her, one of them smashing her arm into the wall until she let go of the cannister.

"Don't you fucking touch me!" she shrieked as she was bodily lifted off the floor and dragged back into the penthouse.

She fought tooth and nail, but the men holding her had a good grip and she'd never really learned how to fight. Not like her mother and sister. She was more the laze-in-bed-and-read-a-novel kind of girl. Now she was paying for her lack of combat skill. Possibly with her life.

They marched her from the stairwell where their comrade was groaning in agony, back through the loft and down the stairs to where Madison and Lord Grayson were looking up at them.

When Madison realized what was going on, she yelled, "Don't hurt her!"

"What the fuck do you care?" Saskia shouted furiously. "You lied to me. You told me I would be safe and I believed you."

The years of friendship fell to dust on the floor as Madison's face crumpled in guilt. Maybe if she'd betrayed Saskia for a better reason, like her father threatened her, Saskia might have been able to forgive her. But a trip to New York? No, after today, Madison was dead to her.

"Calm down, Ms. Koba." Lord Grayson held a hand up as though offended by the commotion.

Saskia rolled her eyes. Was she supposed to go quietly to what might end in a bullet to the brain? Not fucking likely.

"What happened to calling me Saskia?" she demanded, disgust in her voice. "That's what you used to call me when I would run barefoot through your garden, picking wildflowers with your daughter. You remember that?"

He flinched, and she felt mildly better that she'd scored a hit. When Madison had sent out messages to all of Saskia's social media and email accounts, begging her to get in touch after the collapse of the Koba empire, Saskia had truly thought she had an ally in her childhood friend. The betrayal stung. Though not as much as Madison would sting if Saskia could get her hands on the other woman for a few seconds.

"You'll be better off if you go back to your family," Lord Grayson said, his voice low, as though he meant to be soothing. "They're desperate to get you back."

"I'll bet they are!" she snarled. "My father is dead, asshole, and my mother is on the run, afraid for her life, and you're going to send me back to the man who plans on killing her. Excuse me if I don't thank you."

He shook his head in disappointment. "I wouldn't send you back if I didn't think it was safe."

"Maybe we should think about this..." Madison interrupted, indecision in her voice.

Saskia ignored her former friend. "How much is he paying you for my 'safe' return?"

The kindly expression melted away, leaving behind the calculating mask of a man who was putting money ahead of Saskia's life. "You were always a clever little thing."

"It doesn't take cleverness to figure out your motivation

for returning me to the man who killed my father and took over my home," she countered.

"Spare me the poor child campaign, it won't work." He nodded at the men holding her. "Take her. Use the needle, she won't go quietly."

Saskia snorted. "You sound like a Bond villain."

When one of the men pulled a syringe from his pocket and uncapped it, Saskia began the fight. It was useless, though. Both of the men holding her outweighed her by a lot and had far more experience restraining a person than she had in escaping.

"What are you poisoning me with?" she demanded, her voice becoming higher pitched as hysteria took over.

Lord Grayson looked pitying, but not enough to stop what he'd orchestrated. "It's just a shot of GHB to make you more compliant. It won't hurt you."

Saskia fought as hard as she could and twisted one of her arms out of their grip. She swung her fist around, but Lord Grayson stepped up to help hold her while they stuck her in the arm with the needle.

They continued to hold her until she stopped fighting them. "Okay, okay," she snapped. "Let me up."

They'd wrestled her to the floor, but once she was calm, helped her back to her feet. One of them still held her arm in case she bolted. She rubbed the needle prick with her hand and glared at everyone.

"I hope your conscience gives you restless nights for the rest of your damn lives. You're sending an innocent woman to her death."

Madison gasped, but her father shook his head. "Enough dramatics." His gaze shifted to the men. "You can take her downstairs. The drug will take effect in the next few minutes, which should help quiet her."

Each man took an arm and started to haul Saskia away.

Madison stepped into their path and reached out to touch Saskia.

"I'm so sorry – " she tried to say.

"Get away from her!" Madison's father shouted.

It was too late. Saskia slammed her forehead into Madison's nose, producing a satisfying crack and sending her former friend flying backwards into the arms of her father, blood spurting from her nose.

Saskia's head hurt like a bitch and she felt blood drip onto her cheek. Her lips stretched into a feral grin.

"Have fun in New York, Maddy."

"Get her out of here!" Lord Grayson snarled as he reached for his sobbing daughter's face.

Saskia's day might end in a bullet to the brain, but at least she had the satisfaction of knowing she'd fucked up Madison's beautiful face. Bitch had always had more looks than sense.

CHAPTER SEVENTEEN

Shaun woke slowly to the constant shaking of her shoulder. She mumbled and tried to roll away from the annoying thing that was touching her. The sound of a soft chuckle annoyed her further so she pushed herself up in the bed and glared around the room, trying find the source of her ire.

Of course, no one except Jozef was allowed in their bedroom unless there was an emergency, so it was his face she saw, lit by the soft glow of a lamp. She tried to blink away the heaviness of her sleep as she focused on him, the annoyance at being woken up falling away. Jozef didn't wake her unless he had a good reason.

"What's wrong?" she asked groggily.

He began signing and it took a moment for her sleepy brain to catch up and follow his signals.

"Saskia?" she asked, finally picking up on what he was trying to tell her. "Saskia is here?"

He nodded, his expression serious.

Shaun fought with the bedding until she could slide off the bed and stand, wobbling on her feet. As soon as she was steady, she rushed to the closet and pulled her bathrobe off the hook on the back of the door.

She tied the sash and looked expectantly at Jozef.

He escorted her through their suite with a hand at her back.

Shaun was anxious to see Saskia; to lay eyes on the younger woman and make damn sure she was okay. Two weeks earlier, when Shaun had asked after Saskia, Jozef had bluntly told her the truth. Saskia believed her life was in danger and had gone on the run.

Shaun had been shocked, but the more she thought about it, the more she realized it was a natural response. Jozef's clear path to the Koba organization was through wiping out anyone with a claim on it. When Shaun had this realization, she'd demanded to know what Jozef's plans for his cousin were, fearing the worst.

He'd assured her that he only wanted to find Saskia safe and sound and bring her home. He'd been so earnest in his worry over his young cousin that Shaun realized he had no intention of harming Saskia. Her relief had been short-lived though, the longer it took to track her. Saskia was intelligent and resourceful. Part of Shaun thought maybe Saskia's best shot at a happy and normal life would be to disappear for good and have nothing more to do with the Koba family. But pain shot through Shaun as she imagined never seeing Saskia again. The two women had bonded while Shaun had been a captive and again when Shaun was brought back to Prague. If there was one truly innocent member of the Koba family, it was Saskia. She deserved the best of everything but kept getting the short end of the stick.

Shaun and Jozef walked swiftly down the wide, ornately decorated hallway to Saskia's suite. It had been left untouched, waiting for its owner to reclaim it.

When a quick glance failed to produce Saskia, Shaun

continued through to the bedroom. Sure enough, Saskia was laid out on her bed, one arm flung over her head and the other resting against her chest. It looked like she'd been dropped on the bed and left. Havel was standing on one side of the bed while Terek, another member of Jozef's team, stood on the other. Both men looked relieved to see Shaun, who rushed to the bed.

Jozef stood watching from the doorway as Shaun checked Saskia's pulse, which was strong and steady. Shaun sighed her relief and sat gingerly on the bed beside her.

"What happened to her?" she demanded, looking around accusingly at the men.

It was Havel who answered.

"She was picked up in London by a contact, but apparently fought the people hosting her so they drugged her." Disapproval coloured his tone, which made Shaun feel more lenient toward him. "Idiots couldn't handle one small girl with zero fighting experience."

"Do you know what they gave her?" Shaun rested her hand on Saskia's forehead. It was warm, but not unusually so.

"GHB," Havel told her. "Two strong doses of it."

"They gave her the date rape drug?" Shaun asked incredulously.

Havel nodded, then a smirk curved his lips. "Apparently she hit them with pepper spray and broke someone's nose."

Shaun spotted a faint bruise on Saskia's forehead and wondered if that was how she broke someone's nose. Good for her. Even if Havel insisted Saskia couldn't fight, she was scrappy enough to make her hits count.

"Is she going to be okay?" Havel's eyes were on Jozef when he spoke, though the question was aimed at Shaun. She suspected Jozef had been signing behind her.

"I think so, but we won't know for sure until she's awake."

Havel and Terek quietly left the room.

Shaun tried to tell herself it wasn't Jozef's fault. When shit hit the fan a month ago, he couldn't have imagined that the events would lead to his cousin being taken captive, drugged and returned to her family home.

Still, when Shaun finally looked up at him, she couldn't help the accusation in her tone. "Why didn't you just let her go?"

Jozef stepped closer to the bed. *She's a high value target. Always has been and always will be. She's a member of one of the most powerful organizations in Eastern Europe. A prime target for kidnapping.*

Shaun shook her head, still unable to let the lingering bitterness go. Saskia's fate was too similar to her own. "She would've been happier if you'd let her find her own path."

She would have found trouble. She belongs with her family.

"Her family isn't the same family she knew." Shaun tried to moderate her voice, but she felt the heat of suppressed anger licking at her. "Her father is dead, her mother and sister are gone, and you are responsible. I know you didn't want this, but those are the facts. You've brought her home to a mess."

Jozef couldn't argue and didn't try. Instead, he asked, *does she need anything? Will she be okay?*

"Physically, probably. Mentally? I don't know."

Jozef paced, gripping his head in his hands, his shoulders hunched. Some of Shaun's anger melted in the face of his concern for his cousin. "I'll stay with her until she wakes up, and then we should be able to tell if there was any harm caused by the shots she was given."

Rather than leave, Jozef dropped into a chair.

Shaun made herself comfortable next to Saskia on the bed, leaning back against the headboard and brushing her hand down Saskia's face. Shaun felt like she needed the comfort almost as much as Saskia. She couldn't imagine how traumatizing it must've been for Saskia to be picked up and physically held against her will by a bunch of men. Actually, Shaun knew exactly how that felt, which was why she wanted to be there when Saskia woke up.

She settled more comfortably onto the pillows and wrapped her arms around Saskia.

Saskia felt weirdly fuzzy. Like she'd drank the entire Christmas party punch and was trying to sleep off a wicked hangover. Speaking of hangovers... the moment she tried to move, her head started pounding, and she felt like she was going to vomit.

She tried to shove the blankets away, only to find a pair of arms trapping her. Panicked, she tried to smack the arms away as bits and pieces of her memory returned and she realized she'd been kidnapped. Her hands were clumsy and she collapsed back against the bed. She would just have to throw up on whoever was holding her.

"You're okay, it's me." The voice was quiet and soothing.

A woman. If it was Madison, Saskia was going to break her neck this time.

The face in front of hers swam and she had to blink a few times to clear her vision. Shaun was leaning over her, a concerned expression on her face. Saskia reached up to touch her, to make sure she was real.

"You're so pretty."

She didn't realize she'd said it out loud until Shaun's concern changed to amusement. "I think you're pretty, too."

Saskia frowned. "Don't do that," she mumbled.

"Do what?" Shaun asked.

"You know...." Saskia licked her lips, they were so dry.

"That thing when you don't accept a compliment by turning it around."

"Did I do that?"

Something in Shaun's voice suggested she knew exactly what she'd done. Saskia tried to flick Shaun, but couldn't coordinate her fingers. "You're beautiful. As close to perfect as god could get." She felt a burn of tears as her numb mind decided to compare Shaun's body to hers. Shaun's skin was flawless, her eyes sparkled and if that wasn't enough to hate her, she was also tall and skinny. The exact opposite of Saskia.

"You're pretty and that's final." Her words slurred.

Shaun laughed and leaned over to hug her. "I think you're going to be okay."

"Was I ever not?" Saskia asked, confused, then remembered the kidnapping. "Oh right, those assholes drugged me."

A growl from the corner of the room drew Saskia's attention, and she swivelled her head to see what kind of dog got in her bedroom. When she spotted Jozef, her heart leapt into her throat and fear radiated out of her like a beacon.

She scanned him and was relieved to see he was wearing a T-shirt and jeans with no visible holster. Still, she scrambled up in the bed and pressed herself against Shaun. He was far less likely to shoot her if she was wrapped around his girlfriend.

Shaun slipped her arms around Saskia, which made her feel like they were a united front against the threat of Saskia's own family.

Jozef stood and slowly approached the bed, his eyes on her. His expression was one of concern, the same as Shaun's had been. He didn't look angry or like he had any intention of hurting her. Still, Saskia had to be sure.

"What are you going to do with me?" She wished her voice sounded less slurred.

Shaun rubbed her arm.

Jozef shook his head. *Nothing. I'm not going to hurt you.*

"Good, then you can let me go."

I can't do that. You're in the same danger you were in before…

He didn't finish the sentence but looked away.

"Before you killed my father," she finished for him, her voice flat.

He nodded.

I'm sorry, he signed. *I wish it could have been avoided.*

Saskia didn't know what to say, but the grief she saw on her cousin's face was real. It matched hers. The sort of angry grief a person felt when the one they loved didn't have to die. Saskia's father had chosen his path, and though Jozef had been the one to kill him, he hadn't wanted things to end that way.

"What about my mother?" Saskia asked. "Do you… do you have her?"

N-O, he admitted. *But we're looking.*

"What will you do with her when you find her?"

He didn't speak, but his hardened expression spoke volumes.

Saskia pushed out of Shaun's embrace and moved to the edge of the bed, pleading with Jozef. "Don't kill her. I know she's been a pain in your ass…" she glanced guiltily back at Shaun, "and she tried to kill Shaun, but she's my mother. I can't lose both of my parents."

Jozef stared at her. It was clear his heart was warring with his head. Saskia took her advantage and continued to push.

"She raised you and she really loved you, even though she fucked everything up. She's disturbed, Jozef. We've all known it for years, but no one ever talked about it. She nearly killed her own sister over a bout of stupid jealousy. Dad should have locked her up back then."

Jozef's face softened and Saskia knew she had him. She went in for the kill. "We can keep her confined for the rest of her life. I'll even volunteer to be the one who looks after her. Just please don't kill her."

Jozef looked at her with pity. *I'm sorry.*

Saskia collapsed back onto the bed. She understood his reasoning, understood why he had to kill Dasha, but understanding didn't repair the tear in her heart that kept getting bigger.

Her eyes filled with tears as she thought of the way everything had changed. Life as she knew it was over. She had no idea where she was going now or what her place in the family was. Would she be allowed to go back to school? Would she still have to make an advantageous mafia marriage?

She was too tired to ask, but eventually she would need answers to her questions so her future would feel a little less uncertain.

Jozef must've seen the despair on her face because he stepped up to the bed and put his hand on her head.

Saskia crawled away from him, pushing Shaun's comforting hands aside.

"I want to be alone."

CHAPTER EIGHTEEN

"A Mr. Dietrick and a Special Agent Moreau to see Mr. Koba."

Jozef looked up from his desk, paperwork spread across the surface, and tried to reengage his brain. He'd been consumed by Krystoff's meticulous record-keeping, not something he had suspected his uncle capable of. Yet the evidence of Krystoff's obsessive need to record every interaction, be it financial, contractual or personal, filled a small room of file cabinets next to his office.

Jozef had been engrossed in the records surrounding Leeza's marriage when Atlas had interrupted him. Though Jozef had recently found out about Leeza's parentage, it turned out that Krystoff had known for years and her marriage appeared to be based on the knowledge. Jozef couldn't figure out why, unless it was petty revenge against his now-beloved wife. He'd wanted her to suffer in some small way for birthing a bastard into the family and accomplished it by giving the girl away in marriage to a monster. The more Jozef read, the more he realized his uncle had known exactly who and what Adam Horáček was prior to the union. Yet, he still negotiated the marriage, and there didn't appear to be even a hint of blackmail to push him into the decision. No, it appeared to be simply a matter of petty revenge.

Show them in, Jozef signed to Atlas. *Get H-A-V- E-L.*

Jozef had been expecting this meeting. After the death of his uncle, he'd smoothed things over with law enforcement fairly easily. Krystoff had orchestrated the attack on his nephew and Jozef and the 'residents' of the building had simply been defending themselves.

It was a weak story, though it was mostly true. Despite Jozef's attempt to clear the building of anything that could be illegal, he'd been shaken by Krystoff's death and had missed a few things. Though he'd hidden his rocket launcher in the safe room, it was clear his apartment had been blown up by something significantly more powerful than a sidearm. It was also clear that Krystoff hadn't killed himself with a rocket launcher. Still, Jozef had thrown money and promises at the problem and it had gone away. He'd even convinced law enforcement not to pursue any questioning with Shaun.

She'd been surprised by the lack of questions, but Jozef had reassured her they got everything they needed from others and didn't require an additional statement from her. She'd been too traumatized to question him further. Something he was grateful for. She didn't need to know that they'd had to dispose of Giselle's body privately. Or that they suspected someone close to Jozef of killing her.

Though the local police had cleared Jozef and his team of any wrongdoing in the attack, the Prime Minister's office was gunning for him, hoping to use the incident to their benefit. Dietrick would be here on the Prime Minister's behalf, his bodyguard and mouthpiece, and had apparently teamed up with Interpol to add more weight to his efforts.

Jozef recognized the name Moreau. Though it was a common French name, most in the underworld knew of

Interpol bloodhound, Francois Moreau. He was known for bringing down organized crime families.

Jozef's suspicions were proved true when Atlas escorted the two men into his office. Jozef stared hard at Moreau. He was the same man that their surveillance had taken pictures of. According to Jozef's sources, the man had been looking closely at the Koba family.

Moreau must have a set of solid brass balls for walking into Jozef's den like he hadn't a care in the world.

"Koba," Dietrick said coldly.

Jozef wasn't surprised at the chilly greeting. Last time they met, Jozef had put a bullet in the other man's shoulder for endangering Shaun on the highway.

Jozef didn't attempt to communicate, instead crossing his arms over his chest and staring at them. He wanted them to feel the heat of discomfort while they waited for Havel to arrive, which could take anywhere from two minutes to fifteen, depending where he was on the estate.

It was times like this, meetings like this, when Jozef knew how to use his voicelessness to his advantage. Humans were used to using vocal communication. They relied on it so much that many had lost their ability to read body language and nuances. Jozef had spent his entire life honing his ability to read others. Not in what they said, but in what they didn't say.

Dietrick was attempting to put on a brave front, but fear radiated from him in waves. His slightly raised eyebrows, taut forehead and open mouth breathing gave away his fear. He also moved so that the shoulder Jozef had shot was turned away, subconsciously favouring his injury. Like a shark, Jozef smelled blood in the water when it came to Dietrick.

He shifted his focus to the other man, openly staring at Moreau. The Frenchman was more difficult to read. His expression was guarded, and his body language was loose and uninterested, his hands in his pockets, his gaze on the fireplace mantle, which showcased Krystoff's cigar box and a few other trinkets. Of course, Moreau wasn't as casual as he looked. The rapid flicker of his pulse gave him away. Was his elevated heart rate fear or excitement?

Havel knocked once and let himself into the office. Ignoring the other two men, he approached Jozef's desk and signed, *you want an interpreter?*

Jozef gave him a feral smile. *Not just any interpreter. I want you.*

Havel chuckled. *I love you too, bro.*

It was a joke, of course, but it amused both men to laugh privately while their guests stood stiffly waiting for acknowledgment and wondering what the hell was being said.

Jozef cleared his throat, and Havel took that as his cue to step to the left side of the desk. Near the boss, protective, but keeping Jozef in the position of power.

It was all about optics. If they acted like tough guys, then others would believe that they were seeing tough guys. Jozef had a reputation for being brutally efficient, and though he was as his reputation suggested, half of the stories that circulated about him were made up. He and his men did nothing to discourage them.

What do you want? Jozef signed, staring hard at Dietrick.

Havel interpreted.

Dietrick looked uncomfortable and glanced between Jozef and Havel as if trying to decide where his eyes should land. He made the correct choice when he chose Jozef.

"We have some questions regarding the evening of November 29th," Dietrick began. He pulled a notebook from his inside coat pocket, channeling every television detective ever.

I've answered questions. I have nothing more to add.

"I understand." Dietrick tapped the notepad with his pen.

"This won't take long. We just need to clear up a few inconsistencies."

Before he could begin, Moreau spoke up. "Our condolences for the loss of your uncle."

He was staring just as hard at Jozef as Jozef had stared at him earlier. He was looking for micro expressions. For a split second, Jozef wondered if the man knew sign language. His gaze was sharp, and his mind seemed to be working overtime.

Thank you, Jozef signed.

"It must have been terrible for you," Moreau continued. "Being the one to end his life. He took you in as a child, correct?"

I think you know that your information is correct.

Moreau nodded and fell silent, allowing Dietrick to continue. In a few sentences, Moreau had made it clear that he was in charge of any investigation that was happening. Dietrick was a mouthpiece sent from the prime minister's office to open doors for Interpol.

Interesting.

"What were you doing when you first found out the building was under attack?" Dietrick asked, not looking up from his blank notepad.

I was watching TV with my wife and her mother.

Dietrick looked up sharply. "You got married?"

Jozef let out a soft growl before signing, *as good as.*

Havel translated, then added, "You'll want to call her his wife if you prefer your arms attached. He's not big on disrespect."

Jozef's lips stretched into a feral grin, punctuating Havel's warning.

"Please refrain from threatening law enforcement," Dietrick said with as much dignity as he could manage while nearly shitting his pants.

Jozef barked his laughter and signed, *you aren't law enforce-*

ment any more than we are. If your friend here, who is law enforcement, has a problem with me, he can step up and say something.

Moreau nodded at the exchange, his sharp eyes flicking between the men. "No problems here."

Dietrick looked even more uncomfortable, if that was possible. "Uh... so you were watching television with your... wife and her mother. What's the mother's name?"

No comment, Jozef signed while Havel translated.

They would already know Fatima's name, but if they somehow didn't, he wouldn't enlighten them. He would protect the women under his care, no matter who was asking the questions.

"I'm afraid I need you to answer the question," Dietrick pushed.

Jozef placed his hands on his desk and leaned over, narrowing his eyes. *No, you don't.*

Before Dietrick could push his own head further through the noose he was hanging for himself, Moreau stepped in. "Move on, Dietrick."

Jozef snorted, straightening. So Moreau fancied himself the good cop here.

Dietrick pushed forward as if he hadn't had a good portion of his pride crushed by the man standing across from him. "What was your response when you found out your building was under attack?"

I contacted my men and told them to defend our holdings.

Havel glanced at him, as if questioning his blatant honesty, but translated.

Jozef wasn't worried. It wasn't illegal to defend property in the Czech Republic. His building had been stormed and he was a professional security expert. It was only natural that he and his men would act in their own best interests.

"You didn't think to call the police?"

Our building alarm connects with the local police department.

The moment the building was attacked, law enforcement was informed.

"Yet you didn't wait for them. You allowed your people to rampage through the building, killing indiscriminately."

Jozef hadn't credited Dietrick with having enough balls to come out swinging, not when their first meeting had ended badly for the man. He must feel brave with Interpol at his back. Little did he realize, Interpol wouldn't lift a finger unless it helped them with an apprehension.

My people defended themselves and the building they were charged with defending. Jozef paused, as if gathering his thoughts. *Are you implying we should have waited for the police to arrive? We should have allowed ourselves to be killed? I will remind you that there were casualties on both sides.*

"Far more on the other side than on yours," Dietrick countered.

My men are better trained in high-pressure security situations. Jozef crossed his arms over his chest, bulging his biceps, telling the other man through body language to back off this line of questioning.

Dietrick wasn't good at hints.

He pressed on. "You could have detained those men. Your guys left fewer men alive than dead."

Jozef frowned fiercely. *How were we supposed to do that? Politely ask them to hand over their weapons and stand down? I'm not pleased with your implication that we could have done something differently that night. I lost my uncle and a good friend. I have nothing further to say. Unless you plan on charging us with something, leave.* Jozef's expression became derisive as he continued, *but of course, you can't charge us with anything because you aren't actually law enforcement. You're security, just like us.*

If Dietrick ever needed work outside of the Prime Minister's office, he better move clear across the world, because

Jozef planned to make his life very difficult once he lost the protection of his politician buddy.

Moreau took a step toward Jozef's desk. "I have one more question, if you don't mind."

Jozef waved his arm, indicating the other man could ask.

"Do you know the whereabouts of Dasha Koba?"

Jozef stiffened, but otherwise didn't so much as twitch to give away his thoughts. Finally, after a long moment, he answered, *I do not.*

They stared at each other, then Jozef signed, *do you know where she is?*

"No."

Moreau's answer came before Havel could translate. He'd deliberately shown his hand. Jozef wondered if the other man was giving away his ability to put himself in Jozef's camp, or as a warning.

Moreau was a clever man, Jozef knew it in his gut. The man would definitely show up again. The question was, who was he really and what did he want?

CHAPTER NINETEEN

Shaun rifled through her purse, making sure she had everything she needed for a trip into the city. Cell phone, wallet, tissues, tampons, taser, pepper spray, mini first aid kit.

She grinned to herself as she exited her bedroom.

Her life had changed enormously. Two years ago, she would never have imagined carrying a taser and pepper spray. Of course, Jozef was the one who insisted she carry some form of protection. He told her she wouldn't be allowed to leave the house unless she had the correct accessories.

She skipped down the wide staircase, her steps happy and light. She was going to meet Dr. Černý at the hospital to go over the particulars of their upcoming joint surgery. She was so happy to finally get back to work that nothing could bring her down. Or so she thought, until she rounded the bottom of the staircase, heading for Jozef's office to say goodbye before she left.

Standing in the hall was a group of men. Jozef, Havel and two men she didn't know. As she approached, her steps slow-ing, she realized she did know one of them. Or had at least she'd seen him.

His head turned as she approached the group, and she couldn't keep the jolt of recognition from her face, which Jozef saw because he saw everything. His neutral expression turned into a scowl as he noticed her gaze lingering on the man.

"You," she said, stopping in front of the group.

Moreau dipped his head in a nod as Jozef stepped forward, gripping Shaun's arm and pulling her away from the two strangers. Havel shifted so he was mostly in front of her. Frustrated, Shaun shoved Havel, trying to see around him.

"Who are you?" she demanded. "Why were you following me?"

Havel stared at the two men. "Which one was following you? Moreau?"

Shaun nodded. "Yes."

Jozef let out a growl that sent the hairs on her arms and neck standing on end. Her fiancé sure knew how to use the few sounds he could make have impact. Shaun ignored him, focusing her glare on the tall man with sandy blond hair. The man she'd pegged as law enforcement.

Before she could get an answer, Jozef was on top of him, gripping him by the neck and shoving him into the wall behind them. Instead of fighting back, the man held his hands up. Jozef punched him, dropping him to the ground.

"Whoa, what the hell do you think you're doing?" The other man, not Moreau, rushed to his friend's side, helping him to his feet.

Havel's shoulders were shaking with laugher, which made Shaun want to punch him. She reminded herself that she had surgery in less than a week and needed her hands unbroken.

"Jozef!" Shaun said sharply, drawing his attention. "I want to talk to him. Move your goon."

Havel twisted around to glare at her. She'd called him that a few times and he'd made it clear he preferred second-in-command, security specialist, or even bodyguard, over goon.

Jozef nodded at Havel, and when the big man moved from her path, she was able to step forward and examine the object of her interest. She sighed heavily and reached into her purse for a fistful of tissues. She handed them Moreau, who was bleeding in her hallway.

He took them and pressed them under his nose, which was swelling.

"I think it might be broken." Shaun reached for him, but Jozef jerked her away.

She turned a heated glare on her overprotective fiancé. "If you insist on punching strange men in the house, I will treat them. It's not polite to send bleeding people from our home."

Havel didn't bother to conceal his laughter and, after a long moment, Jozef released Shaun's arm and allowed her to examine her new patient.

"Come on, let's get you sitting down in a chair." She ushered Moreau back into Jozef's office and gave him a small push, indicating he should sit by the fireplace.

He'll bleed all over the place, Jozef complained.

"Then you shouldn't have hit him, should you have?" She leaned over her patient. "Tilt your head up so I can see the damage."

She felt the heat of Jozef's body as he hovered against her back. She wanted to tell him to give her space, but the tingles zinging up and down her spine in a dance of pleasure at his nearness held her tongue.

"Yes, it's broken."

She pulled her first aid kit from her purse, opened it and grabbed a handful of gauze and a roll of medical tape. She picked up a garbage can. "Throw the tissues in here."

Her patient did as she instructed, his light blue eyes

following her movements. His expression was neutral, despite the pain he had to have been feeling.

Shaun wondered if he was used to pain. He barely reacted, even as Jozef was punching him. Maybe he was a mercenary, like Jozef and his men. She'd discovered they could take a lot of pain. Of course, once she turned her attention on them, they whined like puppies with hurt paws.

She packed the gauze against his nose and taped it.

"You should go to the hospital. You might need a splint and they can give you pain meds and antibiotics. They'll also let you know if you need a procedure to correct the misalignment."

His expression finally changed, becoming derisive.

"I don't need a hospital." His words were muffled, as though he had a cold.

Shaun shrugged. "That's up to you, but if you want to breathe through those nostrils, you should make sure there isn't permanent damage." She sat in the chair opposite him, shoving her first aid kit back in her purse. "Now, tell me why you were following me."

Jozef growled once again and Shaun threw her arm out, stopping him from attacking their guest. He would be able to easily break her hold, but he allowed her to continue.

"You followed me twice that I saw, though it was probably more. Once when I was leaving Prague after I was poisoned and once more a month ago at the Christmas market. Right before... before..." her gaze sharpened as her mind whirred. "Were you there for the shootout? Were you on the street? If you were following me at the market, it stands to reason you might have followed me to the restaurant."

He sighed, a slight gurgle to the sound from the blood likely dripping down the back of his throat.

"I wasn't following you."

Shaun narrowed her eyes at him. "I know what I saw."

"Why would I follow you? You aren't on Interpol's radar."

"Maybe you wanted me to lead you to Jozef?" She was bewildered. She had definitely seen this man. His eyes had been on her. He must be lying.

"Why would I have needed you to lead me to Jozef?" His eyes had gone blank once more and his voice was neutral, as if he didn't care about what he was saying. "He was already in custody when I first arrived in Prague more than a year ago. Then he was pardoned, no longer a target."

"That's not true," Shaun charged. "Interpol is different from local police. You might still be after him and I would have led you right to him."

Jozef tapped her shoulder and when she looked up, he shook his head and signed, *he knew where I was. I wasn't trying to hide. He wouldn't have needed you to lead him to me.*

Frustration welled up inside her. "Then why were you following me?" She turned her accusing glare back on the man sitting across from her.

"Dasha."

It was Havel who spoke.

"What about Dasha?"

"She was at the Christmas market and she was probably watching you when we met in front of your hotel. She must've followed me when I was dropping off your plane tickets." Havel stared down at the other man, his face carved of granite. "Dasha Koba would make a nice trophy for Interpol, especially if you could've gotten her to flip on her husband."

The air in the room crackled with tension, and Shaun realized exactly what she'd just stepped into. Two men, likely law enforcement, were in their home, essentially at Jozef's mercy, while one of them was being forced to admit that he'd been surveilling the family.

"Is it true?" Shaun demanded.

Moreau nodded, his gaze locked with Jozef's. He must've

read death in Jozef's expression, because the pulse in his throat began hammering and his eyelid twitched.

"I saved your wife." It was clear he was attempting to get the mob boss to stand down before Jozef added to his injuries.

Shaun was confused. "You saved whose life?"

"Yours," his gaze flickered to her. "Outside of the restaurant. During the shootout. You guys were sitting ducks in that car. I did my best to provide cover fire until help arrived."

"You did a shitty job," Havel growled. "We lost two men in that car."

"But she survived."

They remained silent for a few minutes until the other man who Shaun didn't know spoke up. "I think we should be going."

"I agree." Havel looked like a boulder that was about ready to roll downhill, crushing everyone in its path. He looked confused, pissed and deadly.

The two men hurried from the mansion, leaving Havel, Jozef and Shaun by the front door. Jozef stared pointedly down at Shaun's purse, then at the SUV in the driveway with its engine running and Cooper standing next to it with his arms crossed.

You were going somewhere? Jozef asked.

Shaun kissed him on the lips, a quick smack, before backing away so he couldn't grab her and force her to stay. "I told you yesterday, I have a meeting at the hospital." As his brows drew down in displeasure, she quickly added, "I have Cooper and two others to protect me. I've already talked to Dr. Černý and cleared their presence in the hospital."

Take two more, Jozef signed.

Shaun was so relieved he wasn't going to back out of his agreement to let her go to the hospital that she quickly agreed. "I will. They'll have to stay in the solarium though since they haven't been cleared."

Jozef ignored her amendment to his demand. *Come straight home when you finish. I have a surprise for you.*

Pleasure sizzled through her and she grinned up at him. He always gave her the best surprises.

"I'm having an early dinner with my mom." As his brows did the angry thing, she added, "You told me I could see her any time I wanted. But don't worry, I'll be back in plenty of time for your surprise."

Jozef stared at her, forcing her to hold his gaze. After a moment, he nodded. *Go to your mother then, but don't be late or I'll come searching for you.*

She couldn't help herself. "What happens if you have to come find me?"

The look he gave her sent her pulse fluttering and made her squirm in her panties. It might just be worth it to show up late.

CHAPTER TWENTY

The drive to the hospital took about thirty minutes. Shaun chatted amicably with Cooper, her new favourite bodyguard. He was growing on her more and more every day, a bit like a foot fungus. He encroached on her personal space, chattered incessantly and made inappropriate and unfunny jokes. He was one of those people who treated death like it was a hilarious affliction. But he was sweet when it counted, and he was always respectful.

"You think the boss man will have those two assholes killed?" This was from Cooper.

Shaun rolled her eyes at him. They were sitting together in the back seat of an SUV that had been assigned to Shaun for her visits into the city. Two other bodyguards sat up front. Both were straight-faced and uninterested in what was happening in the back seat.

"Why would Jozef tell me he was going to kill someone?" she asked, not bothering to feel appalled by the question. She was getting used to Cooper. "I'm a doctor."

"What does that have to do with anything?"

The American was slouched in his seat, the seatbelt

stretched taut across his broad chest, his chiseled jaw clean-shaven and his blond hair cut to perfection. If she didn't have Jozef in her life, Shaun might find Cooper drool-worthy. At least until he opened his mouth and said something.

An image of him being gagged by a woman before going to bed with her made Shaun laugh out loud. He gave her a strange look but didn't comment. She shook the image away. Jozef was so possessive, if he suspected Shaun of daydreaming about another man, innocent thoughts or not, he would lock Shaun in their bedroom and beat up the man who'd infiltrated her head.

"My oath as a doctor is to do no harm, which I take seriously."

"What does that have to do with your husband killing someone?" His blue gaze was on her face. That was another thing she liked about him. Cooper was direct when he spoke to her, and he looked her in the eye.

"I would prefer not to think of Jozef killing anyone," she said tartly.

"And yet he does. Do you plan on burying your head in the sand so you can pretend it's not happening? That doesn't seem like you."

She flinched.

Cooper had unknowingly touched on the single thing in her relationship with Jozef that could break them. She could look past a lot, including many of his illegal enterprises. She could reason that he was raised to lead a criminal organization. The one thing she couldn't do was absolve him of the sin of murder.

Shaun and Jozef had discussed the ideology of murder more than once in their turbulent relationship. Jozef knew right from wrong. Knew when he took a life that his actions had ripple consequences. Yet, he still killed. Even though she wasn't a part of that side of his life, she was aware it existed.

She shook her head. "I don't have an answer for that yet. Maybe I never will."

"You love him?" Cooper asked.

Shaun nodded. "Of course."

"Then find a way to live with it."

She frowned. "Why should I do that? Why shouldn't he be the one who changes?"

"He has changed," Cooper countered. "I've only known him for a few months, but I knew of his reputation before I started working for him. He's changed, Shaun."

"But he still kills."

Except for the attack on the club, which had been an extreme situation in which Jozef had been forced to defend himself, she actually wasn't sure Jozef still killed. She wondered if Cooper knew something she didn't.

Cooper, being a very candid man, gave her exactly what she wanted, showing her she didn't really want the answers. "Sure, he still kills. He had to take out a few of his uncle's most loyal men so he could take the estate without getting a knife in the back."

Shaun felt like ice water had been poured over her and she had to bite her lip to stop a gasp of shock. She shouldn't be shocked, though. Jozef was a killer, a mob boss now. Head of a Bratva affiliated organization. He had decisions to make and some of those decisions would end lives.

"Then he hasn't changed that much," she said flatly, looking out the window, hoping her tone would shut down the conversation.

Of course, Cooper always had to have the last word. "Keep telling yourself that, princess."

She turned narrowed eyes on him and opened her mouth to blast him, but he flashed her his signature grin and she smiled back. She couldn't stay mad at her bodyguard. He was irrepressible, but more than that, after losing

Karl, she wanted to make sure she had her bodyguard's back.

She knew it made little sense; her bodyguard was there to protect her. It wasn't her job to protect him too, but she couldn't help herself. And it wasn't just Cooper. She watched all the men, keeping an eye on them. She took a more active role in treating injuries and inquiring about their lives.

What she was learning was that many of them had rich lives outside of Jozef's sphere, and Jozef, apparently, encouraged them. He thought having families and family support was healthy.

While treating a sprained wrist, one man had gotten during the attack, she'd discovered the man lived with his parents in the city. He was twenty-one and enjoyed working for Jozef because he could make enough money to buy a place for himself and his girlfriend. Another man had come to her needing treatment and had asked her advice on what he should get his wife for Christmas. It had been an oddly domestic conversation considering she'd been suturing a knife wound.

Jozef and his people were changing her. She felt it, but she also didn't know how to feel about it. Condoning any kind of violence was a slippery slope to travel, and she'd already given up so much of herself to be with Jozef.

As always, her thoughts on this matter left her feeling slightly depressed and without any answers.

Her mood lifted considerably when she saw Dr. Černý's smiling face at the hospital. Elisa shook Shaun's hand warmly.

"I'm so happy you've agreed to come."

Elisa led her to the neurology department, where Shaun looked around with a wave of nostalgia. She loved being in a hospital again. The smells, the sounds, the feel, it all spoke to her soul. Some of her greatest successes had taken place in a hospital similar to this one.

Elisa showed her into an office. It was brightly lit with large windows that showed a view of the parking lot. The other woman caught Shaun looking out the window and gave her a wry look.

"I know, it's not spectacular, but it's mine."

Shaun laughed. "My office in Montreal barely fit two people, and it had no windows. This is a considerable step up."

Though she disparaged her little office, she missed it. It had been hers and she'd worked her tail off to earn the position of Chief of Neurology. It was a coveted position, one that she'd been shocked to learn she'd be given. At first, she'd thought her father had pulled strings, but when confronted he'd denied giving her a leg up over the competition. It had been a combination of her flawless residency, her excellent track record in surgery, and her outside-of-the-box thinking. She'd been the youngest chief in the hospital, but one of the most respected.

"I can't tell you what an honour it is to have you in my hospital discussing a surgery that we're going to conduct together." Elisa looked extremely happy. "I hope that we will convince you to take a position with us once we have completed our surgery."

Shaun grinned at the thought of taking a position at the hospital. She hadn't contemplated her career beyond the surgery. She'd been so grateful for the opportunity that she'd forgotten she was one of the preemptively sought after neurosurgeons. When she worked at the Montreal General Hospital, she would often have to fend off job offers from other institutions. She'd considered them, especially one from UCSF Medical Center in San Francisco. Their neurology department, complete with all the cutting-edge toys for surgeons, was a dream come true to any neurologist.

She'd declined their generous offer, choosing to stay in her hometown.

Now, she had a chance to work with a hospital and staff that were foreign to her. She could learn new techniques and share her own. It was an exciting opportunity.

But would Jozef go for it?

He was already in a tizzy over the single surgery she would conduct in a week's time. She couldn't imagine him being okay with her taking a permanent position.

Regardless, it was a worry for another day. She had a surgery to look forward to, and that was enough for now.

The two women spent several hours going through the procedure, first with each other, then with the three surgical nurses and anesthesiologist who would assist them. They ran through every scenario, making sure that they were completely thorough in their risk assessment.

By the time they finished, the two women were exhausted but satisfied.

"With the surgery we've come up with, I give him 50/50 odds of a full recovery," Elisa said enthusiastically.

Shaun agreed and looked at her colleague. "You know what I love about tumours?"

Elisa laughed. "No two are the same."

"Exactly."

Only a neurologist would love a tumour. It was one thing that bound them. The desire to find, diagnose, and eradicate masses from the brain. It was a strange obsession, but one that they shared.

"I've booked the learning lab for Saturday if you'd like to join me for a dry run."

"Of course," Shaun readily agreed. "We should orchestrate the entire thing from beginning to end. Decide where everyone will need to stand and where the instruments should be. I'm a newcomer to this hospital, so I'd also like to see the surgical room I'll be working in."

"No problem. We can do that now so when we do our practice run, we'll know where everything will be." As they left Elisa's office and made their way to the surgical ward, she said to Shaun, "You've done procedures in less than ideal conditions, I'm sure this will be a treat for you."

Shaun shot the other woman a look. She was talking up her hospital in order to get Shaun to accept a position with them. It would be a feather in her department if she convinced Shaun. It was to her credit that she wasn't letting a sense of competition get in her way. Competitiveness was a common trait among surgeons, which could be both good and bad. It drove them to strive for perfection, but it also made them overlook excellent surgeons and opportunities in their drive to get to the top.

Perhaps that was why Shaun enjoyed working with Doctors Without Borders. The experience was both humbling and forced her to learn new skills. Depending on the camp or city she was working in, she rarely had the resources she would have access to in a hospital with more money at their disposal.

As they approached the surgical ward, Shaun turned to Cooper. "You and the other men will have to remain out here." When it looked like he would argue, she added, "I've already cleared it with Jozef. He understands that there are sanitization risks to having people on this ward. It's locked down tight so no one can enter."

Cooper gave her a skeptical look. "Pretty sure I could easily infiltrate that flimsy door."

His gaze went past her to land on a steel double reinforced door with shatter proof windows and a code reader.

He was already pulling his phone from his pocket before Shaun could suggest he call Jozef. The conversation was brief and Shaun could finally continue without her contingent of bodyguards.

As she and Elisa traversed the hallway, Elisa spoke about the incident. "You seem like a very independent person; these restrictions must be hard on you."

Shaun thought about it and then smiled. "Not really. Jozef wants to keep me safe, but he also wants me to be happy. I wouldn't be here if I was truly restricted."

Elisa stared at her. "But you have to make decisions based on what he wants, don't you?"

Shaun laughed. "I think you just described marriage. It goes both ways, he has to keep me in mind when making decisions too."

"That probably explains why I'm not married." Elisa's tone was dry. "Well, I'm glad you've found someone worth the sacrifice of your independence. I wish you a very happy and long marriage."

Elisa pushed the door open to an empty surgery and waved Shaun in. As Shaun looked around the room, half her mind was on what the other woman had said. She had found someone worth sacrificing for, someone who she could be happy with, and she wasn't willing to let that go.

Shaun grinned to herself, her back to the other woman. She thought maybe she was finally ready to take the plunge.

CHAPTER TWENTY-ONE

Dasha sat on the hospital bed, her back straight as a poker, her face clear of expression as the attending doctor lifted her arm, put his hand against her elbow and pushed, then rotated the arm at the shoulder. He did the motion several times.

"On a scale of one to ten, how much discomfort are you feeling?"

Dasha glared at the man. What a fool. He hadn't given her any basis of comparison. What was a one? A pinch, or a slap? Then a ten must be a severed limb.

"One," she told him, her gaze steady on the wall past his shoulder.

The doctor grunted. "There's no point in hiding your pain, Mrs. Evanoff. I can prescribe something to help if you'll allow me."

Condescending man! Would he say the same if it had been her husband sitting there? Or another man? No, he would not. He would allow them to bear their pain with dignity.

Dasha regretted that she was forced to come to the hospital for her treatment. She would have preferred

Krystoff's personal physician, but the man, along with most of their former employees, had scattered when news of Krystoff's death reached them.

Leeza hadn't even made it to Poland before Dasha insisted she pull the car over. Disgusted, Leeza had let her mother leave. Her daughter's parting words still stung. "If you go back to Prague or pursue any kind of vendetta against Jozef and Shaun, then consider us done. I don't want to hear from you again."

But Dasha knew she'd made the right decision, for both of their sakes. Leeza didn't need her mother shattering what little remained of her life, and Dasha didn't need an over-concerned child hovering over her.

She hoped she would see Leeza again... and Saskia. But some things were more important.

"Okay, I think we're finished here."

The doctor finished re-bandaging her arm.

"You'll need to come back for another session." He pulled up his schedule on the computer in his office. "Does Thursday 10:00 AM next week work?"

Dasha inclined her head in agreement and took his card with the appointment written on it. She'd seen him twice since the accident and was gaining confidence in the use of her arm each time.

She was certain that Jozef would search for her, but she doubted he would concentrate many efforts in Prague. He would expect her to run as far and as fast as she could go, knowing he would be gunning for her.

What he didn't know was that she'd lost everything, and a woman with nothing left to lose had only one course of action left. Vengeance. She wanted to right the wrongs and avenge her husband before she joined him. She wasn't afraid of death, and her motivation to take down the new Koba regime was strong.

She would bide her time until conditions were right, and then she would do what Krystoff could not do. What she herself had been unable to do when she'd held a knife to a five-year-old boy's throat. She would take out the mute mobster and his house-wrecking girlfriend.

Dasha slid off the table and picked up her purse, slinging it across her good shoulder. Each day she regained more and more strength in her injured arm. In order to aid in her efforts, she lifted weights daily, ignoring the agony that ripped through her body.

She stepped out the door and damn near walked into the last person she expected.

Heart hammering, she whirled around and launched herself back into the doctor's office. He looked up, startled. "Did we forget something?"

She forced a smile, her first in weeks. "I have a question, actually."

"Of course." He straightened in his chair, giving her his full attention.

Dasha racked her brain for a question, but her thoughts were on Shaun Patterson, the woman she'd nearly run into in the hallway. She was followed by three bodyguards, any of which could have easily recognized Dasha. It was sheer luck that her head had been down as she adjusted her purse, her hair obscuring her face.

"I... I... when do you think I'll be able to drive again?" she asked quickly, wanting to get out of there and rush down the hall, catch another glimpse of her prey. It was an obsession, beating at her, propelling her forward. She hated that she had to let Shaun leave with her bodyguards.

"It'll be a few weeks yet before I can recommend the use of heavy machinery."

"Uh... sure."

She thought enough time had passed that she could slip

away from the room unnoticed. She said goodbye to her doctor and opened the door, peeking into the hallway. Shaun and her entourage were nowhere in sight.

She stepped into the corridor and looked both ways, indecision warring within. If she turned left, she might get another glimpse of her prey, but she risked getting caught. If Jozef found out she was still in Prague, he would shut the city down and raze it until he got his hands on her. His uncle had taught him too well for her to think he'd allow her to slip away again. He was the guard dog. Once he got a bone, he didn't give it up easily.

Dasha turned right, shoving her sunglasses on her face and dipping her head low so her hair would obscure her features. If Shaun was in the hospital, then it would be crawling with Jozef's men. He didn't take risks with the girl. The last time Dasha had gotten close to her had been through a lot of careful watching and waiting. She wasn't stupid enough to think Jozef would give her another chance at the girl. He probably had bodyguards following her she didn't even know about.

Dasha made her way swiftly through the parking lot to the car she was borrowing. She let herself in and breathed a sigh of relief when she was able to the leave the lot without incident. Still, she looked in the rearview mirror all the way home and held her gun close to her side as she traversed the stairs to the top floor apartment.

It was an old building with four floors and no elevator. The place hadn't been renovated in years. The tiles were cracked and dirty; the furniture was old and falling apart and the windows were so grimy only a small, very determined amount of sunlight could get through.

It was perfect for hiding out.

After coming back to Prague, she'd gone to an old society friend, Cece Mountbatten, for refuge. Cece had set her up in the guest room of her luxury townhouse, but the setup hadn't lasted. At Dasha's request, Cece had gone to Krystoff's funeral reception. Unfortunately, she'd crossed words with Jozef, then come back to the townhouse in a fury over the incident. The idiot woman had no idea how much harm she could have done to Dasha with her carelessness.

Dasha had gotten out just in time and watched from a shadowed garden across the street as Jozef's men paid Cece a visit, having found out she was an ally of Dasha's. Luckily, they left empty-handed, but it had been close.

Dasha had been forced to find a new safe-house to hole up in, and this one was far less posh.

She dumped her purse and a bag of groceries on the counter. She'd avoided going out, but she'd had to go to her physio appointment. If she didn't gain strength, then she wouldn't be effective when she finally enacted her revenge.

She lay down on the couch, covering her face with her hands and taking several deep breaths. It was times like this, when she was faced with how far she'd fallen that she had to hold back tears. Rather than let them fall, she berated herself until they dried. She was useless if she couldn't hold her shit together.

Finally, she rolled onto her side, her bad arm up, dragged the homemade quilt over her body and allowed herself a small nap. Though she didn't like to admit it, her recovery was slow and tedious. She didn't have the same level of energy that she'd had before her injury.

She slept heavily, the shadows of the day gradually creeping through the apartment. She woke with the awareness that someone was in the room with her. She thought maybe Jozef had figured out where she was. Without pause, she rolled off the side of the couch, reaching for her gun at the same time.

She hit the floor, rolled again until she was on her back

and aimed the pistol, preparing to fire. Her eyes met the startled face of Nikolay.

"What the fuck are you doing here?" she growled, shoving hair out of her face and lowering the gun.

When she'd left Cece's, she'd gone to the only person who might actually help her. It was a risk but having a man on the inside was also a bonus. Nikolay helped set her up with the apartment and a car.

Dasha had known well before Krystoff's death that Nikolay was betraying Jozef. She'd first suspected when he started turning up at the mansion after Jozef had moved into his club. Dasha had questioned Krystoff, and he'd admitted that Nikolay was in his pocket.

Though Dasha wanted revenge, wanted to bring the killer of her husband down, she still despised Nikolay for his lack of loyalty. Perhaps it was his generation. None of them had loyalty anymore. If Jozef had been loyal, he wouldn't have gone rogue and the family wouldn't have splintered. The difference between Jozef and Nikolay was that Jozef was up front about his intentions and where he stood.

Nikolay was a sneaky bastard, and she hated having to rely on him for sanctuary while she was in Prague.

"Brought you some things."

He sat on the couch, leaving plenty of room for Dasha to pick herself off the floor and settle back on the couch. Adrenalin was rushing through her, warring with a groggy, sleep-hazed mind. It made her feel light-headed and disoriented.

"New phone." Nikolay placed a phone between them.

Dasha picked it up. It was an old flip phone. She would take the Sim card out when Nikolay left and replace it with one of her own. She didn't trust him not to keep tabs on her.

"Meds." He set a plastic bag with three pill bottles between them.

Dasha picked them up. Dasha hadn't been able to buy her

own medications, so Nikolay had been getting them for her. If the bottles were sealed, she would take them. If not, then she would suffer.

"Any news?" she asked, trying to sound casual.

She was desperate for any tidbits. Not just because she wanted to know what was going on in her enemy's camp, but because she wasn't used to hiding out while life went on around her, without her. Dasha had always been the planner, the one with her finger in every pie. Going dark was a new and frightening situation for her. Though she was fiercely independent, she missed her family.

"They're hiding someone... or something," Nikolay said, annoyance colouring his tones. "One of the guest suites is being used, but no one knows who. Only Shaun, Jozef and a nurse are allowed in the room. I think they might be hiding someone who was injured during the attack."

Dasha perked up. "Krystoff?" Though she knew better, she couldn't help the hope that rang through her voice.

Nikolay shook his head, his gaze on the dingy carpet. "He's gone. I saw his body."

A shaft of pain sliced through her, and it was everything she could do to keep the emotion to herself. Every day was a fresh wound, a fresh reminder that the man she loved, the life she loved, was gone. And every day the pain rushed through her like a tidal wave of suffocation. She wanted to scream and cry and throw her meagre possessions. Instead, she pulled the pain deep into her soul and let it fester, let it drive her.

"They've finished moving into the mansion." She said flatly. Not really a question. She knew it was happening, knew that Jozef would have to take the physical seat of power, along with the figurative mantle. The Koba estate went back 300 years. Generations of people, generations of mafia had lived there.

"Yes."

Nikolay's answers were short and pointed. She suspected he knew how she felt about him. Though she tried to hide her feelings, disdain was one that always managed to slip through the cracks.

She wasn't entirely sure what his motive for helping her was. Could be he thought she would give him a leadership position if she took the organization back. What he didn't realize was that she had no interest in the organization. She wanted to take out the source of all her pain, then she wanted to die.

Simple, basic, bloody.

She had been stripped down to the basics. No home, no family, no money, nothing. She would leave this earth a much different person than she arrived. Death would allow her the peace that her constantly moving brain had never found. She would welcome it.

"I saw Shaun at the hospital today."

Nikolay looked at her sharply.

"Don't worry, neither she nor her bodyguards saw me."

"I should have warned you," he said, leaning forward and placing his elbows on his thighs, slouching his shoulders. "She's doing a surgery there next week."

"What?" Dasha sat up straighter. "You should have told me sooner. This is a prime opportunity."

Nikolay knew what Dasha wanted, though he was pushing her to bide her time until he could build an army and help place her at the head of the family again. She allowed his brief fantasy, though her goals differed from his.

"They don't tell me much," he admitted. "I didn't know she was going until she'd already left the mansion."

Nikolay had mentioned before that he thought he was being treated differently. She'd assured him it was his imagination and he would be safe inside the organization, spying for her. In reality, she was sure Jozef suspected Nikolay of something. In the fifteen years since Jozef had formed his infamous team of mercenaries, he'd kept them close. They worked like a machine. When the head moved, so did the arms and legs. But Nikolay was being left out of the loop. It was a concern, one that perhaps if Nikolay were smarter, he would see.

It didn't matter to Dasha. She was more interested in the comings and goings of the family, not the intricate details of Jozef's work life. She hoped once she was finished with Nikolay, Jozef would take care of him for her. She didn't like getting her hands bloody... with one exception.

"Get me the date and time of that surgery," she told him, then stood and walked to the door, pointedly opening it and staring at him until he got up and left.

CHAPTER TWENTY-TWO

Shaun sat on the balcony of her suite, gazing blindly toward the garden and sipping at her first cup of morning coffee. She wore a heavy sweater with a coat over top and a pair of knit gloves, in concession to the wintery weather. She looked the picture of contentment, but images could be deceiving. Inside, her brain whirred like a squirrel on speed, racing on a hamster wheel.

Her thoughts bounced from her dislike of living in the mansion, to her upcoming surgery, to the dull ache in her chest when she thought of Jozef. The ache was bittersweet. The moments they snatched for themselves were amazing. They came together in a combination of explosive sex, laughter, and signed conversations.

The evening before, Jozef had surprised her with a picnic on the living room floor of their suite. It had everything, from a checkered blanket, to chocolate covered strawberries and champagne on ice. There was an envelope next to the champagne with her name embossed on it.

"What's the occasion?" she asked.

Not that I need an occasion to give my lovely fiancé a gift, but it's Christmas, he signed.

Shaun had gaped at him.

Christmas? She'd forgotten about Christmas?

He'd laughingly told her it was a few days earlier, and, yes, they'd missed it. Shaun had wanted to immediately call her mother and apologize and wish her a belated Merry Christmas, but Jozef had pulled her down onto the blanket, kissed her soundly and assured her they'd sent her mother an extravagant gift. Apparently, he'd seen her mother the day before while he was the Guard Dogs Securities offices and Fatima had reassured him that she wasn't hurt at all by the missed holiday, that she understood they were mourning Krystoff.

When Shaun was satisfied that she didn't need to rush off to call her mother, Jozef had pressed the envelope back into her hands. It was an extremely generous donation to Doctors Without Borders. The letter explained that Shaun was to be the one to decide where the funds were distributed.

She'd flung her arms around his neck and kissed him like she'd never kissed him before. He hadn't done it out of a sense of generosity, he'd done it for her. Maybe she wasn't changing who he was fundamentally, but he was becoming the man she wanted to spend the rest of her life with. She would take his precious gift and hold it close to her heart. It was better than diamonds.

They made love on the floor of their suite, taking time to explore each other, to laugh and to simply be. There was no mafia, no bodyguards, no outside world. Just them.

Jozef lingered over her body, worshipping her with his hands and mouth, playing with her erogenous zones. He nearly made her come when he took her nipple into his mouth and laved it with attention. He refused to let go, driving her higher and higher until finally slipping a finger into her wetness and carrying her home on the wings of a beautiful orgasm.

As she'd drifted back, he found other parts of her body to tease and torture. He spent several minutes on each ear until all she could hear, all she could feel was the rushing of her blood through her veins, the sound of his harsh breathing as he denied himself in his quest to give her as many orgasms as he could before he took his own. He slid his rough fingers over her clitoris, forcing her over the edge with a keening cry.

Finally, after more orgasms than she could count, he took his own. He gripped her face and held her, watching her, as he drove himself home, filling her completely. He kissed her, using his tongue to simulate what his cock was doing. Before she could catch her breath, she was once more thrown headlong over the edge. This time he followed her, pumping into her, filling her with his seed.

They'd spent most of the night on that blanket on the floor, making love, eating, talking to each other in their silent language. The delicious ache Shaun felt in her limbs this morning was testament to the perfection of Jozef's date night planning.

Shaun had never imagined feeling so content with a partner. She'd always thought of herself as too career-driven to satisfy another person in the long term. She hadn't wanted to divide her attention between the hospital and a man.

But now, with Jozef, he made it easy. He slipped into her life, laying anything she could want at her feet. Even the opportunity for this upcoming surgery was because he'd brought her to Prague.

The bittersweet feeling she was experiencing was because the time they had together was few and far between. The more Jozef seemed to settle into his new role as head of the Koba organization, the more demands on his time there were.

Shaun didn't want to distract him, so she bit her tongue and took whatever precious time he could spare. She's seen what could happen when a mobster became distracted. Jozef had been distracted by Shaun and as a result his entire life had blown up. Krystoff had been distracted by Dasha, and now he was dead. One mistake could bring down an entire organization.

Her gaze strayed across the lawn, landing on a building just out of the corner of her periphery.

"What is that?" she whispered, standing.

She moved to the edge of the balcony and leaned over, squinting at the building in the distance. A stone path led from the garden toward a cottage. She wondered if it had been Leeza's home.

A pang hit Shaun as a wave of sadness crashed over her. She hadn't known Leeza well, but the other woman had always been kind to her, if somewhat cool. Perhaps if the family had stayed together, the two women might have become friends. Now, Leeza was on the run for her life, fighting to protect herself and her child. Though none of it was Shaun's fault, she felt responsible.

Setting down her finished coffee mug, Shaun made her way back inside. She picked up her purse and left the suite.

"Morning." Cooper was standing across the hall from her door, leaning negligently between two gaudy paintings and looking down at his phone. When she turned to lock the door, he straightened and slid his phone into his pocket.

"Where are we headed this beautiful morning?"

Cooper was more of a morning person than Shaun. Sometimes his tendency toward chipperness drove her insane, while other times it allowed her to have her morning grumps without the pressure of having to speak.

"We're inspecting the premises."

"That sounds like... fun?"

She laughed when he ended his sentence on a question. "This is my home now; I think it's time I reconcile myself to the situation."

"The renovations to your old apartment should be done in the next few days." Cooper strode down the hall next to Shaun. "Why don't you tell Jozef you want to move back in?"

Shaun stopped and looked at her companion. "I don't think Jozef can move back to the apartment. Appearances are important right now."

"Shame, he had it fixed up exactly the way you wanted." He tilted his head to the side. "If you don't move back in, he'll have to install a mistress in there, and then things will just get messy when you visit your mom."

Laughter burst from Shaun before she could recall it. It felt good to laugh, though. Things had been too serious for too long. She needed to see the lighter side of things or she'd become the nervous wreck she'd been in Montreal.

"Could you imagine that poor man trying to maintain a mistress while he's under all this pressure? Not a chance. He'd have a coronary."

They laughed over the idea together and continued down the hall. Not only did Jozef not have time for a mistress, but his whole being seemed focused on his obsession with Shaun.

At first, his possessive manner had been off-putting, but as she got to know him, it now felt comfortable, like a security blanket. She knew he wouldn't make a single decision without keeping her in mind. He would always put her first, which meant she would always be safe. Having that knowledge was power, one that she intended to keep safe in her heart. She wouldn't take advantage of him, but she would appreciate how much he fought to make her world perfect.

"The stairs are this way." Cooper stopped at the top of the wide staircase leading down to the first floor, while Shaun breezed past him.

"I know," she told him, making her way down the corridor toward Saskia's suite. "We need a tour guide for our inspection."

She smiled at the guard standing stoically next to Saskia's door. Shaun knocked softly and waited. Saskia opened the door a minute later. She looked dishevelled, but not sleepy.

"Am I disturbing you?" Shaun asked, stepping into the suite.

Saskia shook her head. "No, I was watching TV."

Sure enough, the TV was playing, though the volume was so low it could barely be heard.

Shaun took in the suite. It looked like the Cookie Monster had flipped the place in his search for cookies. Saskia had only been back a few days, but her suite suggested she'd been living in her own filth for months.

"Is everything okay?" Shaun asked, concerned.

Saskia shrugged. "What could be wrong? My dad is dead, my mom is in the wind, my sister is god knows where and my grades are plummeting because I'm not allowed to leave the house or even contact any of my professors." She threw herself angrily on the couch. "I wish I'd never been brought back here."

Shaun sat gingerly on the couch, moving a porcelain doll so she wouldn't sit on it. She rubbed Saskia's arm. "It's only for a few more days, until Jozef can make sure it's safe for you to return to campus. He has to make sure the deal your father brokered with the dean of the university is still going to be honoured."

"That's what he says," Saskia charged. "But I think he's keeping me here because I'm a flight risk."

Saskia's frustration was real, but Shaun suspected it wasn't entirely directed at Jozef. Saskia had tasted a moment of freedom and had looked forward to finally having the world at her fingertips. Now, she was right back where she started, but her entire family dynamic had changed.

"Are you a flight risk?" Shaun asked gently.

Saskia chewed on her lip and then swallowed hard, her eyelashes fluttering so the tears wouldn't spill.

"I don't know," she admitted. "Maybe." She exhaled. "Things just feel so different now. It was never awesome living in this house, but at least I knew what to expect when my dad was running things. Now... I don't know what's going to happen. Not to me, or my mom, or Leeza. I hate being back in this stupid house. I feel like I'm suffocating at the same time as being surrounded by memories of my dead father."

Shaun felt guilty at her own preoccupation with not wanting to live in the mansion. It must be so much worse for Saskia and Jozef. Maybe she should do them all a favour and burn the place to the ground.

"It's okay to feel conflicted," Shaun said gently. "You're angry with Jozef and need some time to come to terms with what happened. I don't blame you."

Saskia shook her head. "You're wrong. As much as I hate being cooped up, I don't blame Jozef for any of this. He's a victim. He was always a victim. Right from when his parents were killed."

Shaun felt a rush of love toward Saskia, who could show Jozef compassion, even after he killed her father.

"Come on." Shaun patted Saskia's leg and stood. "We're going for a walk."

Saskia looked skeptical, like she'd had a day of pizza and TV planned and wasn't going to give it up easily.

"Where are we going?"

"I want to go check out your sister's cottage."

Myriad expressions flickered across Saskia's lovely pixie face before she settled on curious. "Why do you want to know what's in there? My sister is pretty one-dimensional.

She likes bleach and yoga, which her house definitely reflects."

Shaun shook her head, trying not to laugh at Saskia's description. "I'm sure your sister is more interesting than that."

"Oh, I know she is, but her house is boring." Saskia stood and reached for her coat, which was hung on an ornate coatrack by the door. "Did you know we don't share a father?"

Of course, Shaun already knew that, but she wondered how Saskia knew something that must've been a monumental secret in the Koba family. "Who's her father if not Krystoff?"

"I don't really know." Saskia shrugged. "If I had to guess, then an old business associate of my dad's. My mom would've had more access to someone my dad was working with, and apparently their marriage wasn't a happy one way back then. I don't remember though. As long as I've known my parents, they were thick as thieves." She snickered at her own joke. "But according to Leeza, they used to fight like cats and dogs when she was younger. I can't imagine them fucking around if they hated each other."

"Saskia!" Shaun couldn't help the admonishment, nor the laughter that followed at Saskia's description of her parent's marriage.

"Well, it's true." She grinned, looking happier than she had when Shaun arrived. The two women left the suite and headed down to the main floor, Cooper and Saskia's guard following them.

"Why do you suspect your sister had a different father? You two look pretty similar."

"Yeah," Saskia agreed. "We look like my mom's side of the family." The chill morning air hit them as they stepped outside the kitchen door, waving at the cook as they wandered through. She didn't wave back. Shaun had offended her during her first week in charge of the mansion by asking for more vegetables with their meals. "I overheard Leeza call someone 'dad' on the phone and tell him she loved him. Leeza never called Krystoff 'dad', and she definitely never told him she loved him."

"Did your sister know you were listening in on her private call?" Shaun asked disapprovingly, easily able to see the younger woman eavesdropping. She probably did it to everyone who lived in the mansion, not just her sister.

"No, she had no idea." Saskia's face grew dark. "It doesn't matter now; I don't even know where she is."

Shaun wrapped an arm around Saskia's shoulders as they picked their way across the stone path toward Leeza's cottage. "Are you worried about her?"

Saskia nodded and blinked rapidly, her voice higher than normal when she spoke. "I'm worried about both of them, Leeza and little Kristoph. Leeza can protect herself, but she has to take care of my nephew too. I don't know what chance she'll have if she's worried about him while fighting to save their lives."

"I'm sure they aren't at risk," Shaun tried to reassure her.

Saskia stopped walking. "Don't you see? In order for Jozef to take this organization free and clear, he needs to get rid of Leeza."

Shaun frowned. "But wouldn't that mean you're a threat too?"

"No. Jozef has more to worry about from Leeza than he does from me. I'm not married, I don't have children, I'm easy to control."

Shaun couldn't help the chuckle that spilled from her lips. "You are *not* easy to control."

Saskia flashed a brittle smile. "No, maybe not, but I'm easy to find or I wouldn't be here."

"I don't think Jozef intends to hurt your sister. It's not like him."

Saskia looked at her pityingly and Shaun wondered if her lack of understanding of the mafia world was showing again.

"I hope you're right," she said grimly.

Shaun vowed to talk to Jozef about Leeza. See if he could do for her what he was doing for Saskia. Bring her back into the family... what was left of it and protect her and her little boy.

Shaun's belly did a backflip as the small dark voice inside her head reminded her of his mafia heritage. If what Saskia was telling her was the truth, maybe Jozef really was trying to kill his cousin. Shaun knew without a doubt she couldn't live with a man who murdered an innocent woman.

A flash of her colleague jumped into Shaun's mind, shot in cold blood by the man Shaun now loved. She was a hypocrite. She'd fallen in love with that murderer and now she was trying to convince herself he was a different person from that man, one with enough compassion not to kill innocents.

She took a deep breath and shook the thoughts away.

As they approached the front door of the cottage, Shaun realized they didn't have a key. "Shoot, we'll have to go back."

Saskia dug in her little purse and came up with a set of keys that would put a caretaker to shame.

"You really have your fingers in everything around here, don't you?" Shaun asked as Saskia unlocked the door and pushed it open.

"I like to stay informed; it keeps me alive." When Saskia attempted to step through the door, Cooper pushed between the two women and shook his head, going ahead of them. They looked at each other, then followed him in.

Cooper did a quick search of the house, while the other guard stayed at the door. "Okay, looks like the place is empty."

"What are you looking for?" Saskia asked, swiping her finger across the large dining table, smearing the dust.

"I don't know," Shaun admitted. "I wanted to see the place and see if there was anything that could help find your sister."

"I doubt it. Leeza's not one to leave paperwork lying around, but if she did have something, it would be in her upstairs safe."

The two women made their way to the second floor, Cooper trailing behind them. Shaun turned to him and asked that he remain in the hall as they entered Leeza's bedroom. It was silly, but she felt like it would be further invading Leeza's privacy if they allowed a man in her bedroom.

He hung back but left the door open, his eyes on them as they looked around.

"In here." Saskia opened the door to the closet.

There was enough room for both of them inside. Saskia sank to her knees on the carpet, shoving hangers with clothing aside.

Shaun sat on the floor next to her and watched in fascination as Saskia opened the safe on her first try.

"Done this before?" Shaun asked sarcastically.

Saskia flashed her a grin and opened the small metal door. It was empty.

Saskia's grin turned into a frown. "She must've emptied it before she took off. I was here right before things blew up and it was filled with cash, passports and a gun."

Shaun wasn't surprised about the gun. Leeza had pointed one at her when she'd tried to run away from a clothing store, shortly after the two women had met.

Shaun and Saskia were so engrossed in their conversation that they missed the panel at the back of the closet sliding open. It wasn't until the smell hit them, sweaty human flesh and rotting food, that they realized there was someone looming over them.

Saskia noticed him first and screamed, diving for her purse and gun. Shaun threw herself in front of Saskia, determined to protect the younger woman when the man lunged for them.

He didn't make it.

Hearing the commotion, Cooper flung himself into the room and got a shot off before the man could touch either woman. The bullet hit him and he went crashing backwards into the hidden room behind him.

Shaun scrambled after him, though Cooper yelled at her to stay back.

"He's hurt," she snapped, crawling up the length of the man and reaching for his neck, relieved to find a steady pulse. "He's alive."

"Yeah, but who is it?" Saskia flicked the light switch on in the safe room and gasped. "Adam."

CHAPTER TWENTY-THREE

"She's here."

Jozef looked up as Havel entered his office. He'd been pouring through his uncle's appointment diary and records. He was about ready for a change of pace. He sincerely hoped the life of a mob boss didn't always include this much paperwork and politics. He was itching to get back into the field with his men. Not just men anymore, not if this meeting went well.

Jozef nodded at Havel to show her in.

Havel hesitated. "Are you sure about this, man? She's... she looks so delicate. Sure, she's got some training, but what does that mean when we're in a combat situation and she can't keep up? I think you're making a mistake."

Jozef appreciated Havel's blunt assessment. It was part of the reason he was Jozef's second-in-command. He voiced his thoughts, whether or not Jozef wanted to hear them. The two men tempered each other. While Jozef was calm and measured, Havel could be a hothead. But the big, bald enforcer also had a sense of when to pull back, when to leave a deal on the table. He was protective and good at his job.

In this case, he was wrong. A woman on the team would be an asset. She would give them access to spaces and people that the men on his team couldn't access. The more Jozef thought about it, the firmer in his decision he felt.

He wasn't surprised by Havel's hesitation, though. The other man tended to disregard women. He was one of those people who wanted his woman in the kitchen, barefoot and pregnant. It was the way he grew up. First, in a traditional household with a father who oppressed the mother. Havel eventually ended up driving his father away, liberating his mother, but he couldn't unlearn what he'd seen. Then, on the Koba estate he saw the traditional roles the women in the family took. What he didn't see was how much power each woman had held. He hadn't lived in the house with them, hadn't seen the conversations that took place where the women's voices were heard. Krystoff might have been head of the house, but Dasha was his voice, and his daughters were given the freedom to speak their minds.

I'm not making a mistake, Jozef signed, standing up. *You'll see.*

"By why her?" Havel argued. "She's too connected. She could get us all killed just by standing in this house, let alone by joining our team. Let's pick another woman."

I will handle her family.

Havel shook his head, still not convinced. "I hope you don't live to regret this."

Jozef smiled grimly. *I suspect if I'm making a mistake, I probably won't live to regret it.*

Havel laughed, the sound rusty but jovial. "Fair enough."

He left the room, returning with their guest in tow.

"Jozef," she cried, rushing toward him. "I'm so glad to see you again."

Jozef caught her as she threw herself into his arms, hugging him. His thoughts on Shaun, he quickly shoved her away. She resisted, tangling her arms around his neck and attempting to kiss his chin. He would have to put a stop to her flirtations if she was going to work for him.

He set her away from him and put the desk between them. She flopped into one of his guest chairs.

"I thought maybe I was in trouble when you sent your guys to come get me, but this one," she jerked her thumb at Havel, who narrowed his eyes in annoyance, "assured me I was still safe. Hey, does my brother know I'm here?"

As she chattered, Ayaan looked around Jozef's office, her sharp intelligent eyes taking in everything in a sweeping glance. When her gaze settled on Jozef once more, he saw the inner workings of her mind flashing through her dark brown eyes. She was curious, but comfortable. She was exactly as Jozef remembered her when they rescued her from Central Africa and flew her to Nice.

Your brother doesn't know that you're here, Jozef signed.

Why? She signed back. *Are you hiding me for some reason? He won't like that, you know.*

Jozef was so startled by the revelation that Ayaan knew sign language that he couldn't help his expression of surprise. Satisfaction lit Ayaan's features as she watched him.

The brat was enjoying herself.

I had nothing to do while I was in F-R-A-N-C-E, she signed, *so I hired a tutor and learned how to communicate with you.*

Her signs were basic and clumsy, but easily read.

Jozef became even more sure about his decision to make her part of his team. It was a requirement that the members learn sign language. Not just so they could communicate with their leader, but to give them an advantage in the field. They could move through enemy territory in silence, using sign language to communicate. The method was extremely effective.

You thought you would see me again? Jozef asked, wondering what the young woman was up to.

She flashed him a cheeky grin, *I hoped.*

Jozef shook his head at her audacity. He would definitely have to curb her tendency toward the outrageous.

I want you to speak verbally while we conduct this interview.

"Interview for what?" She switched easily back into verbal speech patterns, glancing over her shoulder at Havel. "He didn't tell me why I was here."

I requested he keep my reasons private until I spoke with you.

She nodded.

Tell me about your training. Your brother made you a soldier as a child?

"No, I made myself a soldier when I was a child," she corrected him. "Muhammed had nothing to do with that choice. He tried to dissuade me, but I was determined to follow him and his men into battle. He decided it would be safer to have me properly trained and supervised."

How old were you when you began training?

"Six."

Jozef was shocked. A six-year-old had made the decision to go to battle with her brother? Her expression was shuttered, closing him off from the open young woman who'd walked into his office. He suspected she was like him. She'd experienced some kind of violence at a young age that had shaped her decisions, made her determined to follow in Radik's footsteps.

As a child, Jozef had experienced violence. Had watched his parents die, had been stabbed in the throat. He remembered little surrounding the events, but he did remember the desperate desire to avenge his parents. His uncle had used that desire to shape Jozef into the feral dog he later became. Looking back, he realized he'd been traumatized, had perhaps needed coddling rather than the gun his uncle had given him. Regardless, the experience, like Ayaan's, was the catalyst for who he was today.

If you're accepted on my team, you will be expected to follow orders at all times. You will not be given the freedom you were given while working for your brother.

Excitement lit her eyes, chasing away the lingering shadows. "I knew you were considering me for your team! I saw the way you looked when you realized I could handle myself. When's my first job? When can we leave? Are you coming with us?"

Jozef couldn't help the chuckle that spilled from his lips. She was irrepressible. He enjoyed seeing the quality in a young person, but he worried it could get her killed.

New members of my team aren't deployed until they are trained and ready.

"I'm trained," she said excitedly. "I'm ready now."

Jozef shook his head. *It doesn't matter how much training you've had. You must fit seamlessly in with my men. You must have the right attitude and you must understand the way we work. First, you will work closely with H-A-V-E-L, then you will train with the entire team. If you pass inspection, then you will be given a job.*

She glanced frowningly over her shoulder at Havel, who was leaning against the fireplace with his arms crossed, then back at Jozef. "I'd rather work with you."

N-O, I don't work with new recruits, he signed sharply, nodding toward Havel. *He will be your teacher and mentor. He is not an easy man to work with, so I know anyone coming out of his training program will be tough enough to take the rigorous parts of our job.*

"I'm tough enough," she said defensively.

N-O, you aren't. Jozef was blunt, but he needed her to understand how difficult the coming months would be. *You will be beaten repeatedly, with no concession to your size or gender.* Ayaan wasn't a large person at around 5'4", fine-boned and graceful. *You will be forced to sleep in deplorable conditions. You will be woken in the middle of the night and repeatedly put through drills that will make the Russian special forces look weak. You will be sleep deprived, food-deprived and you will reach your breaking point. It is then that we will see if you have what it takes to work with my people.*

She stared at him, her face unreadable. She was a chameleon with her expressions. She carefully orchestrated each one depending on the situation and when she didn't want anyone to know what she was thinking, she hid her feelings. Another asset.

"No," she finally said.

Jozef raised his eyebrows. *No, you don't want to be part of the team? You want us to take you back to N-I-C-E?*

"No," she said again, rolling her eyes. "You are mistaken. I won't be the one taking a beating." She looked at Havel, an irrepressible grin shaping her mouth. "He will. If you prefer your second-in-command unharmed, then let me know the parameters of the beating I am to give him. Should I pull back or break some bones?"

Jozef glanced at Havel who was staring at Ayaan like she was some kind of an alien creature. Then his expression gradually changed to one that told Jozef Ayaan was in for the beating of a lifetime. Jozef wondered if maybe it would be the other way around. He didn't sense false confidence in the young woman. She fully appreciated her combat skills.

Despite his admiration for her, Jozef needed Ayaan to understand how things worked. *You will listen to your mentor and do what he says without question. Hesitation can get you killed. I suspect you were allowed to question your brother. That won't happen here. This isn't a democracy.*

"I understand." She stared at Jozef steadily, allowing him to see her eagerness. "I can listen to orders." She looked at Havel again. "Even if I don't agree with them."

If you are allowed to sign onto my team, then what you think will no longer matter. You will become a cog in the machine. You under-

stand? Now is the time to leave if you wish to leave. Once your training begins, the only way out is death.

"I'm ready," she said without hesitation.

Then your training begins immediately.

Havel straightened. "Come with me, recruit."

Ayaan stood and turned to leave, then hesitated. "What about my brother? He won't be happy that you took me from Nice, and he's going to be even less pleased when he finds out where I am and what I'm doing."

Jozef flashed her a feral grin. *I will take care of your brother; you concentrate on your training.*

She looked at him suspiciously before leaving.

She was right to be suspicious. Jozef hated being cooped up, forced to read through paperwork and restructure an entire organization. He was ready to get back into the field, to lead his men into battle. Though he truly believed Ayaan would make a decent asset to his team, he wasn't sorry he was poking her brother. If he couldn't go out and find a fight, then he would bring one to him.

Jozef stood and stretched, working out the kinks in his neck and shoulders. Too much time spent sitting. He could use a good training session. He was almost jealous that Havel would be the one to work with Ayaan. He could use a good sparring match. Perhaps he would engage Havel for a fight later.

Before Jozef could leave his office, a sharp knock sounded and Cooper let himself in without waiting for permission. Jozef frowned at the other man. He was always in a rush, sometimes forgetting to observe house rules.

"Sorry, boss," Cooper said, catching Jozef's look. "We have a situation down at the shed."

CHAPTER TWENTY-FOUR

Shaun was annoyed with her bodyguard. He'd insisted on bringing Adam to the shed, rather than allowing her to take him to either the hospital, or at the very least, the infirmary up at the house.

She hated the shed. It brought back memories of her first few days with Jozef, which were fraught with fear and anxiety. When she'd been convinced he'd eventually kill her. He'd forced her to spend the night in one of the cells after she tried to escape. The only thing that stopped that memory from being completely traumatic was Jozef coming in during the night and sleeping with her. That was the first moment she believed he truly cared for her. The next morning he'd been cold and unapproachable again.

Adam was laid out on a wooden pallet with his shirt stripped off. He moaned in pain while Shaun treated his wound. He'd been shot, he was lucky; the bullet had grazed him, going in his side and right back out, without hitting anything important. It was a flesh wound, but it would still need sutures and he would have to take antibiotics to stave off infection.

Surrounding Shaun were four guards and Saskia who was staring down at her brother-in-law with a cold calculating expression. Shaun thought it was overkill, considering Adam's condition. And she didn't just mean his wound. He wasn't in peak physical shape. She'd long suspected he struggled with untreated diabetes.

His face was ashen and he was shaking. His skin had a grey tone that shouldn't be present in a healthy person.

"I need my medical kit." Shaun turned to look pointedly at the guards. No one moved. "Now please."

They looked at each other and one finally left to do her bidding.

Saskia raised an eyebrow at Shaun before turning back to Adam.

"Tell me why my sister hated you."

"Saskia," Shaun said sharply. "He's injured. Now is not the time."

When Saskia looked at Shaun, her eyes were glacial, as if she were in some kind of private zone, rather than talking to a woman she'd befriended. "Now is the perfect time. Why do you think he was brought to the shed? He's here for interrogation. It's why the men don't care if you get your med kit or not. You can patch him up, but he'll probably be bleeding again in a few hours."

Both Shaun and Adam flinched, and Shaun's fingers froze over Adam's prone body. "But he was part of the family. Why would Jozef want to hurt him?"

"Don't be so naïve," Saskia said scornfully, then looked down at Adam, who was eyeing her as though she were a viper. "And you, answer the question."

For the first time since they'd discovered Adam hiding in the panic room of his wife's bedroom, he spoke. His voice was surprisingly cool considering he was being threatened.

"I don't know why your sister hated me."

"But you don't deny it?" Saskia hissed, pacing closer.

He shrugged, then winced as his wound stretched.

Shaun pushed harder against the shirt she was holding to his side. She'd snatched it from Leeza's closet, thinking the other woman wouldn't mind. Now she wasn't so sure. Leeza hated her husband? It was clear the two hadn't been in love, but hate?

"I think you do know why she hated you," Saskia pushed. "And you know what?"

Adam stared steadily back at her.

"As soon as I find out, I'm coming back here and cutting your nuts off with a pair of rusty shears."

Oddly, Adam's expression didn't grow fearful or contemptuous. Instead, he looked at Saskia with a new kind of interest. As though she'd gone from someone who didn't register as existing in his world to suddenly worth his notice. Shaun didn't like that look.

"Saskia, please stop talking."

Saskia glared at Shaun. "This man made my sister's life a misery and I want to find out why."

"It doesn't matter right now."

"Yes, it does!" Saskia insisted. "He's the reason..." She trailed off without finishing the sentence.

Adam was still staring at Saskia fixedly.

"Saskia, it's time for you to leave," Shaun said calmly. When Saskia didn't move, Shaun looked over her shoulder at the men. "Please escort her out." When Saskia protested, Shaun added, "You aren't needed here. I'll come find you later."

Saskia sputtered something that Shaun knew she didn't mean. Still, it bothered Shaun that Saskia was now angry with her. It also bothered Shaun that she had so easily switched gears to take charge of what was clearly a mafia situation. It struck her that she'd gone from being unsure in this shadowy underworld to gradually finding her footing.

Probably not that surprising, considering how many life and death situations she'd faced since meeting Jozef. She was learning to think on her feet in these situations.

Still, she was relieved to see Jozef when he walked in the door. The air in the room changed dramatically as his dark-suited figure moved to stand next to her. He placed a tattooed hand on her shoulder and squeezed gently.

Suddenly, despite her hand pressing against a bloody wound and the four extra men in the room, it was just the two of them. Shaun looked up at him, drowning in his velvet blue eyes. He allowed the shutters to fall, allowed her to see his intense love for her.

He lifted his hand from her shoulder and she felt instantly bereft. *You wish to treat his wound?* Jozef signed.

Shaun nodded. "He's injured. He'll need sutures and some antibiotics. I asked for them, but I don't know if they're coming."

A medical kit landed on the floor next to her. Shaun glanced up at Cooper, who'd brought it for her. "I've sent someone for the antibiotics."

Shaun smiled at him and then looked back at Jozef. She licked her lips and hesitated before speaking what was on her mind, switching to sign language so her patient wouldn't be upset. *Do you intend to hurt him?*

Yes, Jozef signed quickly and decisively.

Saskia had been right.

Will it make a difference if I ask you not to?

Jozef stared steadily down at her. *Yes, it will make a difference.*

But you intend to hurt him anyway, don't you?

Jozef didn't speak. He rarely spoke when the person asking already knew the answer.

Shaun sighed. "Well, I'd still like to treat his wound."

Go ahead, Jozef signed. *When you finish, you'll be escorted back to the house.*

Shaun got to work, patching up the wound in Adam's side. She pulled on a pair of gloves and used hydrogen peroxide to wash her hands and for a quick clean of the wound to remove debris. She used soap and water for a more thorough cleaning.

Adam flinched, but otherwise didn't move as she worked on him. He was staring at the ceiling now, perhaps mentally preparing himself for torture.

Torture.

Shaun was going to be complicit in torturing a person. She would know it was happening and wouldn't do anything about it.

Without realizing, her breaths became shallow as her thoughts battered her. Sweat beaded her forehead. She shrugged a shoulder, soaking the sweat with her sleeve.

She finished the sutures and taped gauze over the wound. She took her bloody gloves off and set them aside. She tried to stand, but her legs wobbled badly.

Jozef caught her under the arms and pulled her away from the pallet.

Shaun knew all eyes in the room were now on her, but she couldn't stop the panic attack. It hit her like a cement truck, sucking the air from her lungs. She tried to take in a deep breath, but it strangled in her throat, choking her.

Her fingers flexed and curled, as if they had minds of their own, her nails cutting into her palms. Her legs refused to work, refused to carry her from the room. Her cheeks burned as she felt her dignity slipping.

Why did it have to happen here? In front of all these people?

Jozef lifted her and carried her from the room. In the

corridor, he sat her down on a bench and crouched in front of her. She thought she might see accusation in his eyes. She had shown weakness in front of almost half a dozen men. Even though she was new to the mafia, she knew enough to realize one didn't show weakness. It was like leaving blood in the water for the sharks to find.

She should have known better, though. The only thing Jozef's expression said to her was how concerned he was. It helped her calm down a little. He stared at her, his eyes eloquent while he ran his hands up and down her arms, then her thighs.

He didn't tell her to breathe. He didn't have to. He showed her what he wanted to do by taking in steady breaths, then letting them out. In and out, in and out. With each breath, more oxygen flooded her brain and body, making her feel steadier.

When she finally caught her breath, the tears started. "I'm complicit," she told Jozef. "I'm complicit in whatever you do to him, and I'm complicit by living here. I'm complicit by not turning you into the police." She placed her hand over her chest, over her heart. "I am complicit in harming others, and I swore an oath to do the opposite."

Jozef's gaze became sad, but she could still read his determination. He had no intention of changing.

"I can't do this, Jozef," she sobbed. "I tried, because I love you more than I've loved anyone ever. But I can't do this. It's the opposite of everything I stand for, of who I am."

She didn't know what she was trying to tell him. She couldn't bring herself to tell him she was leaving, or to demand he let her go. He solved her problem in his typical Jozef way.

First, he touched her face, holding her wet cheeks between his palms before leaning forward and gently kissing her, licking the salty tears from her lips. Then he stood, towering over her.

Shaun looked up at him.

You are not complicit. When she shook her head, he tapped her cheek with his finger. It didn't hurt, but the tap was sharp enough to keep her from arguing with him. *You're not complicit because you are my captive. You might love me, you might wish to stay with me, but you are still my captive. I will never let you go. Even if you come to hate me. Even if you run away from me. I will always find you and I will always bring you back.*

She blinked away her tears, the last of the tightness in her chest dissipating. Despite his brutal words, she treasured them. They allowed her peace of mind when she couldn't seem to find it on her own.

You belong to me, he continued. *Nothing you can do will induce me to allow you to leave. I know you believe you can convince me to let you go if you really want to go, but it's time to let that fantasy go. You will never leave. Not now, not ever.*

Shaun nodded, then stood, her hand on the wall for support.

Jozef slipped an arm around her, steadying her. She tipped her head back and stared at him, registering the determination, the truth of what he said in his eyes. He meant every word.

"Okay," she whispered, then stepped back. She turned away from him and left the shed, taking peace in the sunshine flooding the rose garden and lighting the stone path.

Cooper came up alongside her and together they walked silently back to the house.

CHAPTER TWENTY-FIVE

Shaun didn't know what to do with herself once she got up to the house. She felt restless and uncomfortable in her own skin. She hated knowing what was probably happening down at the shed. It helped to know that Jozef was going to do what he wanted to do, regardless of what she wanted.

She searched for their cook, Sona, in the kitchen to go over the week's menu, but found a note saying the other woman had gone grocery shopping.

She tried knocking on Saskia's door, but the younger woman yelled for her to go away. Shaun understood why Saskia was angry, but she hoped the other woman wouldn't hold a grudge. She was one of Shaun's few friends in Prague. Plus, Shaun suspected Saskia's grudges could become painful, depending on how she directed her energy.

"Are we done pacing the mansion?" Cooper asked drily, trailing Shaun from room to room.

She narrowed her eyes at him. "Just for that, I should make you do laps around the grounds."

He flashed her a grin. "You'll be coming too."

Shaun decided to spend some time alone with her cat. He spent most of his time in their suite, though he was allowed the run of the mansion. He hadn't quite gotten brave enough to go exploring yet. Shaun was okay with his timidity. She didn't trust the house guards not to let him outside, and she would be devastated if he disappeared or got hit by a car.

"Fitzy." She bent down to scoop up the cat who met her at the door.

He vocally let her know how much he didn't appreciate spending all day alone, then shoved a paw in her throat, insisting she put him down. She laughed and set him back on his feet, where he proceeded to follow her into the bedroom, treating her to a meowing diatribe.

She lay down on the bed and patted the covers, encouraging him to jump up. After a few seconds' hesitation, he jumped and made his way over to her, rolling onto his back so she could pet his chubby belly.

"How is life, little man?"

He purred in contentment, kneading the air with his paws.

"Not too bad in this giant mausoleum, is it?" Shaun glanced around her bedroom.

It was growing on her. She still hated knowing it had once belonged to Jozef's aunt and uncle, but their ghosts were fading. She pulled her phone from her pocket and tried calling her mother, but there was no answer. She wondered what Fatima was up to and decided to try again later.

She sighed and rolled onto her back, staring at the ceiling. These were the moments she hated, had always hated. She didn't enjoy being alone with her thoughts. She'd never really been a Zen kind of person. She liked to move, to work, to keep busy.

After a few minutes she stood and went back into the sitting room, pulling her binder from its cubbyhole under the coffee table. Fitzy jumped up on the couch beside her, making himself comfortable against her thigh. She curled her legs beneath her and allowed her work to consume her. She read through the step-by-step procedure for her upcoming surgery and referenced the works of several other professionals to make sure she was on the right track. The surgery itself wasn't groundbreaking, but it was complex. The type of surgery other surgeons would refuse to do because the odds of fatality were too high. Shaun enjoyed the challenge. She tried not to let worry over fatality rates stop her from taking on difficult operations.

She wasn't sure how long she poured over the documents but when she looked up the shadows in the room had length-ened and Jozef was sitting in the armchair across from her, his leg crossed over the other at the knee, his elbow on the armrest and his chin in his hand. Fitzy was curled on top of his foot, snoozing on the floor.

Jozef looked serious, but relaxed.

When she first caught sight of him, she yelped, dropped her binder and grabbed her throat.

He chuckled.

"Don't do that!" she said accusingly.

Don't do what? he asked.

She narrowed her eyes at him. *Don't scare the life out of me. Make yourself known next time you want to hang out.*

He shook his head. *I enjoy watching you.*

She glared at him, but her lips twitched in amusement. *You've done this before?*

Many times, he admitted.

She believed him. He was like a cat, entering a room noiselessly, then watching his prey until he was ready for them to see him. But once his presence was known, he filled a room with his energy. It was a strange phenomenon. He was larger than life. A man who didn't need to use his voice to make his presence count.

I should put a bell on you.

His shoulders shook with laughter, *my men wouldn't know what to do if I walked around with a bell all day.*

They smiled at each other until the seriousness of what had occurred inside the shed infiltrated their moment.

Shaun licked her lips and hesitated over what she wanted to ask him. She loved these moments, when they were together, alone and intimate, the two of them in a bubble. She didn't want to ruin the moment, but she needed to know.

What did you do with A-D-A-M?

His response was quick, telling her he knew she would ask. *He's fine.*

When she opened her mouth to ask him to define 'fine', he held a hand up.

I didn't touch him. I interrogated him, but the man knows nothing. He doesn't know where my aunt or cousin are. When he realized the family was under attack, he gathered as much food as he could carry and closeted himself in the cottage's panic room. He hadn't left since until you scared him out.

How do you know he's telling the truth? Shaun was curious about the interrogation. How did Jozef extract information when he needed it?

Jozef snickered, flashing a boyish smile. *I know.*

She frowned. *You said you didn't torture him.*

I didn't. Apparently seeing the direction of her thoughts, he frowned severely. *My men didn't touch him either. You will not disbelieve me when I tell you something.*

Shaun laughed out loud, despite her concern for Leeza's husband. "You can't stop me from having thoughts, Jozef."

He placed both of his hands on the armchair and pushed himself up, uncoiling from his deceptively relaxed position.

Fitzy grumbled, stretched, and sauntered away. After the explosions in their apartment, Fitzy had grown more attached to Jozef. Shaun wasn't sure why, but she was happy to see her future husband and cat getting along.

As Jozef stepped toward her, he signed, his movements slow, so she wouldn't miss a single one. *You won't doubt me because I won't allow it.*

He dropped to his knees in front of her.

"Dictator," she whispered, but her smile took the sting from the word.

He leaned forward and kissed her, taking her lips in a bone melting kiss. He lingered but didn't push for more. This was one thing she adored about him. He never stopped kissing her.

In her other relationships, once sex was on the table, kissing and making out fell to the wayside. For Jozef, the kisses were essential. He took them at every opportunity, no matter where they were or who was looking. For him, the kissing didn't lead to sex. It was an intimacy between them he kept alive.

When he leaned back, she signed, *so how did you get him to confess?*

He flashed her a grin and held up his hand. There was a poorly taped bandage on his palm.

"What happened?" she demanded, grabbing his hand and pulling it into her lap.

She peeled back the bandage and found a cut about an inch long. It was deep enough that it had bled, but it wasn't bad enough that it needed suturing. She looked up at him, bewildered.

He tugged his hand away, re-taping the bandage.

A-D-A-M is sickened by the sight of blood. He damn near fainted when I cut myself. That was all it took to get him to tell us everything he knows, which unfortunately isn't much.

"Hemophobia," Shaun murmured, then shook her head in disapproval. "It's not nice to use a person's fears against them."

Jozef shrugged. *Better than torture.*

He was right. If she was going to pass judgment on Jozef's actions, she had to admit, she would be a lot more upset if he'd resorted to torture.

"He wasn't freaking out about his own blood when I tended to him," Shaun mused as she thought about the man's reaction to being shot. She'd been so concentrated on tending him that she hadn't really paid attention. "Actually... come to think of it, I don't think he looked down at all. He either kept his eyes shut or averted. He was shaking and looked like he was going to throw up, but I attributed his symptoms to being shot. I bet he was reacting to the blood too."

Jozef shrugged, uncaring of how Adam's fear manifested.

"Did you hold back because of me? Is that why you didn't hurt him?" she asked, unsure she wanted to know the answer. Adam wasn't going to be the last time they ran into this issue. Eventually, Jozef would have to do something to someone that Shaun hated. She wasn't sure how she would deal with it, if she would try to justify his actions or if she would decide she couldn't stomach being with him.

If she was being honest with herself, she would admit that it wouldn't be the latter. It would never be the latter. She was with Jozef now.

Yes, it was for you that A-D-A-M wasn't beaten. I didn't want you to think of me that way. I was the guard dog for this family for many years, but you have shown me I can be more.

Jozef's admission hung in the air between them.

Shaun touched his face and smiled sadly. "You were always more than the guard dog. You just needed to see yourself differently."

They stared at each other, wrapped in the moment. She

loved everything about him, even the brutal parts. It was strange… loving a man in a wholly encompassing way, yet still hating some things he did.

She was learning just how messy love could be.

Jozef stood and signed, *come with me, I want to show you something.*

He held a hand out to her and Shaun took it, allowing him to pull her off the sofa.

"Where are we going?" she asked as he grabbed her coat from the closet by the door and tossed it to her.

The gun range, he signed.

She gaped at him. "I hope you don't think you're going to get me to shoot a gun."

You will shoot a gun, he signed, *you already have. This will be much easier than the last time.*

"The last time I was trying to save you from being shot in the back!" Her voice grew in volume as he grabbed her hand, pulling her out of their apartment.

Cooper, who was leaning against the wall opposite looking at his phone, straightened.

"I don't intend to ever hold a gun again, Jozef. That was a one-time deal. I hate the sight of them." He nodded at Cooper, who fell into step behind them, following them down the hall.

Jozef didn't answer her, though he was holding her hand in a firm grip so he couldn't communicate.

"Jozef, no!" Shaun dug her feet into the steps as they continued down to the main floor of the mansion.

He kept walking, which caused Shaun to catapult forward, hitting him in the back. He didn't loosen his grip and he didn't stop walking.

Cooper came up alongside her. "You need to know how to protect yourself. It's Jozef's responsibility to make sure you're safe, and the first step in that process is to teach you how to defend yourself."

Jozef finally stopped walking, but when he turned, his glare was for Cooper instead of Shaun. In one eloquent look, he told the other man without words that he didn't need Cooper speaking for him.

Cooper held up his hands in his typical, 'sorry boss' pose. It was almost funny, the dynamic growing between the two. Cooper was a good man with a lot of annoying qualities that seemed to be growing on both Jozef and Shaun.

A chill ran through Shaun as she remembered what had happened to her last bodyguard. He'd been shot in the head while trying to protect her. Maybe she shouldn't develop a friendship with Cooper.

She looked over at him as they continued out the front door where Jozef helped her into the front seat of his Bugatti. Cooper strode to the SUV behind them and climbed inside. She didn't think it would be possible to not be friends with the man. He was always with her, he was talkative and opinionated and he made of point of being a sympathetic ear.

Shaun glanced at Jozef as he navigated the driveway.

"I don't want Cooper to die."

He hit the brakes so hard Shaun had to brace herself against the dashboard.

Jozef put the car in park and turned to her.

You are not allowed to care about that man, he signed furiously. *I will assign someone new to your personal detail.*

You don't understand, she automatically signed back. *It's not him personally... well, it is a little. But I would grow attached to any bodyguard you assigned to me.*

When Jozef looked angrier, she rushed to assure him.

I'm not going to become romantically attached to the man. He's not even close to my type. But I do like him, the same as I liked K-A-R-L. I don't know if I can handle losing another bodyguard.

Who exactly is your type? Jozef demanded, the thunderous frown still wrinkling his brows.

Shaun shook her head at him. He really wasn't getting past the part where she was discussing another man to see the root of her issue. She cupped his cheek, then gave him a light slap, intended to get him to pay closer attention to what she was saying.

You are my type, idiot, she told him. *I like tall, sexy, protective, sweet and growly. All you, only you. Okay?*

He grinned at her. *Okay.*

Then she added, *now focus. I think you should stop giving me bodyguards. I can't take it when something happens to them.*

Jozef shook his head. *You will always have bodyguards. This isn't negotiable. If you don't want them to get close to you, then I will make sure they protect you without talking to you, except for what they absolutely need to.*

I don't like that solution. If someone has to follow me around, then I would rather become friends with them then pretend they're invisible. It feels elitist to treat them like a paid employee.

But they are paid employees, Jozef argued.

She pressed her lips together and frowned at him.

You're missing the point.

He leaned over and kissed her, then signed, *no I'm not. I understand what you're saying, and I understand why you're having difficulty. L-E-E-Z-A had the same problem with her personal body-guard. They became close and she couldn't stand the idea that he would be in danger.*

What happened to the bodyguard? She asked.

He works for me now. H-A-V-E-L.

Shaun was surprised, but she supposed it made sense. Havel had been with the family for a long time. It would make sense that he would've taken on different roles.

Jozef continued, *this is why you need to learn to shoot.*

So I can protect my bodyguard? She laughed when he gave her an exasperated look.

No, he signed back, *so you can protect yourself, which will free up your bodyguard to eliminate the threat.*

Shaun sighed. It made sense. Her life was with Jozef now, and whether or not she liked it, he was a mob boss. She would become a target. Was already a target.

"Okay, let's do this."

He nodded his satisfaction and put the car in gear.

CHAPTER TWENTY-SIX

The gun range was on the property, but Shaun found out that it was easier to get to it by leaving the property and driving around to the other side of the estate. She truly did not know exactly how large the Koba lands were, but she should probably find out so she wouldn't be constantly shocked. Maybe find out if there was a map.

They drove through the guarded gates on the other side of the property, drove up a hill and came to a stop next to a large wooden building. Outside the building was something that looked like an obstacle course with targets set up at strategic points.

The competitor in Shaun sat up and took notice. She might hate the idea of weapons and the destructive implications behind them, but she enjoyed excelling at everything she tried. Each new skill she developed was carefully honed until she was as close to perfect as possible.

Jozef showed her around the building, starting with a truly impressive armoury. Every weapon imaginable filled the storage room, many of them behind locked and coded cages. She appreciated the safety precautions.

We'll start you off small, Jozef signed as he led her toward one cage. He tapped a code into the panel and opened it. *You'll get the codes to these cages so when you feel like shooting, you can come up here without me. You're always welcome. All staff, including my men, have to book their time in the range, but family can come and go as they please.*

Shaun's heart picked up the pace as Jozef started examining weapons, picking each one up and weighing it in his palm before replacing it. She wasn't sure she wanted to become comfortable enough with the gun range to come and go at will.

Finally, Jozef chose a weapon. He handed it to her, and she reached for it, hesitating, her hand hovering over his for a moment before taking it.

It felt strange to her. She'd held exactly three guns in her entire life, all on the same day. One when Karl had been killed, and she'd been forced to defend herself and then again when she took one from the locker of the panic room and tried to defend Jozef. And last, when she picked up Havel's gun to protect them while he recovered. But those times were different. She'd been in panic mode and reaching for those weapons had been automatic, like a reflex. Now, she was willingly choosing to use a weapon.

"I don't like it," she told Jozef, looking at him and hoping he could see the indecision.

He caressed her cheek, then dropped his hand to sign, *you'll do fine. Imagine it's a scalpel and you need to make very precise cuts in your target. With practice, you'll grow more comfortable and gain confidence. It will become more of an accessory than a monster that weighs on your mind.*

She was relieved that he understood, but she wasn't sure she believed him.

He must have read her continued indecision. *When I first held a gun, it felt foreign. It brought back flashes of my parents' deaths. It took time, but eventually I grew comfortable. Now, it's an extension of myself. Like a limb.*

Shaun had seen the way he was around weapons. They were definitely a part of him. Like he said, an accessory.

"Okay," she agreed. "I'll try."

You won't try, you'll succeed.

She knew he wasn't giving her a pep talk when he said she would succeed. He was telling her she didn't have a choice. She would learn to shoot and she would learn to shoot well because he was going to make damn sure she could.

Unfortunately for Jozef, it turned out that Shaun had absolutely no natural ability.

Twenty minutes later, she growled in frustration. "This is nothing like cutting with a scalpel!"

Jozef chuckled and took the gun from her, setting it on the platform in front of her. He hit the button next to the wall, which called her target forward, then removed the earmuffs from her head.

You weren't any good with a scalpel the first time you picked one up.

She crossed her arms over her chest and pouted. "How do you know?"

No one is good the first time they try something.

"Maybe I'm a prodigy."

Maybe, but you're definitely not a shooting prodigy. He unhooked the target and held it up. She'd used an entire clip and hit her target twice, neither bullet actually hitting the person's outline on the target.

"I think you got mine too."

Shaun turned to find Saskia standing behind her. Her pulse picked up as she noticed the gun held low at Saskia's side. She looked more mature than usual, standing there in ripped blue jeans and a pink hoodie, blue earmuffs around her neck and her gun at her side.

She handed Shaun her paper target. Shaun took it from her and winced as she saw the stray bullet hole in the paper's edge. Saskia's shots had all landed within the outline.

"You're not very good at this."

"It's my first time," Shaun argued.

"It shows."

Before Shaun could say anything else, Saskia stalked away, heading for the armoury. Maybe to check her gun in.

Shaun sighed and turned to look at Jozef. "She's mad at me because I kicked her out of Adam's cell earlier."

Jozef looked at her speculatively. *Why?*

"She was interfering, and she refused to listen when I asked her to stop questioning him." She chewed her lip before confessing her thoughts, "I didn't like the way he was looking at her. Sort of predatory."

Jozef nodded, but his gaze was still on her. It was speculative. Finally, he signed, *keep away from him. I'll tell S-A-S-K-I-A the same.*

They continued practicing until the gun range emptied and it was just Shaun, Jozef and Cooper left. Out of the corner of her eye she caught Jozef knock on the barrier between them and Cooper. When Cooper looked over, Jozef jerked his head toward the door.

Cooper immediately re-holstered his weapon and strode away.

Shaun's heart picked up in speed. She pretended she hadn't seen the interaction and turned back to her target, lifting her gun.

Jozef slipped behind her, pressing his erection against her ass. She was wearing leggings, so she felt every inch of him.

Her breathing became heavy as he wrapped his arms around her, his long reach easily able to cover her hands over the gun. Together they lifted it. He took aim and then kissed her beneath her ear, sending a shower of tingles down her neck. He nodded, and she squeezed the trigger.

She was surprised when her bullet hit the target dead center in the head. He adjusted their aim and nodded again. She took another shot and hit the target in the heart.

"Oh my god!" she exclaimed, turning in his arms. "I hit the target!"

He chuckled, slipping the gun from her fingers. She'd accidentally pointed it at him. She opened her mouth to apologize, but he slid his hand around her neck, capturing her and dragging her into his chest. He took her lips in a ferocious kiss. One that was unmistakably sexual.

He pressed his cock into the cradle of her thighs, telling her without words exactly what he wanted.

He set the gun on a shelf next to them and enveloped her in his arms, his lips coaxing her mouth open. He swept her mouth with his tongue, his growl of pleasure reverberating between the two of them.

Scorching heat cascaded through her as he swept her with his hands. Then she shivered as a chill hit her when he took the hem of her T-shirt and lifted it, baring her stomach and chest. She wasn't wearing a bra and the shirt caught briefly on her nipples, tweaking them, before Jozef pulled it firmly over her head.

He broke their kiss and dipped his head to take her nipple in his mouth. She moaned and leaned back against the shelf behind her, giving him better access as she drove her hands into his hair, gripping his silky strands.

She loved the way Jozef made love. All in, no hesitation. He knew what he wanted and he took it. His entire focus was on their mutual pleasure. There was no better aphrodisiac than a man who took pleasure in the pleasure of his woman.

He pulled at her nipple, rolling it against his tongue then using the edge of his teeth to prick. The sweet aching burn turned rapidly into an inferno of need that sent her hands diving between them, scrambling for his belt buckle. He chuckled against her breast, not helping her as he switched to her other nipple, driving her insane with his play.

"Jozef!" she said desperately.

He released her nipples and reached between them, pushing her fingers aside and undoing his belt. Heat slammed into her at the metallic sound of Jozef's belt as he unbuckled, followed closely by the sound of a zipper.

Their gasping breaths mingled as he lifted her, setting her ass on the shelf, then gripping her neck and devouring her mouth. She met him tongue for tongue, teeth for teeth. She gripped his cock, squeezing and stroking as he tugged at her leggings.

She giggled into his mouth when he struggled. He should've shoved them down her legs before he set her on the shelf. He broke the kiss, glared at her for daring to laugh at him, then pulled her down so she was standing again.

He didn't waste any time. A loud rending sound filled the range as he tore her leggings at the seams.

Shaun's pulse leapt at the sound. His eagerness was taking her own libido to new heights. She couldn't stop touching him, sliding her hands under his shirt and digging her nails into his mouth-watering slabs of muscle.

He gripped her by the waist and turned her around, tearing her panties down her legs. She gasped and looked over her shoulder as he bent down behind her. He bit her ass, hard enough to hurt but not hard enough to break her skin.

She squealed, then moaned as he pushed her ass cheeks apart and dove in face first.

Shaun had never had her ass eaten before, but she'd heard about it and seen enough porn to be intrigued. Jozef showed her just how right she was to be curious.

Sensations shot through her, leaving her shaking and

gasping as he used his lips and tongue on her ass while fingering her pussy. She bent herself over the shelf she was clutching and spread her legs wider.

It was like being loved by a storm. Electric, powerful, unpredictable.

Jozef stood and whirled her around, picking her up and setting her back on the shelf. With a hand behind her neck, holding her steady, he slammed into her. He didn't wait for her to adjust, but started pumping, pushing harder and harder, faster and faster.

Sounds spilled from her lips, but she wasn't sure what they were. She felt incapable of controlling herself. He was too much, too hard. He was everywhere at once, touching her inside and out, driving her toward her orgasm.

Out of nowhere, with very little buildup, it slammed into her.

Shaun let out a scream as her orgasm hit like a tsunami, wave after wave. She couldn't breathe, she was drowning in pleasure.

She barely noticed Jozef finish.

He gripped her hips so hard it would have hurt if she'd been even remotely cognizant of what was happening around her.

Finally, she was able to draw in a breath as his semen shot into her, flooding her with his warmth.

She would have collapsed backwards, but he grabbed hold of her and held her against him.

When they both landed from their respective orgasms, Shaun looked at him with what she knew was a stupid grin plastered across her face. There was an answering one on his.

"I think I'm definitely going to need more shooting lessons."

CHAPTER TWENTY-SEVEN

Shaun arrived at the hospital right on time with her team of bodyguards. Cooper had been cleared to stand outside of the surgical room, while the others would patrol the corridors outside of the surgery ward.

Walking into the hospital, knowing she was about to do the thing she loved most in the world was both heady and nerve-wracking. It was a different hospital, but the same feeling of exhilaration.

She knocked on Elisa's office door and was greeted with a bright smile.

"Come in, I'm just finishing up a few things and then we can go to the patient's room." Cooper tried to follow Shaun through the door, but Elisa stopped him. "I'm sorry, you can't come in. We'll be discussing the details of this patient's surgery, which is private."

"I go where she goes," he said gruffly, crossing his arms over his chest and showing off his impressive biceps.

Elisa didn't look particularly impressed. "The door is made of glass. I'll leave it unlocked. If, somehow, Dr. Patterson is attacked while she's in my office, you can be by her side in under two seconds. Or shoot through the door. Whatever's easiest."

She didn't wait for an answer, but closed the door in his face. Shaun smothered a laugh at his disgruntled expression.

"Have a seat." Elisa waved Shaun to the guest chair. "I have a few things for you to sign."

Shaun sat down, setting her purse on the floor. She'd assumed she would have to sign a non-disclosure agreement given the sensitive nature of the case. Elisa placed several documents in front of her with tabs where she needed to sign.

The two women worked together in comfortable silence. Elisa was concentrating on several files in front of her. As head of neurology, it was her responsibility to review the case files for the staff working under her.

Shaun read carefully through each document Elisa had given her before signing. Sure enough, one was an NDA from the patient. There was another from the hospital, as well as liability waiver. The hospital was not to be responsible for any injury to her person while on the hospital grounds. The last document was for the transfer of her fee for the procedure. She raised her eyebrows and looked up at Elisa.

"We didn't discuss a fee. This is a sizeable sum that I don't particularly need. Given that my fiancé is donating money to the hospital, it feels a little unnecessary."

Elisa smiled. "We have to pay you. Paid staff are covered by our insurance. We don't really have a volunteer program for surgeons."

"But the amount."

"Yes, I negotiated for that on your behalf." When Shaun opened her mouth to argue, Elisa held a hand up and cut her off. "All women should be independent. This is your work, and you should be paid for it. You're one of the best surgeons in the world. Had we borrowed you from your hospital in Montreal, this is what you would have been paid."

Embarrassment flooded Shaun and she quickly signed the last document. Of course, she should accept the money. She was independent of Jozef. It rattled her that she was thinking in terms of a kept woman. She needed to have a stern talking-to with herself when she got home.

When Shaun finished, she pulled a file from her purse and passed it across the desk.

"What's this?" Elisa opened the file, then laughed when she saw Shaun's resume with the cover letter asking for a permanent position at the hospital.

"Consider this my formal request for employment."

Elisa shook her head and set the file down. "This wasn't necessary. We will consider it an honour if you accept a position with us. The hospital director is so pleased by the idea that I think he's ready to offer you my position. He's already printed your identification."

Elisa tossed the ID badge across the desk toward Shaun. On it was the picture the hospital had taken of her when she'd first gone through security one week earlier.

Shaun looked carefully at Elisa. Her comment about Shaun taking her job was pointed. Though any position other than the head of the department would be a step down for Shaun, she had no intention of taking the other woman's job. They inhabited an incredibly competitive field and there were few enough women who made it to the top that Shaun was unwilling to displace one as smart and driven as the woman sitting across from her.

If Shaun were to take a long-term position in the hospital, she would have plenty of room for movement. She was almost twenty years younger than Elisa, who would eventually retire or move on to a director position.

"Your job is safe around me," Shaun assured her. "Honestly, it'll be a relief to not have the responsibility of an entire department on my head. A new position will give me more time for lab work and research."

Elisa nodded, but didn't comment. Until that moment, the natural competitive nature between surgeons had been pushed to the wayside as they forged their way through the planning of a difficult surgery. Now, they were hours away from conducting that surgery and their positions were shifting.

Shaun would take lead on the surgery, but Elisa was technically her boss while she worked at the Prague hospital.

Elisa pushed away from her desk and stood. "Let's go see our patient."

"I thought you would never ask."

Shaun clipped her badge onto her shirt and followed Elisa from the room. She would finally find out who her mystery patient was. So far, all that had been disclosed to her was his age, medical history and current medical condition.

They ran into another issue when Cooper flat out refused to allow Shaun to enter the patient's room without an escort. It was one thing to let Shaun speak with Elisa privately while he watched through a glass door, but quite another when she intended to walk solo into a room with people he hadn't vetted or run by Jozef. He took his bodyguard duties extremely seriously.

They had to wait another ten minutes while Elisa called down to her office and asked for another non-disclosure agreement, which was promptly rushed to the patient's room. Cooper held it against the wall and signed with a pen that Elisa handed him.

"Are we ready now?" Elisa asked, an edge of sarcasm in her voice.

The trio entered the room and Shaun looked to the man on the bed, clad in a hospital gown, his legs crossed in front of him, a stack of papers in his lap. She didn't recognize him, but when her gaze strayed to the other men in the room, she immediately recognized one of them. He'd been in her home a few days earlier.

She stopped in her tracks and Cooper stepped in front of her, his hand going beneath his jacket. He recognized the man too. Alan Dietrick, personal bodyguard to the Prime Minister of the Czech Republic. Which meant the man on the bed must be…

"Dr. Shaun Patterson, this is Branislav Makovsky, our Prime Minister."

Cooper recovered from his shock first. "Absolutely not. This is a setup." He turned and grabbed Shaun by the arm. "We're leaving now."

Dietrick and the other two bodyguards stepped forward, but it was the Prime Minister who stopped them.

"Please." His voice was firm, despite his fragile condition. "Let me speak with the doctor before you take her out of here."

Shaun looked at the man, saw the sincerity in his eyes. In a low voice she said to Cooper, "He won't hurt me in a hospital full of people."

"You don't know what this man is capable of," Cooper countered, not lowering his voice. "Jozef wouldn't approve."

Shaun shook her head. "I am a doctor and this is my patient. Period. He is not the Prime Minister."

"I don't know about that," the Prime Minister said drily.

Shaun narrowed her eyes at him. "I will leave and your odds of surviving this surgery will go down drastically."

He took a sharp breath and stared at her, as if trying to see into her soul. She knew what he was looking for. Answers to his own mortality. He wanted to know if the fiancé of his rival could actually set aside any preconceived notions and work to give him a few more years of life.

"So I've been told," he said quietly, his gaze switching to Elisa. "Dr. Černý has indicated that this surgery cannot go forward without you. Please, I only have a few months left. I... I want more time with my grandson. He was born only a few months ago."

Shaun heard the hesitation and the sincerity in his voice. He didn't want to appear weak in front of his men, but he was willing to say whatever it took to get Shaun to agree to do the surgery.

She stepped away from Cooper, giving him a stern look as she approached the hospital bed.

"You know that your survival is uncertain, even with me conducting the surgery."

"Yes, I've been informed." Again, he glanced at Elisa. Shaun sensed he trusted the other woman, which made Shaun trust her a little less.

"You understand that this surgery is designed to extend your life, not save it?" Shaun was being far blunter that she might have been with other patients. As much as she wanted to be completely impartial to her patient, she couldn't forget that he'd tried to blackmail Jozef into working for him. "The tumour has a high chance of coming back in three to five years, at which time you probably won't survive another surgery."

Branislav looked at her steadily. "Three years is better than the three months I've been given. Please, Dr. Patterson, I need you."

She stared back at him and finally nodded. She looked at Elisa. "I think we're ready."

It turned out that Dietrick had been given the same permission as Cooper to stand outside the room while the surgery was being conducted. The rest of his men would have to remain off the surgical ward.

Branislav was moved onto a gurney and wheeled to his

surgery ahead of his doctors and bodyguards. Several nurses and an anesthesiologist began preparing the patient while Elisa and Shaun scrubbed their hands and arms.

"Can you be objective with this man?" Elisa asked.

"Of course," Shaun replied quickly. "Aside from my professional background speaking for me, I am completely objective. I don't know this man, hadn't met him before today and don't particularly care about him one way or the other, except as a human being."

"But he must have some business with your fiancé," Elisa persisted. "You won't hold this against him?"

Shaun smiled grimly. Of course she would. If holding the man's life over his head stopped him from harassing Jozef, then she would do it.

She stopped scrubbing and stared at her reflection in the glass separating the scrub area from the surgery. She was proposing harm. Not physically, because she would never actually harm the man, but she would withhold the surgery if he persisted in going after Jozef. The thought should have sickened her, but it didn't. It gave her a strange sense of power over the situation.

She was in her element. In surgery, she was in charge. She was powerful and he was at her mercy.

She was changing. Just as Jozef was changing, becoming more thoughtful because of her, she was becoming more ruthless. Her life had been put in danger several times over the past year and a half. She was done being the victim. It was time to take charge of her life again and she would start by ensuring the safety of herself and her family.

The two women finished scrubbing and put on their gowns, masks and gloves. Upon entering the room, Shaun took her seat on the stool next to the patient. While Elisa redirected the placement of the implements, Shaun leaned over to speak to her patient.

His dark brown eyes met hers and she read understanding in them.

He knew she was about to throw down an ultimatum.

"If this surgery is a success, then you will owe me, and I promise, I will collect." Her voice was low so only the Prime Minister could hear.

He stared at her, his dark eyes assessing. "You have my word. Just cut this thing out of me and give me a few more years with my grandchildren."

CHAPTER TWENTY-EIGHT

Havel grunted and stumbled back as he absorbed Jozef's blow.

Jozef was beating the shit out of him, while he'd only landed a couple of blows. It went this way every time they sparred. Havel was heavy with muscle, while Jozef was light on his feet and wiry. Muscles roped the younger man's arms as he danced before landing each blow.

Havel was next only to Jozef. No one else could beat him, which was his only consolation after a good ass-whooping courtesy of his best friend and boss. Jozef didn't pull his punches but attacked full force and danced away before Havel could land a single blow.

Havel was still catching his breath when he saw Jozef come at him out of the corner of his eye. He held up his boxing glove and shouted, "Mercy."

Though the sound was muffled through his mouth guard, Jozef heard him and stopped his advance.

Havel dropped to his knees, spat out his mouth guard and sucked precious air into his lungs. Each breath sent a blast of nausea rushing through him, but eventually his stomach settled.

"Stay the fuck away from my stomach." Havel glared at Jozef, who'd dropped onto his ass and was leaning back against one of the posts, resting his arms across his upraised knees. Fucker was barely winded while Havel was dry heaving and trying to keep his breakfast down while shards of pain ripped through him.

Jozef stripped the tape from his gloves and pulled them off, dropping them to the mat and flexing his fingers.

Once he was able to catch his breath, Havel mimicked Jozef's pose, sitting on his ass and leaning against the post behind him.

You're getting old, Jozef signed. *Used to be you were the one handing me my ass on a platter.*

Havel snorted. "Yeah, it was stupid of me to teach you everything I know."

They stared at each other. Though they were joking around, the atmosphere was heavy. Havel had taught Jozef everything he'd known, taking the boy under his wing when Havel joined the Koba organization. Now Jozef used those skills to rule his new kingdom with an iron fist.

That wasn't what their current boxing session was about, though. Jozef liked to box when he couldn't keep his mind on his work, and today he was useless for anything except fighting.

"Your lady doctor will be fine. She's surrounded by guards and she's spending most of her day in the most protected wing of the hospital." Havel repeated the same words he'd said to Jozef forty minutes earlier and about two hours before that when she left for the hospital. "Nothing can happen to her."

Nothing was supposed to happen to her when she went Christmas shopping, but my aunt somehow slashed her up and started a war. She should have been safe under this roof one year ago, but she was poisoned. Jozef's frustration showed in the jerky movements of his hands as he signed. *How can I keep her safe when she's not with me? Yet, I know I can't keep her with me at all times.*

Havel nodded his sympathy.

Jozef wore his heart on his sleeve when it came to Shaun. He was one scary motherfucker with almost every other aspect of his life, but for Shaun, he was practically psychopathic. His need to have eyes on her, his desire to murder anyone who came within feet of her, his obsession, it consumed him. Yet, it also somehow made him better at his job. He had a focus now that he'd never had before, and it made him brutally efficient.

Havel hadn't understood Jozef's attraction to the doctor when they'd first picked her up more than a year before. Hell, he didn't totally understand it now, but he knew enough to keep his mouth shut and show respect for the lady of the house.

"She's smart. If she finds herself in trouble, she'll think her way out of it." Havel tried to sound reassuring. "And if that fails, she has her gun. She can shoot her way out."

Havel had been impressed with Shaun's willingness to learn how to shoot. He hadn't thought she would have it in her. He thought a weapon would interfere with her precious 'do no harm' rule. It surprised and pleased Havel to see her accepting her position as the wife of a mobster in a way he hadn't thought her capable of.

She can't hit the broad side of a target, Jozef signed, disgust clear in his expression. *We've been out shooting three times and I think she's getting worse.*

Havel chuckled. "I saw her last target sheet. She hit the edge of the outline. Maybe if she unloads her weapon, she'll get her attacker in the arm."

Both men chuckled over the image of Shaun shooting an entire clip at a guy and missing anything vital.

"I checked in with Cooper before we started our match. He says she's inside the surgery with her patient, three nurses, an anesthesiologist and her doctor friend. She couldn't be safer." Havel left out the part where Cooper had also told him the identity of Shaun's patient. He didn't think that knowledge would make Jozef feel any better about letting Shaun out of the house. They could have that discussion later. "All of them have been thoroughly vetted and passed our checks. Not even a speeding ticket among them."

Jozef nodded, though he didn't look any happier.

Any news on our missing Phantom? Jozef changed the subject.

"No," Havel said shortly.

The subject of Leeza being the Phantom irritated Havel all around, though he understood Jozef's interest. Leeza was Jozef's cousin and a potential threat to his new position as head of the Koba family. Until they found her and locked her down, she had to be considered a wild card.

Havel probably knew Leeza best, yet he hadn't had a clue as to her true identity. He hadn't known that her father wasn't Krystoff Koba, hadn't known of her alternate identity. Hell, he hadn't even known the extent of her combat skills until he heard details of her escape from the mansion and, later, once they figured out what the hell had gone on at the hospital, of her rescue of her mother.

Havel was both impressed and infuriated by this new Leeza. The woman he'd known intimately several years earlier no longer seemed to exist. Yet, in his heart, he knew she was in there somewhere. The wide-eyed, vulnerable girl who'd loved him as passionately as he'd loved her.

When she'd broken his heart by choosing Adam Horáček over him, he'd been too furious to look deeper into her decision. He'd allowed his hurt masculine pride to guide his actions, turning his back on her. Now, he was discovering that she'd had a secret life and a shitty marriage.

He felt responsible for allowing her life to crumble to where she felt desperate enough to invent the Phantom. He'd been in love with her, obsessed with her, and though those feelings never died, he'd shoved them so far down into his black heart he couldn't see a way to reach her. Didn't want to bother.

It wasn't until Jozef had ordered her to be killed along with her mother and father that Havel realized he still had feelings for her. Strong feelings. He'd buried them and accepted that she would have to die.

Now Jozef was handing him the opportunity to take the one thing he'd always wanted: Leeza Koba on a silver platter.

What do you have so far? Jozef persisted.

Havel scrubbed a hand over his face, flinching when his boxing glove touched an open cut on his cheek.

"Before you discovered her other identity, she was using Vasiliy's resources to travel and make trade deals throughout the underworld. She was small scale enough that we didn't notice her until recently. Then she took your uncle and set all this in motion."

Jozef nodded thoughtfully. *Why do you think she took my uncle? She cut off his small finger, but that was all. She didn't torture him or try to get information.*

Havel shrugged; he had an idea.

Leeza had always been passionate, full of life, intelligent and driven. When Krystoff had brokered a deal with the mob accountant for her hand in marriage, the life had been sucked out of her. Or so it had seemed. Now Havel wasn't so sure. Perhaps, like he had buried his feelings for Leeza, she'd buried her joy for life. Carefully hiding and nurturing it until she could bring it back into the light. Perhaps her creation of the Phantom was a combination of her passionate nature and her desire to be seen and heard in the world where she grew up. A world that could be hard on the women who were negotiated for and traded like commodities.

Of course, this was all speculation. Until he got his hands on her, he would remain clueless. Instead of giving away his suspicions to Jozef, he gave him a version that was still probably true. "Revenge. Krystoff sold her into a shitty marriage, and she wanted to show him he wasn't an invulnerable god sitting on his throne. He was fallible and she wanted to make him feel weak."

That would explain why we were so easily able to release him from Vasiliy's prison. Jozef's gaze was laser sharp as he stared at Havel, as if trying to divine his thoughts. Havel, who was used to hiding his emotions, didn't bother with Jozef. Jozef had a sixth sense for the emotions and intentions of others. *You will question her when you capture her. I want answers to these questions.*

"Yes, boss," Havel assured him. He'd intended to interrogate Leeza the moment he got his hands on her. Well, perhaps after he'd had his own revenge for the suffering she caused both of them years earlier when she'd chosen her father's wishes over Havel's heart.

I'm having her father's place watched, but it's unlikely she will go back there.

"Too smart," Havel agreed. "She would know that you're monitoring Vasiliy."

Maybe we should threaten the father.

Havel kept his flinch from showing on his face. If they threatened Leeza's father, then she might become reckless in an attempt to get at him. They could capture her easily, but she would be angry and vengeful. Havel wanted to avoid that scenario.

"I think we should wait, see if she comes to us. She's in a bad spot. Can't use Vasiliy's resources anymore because she knows we're tracking them. She can't travel far with a child in tow. Eventually, she'll have to come to us, or spend the rest of her life hiding."

I will leave it in your hands, but I don't like having loose ends running around unaccounted for. My aunt and her daughter must be brought in.

"It'll get done," Havel agreed.

He was going to have to press his contacts harder, try to get his hands on Leeza before her cousin did. He was loyal to Jozef, but he'd loved Leeza since she was young. He would do what it took to keep her and her boy alive. He would have to balance his loyalties, and hopefully things would play out in a way that he wouldn't have to make a devastating choice.

CHAPTER TWENTY-NINE

"That was amazing!" Elisa said enthusiastically, stripping her gloves off and shoving them into the hazardous materials bin. She flung her mask in next, revealing a toothy grin. "You were phenomenal. What a success!"

Shaun smiled ruefully, stripping off her own mask, gown and gloves. "We won't know until the patient wakes up and goes through the after surgery protocols."

Elisa rolled her eyes. "You know it was a success. You're as much a surgeon as I am. You know the feeling when something goes really well and your patient comes through with flying colours. We may have bought Branislav more than a few years."

"Yes, I know that feeling," Shaun agreed, her tone still serious. "And I've been wrong before. I'll wait for the patient to wake up and start talking before I pass judgment on the success of the surgery."

"You are such a... what is that American term?" Elisa looked thoughtful before coming up with the answer. "A party-pooper. You are pooping on my party."

The way Elisa spoke, almost child-like in her excitement,

made Shaun laugh. She was definitely more reserved than her friend, but she'd learned the hard way not to count her eggs before making sure the chicken survived.

"What if we have a celebratory cup of coffee in the cafeteria?" Shaun suggested. "I'll pay; a thank you for assisting in a fantastic surgery."

"Ah ha!" Elisa crowed. "You admit the surgery was fantastic. Yes, we must celebrate. They have a very mediocre chocolate pudding in the cafeteria. I will allow you to buy me one of those too."

Shaun laughed out loud and shook her head. She walked out into the corridor, looking around for her bodyguard. Cooper stepped away from the wall, along with the Prime Minister's bodyguard.

She directed her words to Dietrick. "Branislav is still under anesthetic. We should know in a few hours how the surgery went."

He nodded his understanding but said nothing. His gaze was blank.

She supposed it made no difference to him other than a paycheck. Her observation of the Prime Minister and his bodyguards was that there was no love lost between them.

Cooper followed as she and Elisa continued to discuss the surgery.

When they left the surgical ward, Shaun said, "I'll meet you in the cafeteria. I want to grab my purse."

Elisa smiled and continued on.

Shaun was still flying high from the success of her surgery when she and Cooper arrived at Elisa's office. Cooper automatically stayed on the other side of the glass wall while Shaun flashed her ID badge across the metal scanner to get into the office. As she bent over to pick up her purse, she heard a voice behind her.

"Hello Shaun." She jumped and would have whirled around, but the voice stopped her. "Don't react!"

Her heart rate sped up and she had to gasp to catch her breath. Her initial thought was that Dasha had somehow found her, but the voice was male.

"What do you want?" She tried to strengthen her voice, but she felt like a trapped mouse. The only way in and out of Elisa's office was through the glass door. The voice was coming from the direction of the windows. Whoever he was, he could easily stop her from leaving the room before she made it to the door.

"I want you to reach into your purse and collect your phone. Then you'll pretend that you're calling your mother."

Every instinct told her to resist, told her she was in danger and that she should run. But Shaun now had plenty of experience with extreme situations. She could force her breathing back to normal, which supplied enough oxygen to her brain that she could think through what was happening. Whoever was talking to her wasn't interested in hurting her. Or at least not at the moment. They wanted to talk to her without the interference of her bodyguard, which piqued her interest.

She reached into her purse. Her phone was on top. He must've gone through her things. Anger rushed through her, but she pulled the phone out and held it up to her ear.

"Now what?" she demanded.

"Turn around and wave at Cooper, let him know you'll be a minute."

She turned, but instead of looking at Cooper, her gaze zeroed in on the man standing opposite her, in the corner between the cabinet and the windows. The only spot in the office where he wouldn't be visible to Cooper.

"Hello again, Shaun."

It was the Interpol agent, Francois Moreau. Jozef had told her his name, told her to watch out for him and to contact

Jozef immediately if he turned up and tried to talk to her. Jozef had certainly predicted this moment.

"My name is Dr. Patterson; I would appreciate if you do not refer to me on familiar terms. We are not friends." She wanted to set her boundaries before finding out what this man wanted. She was curious, but not enough to allow him to manipulate her.

Men often pegged women of her profession and experience as a soft touch. They saw her as a helper, compassionate and caring. While she was all those things, she was also a surgeon. She was egotistical, obstinate, and stubborn. She'd learned to use the misjudgment of men to her advantage. If they undervalued her work ethic, they would be left in the dust as she rose through the ranks of the world's best surgeons.

Rather than showing insult at her comment, he dipped his head in acknowledgment. "Dr. Patterson."

Her eye caught on a movement as the door to Elisa's office opened and Cooper's head popped inside. "Everything okay?"

"Yes," she blurted. "I'm on the phone with my mom, just telling her about the surgery. She wanted to know."

A shaft of guilt forced her to drop her gaze. She'd been building trust with her bodyguard for weeks, and now she was lying to him. She hoped the information she could get from Moreau would be worth the lie.

"Be sure to tell her what a rockstar you are for saving the Prime Minister from his brain tumour." She smiled as he pulled his head from the office and turned his back to give her privacy.

Shit, now she would have to tell Fatima about the surgery before Cooper saw her again. This was the problem with lies, they were too easily unraveled.

Her annoyance at Moreau made her voice sharp when she

spoke to him. "Tell me what you want and make it good, or I will call Cooper in, which you obviously don't want."

He shrugged. "Getting to you is like breaking into the Louvre. Very difficult and a little dangerous. If your bodyguard allowed you to have a conversation with me, he wouldn't be doing his job."

Fair enough, though Shaun still didn't like his methods. "If I'd wanted to talk to Interpol, I would've contacted you myself. I have nothing to say."

"You may have nothing to say to us, but we have plenty to say to you, particularly on the subject of your future husband."

Red hot fury rushed through her, along with the instinct to protect Jozef. "I have nothing to say to you, Mr. Moreau. If you want to speak with my *husband*," she stressed the word, daring him to point out her lack of marriage certificate, "then you can talk to him yourself."

"Your husband is mafia; he's been taught since birth not to talk to the police. I want to talk to you because I think you will be more open to negotiation."

"Then you're wrong," she snapped. "I won't speak with anyone without first talking to Jozef."

"I thought you were more independent than that," he chided. "Pity. I was looking forward to having an intelligent conversation with an intelligent woman."

"If you think insulting me through fake flattery will work, then you haven't done your homework on me at all." She picked up her purse and dropped her phone inside. She was done and she was done with pretending. She headed for the door, intent on capturing Cooper's attention and telling him about her shady visitor.

"Even if it saves your husband from a long prison sentence? Or even death?"

She stopped walking and turned a ferocious glare on the

man. "If you had anything on Jozef, you wouldn't be here talking to me. You'd have him in custody already."

He smiled grimly. "That is a naïve position to take. While I admit we don't have a lot of evidence linking your husband to illegal foreign operations, we have enough to bring him in for questioning. We probably have enough to hold him for a while, which could cripple his takeover of the Koba organization. He's in a delicate position at the moment, it wouldn't take a lot to destabilize him."

Now Moreau had her attention. Jozef rarely talked to her about his takeover. She thought it was sort of an unspoken agreement between them. Jozef didn't want her involved in his criminal activities, and she didn't particularly want to hear the grisly details. Yet, she was curious. Especially because she saw the recent changes in him. He was becoming more serious and he disappeared at all hours of day and night.

"I won't help you bring in my husband, if that's what you're looking for."

He shook his head. "Actually, Jozef's work has caused more good than harm. Though he's definitely involved in illegal activities, some of which we can prove, he's also responsible for helping stabilize the governments in this region of Europe."

Shaun was surprised to hear that Jozef had anything to do with politics. But then, maybe she shouldn't be. She knew the Prime Minister wanted Jozef on his side. Perhaps this was what Moreau meant.

"If you don't want to arrest Jozef, then what do you want?"

"His aunt." The answer was blunt, and it took Shaun a moment to realize who he meant.

"You want Dasha?"

He nodded. "Dasha Koba has been known to us for a long time. Since before she became a Koba, in fact. Her father was not only high up in the Bratva, but he was also a government official. Dasha has danced the line between the two worlds since she was a child. She has become the driving force behind her father's political decisions. She chose her own husband from among the most powerful men in Eastern Europe."

That was a shock to Shaun. As far as she knew, Dasha had been given to her husband in marriage and they had suffered an unhappy relationship for years before reconciling. If what Moreau was telling her was correct, then Dasha had been responsible for her own marriage. She had made the decision based on her own politics. It was a stunning revelation. Rather than a victim, Dasha had been the queen, moving everyone else around the board like chess pieces.

"How do you know?" she asked, but she didn't really need to. Everything she'd seen and experienced at Dasha's hands led Shaun to believe Moreau's version of the older woman.

"Her father was extremely forthcoming about the entire family when we picked him up for his involvement in a prostitution ring."

Shaun wrinkled her nose in disgust. "Please tell me that man is rotting in prison somewhere."

Moreau gave her that pitying look that told her he thought she was hopelessly naïve. Perhaps she was. After her time spent with Jozef and among the Kobas, she really shouldn't be shocked by anything anymore.

"He didn't make it long in the system. He tried to flip on some of his colleagues. They found out."

Shaun was both fascinated and horrified by what she was hearing. It was a glimpse into Dasha's life, which helped explain why she was the way she was. It sounded like she was as calculating and corrupt as her father.

Shaun glanced at Cooper who was looking at her curiously through the window, a slight frown on his face.

Shaun held the phone up and wiggled it, holding up one

finger to show she would be another minute. He nodded and turned away.

"What do you want from me?" Shaun asked again. "Cooper won't stay out there forever."

"We want you to help us bring in Dasha Koba. We have information that she may be in the city. It's a fair assumption that she might come after you again. She seems single-mindedly focused on your demise."

A shiver went straight through Shaun. She was certain if he was correct and Dasha was hanging around Prague that it would be a matter of time before she got Shaun alone again. She had a knack for creating situations to her advantage.

"And what happens if she comes after me. You guys bust the door down and arrest her? How do you intend to do this without my bodyguards noticing? They don't stray far from my side." She stared at Cooper through the door. His pose was deceptively relaxed, but she knew if she called out to him, he'd be in the office in seconds.

"We can take care of that," Moreau assured her. "All we need you to do is to get her talking."

Shaun remembered the last time Dasha confronted her. The other woman hadn't spoken during the entire attack. Shaun shook her head. "She won't talk to me. She'll get me alone and do her best to kill me."

Shaun felt nauseas as memories flooded her. The poisoning, the stabbing in the washroom. Dasha was brutally efficient. She wouldn't waste time talking.

"Flatter her intelligence," he suggested.

Shaun shook her head. "She won't talk to me."

Moreau frowned. "You'll have to find a way. It's her or Jozef, Dr. Patterson, and we'd rather take the aunt. She's had her fingers in the Bratva for so long, directing first her father's activities, then her husband's, that she would be very valuable to us. However, if we can't bring her in, we'll go after the next best person, her nephew."

Now the Frenchman was negotiating, trying to play on Shaun's desire to keep Jozef out of prison. She was about to tell him to go fuck himself, but Moreau decided on a different tactic.

"What do you think Jozef will do to his aunt if he gets his hands on her before we do?"

A shiver snaked down Shaun's spine. The image of Jozef's uncle, shattered and dying on the floor of their apartment. That was nothing compared to what Jozef would likely do to the woman who'd orchestrated the entire situation. She didn't want him to have to live with that; to live with being responsible for the death of the woman who raised him.

Moreau went in for the kill. "We can protect her. She will remain in custody for the rest of her life, but if she cooperates with us and gives us the information we need, we can make the rest of her life very comfortable."

Shaun bit her lip. He had her. And he'd been correct in his first assessment of her, she was a compassionate idiot. She was going to work with this man, work with Interpol, because it would save Jozef from a lot of pain.

"Alright," she said. "Tell me what you want me to do."

CHAPTER THIRTY

Saskia's ears were covered with the bright blue mufflers she used when she was shooting. She'd been shooting more than usual, trying to release some of the tension that had been building up over the loss of control of her life.

She was going back to school again, but if she'd thought her father went ridiculously overboard on the protection detail, Jozef was on a whole other level. He wanted the entire campus crawling with their people, protecting her and, in her opinion, keeping her prisoner.

In the house, she felt like a stranger. It looked the same, but it wasn't. Her parents were gone, her sister was gone, and in their place was Jozef and Shaun. She loved and respected her cousin, but she knew he was hunting her mother.

Her mother!

The bitch who gave birth to her and then ruined all of their lives. Still, she didn't want her mother to die. She'd pleaded with Jozef to allow her to take care of their mother, to imprison her and keep her safe. Of course, he wouldn't. He couldn't. Saskia could accept that, but she couldn't find it in herself to forgive.

She suspected Jozef knew what was in her heart. He watched at all times and doubled her guard when she was around Shaun.

Shaun was complicated. Well, actually, she wasn't particularly complicated. She was a do-gooder with a big heart who was navigating a new and deadly world. Saskia felt for her, but she was also impatient.

The things Shaun was learning to come to terms with were things that Saskia had learned as she learned how to walk, talk and navigate a dark world of illegal dealings. She'd watched and absorbed as much as she could while she grew.

Shaun was an unexpected wrench in the Koba operations, but also a breeze of fresh air. She'd led to the downfall of the family, but she was also responsible for bringing to light secrets within the family.

Complicated.

Shaun thought Saskia was being cool and taciturn because of the incident in the shed when Shaun had kicked Saskia out rather than allow her to question Adam. Though she'd been angry, she hadn't stayed that way. Instead, she'd been proud of the way her soon-to-be cousin-in-law had handled herself. Tough and in charge of the situation. She'd managed the guards like she'd been born to it. Like Saskia would have done in her place.

No, Saskia was keeping her distance because she had her own shit to figure out. Where was her place in this family? Where was her sister and her mother? Should she stay and continue with her studies? Should she try to find Leeza or Dasha? Or should she disappear? For good this time.

She was so absorbed by her thoughts and her shooting practice that she didn't notice anyone come into the gun range. It wasn't until she stopped to replace her clip that a tap on the shoulder jarred her back to her surroundings.

Saskia slammed the clip home and spun, raising her gun.

A woman she'd never seen before stood opposite her.

She was young, maybe around Saskia's age. Though she was beautiful, her features were serious and her eyes were hostile. She had ebony skin, short, black hair and wore combat clothes. She stared down Saskia's gun as though daring her to shoot.

Saskia lowered her weapon, assuming the other woman wasn't a threat, or she would have shot Saskia instead of tapping her on the shoulder.

She dragged her mufflers from her ears.

"Who are you?" she demanded.

"That's what I want to know," the other woman responded, her eyes narrowing as she looked Saskia up and down. "I haven't seen any other women around this place. I know you are not Dr. Shaun Patterson, so who are you? A guard?"

Saskia laughed, unable to help herself. She was as far from a guard as you could get.

Saskia was wearing a pair of low-riding jeans with a rainbow ribbon for a belt and a black T-shirt that sat just above her bellybutton. The shirt was emblazoned with one of her favourite metal bands, Mechanical Poet.

The other woman looked like more of a guard in her green fatigue pants, tight black T-shirt, and combat boots.

"I'm Jozef's cousin, Saskia." She held out her hand.

After a moment's hesitation, the other woman took Saskia's hand, squeezing it in a tight, no-nonsense grip, before dropping it. "Ayaan Radik. I am the new hire for Mr. Jozef Koba's elite team."

Saskia's brows went up along with her esteem for her cousin. He really was bringing the Koba organization into the 21st century.

Apparently catching Saskia's expression, Ayaan scowled, misreading Saskia's surprise. "You don't think I can handle myself with these men?"

In fact, Saskia thought the opposite. There was no way Jozef would hire anyone, let alone a woman, if she couldn't handle herself. Still, Saskia couldn't let this chance for mischief pass. She wanted to see exactly what Ayaan was made of.

"Pick a gun." Saskia ducked her head so Ayaan wouldn't see her grin.

Ayaan turned on her heel and strode toward the weapons room, jabbing her fingers into the pad next to the door, entering the code, showing that she had indeed been approved to be on the estate.

Saskia trailed after her, watching as the other woman stalked the room, eyeing the weapons. She stopped in front of the cage that held the heavy artillery. Saskia watched in fascination as Ayaan once again flawlessly entered a code and opened the door.

She didn't waste time but chose an Uzi. She set it on the shelf next to the cage and searched until she came up with the correct magazine. Slamming the cage shut, she reached for the next one, entering the code, walking in and returning with a rifle and a box of ammo.

"Don't close it." Saskia stepped forward and entered the cage, choosing a rifle for herself. If Ayaan got to have some fun with the heavier weapons, then Saskia wanted in on that action.

She slammed the cage shut and hefted the rifle across her shoulder. "Let's go."

The two women left the artillery and walked through the indoor range to the door that led outside.

Saskia suppressed a shiver as a blast of cold winter air

slapped her in the face. She jogged to keep up with Ayaan who was taller and faster. She seemed in a hurry to establish her skills. Saskia wondered what she was trying to prove and who she was trying to prove it to. She wanted to know everything about this mystery woman.

Ayaan set herself up quickly on the range, showing no awkwardness. She was clearly comfortable with the weapons she'd chosen and the range itself. She'd used it before.

Saskia wasn't surprised. All of Jozef's team members went through rigorous training. A woman would be no different. But her place on his elite team meant he was making significant changes. Shaun's influence, no doubt.

Ayaan pushed her mufflers over her ears and picked up a pair of safety glasses. She hefted the Uzi up, set it on one of the wooden benches and kneeled to load it. Once the magazine was in place, she stood and brought the weapon to her shoulder, hunching to look through the sight.

She was breathtaking. Saskia couldn't take her eyes off the other woman. When the hell had she learned to use a weapon of war? She looked like she was born to it. She had to be tough as nails.

The first blast of gunfire reminded Saskia that she needed to cover her ears. She set her own weapon down and pulled her blue mufflers on. She watched in fascination as Ayaan aimed at each target, then shredded it with a volley of bullets. Though an Uzi wasn't considered a precision weapon, Ayaan's aim was impeccable.

When she'd finished with her targets, she set the weapon down, careful to point the muzzle away from both women.

Saskia gave her a slow clap and flashed her a smile. "Well done."

"That was nothing."

Ayaan picked up her rifle next. She knelt on the ground

and took careful aim at a target that was clear across the range. Saskia knew that some of Jozef's men would struggle to hit the target Ayaan appeared to be aiming at. Somehow, Saskia had confidence that Ayaan wouldn't miss.

The blast shook Ayaan's body, but she held steady. The top of the target disappeared as it was shot clear off. Ayaan glanced over her shoulder at Saskia to make sure she was watching, then she stood and jogged over toward a barricade, lunging behind it, then taking aim at the next furthest target. She repeated the process until she'd reached the end of the obstacle course.

Saskia followed behind at a slower pace, admiring Ayaan's form and skill. The other woman could out-shoot most of the security experts on the estate. Truly impressive.

It was a hike to reach the last target where Ayaan was waiting for her. She was rolling her shoulders back and tipped her head from side to side, working out some kinks. Her warm breath was creating puffs in the cold air. She looked more relaxed than she had when the two women met, like she'd needed to work through some tension.

"Feel better?" Saskia asked, leaning on the fence at the edge of the property line. Out of the corner of her eye, she caught one of the guards watching them.

"I'm fine." Ayaan scowled at Saskia.

"You don't have to talk about it if you don't want to."

Ayaan stared at her, then sighed and dropped to the ground, sitting cross-legged.

"It's my brother. He's found out that I've left France and he's furious. He's demanding that I go back immediately."

Saskia sat down beside her, cringing as the cold hit her backside. "Are you afraid he'll come find you? This place is crawling in security, he'd have a hell of a time getting inside."

Ayaan smiled grimly. "He is more than capable of cracking

this place wide open. Who do you think taught me to shoot? No, he won't attack while I'm here. He won't risk hurting me. I'm afraid that he will find out who I am staying with and make life difficult. I'm afraid that... that Jozef will insist I must leave. I'm happy here, maybe happier than I've been since I was a child. I finally found a place where I fit in and I don't want to leave."

Saskia felt a sharp pang in her chest. She knew how that felt. She'd never felt like she belonged in the Koba family. She wasn't like the rest of them. She had no interest in the mafia world. She didn't want to be arm candy for some old man who bought her through a family merger.

"Jozef knows who you are, right?" Saskia asked. "He knows about your brother?"

Jozef wouldn't leave any stone unturned in checking background on his hires. There was no way he would hire Ayaan without knowing about her baggage.

Ayaan nodded. "Yes, he knows. He met my brother a few months ago."

"Then you're good," Saskia said dismissively. "He won't give you back just because your brother demands it. If Jozef wants you for his team, then it's done. You're part of the family. That's how he works. You will be protected until the day you die."

Saskia pushed off the grass and stood, brushing the back of her pants. The ground was cold enough to be uncomfortable to sit on. A recent snowfall had melted, but the ground still froze each night. She didn't know how Ayaan stood it.

She reached a hand out to the other woman. "Come on, let's see if you have any hand-to-hand skills."

Ayaan took her hand in a firm grip and allowed Saskia to pull her to her feet. Saskia suspected Ayaan was more than competent in hand-to-hand combat and that she was about to get her ass handed to her. It was worth it to see such a formidable woman in action.

Ayaan gave Saskia hope. If Ayaan could break free of her oppressive life, then so could Saskia.

The two women moved together in fluid unison, taking out targets as they made their way back across the range.

CHAPTER THIRTY-ONE

Two weeks.

That was how long it took Dasha to get to Shaun. She'd had to be patient for two solid weeks as the other woman came and went, free as a bird. Dasha's fantasies of murder and mayhem became bloodier and bloodier with each passing day.

Shaun killed her husband.

Shaun took her home.

Shaun twisted her nephew, turning him against his family.

It was all Shaun's fault.

The mantra repeated itself in her mind over and over until she wanted to scream. She didn't, of course. She kept it all in, the same as she kept everything in from the moment she realized, as a child, that watching, waiting and learning was the best way to get to what she wanted.

She wouldn't fuck up this time. Everything had been timed down to the second. She wouldn't wait for Shaun to get the upper hand, she would take her out quickly and walk away, like the ghost she'd become as she flitted around the hospital, avoiding cameras and guards.

Shaun walked confidently through the front doors of the hospital, her purse over her shoulder, her four bodyguards with her. One stopped in the conservatory, taking his usual post where he could see the front door. The others would patrol the hospital, checking in with each other and making sure no one got near their principal.

Cooper was the one Dasha would have to worry about most. He was diligent, sharp, and he never left Shaun's side. He watched the woman like she was the baby chick to his mother hen.

Dasha had learned about him and the rest of Shaun's detail from Nikolay. He despised the American bodyguard, taking every opportunity to badmouth the other man. Jealousy clouded his judgement though. Where he thought Cooper was lazy with slow-reflexes, Dasha soon discovered were simulated character traits used to lull those around him into a sense of calm. She suspected the bodyguard could strike with lightening efficiency and deadliness.

He was the one she'd have to get past.

She'd come up with plan after plan and discarded them all as impractical with a high chance of failure.

This wasn't like the poisoning or the attack in the restaurant. She no longer had the element of surprise on her side. Shaun was well prepared for round three, surrounded by experts in security, working in a highly secure wing of the hospital.

Dasha had a plan though, one that would work.

Though Shaun's security team did their best to make life as safe as possible for their charge, there were always loopholes. It was impossible to cover a person at all times.

Dasha had something else on her side. Her fatality meant nothing to her. If she had to die to reach her goal, then so be it. She had little to live for anymore. Even if she could reestablish relationships with her daughters, she would have to rely on them for handouts for the rest of her life. She would rather die than have to beg for every scrap of food.

It was time to enact her plan. She'd been perfecting it for long enough that it felt like clockwork. As Shaun passed Dasha in the hospital corridor, her head down, reading something from the file she was holding, Dasha waited three seconds for Cooper to pass before stepping out of her alcove and following them.

In her stolen lab coat, Dasha fit in perfectly. She held her head up and walked with confidence. She wore large, thick-framed glasses that helped obscure her face, which was scrubbed of makeup. She looked as far from her former self as she could get.

Turning the corner, she followed the two toward the imaging center, where Shaun would spend some time examining x-rays and carefully choosing her patients.

Dasha had considered taking Shaun out in her new office but had discarded the plan. The office was small with only one entrance. The door was locked and coded with a code specific to Shaun. If Dasha had managed to get hold of the code, then she would have gone with the office plan. She would have stood in the shadows and the second the younger woman entered she would have put a bullet in her head. Cooper would likely have taken Dasha out immediately after, but that didn't matter.

Instead, she was forced to go with a more difficult plan that had a higher probability of success. Once Shaun and Cooper disappeared into imaging, Dasha flashed the identification card she'd stolen from a radiologist in the cafeteria that morning.

She'd had to be careful when stealing ID badges. So far, she'd gotten her hands on three. The first two were cancelled within 24 hours of their owner's discovering them missing, which made Dasha realize she would have to work quickly.

She'd taken the first badge as an experiment. When it had been cancelled, she'd used the second badge to map out every section of the hospital Shaun frequented, deciding that imaging was the best place to launch her attack. The hallways were wide. Even if Cooper stepped through the door ahead of Shaun, she should be able to get past him quick enough to put a bullet in Shaun.

She'd stolen the third badge that morning, which meant she had to go through with her plan or risk having the badge become inactive. Eventually the hospital was going to catch on, making it more difficult for her to get her hands on more badges.

Her heart hammered in her chest as victory seeped into her veins, pumping excitement through her. She was so close, so very close.

She closed her eyes and took a deep breath, coming to peace with her own demise. She would join her husband in death. She would tell him of her victory. Tell him she had avenged the family. She would spend eternity with her lover.

She pretended to study the file she was holding as she walked toward the imaging center where Shaun would pick up her case files before heading back to her office.

Four minutes.

That was the average time it took for Shaun to chat with the imaging technician before she left the office. Cooper would step out ahead of Shaun, clear the hall, then allow his charge to go ahead of him. Dasha would walk past him as he swept the hall, and she would kill his principal before he could step in front of Shaun.

If he got in front of the girl before Dasha could get to her then she would shoot him in the knee, sending him to the floor, kill Shaun then finish the bodyguard. She couldn't risk shooting him in the head in case he toppled backwards into Shaun, accidentally covering her and forcing Dasha to lose precious time. The knee was best, it would send him straight down or forward.

The door to the imaging center opened.

The scene crystallized in front of her, and it felt like everything slowed down as Cooper walked through the door, exactly how she'd predicted. His gaze swept the hallway and landed on her, paused, then moved past. No recognition.

Shaun stepped out behind him, her head down as she scanned the images on the page in front of her.

Dasha strode down the hall as though she owned it, her hand sinking into her pocket and wrapping around her gun. It was small, but it packed a punch. It would drill a hole through Shaun's skull, turning her brain to mush.

Cooper eyed Dasha coldly as she walked toward them. She smiled slightly. She could sense the moment he realized there was danger, but it was too late. She'd already passed him and could see Shaun out of her periphery.

Dasha pulled the gun out of her pocket and swung her arm around, her finger tightening on the trigger.

Before she could get a shot off, Shaun leapt forward, grabbed hold of her wrist and pushed her across the width of the hall, slamming her into the wall. Dasha was so stunned by the sudden counterattack that she lost precious seconds to the other woman, who used them to slam her injured arm into the wall again, forcing Dasha to drop the gun as agony ripped through her.

Dasha stared at Shaun with incomprehension.

Except the other woman wasn't Shaun.

A decoy.

Not as tall or slender as Shaun, but compact, fast and strong. Her hair had been done in Shaun's style, a short afro pinned at the sides. She wore heavy makeup, reshaping her face in Shaun's image, but now that Dasha was up close and personal with this woman she could see the differences.

Her plan had failed.

Jozef must've known that she'd been stalking Shaun at the hospital and had set her up.

Well, she wasn't going down without a fight. She'd rather die here and now than risk being taken back to Jozef. She'd seen his handiwork in the shed, and while she could stand a lot of pain, she knew she wouldn't be able to stand up against his brand of torture. He tore people to pieces over days and weeks, piece after piece, never allowing them the death they would come to crave. And those were the people he had no feelings for. Dasha was his aunt, a woman who had loved him and then betrayed him.

Dasha recovered quickly from her shock, sending her fist flying into the mystery woman's throat. The woman ducked it and sent a fist back into Dasha's chest, then her face, flinging her back against the wall. Dasha pushed off, flying toward the other woman, but met with Cooper's fist when the woman ducked again.

The last thing Dasha heard was the sickening crunch of breaking cartilage as her nose shattered, then blackness overtook her and she sank to the ground.

Cooper stared down at Dasha, glad that the operation was finally over. It had been exhausting spending half his days at the hospital following first Shaun around, then tucking her safely in her office with a three-man guard, then following Ayaan around for a few hours hoping to draw Dasha out.

"I thought she'd put up more of a fight," Ayaan pouted, stepping back as Interpol filled the hallway.

It was just like law enforcement to show up after all the excitement had ended. Too much red tape and rules to actually accomplish anything.

"Go fight Havel, you'll feel better," Cooper drawled as they leaned against the opposite wall while a doctor looked Dasha over before pronouncing her fit to be moved.

"I can't win against him; I'd rather fight someone I can win against." Ayaan watched with disappointment as Dasha was hauled away.

Cooper had known the moment Interpol connected with Shaun in Elisa's office. They'd been watching her for a while, setting up a rotating team of men to give them the best chance at making contact. Once they finally did, Cooper had texted Jozef while Shaun was talking to the agent hiding in Elisa's office.

Jozef had refused to use Shaun as bait, but appreciated the opportunity to take his aunt into custody. He didn't care how it was done, as long as she could no longer threaten Shaun. Even better if Dasha took the fall for the criminal activities of the Koba family. Then he would be clear to move forward with his plans for the organization without Interpol breathing down his neck.

Cooper admired the way his boss worked through a problem. Instead of hotheadedly taking Dasha out at the first opportunity, he waited and watched, like the spider carefully weaving his web to trap the fly.

Now she was in Interpol's custody and no longer their problem. She was still alive, which would please Shaun as well as Jozef's cousins.

Cooper pushed away from the wall. He could finally get back to his actual job of tailing Shaun and setting up an impenetrable wall of security around her. He lived to protect. He'd worked as a secret service agent in the United States before quitting in disgust when politics overrode his ability to do his job. He'd been working as a mercenary-for-hire for several years before Havel picked him to fill out the team at Guard Dog Securities.

Cooper had finally found his home with the Koba organization. He had access to weapons, got paid quadruple what he'd been paid as an agent and had the freedom to make his own decisions as long as they aligned with Jozef's idea of safety for his wife.

Cooper wasn't going to do anything to fuck up this job.

CHAPTER THIRTY-TWO

"Interpol is taking her in now. I talked to Moreau and he's assures me that she'll be processed in country."

Jozef grunted his acknowledgment and hung up. He preferred text, but this was one of those rare times he'd insisted on a phone call. He'd wanted to know the moment Dasha was taken into custody.

Instead of elation, he felt a heaviness that had been growing over the past few weeks. Not about having his aunt arrested. She was lucky to get off so lightly. If he'd gotten his hands on her first, she'd spend her incarceration in his shed, dying inch by inch, a little more each day.

The heaviness came from his disappointment in Shaun. She'd kept a secret from him. She'd arranged for Dasha's arrest behind his back. Thanks to Cooper, Jozef had known from the inception of Moreau's plan, his first meeting with Shaun.

Jozef had gone out that night to confront Moreau about his use of Shaun in what could be a potentially dangerous situation. Dasha had nothing to lose. Her life meant nothing to her without her husband, family, home or fortune. Jozef had no doubt that her plan was to take Shaun out, then put herself in the position to be killed quickly.

Moreau had backtracked quickly on his original plan and had agreed to work with Jozef instead of Shaun. Jozef hadn't given the man a choice. Moreau was smart enough to realize that if he continued to contact Shaun, Jozef would make his broken nose look like a playground injury. The only thing stopping Jozef from putting a bullet in Moreau was his desire to use Interpol to trap Dasha.

But why hadn't Shaun come to him when Moreau first contacted her? He had his suspicions, but she would have to answer the question herself.

Living in a world of intrigue and betrayal, Jozef should have been immune to Shaun's betrayal, but it cut deep. She should trust him to take care of her, to listen to her and hold her opinion in high regard.

Jozef was tempted to search out his fiancé and demand the truth, but he knew he had to wait. Had to calm down so he wouldn't terrorize her. He might say or do something he regretted, and he was learning to step carefully with the woman he loved.

He would be lost without her and he wouldn't risk losing her. He would give himself time to calm down, then he would confront her.

He would also close the loophole to her escape from the life he'd pulled her into. She wouldn't be happy, but he needed to tie her to him as tightly as he could before he was comfortable giving her more leash. She wanted a job at the hospital, then she would have to give up any escape from the mafia. She would have to learn to tell him the truth at all times.

Jozef settled into his office chair and continued to peruse the map in front of him. It was a layout of all the trade routes open to the Koba family. Some were marked out as they'd been closed off by rivals. Jozef studied these and calculated the loss in revenue if he couldn't get the routes opened to him. Only two were valuable enough to negotiate over.

Jozef texted Havel, requesting his presence.

Jozef would send his team, with Havel leading, to 'convince' the men holding these routes hostage that it was in their best interests to work with Jozef. If they didn't, then they would find their organizations liquidated and rolled into the Koba organization.

Jozef wouldn't play nice, especially not now. He had too much to prove. If he came across as weak, the Bratva would have him killed and replaced, which he couldn't allow. If he was killed, then Shaun's existence would come into question.

Jozef rolled his shoulders back before reaching for the next file. He wasn't used to being in the office this much. His role had shifted from the field to largely organizational. Once things settled, he intended to resume some of his out of country work with his team. In the meantime, he would take out his frustrations on Havel in the boxing ring.

Before he could open the file, his phone rang.

Jozef looked at the number to see the country code for the Central African Republic.

Radik.

Jozef was surprised it took the man this long to track his sister down.

Luckily, Havel arrived almost as soon as Jozef answered the call.

Jozef put the phone on speaker and set it on his desk.

Havel frowned as Radik's booming, deep voice and unmistakable accent filled the office.

"Koba, are you there? Grunt or something, so I know you are listening. I hate to waste my time threatening some underling."

Havel sat on the edge of the desk and leaned forward. "He's here."

"Ah, and you are his second-in-command, Havel."

"Yes," Havel acknowledged. "We're both here."

"Good, it has come to my attention that while Koba has recruited my sister into your organization, you are the one training her... touching her."

Radik's rage came through the phone loud and clear. Havel winced, which was rare for the big man. Jozef didn't blame him. Radik was one of the few men on planet Earth who might be able to shake Havel's rock-solid confidence.

"No one is touching your sister inappropriately," Havel said calmly. "She's in control of her situation and happy to be here. What more could a brother ask for his sister?"

Havel should've known better. It was like baiting a tiger.

"I could ask that my sister not be deliberately put in the line of fire!" Radik shouted. "You have pressed her into the service of a team of mercenaries." The man spat the last word like it was poison.

Jozef signed, *you hired that very same group of mercenaries, trusting them to take your sister to safety.*

Havel translated.

"Yes, I did trust you to take her to safety, and paid an exorbitant amount to make it so. Now you have dragged her away from the safety of France, turning her into a soldier for hire."

She was a soldier for hire before we ever got to her. I'm simply using her considerable skills and paying her a large salary. You should be happy for her.

"Would you be happy if one of your cousins was deliberately placed in the line of fire? Your doctor fiancé perhaps?"

Jozef growled the moment Shaun was mentioned. He couldn't help himself. He didn't care if it made him a hypocrite. No one was allowed to use her name, especially not a man of war like Radik.

"I wouldn't mention the good doctor again, if I were you," Havel drawled, shaking his head at Jozef.

"I don't give a fuck if I've upset the boss. I want my sister sent back to Nice immediately."

"Your sister doesn't want to go back to Nice."

"My sister is young and impetuous. She doesn't get to decide what she wants." Radik's voice turned from rage to ice. "You will put her on a plane, or you will go to war."

You don't want to go to war with us. I have become far more powerful than when we met. Jozef signed while Havel translated.

"Good, then you will give me a worthy adversary when I come to crush you."

Stay out of P-R-A-G-U-E, you won't receive a welcome. Don't forget that I have your sister under my control.

Havel shook his head as Jozef took things to the next level, but translated word for word.

Predictably, Radik didn't handle the threat well.

"You will fucking die for this, Koba. I will crush you and yours, that is a promise."

He hung up before either Havel or Jozef could respond.

"I think you need a course in negotiation. I believe the accepted practice is not to escalate the situation."

Jozef chuckled. *I'll keep that in mind the next time a warlord wants to burn my house to the ground.*

Havel stood up. "I'll have the guard on the women doubled."

Jozef nodded and waved Havel to the chairs by the fireplace. He picked up the maps from his desk and sat with his second-in-command.

CHAPTER THIRTY-THREE

Shaun stared down at the stick in her hand, waiting and watching, trying not to shake it. She sighed heavily and forced herself to set the stick on the edge of the sink. She stood, pulled up her leggings and washed her hands, splashing water everywhere because she was too busy staring at the pregnancy test.

She'd never taken one before, but the instructions were easy to follow. It was the wait that was difficult. Two minutes felt like an eternity and every second that ticked by was torture.

Her period wasn't late, though it had been a little wonky lately, so she'd bought one of those early pregnancy tests. She and Jozef had been having unprotected sex since they met, and Shaun assumed she kept getting lucky by not getting pregnant.

Damn it. How long had it been? One minute, two, three? Why hadn't she brought her phone in with her so she could time it?

She paced the length of her washroom, back and forth, trying not to look at the stick. It was a sizeable washroom, so she had room to pace. She was at home, having gotten off work from the hospital a few hours earlier.

She'd been working on her research on laser guidance technology when she broke down and used the test she'd asked Dr. Černý to pick up for her. It was the only way she could get her hands on one without Jozef finding out.

Shaun wasn't ready to have that conversation with him yet. Mostly because she had no idea where her own head was at when it came to pregnancy. She didn't think it would be responsible to bring a child into their current situation... yet she couldn't bring herself to start using birth control.

She knew she should talk to Jozef, but he'd been so overworked lately. When they finally got to spend time together, he seemed grateful to just be with her, whether they were eating a meal, watching TV or reading together.

Somehow, Shaun thought bringing up the possibility of a baby might add to the already heavy weight he carried. Yet, she was positive he wouldn't want her on birth control. He was so possessive, so completely wild when it came to her. She suspected he wanted to have a baby with her as quickly as they could manage, whether or not it was the responsible choice.

Shaun picked up the pregnancy test. One line. She double checked the paper that came with the box. One line meant... not pregnant.

Tears sparked in her eyes and she collapsed onto the toilet. Doubts flooded her mind, along with self-condemnation. She should be happy, but she wasn't. What was wrong with her? Bringing a baby into their situation was a terrible idea.

But what if there was actually something wrong with her? She was thirty-five and a half. Maybe her eggs were running out. Maybe she was going through early menopause. Maybe the stress of the past several weeks had caused her reproductive system to go on strike.

Damn it! Why was she stressing this? She was a normal, healthy woman. A doctor. She knew damn well there probably wasn't anything wrong with her. Her body sensed her elevated anxiety levels and knew it was better to hold off on a baby until she could confidently carry it.

Should she have a baby at all? She'd always wanted to have one someday, but it had been a distant, fuzzy goal in her career-driven world. She'd consoled herself that if she reached the age where she couldn't have a viable pregnancy, then she would adopt. Now, she faced a situation she never could have imagined.

She tossed the test into the garbage and left the bathroom, walking straight into Jozef who was standing on the other side. He gripped her arms, steadying her.

"Jozef!"

Her smile at seeing him died as she looked into his face. He was furious.

"What's wrong?" she asked as he dropped his hands and stepped away from her. "Did something happen?"

She imagined every terrible scenario as he stared at her, his icy blue eyes unforgiving. Had the club been attacked again? Was her mother in danger? Was Saskia injured?

"Please tell me what's going on."

Maybe you should tell me, he signed. *You're the one keeping secrets.*

Shaun frowned. Keeping secrets? What was he talking about?

"I don't know what you mean, I tell you... everything," she lied. She didn't have much choice. Jozef was always watching her. Even when he wasn't with her, he was watching through his bodyguards or the cameras installed through the mansion.

D-A-S-H-A. He spelled each letter of her name with quick, vicious movements.

Shaun's heart sank. She *had* been keeping a secret from him, but it was sort of accidentally on purpose. Her schedule at the hospital was becoming increasingly more demanding and Interpol hadn't connected with her except for the first time. She thought they'd either forgotten about her or were waiting for another opportunity, so she let the whole thing go.

"I'm sorry," she said in a conciliatory tone. "I didn't think about what it would mean to you."

What were you thinking? Even in sign language, she could tell his tone was scathing.

"Jozef, I'm used to making independent decisions. I've never had to run my every thought and action by anyone before. I'm sorry this has upset you, but I really hadn't thought it through. I was preoccupied with the hospital and settling into this mansion."

That's why you can't keep secrets from me, he signed, pacing in front of her. *You don't know how to keep yourself safe. You don't understand the danger all around us.*

"I'm not a child," she snapped, losing some of her calm. "I knew how to take care of myself just fine until I met you."

His eyes glowed with icy fire as he glared at her. *You have proven repeatedly that you aren't capable of keeping yourself safe. I've kidnapped you twice, my aunt attacked you twice, and you allowed Interpol to get to you without saying a word to me.*

She crossed her arms over her chest and glared back at him. "You really want to talk about the time you kidnapped me and then dragged me into a family intrigue that has had more of a destructive force in my life than anything else that's ever happened to me?"

He flinched, but he didn't calm down.

He pointed at her. *You are not in control here. I am master and you will listen.*

"Is this really how you want our relationship to go?" she answered back, furious. "Because I refuse to participate in a household where only one voice counts."

You have no choice.

"I always have choices."

You either choose to follow the path I lay at your feet or you will live in a gilded cage. No hospital, no trips into the city to visit your mother. Nothing but the safety of the mansion.

"You wouldn't do that to me."

He stalked toward her.

Shaun did her best to hold her ground. She knew he wouldn't hurt her, but the storm of anger surging towards her was terrifying. She could imagine what his enemies saw when he attacked.

I will always do what is best for your safety, whether you like it or not.

Shaun's heart melted a little. She was in the wrong and she knew it. She'd put herself in a dangerous position by not immediately telling Jozef about Interpol.

"I'm sorry I didn't tell you about the agent who came to see me." She sat on the bed, her hands twisting in her lap. "I thought it would be better if your aunt was arrested. I didn't want you to have to deal with a woman you thought of as a mother."

You took the decision from me. You didn't allow me the chance of deciding what I would do with the woman who betrayed this family. Jozef sank down to one knee in front of Shaun. The position should have put him at a disadvantage, but it didn't. He almost looked scarier. Like the tiger who looked relaxed before biting down on the neck of his prey.

"I'm sorry," she whispered, not knowing what else to say. She saw his perspective and understood the magnitude of her secret. Would she do it again if given the opportunity? She didn't know. Regardless of what her keeping a secret meant to Jozef, she stood by her reasoning.

She'd seen the look on his face, the utter devastation after he'd been forced to kill Krystoff. The heartbreak had been visceral and unbearable. She'd shared the moment with him and it had shredded her heart. She wanted to save him from having to go through that all over again with his aunt.

She blinked as she realized he was signing.

... just a word. Words do not prove loyalty.

She'd missed something, but it sounded like he was rejecting her apology.

"Then what proves loyalty."

Actions.

He stood and stalked to her closet, jerking the door open.

Shaun quickly swiped at her eyes, drying them. Jozef hadn't been very harsh with her. He was incapable of it. But still... it hurt that she'd lost his trust.

Jozef walked out of her closet with a handful of clothes, tossing them on the bed.

She looked from the clothes up into his lake blue eyes, drowning in the anger she saw there. Living in the mafia world, in Jozef's world, felt like learning how to swim all over again and she kept sinking below the surface of the water. Maybe she would never learn how to navigate Jozef's world. Much as she tried, she kept screwing up.

She was living in a place that felt cold and oppressive with a contingent of bodyguards who were always in her space. Cooper shadowed her constantly while Atlas announced guests like he was the royal crier. She'd been harassed by Interpol and had to live knowing there was a woman out there, too close for comfort, who wanted to murder Shaun. In short, her life had become a big mess from the moment she'd met Jozef.

Yet, even now, with him looking at her through a lens of betrayal, she couldn't bring herself to regret a single moment with him. She didn't want out. She didn't want to leave. She just wanted him.

"What do I have to do to prove my loyalty?"

Pick a dress. He pointed at the pile of clothes on the bed and left the room without another word.

CHAPTER THIRTY-FOUR

Jozef shook his head as he strode away from the master suite, trying to cast off the anger. He knew his response was over the top, but he couldn't help the sense of betrayal that he got every time he thought of Shaun deliberately placing herself in danger to trap his aunt.

He'd gone in to talk to her, to tell her that Dasha had been taken into custody. He'd been determined to keep his temper, but every step that brought him closer to her reminded him that yet another person he loved had betrayed him. He tried to tell himself that Shaun didn't understand his world, didn't understand the loyalty that was expected of her.

Then he'd seen her and forgotten everything except how it could have easily been her instead of Ayaan staring down the barrel of Dasha's gun that morning.

If her bodyguard hadn't been quick in both thoughts and actions, Jozef might not have known what was going on. Dasha was highly intelligent and had been coming and going from the hospital pretty much from the day after Krystoff's death onward.

Jozef had gotten his hands on the hospital CCTV tapes

and had traced her every step. Dasha was good at hiding, very good. She was also aware of where every camera was and the angles they could reach. She'd carefully maneuvered through the hospital like a dancer on a stage. Sometimes Jozef would lose her only to pick her back up again when she reappeared on a different floor, unable to avoid all the cameras.

Of course, he could have gotten to Dasha at any time. She was staying in an apartment in the city, and though she did her best to cover her tracks as she moved through Prague, Havel was the best tracker on staff. He'd pinpointed her location almost from the moment she'd started using the tiny apartment as a home base.

Jozef had chosen not to grab Dasha for a few reasons. Though he wanted her dead, he appreciated the poetic justice of forcing her to take the fall for the entire Koba family. He wanted her to languish in prison, knowing that if she hadn't betrayed Jozef, he would have protected her until the day she died. She had helped raise him, turning him into the protector he eventually became. But rather than taking advantage of his protective instincts, she turned on him.

Now, he would turn on her. He would allow others to torture her with confinement until he was ready to strike.

The second reason he didn't outright kill his aunt was the more important one. He didn't want Shaun to look at him differently. Interpol had alerted her to Dasha's presence. If Dasha disappeared and Interpol came after Jozef, Shaun would find out.

She thought he couldn't live with Dasha's death on his hands, but she was wrong. Dasha's death would satisfy the beast in him who craved justice. A twisted version of justice, yes, but justice, nonetheless.

What he couldn't live with was knowing the woman he loved above all else would look at him and see a killer. Somehow, miraculously, she did not see him as a murderer now.

Though logically she knew it was true, she still allowed his hands to touch her body, allowed his love to live in her heart.

If he killed his aunt and Shaun found out, her feelings would change.

Like her body, he was also responsible for protecting her heart and her soul. As angry as he was with her, he wouldn't do anything to shatter her feelings for him.

Instead, he would bide his time and allow Dasha to rot until he was ready to make a move that wouldn't involve Shaun or his cousins.

His anger gradually dissipated as he reminded himself of the reasons he'd allowed Shaun her subterfuge at the hospital. He despised her lack of trust in him, but he couldn't fault her. Not really. He kept secrets too.

Havel met him at the car, which was idling out front of the mansion. Havel's gaze was irritated as Jozef descended the stairs.

"Can't you make a single move with this woman that doesn't mean disrupting the entire household?" Havel complained.

Despite his anger with Shaun, Jozef grinned. *You're just angry because you won't get to throw the bachelor party.*

"Fuck you," Havel grumbled. "I was getting my ass handed to me by your recruit when you texted. I didn't even get to change out of my gym clothes. It's on you if your new bride isn't happy with your best man's lack of tuxedo."

Havel was wearing sweatpants and a sweaty T-shirt that clung to his broad chest and muscular arms. His bald head was shiny and beaded with sweat. He held a leather jacket in his hands, too hot from his recent workout to put it on, though they were firmly in winter with snow on the ground.

Jozef frowned, maybe he should send Havel to his suite in the barracks to change.

Before Jozef could do that, Havel's eyes went past him and landed on something behind Jozef. Or someone.

Jozef turned to look at his bride-to-be.

She was stunning, radiant, beautiful, though she looked much the same as she did any other day. She wore one of the dresses Jozef had handed her and a puffy winter coat. It wasn't the way she looked but the knowledge that they would finally tie themselves together in name, spirit and love, that captivated Jozef, making her shine with a new beauty.

Shaun was holding a small bouquet, likely taken from one of the vases that filled the mansion, a holdover from Dasha's reign. His aunt used to ship in flowers from all over the world to brighten the mansion and give it a floral scent.

The flowers told Jozef that Shaun had worked out what was about to happen.

She glided down the stairs, graceful in her heels, and stopped in front of Jozef, glaring at him. They were eye level.

"I decided weeks ago that I wanted to marry you, so don't think I'm doing this because you told me to." She poked him in the chest with the flowers. "You're a bully and it's a lucky thing that I'm in love with you or I'd be setting fire to this mansion rather than marrying your sorry ass."

She turned to climb regally into the car, but Jozef gripped her arm and swung her around. He forced her back over his arm and kissed her, taking her lips in a passionate kiss that he would normally save for the bedroom.

Every ounce of the anger he'd felt earlier dissipated as their lips met. She loved him, and that was what mattered. She'd kept secrets from him to protect him. It was something he couldn't allow her to do in the future, but he appreciated the motive behind her secrecy.

"I think you're supposed to speak the vows first, then kiss." Havel's voice was dry but amused. "Not that I'm an expert on marriage."

Jozef set Shaun back on her feet, sliding an arm behind her back to steady her when she swayed. He helped her into the car and took the seat next to her. He picked up her hand and kissed the knuckles.

The bridal car left the mansion with the groom, the bride, the best man and a bodyguard. The car behind them held several more guards. Jozef wouldn't take a chance on Shaun's safety, especially not on their wedding day.

"My mother?" Shaun asked as Havel maneuvered the car onto the freeway.

Her bodyguard has informed her of our upcoming union. She's agreed to meet us at the church.

Shaun sighed. "Well, I suppose that's something. What about Saskia?"

I texted her. If she makes it to the church, then she makes it.

"I don't want to get married without her in attendance," Shaun argued.

Jozef took her face in his hands and kissed her lips before dropping his hands. *Then I will have her guard pick her up and bring her to the church.*

He picked up his phone and started texting. Shaun snatched his phone away from him. "Would you stop kidnapping people!"

Shaun unlocked his phone, using the passcode he'd given her. He suspected she didn't want to use her own phone because she was worried Saskia, who had been avoiding her, was still angry over the incident with Adam.

Jozef had kept out of their relationship and wasn't sure where they stood with each other. He was pleased by their attachment though and hoped they would work it out.

Shaun texted: **Please come to the church to attend our wedding. Sorry for the short notice.**

A few seconds later Saskia sent her response.

I know this is Shaun. If it were Jozef, he'd have just

demanded I show up, then send his bodyguards to make sure I complied.

"She knows you well," Shaun said with a laugh.

Okay, yes, this is Shaun. Please come. I want you to stand up with me.

Her response was quick: **really?**

Of course. We love you and want you with us when we get married.

If it was an important occasion, you wouldn't be doing it last minute. I'm on my way. Don't get hitched without me.

"She has a point." Shaun looked over at Jozef who was reading the texts along with her.

No, she doesn't, he signed. *Our wedding was always going to be like this. I would never put you in the vulnerable position of being out in the open at my side during an important event.*

Shaun stared at him. He suspected she was thinking over the past month and realizing he hadn't been going out in public with her. When he left the house, Shaun was at home. When she was at the hospital or her mother's, he was at home.

Jozef had learned the tactic from his uncle, who rarely left the house with his family members, except Jozef. Jozef had taken the risk with Shaun when they'd first gotten together, before he realized the depth of his attachment to her. He'd wanted her to love Prague as her attachment to him grew, so he'd taken the chance of taking her out on a date and to the club.

Jozef explained, *I am a target. My uncle was a target. When he was taken by V-A-S-I-L-I-Y's people, had my aunt been with him, she might have been killed or taken along with him. In my heart I want to be with you at all times, ensuring your protection. In reality, I put you in more danger when I'm seen with you. You are far safer with your bodyguards than with me.*

Shaun blinked rapidly. She switched to sign language. *Is this it then, the rest of our lives? Married, but never able to leave the house together? What about children? I can't imagine never going out together as a family. No picnics, no restaurants, no shopping. I don't know if I'm ready for this.*

She dropped her head into her hands.

Jozef rubbed her back, waiting for her to think her way through this fresh problem. She had grown in leaps and bounds over the past few months, in her knowledge, understanding and acceptance of his mafia life. But sometimes, like now, she learned something that was more difficult to accept.

He understood. He wanted all those things. Picnics, restaurants, shopping, vacations. He wanted everything. But from the moment he became old enough to understand his place in the world, he knew he was different.

Unlike Shaun, he'd never known the things she mentioned. He'd never in his life gone on a picnic, except for the one he arranged for her on the floor of his apartment, a suggestion he'd gotten from her mother.

But Shaun made him want picnics. She made him want everything he'd never known before.

He touched her face, bringing her gorgeous golden eyes back to him. Worry wrinkled her brow and her pulse fluttered in her throat, giving away her nervous tension. She may have decided she wanted to marry him, but she wasn't without reservations.

You will be happy with me.

She laughed, the sound fragile. "Is that an order?"

Her voice was husky and low, meant for his ears only.

That is a promise.

CHAPTER THIRTY-FIVE

Shaun had never really been one of those girls who pictured her wedding day. No poufy white dress, no church filled with guests, no reception with speeches and clinking glasses. All of her fantasies had been directed at her career path. Even as a little girl, in her mind, she wore the white doctor's lab coat, a stethoscope and held a clipboard. Her teddy bear patients would get a diagnosis and then they would take the medicine she administered.

As she hit her teen years, she began dissecting her teddy bears, carefully pulling the fluff out, examining their insides, then putting them back together. Her father had taught her how to make stitches, so she'd meticulously suture each of her teddy bear victims, giving them horrific scars in the process. Her mother had been concerned by her preoccupation with cutting into her toys, but her father had stood by watching proudly, declaring he had a future surgeon on his hands.

Now, as Shaun stood at the head of the church, next to the man she was seconds away from marrying, she realized that despite her lack of vision for her wedding day, that this was exactly what she would have imagined. The man she loved looking at her as though she were the only person on the planet. Her mother in the front row next to Cooper. Saskia standing next to her, holding her bouquet.

Saskia was outfitted in what could only be described as maid-of-honour gothic. She wore black leggings under a black dress with a corset bodice and crinoline skirt. Her hair had been spiked across the front and pulled back in a tight pony-tail in the back. She looked beautiful and very out of place in the sixteenth-century church.

Shaun barely heard the priest as he spoke. Her eyes were on Jozef. The ceremony was more old-fashioned than she thought it would be. Jozef wasn't religious and neither was she, but the ceremony had an elevated religious tone to it that felt both very official and somewhat oppressive. Maybe this was the best Jozef could do on such short notice, though he'd told her he'd been planning it for a while. The church was small, tucked out of the way, on the edge of the city.

Jozef must have caught her looking around the church as the priest spoke, because when she looked at him, he signed, *H-A-V-E-L suggested it. I have no particular attachment to any church or place of ceremony, but he is a brother to me and it's my honour to use his family church.*

Shaun was glad he was explaining to her, but he could have picked a better moment. She almost laughed out loud at the disgruntled expression on the priest's face as he continued to speak.

She caught Havel's eye and he winked. She smiled back. It had taken time, but they were warming up to the idea of friendship, their mutual love of Jozef thawing them.

When it came time for the vows, Jozef spoke first, using his hands to express his love. Shaun did laugh out loud this time, when he refused to repeat a single word the priest was saying, but came up with his own vows. The priest sent her a sharp look and continued speaking.

Shaun quickly sobered, her smile wobbling as tears flooded her eyes. She blinked them quickly away so she could read every single sign.

From the moment I saw you, I knew we were connected. Your kindness toward the child on the streets of L-U-H-A-N-S-K, your giving soul, it shone so bright it nearly blinded me. You have forced me to examine my existence, to find what was lacking and empty, then you helped me fill the wound with love and sunshine. I give myself to you, heart, body and soul. Just as I take you, heart, body and soul. I will love and protect you, as you will love and protect me.

He finished by giving Shaun the special sign of their love.

Fatima let out a watery sob, the sound echoing in the church. Saskia reached into her skirt pocket, pulled out a pack of tissues and lobbed them at Shaun's mother. Then she used her sleeve to wipe her own face as tears trickled down her cheeks.

When it was Shaun's turn, she followed suit, handing her bouquet to Saskia. Ignoring the priest's instructions to repeat after him, Shaun used Jozef's language to profess her love and dedication.

J-O-Z-E-F. She deliberately signed each letter of his name, though the two had found shortened signed versions of their names to use with each other. *You have given me a life I never could have imagined, and, while sometimes I doubted you, you've shown me how much I was missing. You have given me yourself and a love that I would never have found on my own. Now, I am giving myself to you, heart, body and soul as I am taking you for myself, heart, body, and soul. I will love and protect you as you will love and protect me.*

She finished by signing her love to him.

Fatima was now openly weeping while they exchanged rings.

Jozef slid a simple gold band over Shaun's finger, trapping his mother's engagement ring. Saskia handed Shaun a matching band that was slightly thicker. Shaun took it and slid it onto Jozef's finger.

She wasn't sure what the priest said next because Jozef lunged for her, gripping her face and staring into her eyes for long seconds before smashing his lips down on hers. In those seconds she knew his utter devotion to her and it stole her breath.

With his lips, he told her of a love that would last for a lifetime.

Images rushed through Shaun's mind as she remembered their first meeting. She had been so focused on the boy that she hadn't remembered walking into the handsome stranger in the leather coat.

Now she remembered. The power of his gaze as it touched hers was like the physical meeting of their souls. They'd recognized each other before they met. That meeting had led to this moment, when they made official what they'd never been able to deny; that they would love each other long after they left the earth.

Saskia let out a whoop as Jozef finally released Shaun.

Jozef decided they would have the reception at the mansion where the wedding party would be safer.

He'd already told their chef to prepare a large meal with their favourite dishes. Rather than eating at the large formal dining table, they ate in the kitchen with many of the house staff and Jozef's men dropping in to the congratulate the couple. After greeting each of them, Shaun realized she had gotten to know many of the people who worked for Jozef... for both of them.

As the evening progressed so did Shaun's exhaustion.

She'd had a long a day and wanted nothing more than the softness of her own bed at her back. Looking at Jozef though, she didn't think she'd be allowed to sleep any time soon.

She felt a little like she was standing on quicksand with him. She could tell by the hard glitter in his eyes that he had not yet forgiven her for her transgression. Shaun had learned from Cooper that Dasha had been captured by Interpol. The relief that Shaun felt at hearing that told her that, while she shouldn't have kept a secret from Jozef, her intentions had still been good. Dasha was safely behind bars, and Jozef wouldn't be forced to make a grim decision regarding his aunt.

Still, the stiffness of his body and the way he touched her carefully, as though afraid to break her, told Shaun he had more to say about the incident.

It was around midnight that the last of the guests left the mansion. Jozef's men went back to their barracks or into the city where they lived with their families. Cooper and Terek had offered to take Fatima home.

With a hand on her back, Jozef escorted Shaun up to their bedroom.

Her heart hammered with each step and she had to remind herself that Jozef would never hurt her, that he loved her and wanted to make her happy.

Still, he was acting stiffly formal as they entered the bedroom.

She turned to find him already unbuttoning his shirt, his strong veined hands flashing as he pushed each button through the hole.

"Can we talk first," Shaun said, holding up a hand. They'd been intimate many times, but the coolness coming from him made her uncomfortable. She wasn't ready to be intimate until they sorted through his anger.

He dropped his hands so he could sign, *it's time for me to show you what loyalty means.*

"You think this is the way to get my loyalty?" she asked incredulously, backing away from him as he removed his shirt, tossing it aside.

His expression was blank, refusing to give her a hint of his intentions.

She bumped into the side table next to the bed. There was nowhere else for her to retreat.

She shouldn't have to run from him anyway. This was her bedroom, in her house, with her husband. She shouldn't have to feel afraid. She opened her mouth to tell him so, to tell him to back off until they'd sorted a few things out, but he grabbed her hand and lifted it.

"Jozef..."

He placed her hand over his shoulder.

She frowned, then realized she felt something. There were ridges of raised flesh on his shoulder, surrounding a new tattoo. Forgetting her fear of a moment earlier, she stepped closer to him, fingering the fresh ink of an eight-pointed star.

Shaun knew exactly what it meant. Karl, her former bodyguard, had taught her the ins and outs of the Bratva. Jozef was branded with the mark of the Vor. He had a matching tattoo over his opposite shoulder.

"What does it mean?" she whispered, looking up into his eyes. "Why now? What's changed?"

It had been six weeks since the attack on Jozef's club. As far as she knew, he'd claimed the title of Vor even before that, while he was still in prison. Why get the tattoos now?

You have changed me, he signed, then reached for his belt buckle.

She was no longer afraid he might try to have sex with her when she wasn't ready. Now she was curious.

He dropped his pants, stepping out of them and kicking them away.

Shaun saw the new tattoos immediately. Two eight-pointed stars, one on each knee. Other than a serpent tattoo snaking across his hip and disappearing into his pubic hair, he'd had no tattoos on the bottom half of his body until now.

"You've pledged your loyalty to the Bratva, haven't you? That's what the stars mean." She frowned. "What does this have to do with us?"

He shook his head. *I haven't pledged my loyalty to them. They are a means to an end. These stars are for you alone. My entry into their world ensures your safety. The higher I climb, the safer you are. You are my only motivation.*

CHAPTER THIRTY-SIX

Shaun looked up at him wonderingly as he placed an enormous responsibility at her feet. She was his motivation for taking on a mafia empire. She was his captive, she was his love, and she was his reason for being. It was heady. It was exhilarating.

And he wasn't done.

He dropped to his knees on the floor, surprising her.

He looked powerful, godly, and completely at her mercy. His expression had shifted from the cold mob boss to passionate lover.

I am loyal to you alone.

Tears leapt to her eyes. "I know."

He took her hand and held it over his heart before signing, *you are the only thing is this world that can break me. You can destroy everything I've built. One bad decision, no matter how small, can bring down this empire. I must have your loyalty.*

A tear trickled down her cheek and she felt worse than ever for keeping a secret from him.

"What do you want me to do?" she whispered.

Trust me.

She was about to say 'I do' but she hesitated. He'd told her that actions spoke louder than words and her actions had shown him he couldn't trust her. She had to show him she meant what she said and that would take time.

She dropped to her knees in front of him and lifted his hand to her heart before signing, *I will never give you reason to doubt me again.*

His eyes pierced hers as he searched for truth, finally nodding.

As an adult, Shaun had never felt the need to explain herself to a partner before, but Jozef was changing her. She wanted his approval, his loyalty and trust. She wanted the things that had never mattered before and she wanted them because he loved her. He trusted her to make the right choices. She didn't want to break that trust again.

He pulled her onto his lap, kissing her hard, sealing their pledge of trust. She wrapped her arms around his neck and held on, kissing him back, showing him that she was ready to take the journey into their future together.

He stood with her, easily lifting her in his arms without breaking their kiss.

She wrapped her legs around his waist, feeling the press of his cock against her dress.

Jozef dropped her on the bed, coming down on top of her. He framed her face with his hands and searched, his eyes glowing with wonder.

My wife, he mouthed to her because there was no room between them to sign.

"My husband," she whispered back.

The moment was powerful. It was the beginning of a new chapter for them. One that they'd entered willingly, rather than being forced together through circumstance and family ties.

Shaun wrapped her arms and legs around Jozef, pulling him into the private bubble where she pretended no one else existed. It was just them and the way they felt about each other.

"I love you," she told him.

His gaze became grave, and he nodded, telling her he took her love seriously.

"I want you."

He needed no more encouragement.

Shaun was ready to celebrate her wedding night properly. She wanted to explore Jozef's body with the knowledge that he was her husband now. He belonged to her and it was official.

She'd never much cared about tradition, but it suddenly meant so much more to her. She was glad that there was a certificate tucked away in Jozef's safe that announced them a couple in the eyes of the law.

Jozef tried to pull the straps of her dress down her arms, but the bodice was too tight. He frowned and flipped her over, making Shaun laugh as her face was pushed into the bedding.

She felt him tugging at the zipper and, when it didn't immediately give, he gripped the sides of the dress and tore. It fell apart like paper in his hands.

When he'd finished dragging the dress from her body, he flipped her back over. His eyes lit with a new appreciation as they travelled down.

She loved the way he worshipped her with a single expression. He didn't hide what he was thinking; he loved every inch of her. He followed his gaze with his hand, caressing her in sweeping motions.

She lay beneath him, one leg bent, while he explored. It was different. There was none of the frantic energy that always snapped in the air between them. Instead, it was replaced by a new kind of awe.

"Jozef," she whispered, catching his attention. "I want you... now."

His eyes darkened with lust and his breathing grew heavier. He reached between her thighs, touching her, stroking, then pushing his fingers inside. She was more than ready for him.

She opened her legs to him and beckoned him to her.

He lay across her body, holding himself up on an elbow and reaching down with the other to stroke his cock, using the wetness from her body to lubricate himself.

She thought there was nothing sexier in the world than watching Jozef pleasure himself while using her body for inspiration.

"Fuck me," she whispered.

He groaned in response, then leaned into her, lining himself up. He pushed himself home slowly, making her feel every inch as he filled her.

He was big enough that it always took some adjustment, but she was used to the feeling and gave him the anticipated gasp of pleasure that always erupted from her throat when he bottomed out.

When he was there, he pulled back and thrust again, harder this time, forcing another gasp from her. He paused, watching her face.

She grabbed his head and dragged him down for a kiss, thrusting her tongue against his, begging him to move, to fuck her, to give her the orgasm that always hovered on the horizon when he was inside her.

They moved together in unison, their bodies locked, their eyes locked. Jozef placed a hand on her head, touching her face gently, then tangling his fingers in her hair. Anchoring her.

The small bite of pain shot her pleasure higher, and she lifted her hips, loving the way he fit her perfectly. The slap of their flesh, the sweat beading on his brow as he used his strength to hold himself from crushing her while loving her body.

She'd never felt more connected to anyone. It was engulfing, completely overwhelming. Like being wrapped in a blanket and held so tight she could never escape.

"Jozef..." she whispered his name as he drove her higher and higher. She saw the spark of pleasure in his eyes as she said his name, so she said it again, louder. Repeating herself over and over.

"Jozef, Jozef, Jozef."

Like a mantra, or a promise. She was his and he was hers.

She didn't know how long they stayed entwined, making love, each thrust slow and measured, but eventually her climax built to the point that she could no longer hang on.

She cried his name one last time, digging her nails into the flesh of his shoulders as she hurtled through space and time on the wings of her orgasm.

He finally broke eye contact, dipping his head into her shoulder and biting down as his hips slammed into hers, faster and with more purpose than before. He reached his orgasm, flying high in her arms as he grunted his pleasure in her ear.

She held him tight as his movements slowed and he relaxed on top of her. He still held his weight up, but she could feel the softening of his muscles. She smiled. His back was to the door and he didn't twist his head around to keep an eye on it.

He trusted her.

And she needed to trust him.

"I love you," she whispered in his ear, blinking back emotional tears of joy. "So much."

He rolled off her and onto his side, then he signed, *I will love you until the end of time.*

His eyes were dark and serious as they met hers. He gripped her chin and held her face as he leaned over to seal his promise with a kiss.

CHAPTER THIRTY-SEVEN

Six Months Later

Shaun flung the door of her car open and climbed out. She handed her keys to Cooper who gave her a grim look. He'd pulled up behind her with the rest of her bodyguards.

"I know!" she said desperately, clutching her purse and racing up the stairs to the mansion.

She cringed when she saw Jozef standing at the top waiting for her. His arms were crossed over his chest and his eyes were narrowed on her. She tried to concentrate but he was wearing faded blue jeans with a black T-shirt stretched taut over his chest, a thick leather belt and work boots. She wanted to lick him all over, but if his frown was anything to go by, she was more likely in for a spanking and not the fun kind.

"I know, I know," she mumbled as he opened the door for her, and she slid past. "I can be ready in ten minutes. Promise!"

She raced up the stairs to her suite.

"Where have you been?" Saskia appeared at the top of the stairs. "You're supposed to be halfway to Russia by now."

"I know!" Shaun shot past Saskia who fell in step behind her. "I got held up at the hospital. The surgery was more complicated than I expected, then I had to wait for the patient to come out of anaesthesia."

"I don't think the Russians will care much about your bedside manner when they ask Jozef why they were kept waiting."

Saskia followed Shaun into her room and flopped down on the bed as Shaun rifled through the walk-in closet, throwing an empty suitcase out, followed by handfuls of clothes, which landed all over the floor.

"What do you think I should pack?" Shaun's voice was muffled. "Casual, formal, beachwear?"

"Formal, definitely formal. The Bratva aren't known for their casual attitude toward anything, let alone the foreign wife of one of their newest members. Maybe if you look hot enough, they'll forget about your tardiness."

Seconds later a series of evening dresses, cocktail dresses and business suits were thrown from the closet. Shaun leapt over them and reached down to pick the pile up, tossing everything haphazardly into the suitcase.

Shaun glanced around the bedroom, wondering what she was missing.

"Hair products, makeup, shoes, tampons." Saskia listed off the things Shaun hadn't thrown in the suitcase yet.

Shaun snapped her fingers and lunged back into the closet, tossing out a couple pairs of heels and a pair of running shoes. She ransacked the washroom, tossing her makeup bag through the door and hoping it would land on the bed. She looked over her hair products and selected the ones she would need.

They were going to Russia for five days to meet with some of the higher ups in the Bratva. Jozef was confident, Shaun was nervous. It didn't help that Havel had spent the past few days following her around the mansion, giving her advice. Only his advice made her even more worried.

"Don't speak when you haven't been spoken to. Don't give your opinions. In fact, don't have any opinions. In fact, don't speak at all, to anyone. You must remember that you're a representative of the Koba organization. You can't have any slipups with these people."

Jozef had wanted to take Havel with him, but ultimately decided to leave him behind. Jozef had spent the past several months reorganizing and reestablishing the Koba organization, and he didn't want to risk a single problem while he was away. He trusted Havel to keep things in order while they were gone.

Shaun had learned a new respect for Havel over the past few months, while watching him work as hard as Jozef to create a solid foundation for their empire. He was loyal and he took his job seriously. On more than one occasion, Jozef had commented that the other man was invaluable, and he didn't know what he'd do without Havel.

The door to the suite banged open just as Shaun was zipping her suitcase.

"I'm ready!" she called out, then turned to Saskia. "Distract him while I change."

Saskia gave her a mischievous grin. "Of course!"

She slid off the bed and launched herself out the door, using a singsong voice as she called out, "Jozef, will you bring me back a souvenir? I want one of those little dolls you and Shaun have."

Shaun peeled off her top as she headed for her closet, grabbing for a shirt at random.

She pulled it over her head and reached for her scrub bottoms, shoving them down her thighs as Jozef opened the closet door wider and stared in at her. His eyes immediately went to her panties and she flashed him a teasing grin before deliberately turning and bending over to grab the pair of jeans she'd chosen for their trip north.

Jozef growled and slammed the closet door shut, reaching for her. She giggled as he filled his hands with her ass and kissed the side of her neck. He reached around her and cupped her breast through her shirt.

"We're going to be late," she said, her voice husky as he kissed a path from her neck down to her shoulder, shoving her shirt aside so he could get at the bare skin.

He turned her around and gave her an accusing look.

"Okay, yes, my fault," she admitted. "But you knew that I would have the occasional late shift. I warned you, I won't leave the hospital until my patient wakes up."

He swooped in for a kiss, telling her with his tongue and mouth his feelings on her working late.

Jozef gave her hell every time she worked late at the hospital. To his credit, he hadn't once threatened to terminate her job. In fact, since she'd started working at the Prague hospital, Jozef had been surprisingly supportive. He enjoyed listening to her talk about work and bragged to anyone who would listen that he was married to one of the world's preeminent neurosurgeons.

Though he was proud of her, he was also jealous of her time and paced like a caged tiger when she was even a minute late getting home, let alone the hours of overtime she'd put in today. They were taking Jozef's private jet to Russia, so she didn't feel too guilty about making them late.

Still...

"Jozef..." she whispered, then repeated herself louder when he refused to stop kissing her neck and ear. "We have to go."

Jozef sighed deeply and backed up enough to give her a look that promised a good fucking later when they settled at the Bratva palace.

Shaun grinned back and signed, *that better be a promise. You said this would be like a vacation and people get to have sex on vacations. I feel like it's been days...*

Jozef growled and shoved the closet door open, escorting her into the bedroom.

It had been a sore point to both of them that their busy schedules made it difficult for them to get any alone time. When Jozef had first announced this trip, Shaun had been leery. She wasn't sure she wanted to get any deeper in with the Russian mafia. It was a ridiculous concern though, since she was married to the underworld boss of the Czech Republic. The Russian mafia knew exactly who she was and how she got there.

She was still nervous, but Jozef had assured her nothing would happen.

"What if they don't like me?" she'd asked, "I feel certain these are the type of people that get rid of someone they don't like."

They will love you as much as I do. Be yourself and they won't be able to resist falling in love.

She snorted her skepticism. He made the Bratva sound like a bunch of easily won puppies. Still, his confidence bolstered her. Jozef wouldn't take her into a pit of vipers if he thought she might get hurt. It was simply not within his DNA makeup. He was the family protector.

An hour later they boarded Jozef's private jet and settled in for the three-hour flight to Ivanov's palace.

Shaun twisted in her seat to see who would be accompanying them. Cooper was the first one to catch her eye. She wasn't surprised to see her personal bodyguard; she rarely went anywhere without him. Only once in the past six months had Jozef recalled him to fill out his team for an out-of-country mission. Cooper had come home in high spirits and ready to resume his work with Shaun.

She appreciated having a bodyguard who was also a friend. It had taken a few months, but finally Jozef was able to set aside his jealousy and forge a friendship with the other man.

Shaun suspected it helped his ego that she had eyes for no one but her husband. Marriage suited both of them. She'd never put much stock in the piece of paper and vows that bound people, but there was something about having Jozef as her husband that just did it for her. He was handsome, driven, intelligent, creative and special.

Next to Cooper was Ayaan.

It had taken Shaun some time to warm up to the girl, especially when Jozef's men had jokingly told her that the younger woman had once asked Jozef out. The two women had warily stayed out of each other's way until a nasty cold had taken Cooper away from his bodyguard duties for a few days. Ayaan had been chosen to replace him.

Shaun had thought the two women could continue their awkward avoidance dance. Ayaan had different plans. She'd insisted on having eyes on her principal at all times, except when Shaun needed to use the washroom.

Shaun had been watching Grey's Anatomy with a bowl of popcorn, crying her eyes out, when Ayaan had plopped onto the couch beside her, taken a handful of popcorn and proceeded to ask Shaun every medical question that popped into her head as the two women plowed through season six together.

It helped that Saskia and Ayaan had become fast friends, shopping together and hanging out when Ayaan wasn't working and Saskia wasn't in class. It made sense. The two women were the same age and they had plenty in common. Shaun had felt a little left out but had gotten over it quickly.

Once Shaun was past her jealousy, she was open to a friendship with the other women. It made life at the mansion easier to have friends.

Fatima visited as often as she could, but she'd discovered a true joy in spending Jozef's money and flying all over the world on his private jet. Once she'd agreed to a security detail, Jozef was more than happy to indulge his mother-in-law to her heart's content.

In short, life couldn't be better.

Shaun could never have imagined being in the position where she could have it all, but here she was, wife, doctor, daughter and friend. The only thing she was missing was a baby.

She touched her fingertips to her stomach but quickly dropped them away when Jozef turned to hand her a cup of tea he'd requested from the flight attendant. She smiled her thanks, swallowing the lump in her throat. He always took care of her.

She knew he was worried by their lack of pregnancy too, but he never gave a single indication. He was constantly supportive and reassuring. When she'd gone to the fertility clinic, after being referred by Elisa, who had become a great friend to her, Jozef had attended every appointment. He'd held her hand while Shaun went through a series of procedures.

Jozef had gone through a few himself. As of yet, they had no answers. The specialist had told them to be patient. Had told them eight months wasn't really long enough to tell if they could pregnant or not.

Shaun couldn't help but worry. She did her best to keep it from Jozef, who had enough on his plate without adding one more problem.

Perhaps her lack of pregnancy was fate's way of telling her they shouldn't bring a child into the dangerous world of the Bratva. But no matter what she told herself, Shaun couldn't seem to get her heart to agree. It felt like she carried a tiny hole in the organ, and it grew larger with each passing month, each period, each disappointment.

She rolled her head to the side to watch Jozef. He was sitting with his ankle crossed at the knee, his laptop balancing on his legs, his gaze steady on whatever he was reading. He wore his glasses, which she thought were sexy as hell. She hadn't known about them until one night, a few months ago, when he'd come to bed and settled against the covers, opening one of his Russian language books. He'd pulled a pair of glasses from his nightstand and put them on as if he'd done it every night since they met. Only he hadn't.

Shaun had immediately climbed on top of him and coaxed him to put his book down and leave his glasses on while she rode him.

She'd later found out that he felt self-conscious wearing them. Although he didn't consider his lack of voice to be a disability, he knew others thought that, and he didn't want to give away another potential weakness.

Shaun had teased him, saying that approximately thirteen percent of the adult population had eye troubles, but Jozef had been serious. He'd told her that a potential assassin would look at any weakness as an opportunity to take advantage. Jozef needed to portray strength, especially since he was master of his own section of the underworld, and everyone who knew of him knew he didn't have a voice.

She glanced at his screen and saw a spreadsheet open with columns of numbers that made no sense and a language she didn't recognize. It amused her that half of Jozef's job was business. It felt strange to her that the mafia crunched numbers and created business plans.

Shaun pushed her seat back and grabbed the blanket Jozef had requested for her. She stared at him until the gentle hum of the aircraft lulled her into a nap.

CHAPTER THIRTY-EIGHT

J ozef woke Shaun shortly before the plane landed.

She grumbled at him for making her sit up and put her seatbelt back on.

"We're on a private jet, I should be able to sleep through the landing."

You can sleep but you have to do it sitting up with your seatbelt on.

"And my tray table in an upright and locked position. Blah, blah, blah. You own the aircraft, you can suspend a few of the rules." She patted her hair, wincing when it felt as bad as she suspected it looked. That was the problem with wearing an afro. She had to have an emergency recovery effort whenever she slept. "I worked a twelve-hour shift at the hospital with four of those hours on my feet in surgery. I need to get my beauty sleep before I have to dodge mafia bullets."

Not funny, Jozef signed, pulling the blanket from her lap, folding it and setting it aside.

She found it endearing that Jozef tended to be the more domestic of the two of them.

I won't compromise with your safety. You wear your seatbelt, you follow the rules, or I will take your driver's license away.

He'd returned her driver's license to her and given her a car once she'd settled into a routine at the hospital. As long as she promised to have a contingent of bodyguards on her tail and Cooper in the car with her, he was fine with her driving. Shaun loved to drive and did it like she performed surgery: with precision, by her own rules, and creatively when necessary.

I don't know what my driver's license has to do with not wanting to wake up until we've landed. Now that she was waking up, she switched to signing. These days she signed more than spoke, though she often caught herself doing both depending on who they were with.

If you won't wear your seatbelt on an airplane, then I can't trust you to wear one in the car.

"That's bullshit and you know it," she grumbled.

He leaned over and kissed her scowl away. When he continued to linger, Shaun smiled against his lips and pushed herself against his chest, deepening the kiss.

A whistle sounded from the back of the plane that had Jozef whipping his head around to glare at his men. Only it wasn't his men grinning at them and catcalling, it was Ayaan.

Shaun giggled as Jozef turned back around with a frown.

Ayaan definitely got away with more than Jozef's men could. She was incorrigible, which got on Jozef's nerves, but she knew when to draw the line and be serious.

Shaun suspected Jozef was seeing the young woman as a little sister. She wondered if his protective instincts would interfere with his ability to send Ayaan on dangerous missions. She noticed that occasionally Jozef sent his men away without Ayaan, much to the girl's consternation.

When the plane landed and came to a safe halt, Jozef stood and took Shaun's hand. Instead of leading her off the plane with the rest of his people, he pulled her to the back of the plane where their luggage was stored. He pointed at a set of fancy blue Ralph Lauren suitcases.

Shaun shook her head, bewildered.

He picked up one of the garment bags and slung it across a row of seats, unzipping it. She gasped as he pulled a handful of hangers with some of the finest clothes she'd had ever seen.

A gift, he signed.

She touched the fabrics and quickly checked the labels. They were all her size and, as she rifled through them, all a twist on her usual style. They looked comfortable, but with a fine finish that gave them the illusion of being extremely chic and in fashion.

I love them, she signed enthusiastically. *But why did you get me to pack my own bag if you already had clothes for me?*

You didn't give me a chance and your bag was already packed by the time I reached the bedroom. He pulled an outfit from the bag. It was a dark purple skirt suit, with a pencil skirt and a cream-coloured blouse with a lace panel at the cleavage. She touched the fabric, feeling the waterfall of silk slide through her fingers.

"It's beautiful." Her voice was hushed. "Do you want me to put it on?"

He nodded. *You are lovely as you are, but I think this will make the statement that I am in the company of a beautiful, intelligent doctor and if anyone touches me, you will cut them.*

Shaun burst into laughter and hugged the fabric against her chest. "Where should I change?"

Here is fine, I will make sure no one comes up the ramp.

Jozef went to stand in front of the door, blocking the view of Shaun as she changed. Suspecting he'd bought her a complete outfit, she dug through the other bags until she found shoes. She chose a pair of matching soft purple heels.

She changed quickly, ducked into the bathroom, and patted down her hair, which made absolutely no difference, then met Jozef at the door. As she looked at the tarmac, she caught sight of several cars, all black with tinted windows.

"Are those for us?"

Yes, they will be our escort to the palace and our bodyguards to a nearby town. Jozef must've caught her worried look. He cupped her face in his hands and kissed her before signing, *they're here for our protection. We are assets and we are in Bratva territory. If anything were to happen to us here, it would be an embarrassment to the organization.*

She shuddered, the old feeling of being out of her depth creeping back over her like an icy blanket. She hated that feeling. She was no longer balancing between two worlds. She had chosen which side she was on, and her choice was to be wherever Jozef was.

She slid her hand into his and squeezed, giving him the best smile she could manage. "I trust you."

His gaze softened for a split second before hardening to his usual unreadable expression. It was time to put on his business face.

As they walked down the ramp, Shaun teased, "Of all the places I'd imagined our honeymoon to be, this wasn't one of them."

Jozef's face was set in serious lines, but his eyes danced for her. He dropped her hand so he could sign to her. *When we have our honeymoon, you will know it. This is business.* He seemed to think about it and then signed, *although you should reserve judgment until you see the palace. You might think this is a relaxing holiday before we're through.*

Somehow Shaun doubted it, but she appreciated his attempt to ease some of her tension.

Jozef was correct about the palace. It was the most spectacular building Shaun had ever set eyes on. Though Canada was a relatively young country compared to most European countries, there was some beautiful architecture in Montreal. Nothing could compare to the palace, though. It was a step out of time and reality. With its blue spires, stained glass domes and white painted brick walls, it looked like it should drift in the clouds somewhere.

"How much do you suppose a place like this would run?" Shaun asked, taking Jozef's hand as he reached to help her from the car. "For a summer home, I mean."

Jozef chuckled. *I am a wealthy man now and I would happily set the world at your feet.* He shook his head. *But this place? It would take more than my current fortune.*

Shaun shrugged. *I prefer a cottage in the countryside anyway.*

That is why I love you, my beautiful wife.

That's the only thing? She arched a brow at him.

He seemed to think about it. *What else is there?*

She laughed and smacked his bicep before sliding her hand across his arm and allowing him to escort her inside.

Though the palace was indescribably beautiful, it held a chilly feeling to it that Shaun couldn't shake as they were shown through the corridors to the guest wing.

The suite that they would call home for the five days they would be in Russia put the Koba mansion to shame. It gave opulent a new name.

Shaun slid her hand across a marble column inlaid with gold, speculating that she probably didn't need to ask if it was genuine gold. She shook her head as she imagined the many uses the money that had gone into decorating the mansion could have gone to. With the columns alone, Doctors Without Borders could say goodbye to their funding problems.

She followed Jozef and their footman into the bedroom where their luggage was being dropped off.

Jozef was handing the footman some cash, then he handed over his phone, placing it in the footman's palm.

Give him your phone, Jozef told her.

She frowned and reached into her purse. Jozef had warned her on the airplane that she would have to give up her connection to the outside world. The official stance of the palace was that it was a vacation home and phones would interfere with the ambience. Of course, Shaun didn't believe that for a minute.

Her heart beat a little faster as she gave up her symbol of independence, her ability to call for help, her connection to the people she loved. Honestly, she told herself, it was silly to get so worked up. If the Bratva intended to kill them inside the walls of the palace, they wouldn't be given the opportunity of calling for help.

As always, Jozef read her mind. *They won't kill us here. This place is far too nice to stain with our blood.*

Shaun laughed but glanced at the footman who remained by the door pretending not to look at them.

You need to be careful what you say. We must assume that everyone here understands sign language. Nothing we say is private.

Jozef's expression changed. Not to one of surprise, but to one of satisfaction. *My wife is both beautiful and intelligent.* He looked toward the footman, signing, *isn't she?*

The footman looked Jozef in the eye and spoke in deeply accented English, "Indeed she is."

That one sentence told them everything they needed to know. Their communications would not remain private while they were in the palace, no matter what language they used to communicate in.

"You can leave," Shaun said coldly in flawless Russian.

Shaun held the man's gaze as he stiffened and fought to keep the expression of surprise from his face. No doubt, the palace staff had been told that the foreigner wife of Jozef

Koba spoke only English. Perhaps it was stupid to give away her new skill.

"I am to remain in case you need anything, Mrs. Koba."

Shaun narrowed her eyes and rolled her shoulders back, straightening to her full height. In her heels, she was easily taller than the man standing across from her.

"It's Dr. Koba, and we require nothing from you except your departure. Our flight was long and we want to sleep." She gave him a hard stare and tried on her best mob wife voice. "You may leave."

The footman held his ground until Jozef placed a hand on Shaun's shoulder and stared at the man, promising him death if he continued to ignore Shaun's commands.

The moment he left, Shaun flopped backward on the bed, covering her face with her hands. She bounced off the high mattress and slid to the floor.

Jozef grabbed her and dragged her up the bed while she giggled at the ridiculousness of it all. "I feel like I've time travelled a few hundred years into the past. I'm the only woman of colour living among the aristocracy and fighting my way up the ladder to the top while dodging servants who treat me like I'm nothing more than a bug to be squished."

Jozef climbed onto the bed, straddling her legs and staring down at her. *You will shake the aristocracy to its core.*

She stared back at him. The moment should be playful, but it felt serious. They were deep in Russian Bratva territory, guests at the palace where meetings deciding their future were about to take place.

Yes, I will, she signed. *I will fight for us.*

Jozef kissed her, pushing his hands into her hair and anchoring her head. She wrapped her arms around his neck and kissed him back, pouring her heart into the kiss. It was their one flawless method of communication. Both of them spoke as one when their lips met.

Finally, Jozef broke the kiss, staring down at Shaun with love and lust in his eyes.

"You have a meeting," she whispered.

Jozef nodded, gave her one last kiss, then climbed off the bed and strode from the room, straightening his suit jacket as he walked away.

A shiver ran through Shaun. His switch from loving husband to deadly mobster was instant. She knew without a doubt that the man leaving their room was not the man she married, but the one who'd kidnapped her nearly two years ago.

avel's steps were muffled as he navigated the path from the mansion to Leeza's cottage. Leeza and Adam's cottage, he corrected himself. The home that they'd built together. The place where they'd created a family.

After Adam's discovery in the closet safe room, six months earlier, it had been decided that he wasn't a threat. He was allowed to return to his cottage, allowed to resume his work.

Or so Adam believed.

In reality, Jozef and Havel had decided that no decisions would be made about the other man's fate until Leeza was found and brought home. Jozef thought perhaps she would try to contact her husband and they could trace her.

Havel knew better. Leeza wouldn't contact Adam. She hated the man. No, that wasn't true. She used to hate him. Now, she didn't think enough of him to hate him. She wouldn't contact Adam because she wouldn't think of it. As far as she was concerned, the man she married all those years ago was useless to her.

Havel knew how her mind worked, had always known.

He'd allowed bitterness over her choice to break up with him to cloud his judgment, but the fog was clearing and once more he could see her again. See the woman he loved for who she was. Strong, capable, frightened.

Havel had avoided visiting Adam until now. Though Jozef had asked his second-in-command if he wanted to interrogate the accountant, Havel had declined. While Leeza felt nothing for her husband, Havel felt everything. He wasn't sure he could contain his rage.

Now, with Jozef out of town, Havel had decided it was time to have a talk with the accountant. Man to man. As the man who loved Leeza to the man who married her.

He stopped outside the cottage, giving himself one more chance to walk away. Did he have the self-control not to kill Adam Horáček? He was about to find out.

He unlocked the door and let himself in, his hand falling to the butt of his pistol. He didn't need to worry though; Adam was sitting at his dining room table eating his evening meal.

He looked like the prince of his kingdom, as if he hadn't a care in the world. He was seated at the head of the table, a candelabra lighting the immediate area surrounding his place-mat. All other lights had been turned off.

Adam was a weird guy and always had been. He seemed unflappable, even in the direst of circumstances. Though Havel hadn't interrogated the accountant, Jozef had. He'd sat across from Adam, asking question after question, with Havel trans-lating. Every man in the room had become fatigued by the process, though they knew better than to show their feelings.

Only Jozef and Adam had remained unfazed, each completely focused on the other. Interrogator and prisoner. One wanted information, the other... had no motive that any of them could see.

Except Jozef had a secret weapon, a file detailing Adam's life from childhood to adulthood, including his marriage to Leeza.

It had been hard to retain an impassive face and a level voice when the subject of Leeza came up during the interrogation. Especially because Jozef was dropping bombs that Havel hadn't known. Jozef knew that Havel cared about Leeza, but he hadn't known the depth of their relationship before Adam entered the picture.

When the interrogation had ended, Adam had been allowed to resume his old life in the comfort of his cottage. He would remain under surveillance and his position would be suspended until after Jozef met with the Bratva, since Adam was a Bratva sanctioned accountant and related to one of their top men.

"I was expecting you sooner. Months ago, in fact."

Adam continued to eat his meal without looking up.

Havel pulled a chair out on the opposite side of the dining table and dropped his heavy frame into it. The chair creaked and then held.

"Why is that?" Havel kept his tone level and his eyes unreadable.

Adam reached for his glass of wine, taking a long sip of the rich liquid.

"You were in love with my wife. I assumed you would want some kind of payback since I stole her from you." Adam finally lifted his gaze from the table. Havel read triumph there.

Not an ounce of fear. The man was either sociopathic or he somehow thought he could win this confrontation.

Havel laughed coldly. "You don't know your wife if you think she would allow herself to be stolen."

A flash of something rippled across Adam's face before he

fought to control his emotions. Havel thought it was anger at being told he didn't know his wife.

"Yet she still became my wife."

"Yes," Havel drawled. "Why is that? What did you say to Krystoff to get him to agree to a merger between his eldest daughter and someone who is so much lower than her?"

Adam didn't react to the insult. Instead, he picked up his napkin, wiped his mouth and tossed the napkin down. "He was ordered to allow the marriage by Stellan Jovanovich."

"You're related the Bratva accountant."

Adam nodded. "Yes. Stellan is my uncle."

"Stellan Jovanovich? Well, no shit. Maybe we should give your uncle a call and see if he thinks we should continue to pay for your room and board, or if he'd rather you make a quiet exit from the organization. Word has it, you've been an embarrassment to your family." Of course, Havel already knew about the association. It'd been in the file Jozef found in Krystoff's things.

Adam's throat bobbed, giving away his fear for a split second. So, not a sociopath, just a Bratva connected man with some very sick proclivities.

"You can't kill me," Adam said quickly.

"Why?" Havel leaned back in his chair and crossed his arms over his biceps.

He was surprised that rage wasn't making this conversation more difficult. Instead, he felt satisfaction as he played with his food. He might not kill Adam today, but he would eventually. One day. And it was going to be awesome, glorious and satisfying. It would be everything he'd wanted to do to the man since Leeza broke his heart. Every fantasy come to life.

"Jozef won't allow it." Adam pushed his chair back and gripped the edge of the table but didn't rise. "The Bratva won't allow it."

"Is that what you think?" Havel chuckled. "One day soon, Jozef will give you to me on a silver platter. And the Bratva? You've caused them more problems than you've solved."

"I... I don't know what you mean."

Havel's smirk disappeared and he straightened in his seat, placing his hands on the table and deliberately rising slowly, with menace.

"Don't you?" Havel let his question hang in the air before continuing. "The Bratva doesn't like when attention is brought to them unless they deliberately ask for it. You were given to this family to get you out of Russia and away from your highly positioned uncle. You were drawing too much negative attention to him. Now, what could you possibly have done that was so bad not even the Bratva could sanction it?"

Havel shoved away from the table and strode toward Adam, who leapt to his feet in alarm. He tried to stand his ground, but the hulking, muscular, tattooed thug bearing down on him gave him nowhere to go.

"This is ridiculous," Adam said, his voice shaking. "You don't know anything."

"You think not?" Havel came to a stop uncomfortably close to Adam. Havel was several inches taller, bringing his collarbone in line with Adam's eyes.

Adam was forced to look up when he answered.

"There's no evidence."

"There's always evidence," Havel countered. "As an accountant, you should know that. No one gets away with their crimes forever."

Adam scrambled back, hitting the wall behind him then sliding toward the staircase leading to the top floor.

"What about you?" Adam tried to sound tough but failed. "What about your crimes?"

"That is between me and God."

Havel believed he would one day face judgment, then

spend his eternity in purgatory. He was at peace with that. He was not at peace with monsters like Adam getting away with their crimes while still living on the earthly plane.

"But you..." Havel stalked the man across the room, their movements made eerie by the candlelight. "You are a killer. You will burn in this world before I allow you to go to the next."

"You're a killer too!" Adam protested. "What's the difference?"

"I don't murder innocent women."

The truth lay in the air between them. Up to that point, Adam hadn't known how much Jozef or Havel knew about his proclivities. Havel thought it was about time he lay his cards on the table. He was done with Adam living in his little cottage, enjoying his candlelit meals. Havel was going to give him something to worry about until the moment he was ready to end things with the accountant. He would torture the other man's thoughts, drive him to the edge, then he would do it some more before finally taking his life.

Havel wasn't doing it for any noble reason. He wasn't doing it for the women whose lives Adam had stolen prematurely. No, he was doing it for himself. He wanted vengeance for the innocence this man stole from the woman he loved.

"Those women weren't innocent," Adam protested. "They were all prostitutes. They sold sex. They deserved – "

Havel reached for his gun, pressing it to Adam's temple. "Finish that sentence, accountant."

Adam chose to remain silent.

Havel stepped back, tucking the gun back into his holster. "We'll finish this conversation another time."

CHAPTER FORTY

Jozef greeted the Bratva with nods and handshakes as he accepted his place among them.

He'd been led by their footman to the 'study' where business was conducted during those times when it absolutely must occur on palace grounds. In general, the palace was used as a vacation home for the top members of the Bratva, not business.

Jozef believed the Bratva had brought him to the palace to make a statement. They wanted him to know that he was welcome among them. If they'd been trying to intimidate him, they would have invited him to Moscow. If that had been the case, Jozef would've left Shaun behind, despite the invitation making it clear that her presence was mandatory.

Jozef didn't care if he went to war with the entire Bratva organization, he would protect his wife with the last breath in his body.

Fortunately, for their sake, it seemed the Bratva didn't want him dead.

There were eleven men in the room. Jozef recognized all of them. The eldest member, a ninety-eight-year-old mobster by the name of Ivan Siberia, was the top voice of the Bratva. They called him Siberia because no one knew his actual name. Not even Ivan knew. He'd gone into a Siberian gulag as a teenager in the 1930s. He'd been among the first Bratva to rule the prisons. He'd had a reputation for blood-thirsty brutality that had only grown over the years. There were rumours that held he'd had enough men killed to fill a modest-sized city.

Ivan Siberia was the reason many of the Bratva of his age didn't have families. He would use women and children for leverage, then kill them for sport. Despite his terrible reputation, or maybe because of it, he'd become a figurehead in his old age. And though the old man insisted that mobsters should never have families, rumour had it, Ivan had sired many illegitimate children over the years. He kept them well hidden from the organization he'd helped found.

Along with Ivan, the heads of seven families were present, each responsible for their own region of control. Also present were the two men who'd met with Jozef on the day of his uncle's funeral: Alexei Ivanov and Yuri Antonovich.

Jozef was handed a glass of his favourite brand of vodka and a cigar. He accepted them, though he set the cigar aside. As he took a drink from the crystal glass, one of the family heads, Stellan Jovanovich, took the seat next to him.

"How is my nephew?" Stellan greeted Jozef, sitting in the plush chair next to the younger man.

Jozef contemplated Stellan before answering. Finally, he signed, *for the moment, A-D-A-M remains unharmed.*

A nearby footman translated.

"Pity." Stellan lit his cigar while another footman discreetly opened a set of French doors.

He offered Jozef another cigar, which Jozef declined. Jozef had always detested smoking, had tried to convince his uncle to quit for his health. Ironic, considering it had been Jozef who'd ended Krystoff's life, not cancer.

What do you want for your nephew? Jozef asked curiously.

Stellan thought about it. "I don't wish to repossess the boy, if that's what you mean. He was a fuck-up here on Russian soil, and from the reports we received from Krystoff, he was the same in Czechia."

Jozef had been shocked to learn, upon reading Krystoff's file on Adam, that the man was a rather prolific serial killer. Jozef was under no illusion that they weren't all serial killers. Every man in the room had either killed, or had killed, multiple people in their lifetimes. But that was in the name of business. Adam divined a kind of sexual pleasure from his kills. He chose his victims from the weak, the helpless, society's undesirables. Women who wouldn't be missed.

From the pictures of their bodies, each one attached to a police report that had landed in Krystoff's possession, Jozef could tell that Adam had played with his victims for hours before releasing them from their lives. He bruised and broke them without spilling a single drop of blood before strangling them to death. Disgusting and depraved were too kind to describe the monster who'd been allowed to marry Jozef's cousin.

It was after he read the file that Jozef realized he couldn't kill his cousin. She was as much a victim as the other women. Years of abuse were documented in the reports. But what Jozef hadn't understood was Krystoff's motive for marrying his eldest daughter to such a monster. At least, he hadn't understood until he learned that Krystoff was not her father.

Jozef suspected that, while Krystoff had forgiven his wife for being unfaithful, he hadn't been able to forgive Leeza, his supposed first born, for being illegitimate. It was twisted logic, but Jozef knew how his uncle's mind worked. Knew how petty the man could be.

Now, sitting among the Bratva's elite, Jozef felt as though he belonged. He felt no fear because he knew he was an asset. Every step of his life had been in service of reaching this point. He could never have imagined it would be through the death of his uncle at his own hand, but he knew that one day he would sit in this spot.

He spoke to the men surrounding him as equals, with confidence. He had trade that they wanted. He had an elite team of mercenaries that they wanted. He had control of an entire country. He would live and work among these men. He was home.

Shaun spent her afternoon ensconced with three of the wives of the men who were meeting with Jozef. The conversation was stilted at first, but gradually the curiosity of the other women outweighed their reserve of the stranger in their midst.

"And you work?" Tatiana Ivanov asked in Russian. "As a doctor?"

The women looked so shocked by the notion that Shaun had to hide a giggle. She nodded solemnly, as though agreeing that it was definitely strange for a woman of her position to be working.

Shaun answered in Russian, choosing her words carefully. "I do. I recently took a position with the Prague General Hospital."

The women looked at each other.

Tatiana, the spokeswoman for the three asked, "You work with people's brains? Is that correct?"

"Da," Shaun agreed. "I am a neurologist."

"Perhaps you can help my little Niki. There's something wrong with his brain. He's not quite right."

"Uh… is his problem behavioural or physiological?"

"You tell me!" The woman threw her hands up in the air. "He wants nothing to do with the family business. He spends all of his time with his musician friends playing his silly guitar. He says he wants to be famous, to play heavy metal. What is that I ask you? He is definitely damaged in the brain."

Shaun caught the amused eye of Yelena.

"I don't think your son needs Mrs. Koba's attention," Yelena said softly, hiding her smirk. "Perhaps he needs his father's attention more."

"That is another issue," Tatiana grumbled. "Alexei is hardly ever home. He goes out to the clubs and says it is business. Ridiculous. Who needs to do business with the thumping music and the dancing whores?"

Shaun choked on her drink, a vodka soda.

She carefully placed the glass on the marble side table next to her chair.

"Jozef does his business in a club." Jozef had once explained to her that the club was an easy place to meet clients. There was a casual feel and being surrounded by people made them feel safe.

"You see." Tatiana looked around at the other women, her voice hushed. "These men, they are always cheating."

Yelena rolled her eyes and sipped her drink, not commenting. Shaun didn't say anything either. Jozef's devotion to her was unquestionable. She had no doubts when it came to him and other women.

When another round of cocktails was brought in, Shaun declined and asked for a sparkling water. Shortly after, she excused herself from the women, citing exhaustion. It wasn't a lie, she was tired. Her early shift at the hospital, the plane trip and having to speak Russian all day had taken a lot out of her. She was glad when the women were told that the men would continue to meet well into the evening and that their suppers would be served separately.

In her room, by herself, Shaun ate a delicious meal of two kinds of salad and a side of roast beef. She particularly enjoyed the salad with the potatoes, mayonnaise, beets, onions and what tasted like pickles. She noted the ingredients, wishing she had her phone so she would take a picture. She wanted to ask their cook at home to make it.

She thought she would get bored without access to internet or TV, but she found that exhaustion had creeped up on her enough that, after a leisurely bath in a tub that was so huge it could easily cross over into swimming pool territory, she was ready for bed.

She pulled on a gorgeous lacy shorts and tank top sleeping set that she found in her new luggage and crawled beneath the cool sheets of the bed. She propped her head up on a fluffy pillow and watched the moon and surrounding stars until she fell asleep.

She didn't how long she'd been sleeping, but she was groggy when the banging of a door woke her.

Sitting up, she reached for the lamp, her heart pounding in fear until she caught sight of Jozef clinging to one of the marble columns.

He looked confused, like he'd stopped to use the column for balance while he figured out where he was going.

"Are you drunk?" she asked in consternation.

For as long as she'd known him, Jozef rarely drank, and he'd never gotten drunk.

She flung the covers back and slid off the bed, rushing to help him. Unfortunately, he launched himself at her when he caught sight of her, gripping her around the shoulders and trying to kiss her as they both went crashing backwards.

Luckily, Jozef's reflections were excellent, even while he

was inebriated. He twisted as they fell so he ended up taking the brunt of the hard fall and she landed on top of him.

He grinned at her and a wave of vodka breath hit her in the face

"Oh god, Jozef!" she exclaimed, rolling off him.

As she tried to climb back onto the bed, he gripped her around the waist and hauled her back down to the floor. She clung to the blankets, dragging them off the bed. She laughed wildly as he rolled her underneath him.

It was so weird to see Jozef drunk that she didn't quite know what to do except laugh. She touched his face, which was warm. She checked his pulse. It was rapid, but nothing out of the ordinary.

He pushed her hands away from his face and buried his nose against her neck, making a growling sound. He began sloppily kissing her while his hands roamed down her body.

"Not a chance." She shoved at his shoulders, but it was like trying to move a boulder. "Get off me!"

He ignored her, clumsily exploring her body. She sighed, then reached up to pull his ear hard enough to gain his attention.

He swung his head around to glare at her, which allowed her to sternly say, "Get off me right now, Jozef Koba."

He rolled off her and sat up against the side of the bed. He rubbed his hands over his head, then looked up at her and grinned. It took her breath away. The man had dimples and she hadn't even known. He smiled rarely and when he did it was always tight, controlled and quick. This was a whole-hearted, boyish grin and she adored it. She cupped his face and leaned over to kiss him.

"I love you," she murmured against his lips.

He brought his hands up to sign and smacked her in the chin.

She laughed and pushed off the floor, standing over him. She held her hand out. "Come on, I'll help you up."

He took her hand and nearly pulled her back down to the floor. She had to brace herself to help him up. As he stood, he swayed so wildly that she thought he was going to fall over again.

She slid her arm under his and pushed him toward the bed.

He landed on his back; his arms flung over his head.

She thought about trying to get him out of his clothes, then decided against it. He was heavy and she didn't want him thinking they were going to have sex. As much as her body responded to him, even in this state, she wouldn't do something that intimate while he was inebriated.

Shaun climbed over Jozef's sprawled body and tucked herself into his side. She was about to close her eyes when she realized he was signing... or trying too.

She propped herself up and watched until she finally caught what he was saying.

She smiled down at him and whispered, "You're the best thing that ever happened to me, too."

She reached out to shut the lamp off, tucked herself back in and fell asleep to the sound of Jozef's drunken snores.

CHAPTER FORTY-ONE

Shaun slipped from the bed, pulling on a fluffy bathrobe provided by their hosts as she hurried to the door. She didn't want the knocking to wake Jozef, though he was sleeping heavily, snoring loud enough to wake the recently departed.

With a hand at the top of her robe, she opened the door.

"Yes?" she asked sleepily.

"Your morning repast, Mrs. Koba." A servant spoke in halting English, waving toward a cart with covered trays.

Shaun stepped back so he could wheel the cart inside.

He placed the covered trays, a pot of coffee, cream and sugar on the small table next to windows with panoramic views of the rear mansion park. Shaun could definitely get used to this kind of service.

"This is for you, ma'am." The servant held a card out to Shaun.

Shaun sat at the table, opening the envelope, her curiosity peaked.

It was an invitation, quite fancy, considering the contents. It was written in English, in sprawling calligraphy.

. . .

Mrs. Koba,

Please allow me the pleasure of hosting you for tea in my private suite at 11:00 AM. You will be treated with the utmost respect. Kindly send your response with Philip.

Your friend,

Ivan Siberia

The invitation was clear that only Shaun was being invited to meet with the highest man in the Bratva organization. She glanced at the bedroom, wondering what she should do. She'd promised Jozef she wouldn't keep any more secrets from him, but she didn't think the invitation was one she should decline. She wished she could talk to Jozef before deciding.

Shaun looked at the servant. "Philip?"

At his nod, she handed him the invitation. "Please tell Mr. Siberia that I would be delighted to meet with him."

Shaun took her time showering, dressing and snacking off the tray Philip had left for her. There were plates of fresh fruit, whipping cream, and chocolate pudding.

After she finished eating and grooming, she curled up in the chair by the window with a stack of files she'd snuck in her purse. Jozef had told her she wasn't allowed to work, that she must consider their time in Russia to be a vacation.

Jozef was starting to understand that if given the opportunity, she would always choose work. She found perusing images of brain tumours relaxing. Her quick mind immediately set to work trying to figure out how to extract the mass.

One at a time she went through the files until she hit upon the one she would take as her next surgical candidate. She read through it thoroughly and then reached for her cell phone to text Elisa with confirmation. Then she remembered her phone had been taken.

Damn it, they were going to be in Russia for four more days. Could she go that long without her phone? She was already getting withdrawal from a lack of spider solitaire. She wondered if she would be shot by the big Russian guards who she'd seen patrolling the estate if she tried to break her phone out of wherever it was being held hostage. Maybe she should negotiate with Ivan Siberia for her phone. She was willing to do a lot to get her hands on the device.

Speaking of Mr. Ivan Siberia... she glanced at the ornate clock on the wall. Assuming it was correct, she was expected in his suite in five minutes.

Shaun walked gingerly into the bedroom where Jozef was still sprawled out on the bed. The blanket had slipped off and he was gloriously naked. Her eyes immediately went to his still-impressive-while-flaccid cock. She glanced down at the pile of clothes next to the bed. He must've woken up enough at some point to take them off.

"Jozef," she whispered, approaching the bed. She chewed her lip.

To wake him up or not, that was the question. She loved the way he looked while he slept. Boyish, innocent, the implacable lines that played about his eyes and mouth gone.

When he didn't stir, she got a little closer, tracing her fingers across the rippling muscles of his stomach. Still no response.

"I'm going to have tea with the man you told me is responsible for the entire Bratva. I'm really hoping he won't try to kill me. You did say it was unlikely they'd murder us in this lovely palace." Still no movement. She strode into the washroom, filled a glass with cold water and set it on his bedside table. She leaned over and pressed a quick kiss to his lips. "Wish me luck."

Philip was waiting in the corridor for her, his frowning gaze fixed to the smart watch on his wrist.

"Nice watch," she said with an innocent smile. "We should probably hurry. I would guess Mr. Siberia doesn't like to be kept waiting."

Philip's gaze became even chillier. "No."

He turned on his heel and marched ahead of Shaun. She would have loved to take out her newly discovered badass mafia wife persona and knock this guy down a few pegs, but she wasn't entirely sure where he stood in the Bratva regard. She should probably hold off on pissing off the servants until she had more information.

Philip showed her into a suite with a surprisingly warm atmosphere. The pomp and lavishness of her suite was discarded in favour of a cluttered, bright and comfortable group of rooms.

Shaun was surprised, the place looked lived in. Like really lived in. She thought the palace was for weekend getaways and hosting. Or at least, that was the impression that Jozef had given her. But Ivan's suite was more like an elderly retiree's home.

A walker sat next to a well-worn armchair, a TV opposite, and a stack of books was laying haphazardly across a table on the other side of the chair. She watched in amazement as a man, using a cane, walked painfully into the room, moving slowly and with some difficulty.

Shaun immediately broke into a cold sweat. It didn't matter that this man wasn't personally capable of swatting a fly, he could have someone swat her if she became a nuisance to him.

"Please, sit down, Mrs. Koba." Ivan's voice was strong as he turned around and carefully sat in the armchair.

Shaun hesitantly approached the couch adjacent to Ivan's

chair. It was covered in newspapers, magazines, cat toys and a cat bed. She glanced around for the cat but didn't see one. Moving a few items out of the way, she sat on the couch.

Philip wheeled in a tray seemingly from nowhere, set the tea service on the coffee table in front of Shaun, then left the room.

"Would you mind pouring?" Ivan asked, hooking his cane on the walker next to his chair.

"Of course." Shaun leaned forward and poured a rich dark liquid into the two teacups. "Cream or sugar?"

"Both, spasibo."

His English was so flawless, his Russian 'thank you' almost took her by surprise.

She handed him his cup, which he set on the table next to him.

Shaun settled into her chair and held her cup, watching him carefully. She wouldn't take a sip until he drank from his cup. As if noticing her discomfort, he picked up his cup and took a long sip, his dark brown eyes on her face.

She smiled her relief and sipped her own tea.

"How are you settling in, Mrs. Koba?" he asked, pushing his chair into a reclining position.

It felt strange to be in the presence of such a top Vor, but without the formal accoutrements that seemed to surround his fellow Bratva.

"The palace is lovely," she said, unsure if that was what he meant.

He shook his head and studied her. "Let's speak plainly, Mrs. Koba. I don't have a lot of time left and I dislike wasting minutes on pointless speech."

There wasn't a lot that Shaun could say to that, except, "Of course. Please say whatever you like to me."

She didn't entirely mean it. She sincerely hoped he

wouldn't tell her there was a pit of hungry alligators under-neath his living room floor, ready to feast on her flesh.

"Two years ago, Jozef picked you up in a hospital in Luhansk, Ukraine. You were meant to die that day, but you didn't."

CHAPTER FORTY-TWO

Shaun sucked in a breath as images from that day slammed through her. She had worked with her counsellor on mitigating their impact, but when the head of the Vor told her she was meant to be dead, it was like a fresh wound being ripped open again.

"So I've been told," she murmured, bringing her teacup to her lips with a shaking hand.

"You survived." He didn't sound either approving or disapproving, and Shaun wondered where the direction of the conversation was going. "You were poisoned, and you survived. You were attacked, stabbed, and you survived. Your husband was attacked, many within the building fell, yet you still survived."

A chill ran through Shaun and she felt nauseous. She desperately wished she'd told Jozef where she was going. Was Ivan angry over the deaths that seemed to follow Shaun? Did he blame her for what happened to Krystoff?

She didn't know what to say to Ivan, but he'd paused, seeming to expect some kind of response. "Yes, I survived."

"You are a survivor, Dr. Patterson, and you are a very

skilled surgeon, which makes you an asset to my organization."

It was the first time he'd acknowledged her profession.

Again, she didn't know what to say, so she remained silent.

"I have had my people look into you." His gaze was sharp, his words sharper, though his body appeared frail. It was such a strange juxtaposition that Shaun was forced to rethink the way she looked at the mafia being full of raw male machismo. She would bet her stethoscope this man had never made a hot-headed decision in his life. He'd coldly, calculatingly made his way to the top of the Bratva, shaping its future along the way.

"What did they find?" she asked coolly, setting her tea cup down on a side table and clasping her hands in her lap to stop the shaking. If he could sound strong but appear fragile, then so could she.

He leaned forward in his chair, pushing it down with his legs. "You are at the top of your field. Unparalleled in skill and intelligence. You are at the head of innovative technological medicine."

Shaun sucked in a breath. "That's flattering, but hardly true. I share the field with many skilled surgeons."

"Humbleness has no place here," he told her sharply. "This is a warning. You are among the wealthiest and deadliest people in the world. Do not misstep by trying to fade into the background. Make yourself indispensable to the Bratva and your position will remain secure."

"It's not now?" she couldn't help the quiver in her voice.

"It is not," he said bluntly. "Your husband has long been admired by the Bratva. If he hadn't found his way to the top of the Koba food chain, we would have found a way to get him there."

Shaun wondered how they would have gone about that,

but then shoved the thought away. She didn't need to know, and it was a hypothetical since Jozef had the position.

"You, however," Ivan continued, "have become a concern. A witness who was allowed to live, now a wife who pursues a high-profile, highly competitive profession. We rarely allow our women to take positions of power. For good reason, they could become targets. If your existence is not known, or if you remain hidden, you will not be in danger."

Shaun nodded, and unable to help herself, cut in, "Mr. Siberia, while I appreciate your concern, I have worked in war zones on multiple occasions. While I admit, being shot at isn't my favourite past-time, I can handle myself."

He stared at her, a chill in his gaze. "I am aware of your work history, Mrs. Koba."

"Sorry," she mumbled, feeling chastened. She wasn't entirely sure why, or where their conversation was going, but she could shut up long enough to hear an old man out.

"As I said, I would like to consider you an asset." He stared at her; his words heavy in the air between them. "I would like to know where you stand now, Mrs. Koba. Are you an asset or are you a victim?"

Shaun didn't need to think about it. She lifted her chin. "I am an asset, of course."

"Excellent." His face smoothed into more pleasant lines as he waved her toward the coffee table again. "Please take the two files on the table. Read the first and tell me what you see."

She picked up the first file and flipped through, realizing right away it was medical records. There was no name attached, but a glance gave her the age, which left her with the assumption it must be Ivan Siberia's medical history.

She relaxed into the couch as she read and looked at images. The file was surprisingly complete considering she'd only just met the man. He was being forthcoming with her so she would be forthcoming with him.

"You have colorectal cancer. You were diagnosed two years ago, went through five rounds of radiation therapy and one surgery to remove a section of your intestine. The cancer has returned and now..." she drifted off as she flipped through the images and notes, "Your doctor says you have less than six months."

"Would you agree?" Ivan asked curiously, without a note of fear or censure in his voice.

She shook her head. "Given your age and current liver and kidney functions, I would revise that down to two to three months."

He sucked in a breath, showing that he was rattled for the first time since they began their conversation.

"Thank you for your honesty."

Shaun watched him, making sure he meant what he said and wasn't threatening her.

"I'm always honest when it comes to medicine. What's the point in telling a dying man he'll live longer than he will? This way, you have the time to make arrangements and be with the people who matter most to you."

He didn't respond to her comment, but waved his hand at a second file sitting on the table. "Look at that one and tell me what you see." Before she could reach for it, he asked, "You value confidentiality?"

"Of course," she answered.

"Good. No one must know who this patient is..." he hesitated before continuing, "to me."

"As both a doctor and a human being, you have my word that nothing we discuss will leave this room unless you want it to." She paused and then added, "Except for Jozef."

He dipped his head in a nod. "That will have to be good enough."

She picked it up, flipped it open and began reading. The more she read, the more alarmed she became. The patient was a three-year-old male with a degenerative heart condition. "This will be fatal if he doesn't get surgery immediately."

"Yes, that's what his doctor told me," Ivan sat up in his chair and leaned forward. There was a flash of terrible fire in his dark eyes. "Unfortunately, he botched the procedure, and my great-grandson is now on life-support with little chance at survival."

"I'm so sorry," Shaun murmured, meaning it. Though this man had undoubtedly done terrible things throughout his life, she couldn't help but feel for an old man who might outlive his great-grandchild.

She continued to peruse the images and notes, both pre-surgery and post. She studied the blown-up image of the child's heart, holding it up to the light so she could see every nuance.

"What are you thinking?" Ivan demanded.

Shaun lowered the image, tucking it into the file. She stared at the old man. "This is why I'm here, isn't it?"

"Yes," he said, not bothering to cover his true intentions. "This child is my legacy. Even if his parents have more children, none of them will be my Petr. I've spent many years hiding the existence of my family but have recently connected with them. Little Petr has given me more joy than I thought possible in the past three years. I can't watch him die in a hospital bed."

She thought about what she would say next. She had to step carefully with this man, or she might end up in the same position she'd been in two years ago, a woman with a gun to her head and nowhere to run. She suspected the doctor who had botched the boy's surgery was no longer among the living.

"I can't help you." She saw the thunderclouds gathering

on his face and suspected she was about to meet the real Ivan
Siberia. She was quick to add, "As you must know, I'm specialized in neurology and a repair surgery this delicate will
require a top cardiologist. I may not be able to help you, but I
know someone who can."

Ivan released a breath and relaxed back into his chair.
"Thank you."

"I can give you his name under two conditions." She
ignored his sharpening gaze. "You will not threaten or harm
this doctor, no matter the outcome of the surgery. Your great-
grandson has a major surgery ahead of him and he's very
fragile."

Ivan nodded. "Of course. I am not a monster. I wouldn't
bring harm to a person who is trying to help heal my grandson. What is your second condition?"

Shaun chewed her lip, trying to think fast. "You pay him
two million dollars for the consultation and another five if he
agrees to the surgery." Was seven million dollars too much?
Would he laugh at her and then torture her for the name of
the doctor?

"Done." Ivan's answer was so quick she rather thought she
should have asked for more. As if reading her thoughts, he
added, "I will pay any amount if someone gives me the gift of
my great-grandson's life before I leave this earth."

Shaun smiled. "His name is Dr. Sebastian Ngammi, he
lives in South Africa. I met him at a refugee camp in Mozam-
bique. If you give him my name, I'm sure he'll be happy to
help if he can. If your people could give me my phone, I can
write his information down for you."

Ivan made a call and five minutes later, Shaun's phone was
returned to her. She was relieved the battery had enough of a
charge that she could access her contacts. She wrote the
information inside the file, closed it and placed it on the
coffee table.

"Is that all, or was there something else you wished to discuss? I should get back to Jozef."

"Of course." Ivan pushed himself slowly and painfully to his feet. It was hard for Shaun not to help, but she suspected he wouldn't appreciate her acknowledgment of his weakness.

He used his cane to walk her to the door, taking her hand in a light grip and squeezing it in his shaky hand. He didn't immediately let go.

"There was one more thing I wanted to ask you." His calculating look sent a shiver down her back. "I know you have been researching methods of repairing a damaged larynx. You've gone so far as to research top surgeons in the field of voice recovery, yet you haven't taken this information to Mr. Koba. Why is that?"

Shaun swallowed hard and gently extracted her hand from Ivan's. She thought about how to answer him. She didn't think he gave a shit about Jozef's lack of voice. No, he was telling her exactly how invasive the Bratva were. They were keeping tabs on her laptop at work. That wasn't the scariest part, though. The only way the Bratva could know that she hadn't talked to Jozef about fixing his voice, was to have eyes and ears on everything, every aspect of their lives, including the bedroom.

Still, she had to know. "How do you know I haven't talked to him?"

Ivan gave her a tight-lipped smile that told her to tread carefully. "I know."

She nodded and answered the question in the spirit of complete honesty. "Jozef uses his lack of voice to his advantage. It was never a disability to him, and I'm convinced if he could speak, he would lose an important part of who he is."

"And you feel you should make this choice for him?"

Shaun could feel her face heating. Another secret. But this one was different. After finishing her research, Shaun had concluded that Jozef could have done the same digging if he'd wanted. It was telling that he'd never made moves to have his voice box repaired. Shaun didn't want him to ever think she saw him as less than he was because he communicated differently.

Yes, a secret, but not one that would damage Jozef's trust in her. One that would protect his feelings.

Ivan studied her face and finally, when it was clear she wouldn't respond, he said, "Perhaps you will fit in better among the Bratva than I originally thought. You enjoy playing god, don't you? Good day, Mrs. Koba. My regards to your husband."

CHAPTER FORTY-THREE

Fatima giggled at Shaun's description of a drunk Jozef.

"He must've been a bear the next morning," Fatima mused. "It seems so out of character for him to overindulge."

Shaun laughed and sipped the rich burgundy liquid from her wine glass. "He was certainly growling like a bear. It took a lot of convincing before he would let me take care of him, but I finally got some painkillers and toast into him and he turned back into a human. Later, he told me he rarely drank that much and didn't plan on ever doing it again."

"Famous last words."

"Yes," Shaun agreed. "Though Jozef is usually pretty responsible. I think it was the excitement of meeting with the other Vor for the first time. I wonder if the other wives discovered drunk husbands in their rooms that night?"

Shaun was filling her mother in on the details of her trip to Russia with Jozef. The five days spent at the palace were indeed the vacation Jozef had suggested they would be. Except for evening meals and one more meeting for Jozef, they were left alone to occupy themselves. Shaun rode a horse for the first time in her life and discovered she much preferred looking at them than riding on them.

She and Jozef made a trip into the town to shop for souvenirs, meeting with Cooper and Ayaan and taking in the local sites. Truly, Shaun had enjoyed her time in Russia far more than she thought she would.

She hadn't seen Ivan again after their meeting, but the shadow of their conversation never quite left her until she and Jozef were in the air on their private jet and on their way back home. She understood why Ivan Siberia was once known as the fiercest mobster in Russia. Even at his current age, he still held sway over the rest of the Bratva.

Shaun was sitting at the stool in her mother's kitchen enjoying the sights and smells of one of her favourite dishes. Shaun's father had also loved bademjan, an eggplant and tomato stew.

Fatima loved to cook. She'd often told Shaun that it was how Persian mothers showed their love, by stuffing their children full and sending them to doctor school. Shaun had risen to the occasion on both counts. She loved her mother's cooking and she'd become a surgeon.

"Tell me," Fatima said in the tone of voice that suggested Shaun was about to hear something she wouldn't like. "When will I see my grandchildren? I've been waiting for months and still I don't detect a bump or a glow."

Shaun winced and took a long drink of her wine before replying. "The glow is a myth. Most women sweat more because they produce heat from carrying the extra weight. The sweat can bead on the forehead, causing a glow."

"Don't change the subject," Fatima said sharply.

"I'm sorry, mom. It's just not something I really want to talk about."

Fatima must have caught the wistful note in Shaun's voice

because she turned from the stove and looked at her daughter carefully.

"Is everything okay?"

Tears formed in Shaun's eyes and she almost started sobbing. It was a simple question, but she couldn't answer it because she knew if she opened her mouth, a wail would come out.

Fatima saw her distress and rushed around the island, wrapping her arms around her daughter. "Tell me what's going on."

Shaun twisted on the stool, hugging her mother back. The tears began falling despite her effort to hold them back.

"Come on, let's sit on the couch where we can be comfortable."

Fatima held Shaun's hand as they sat, stroking her arm gently.

"I just…" a sob escaped, and Shaun swiped impatiently at her tears. "I'm a world-renowned surgeon! I can fix tumours that are supposed to be inoperable. I save lives. I travel to impossible places and do impossible things, but I can't have a baby!"

It was a jumble of words that probably didn't make much sense, but Fatima seemed to get the gist. "How do you know you can't have a baby?" she asked softly.

"Because we've never used birth control and we have plenty of… " Shaun drifted off, pressing her fingers under her eyelids. "We should've gotten pregnant by now." Again, she paused, then added, "I didn't even know I wanted kids. My career has always been so important, I didn't want to think about taking time off for babies."

"And now that you're married and have the income to support a child while working, it feels like a real possibility."

"Yes," Shaun said, misery lacing her words. "I'm almost 36. What if I've waited too long?"

Fatima sighed and took Shaun's hand, squeezing it. "You're the doctor, you tell me."

Shaun stared at her mother, then wiped away the tears and tried to get her brain to work. "I suppose there are plenty of women having babies later in life now, in their late thirties and forties. With health care and medicine where it's at, women can have babies later and still carry to term." Shaun shook her head. "But that doesn't explain why I can't get pregnant."

"How do you know you can't get pregnant?" Fatima asked, her voice taking on a scolding edge. "You haven't been trying for very long and you've had some traumatic years. Your body might not want you to get pregnant as long as you're in fight-or-flight mode. Have you seen a gynecologist or a fertility specialist?"

Shaun nodded. "We're waiting for results."

"Then you're worrying about nothing, because there's nothing you can do until you know."

Shaun opened her mouth, then closed it. Her mother was right, but the lack of pregnancy wasn't all there was to it.

"It feels wrong to deliberately bring a child into the Bratva, mom." Shaun glanced over her shoulder at the door. Jozef was downstairs with his men. He'd promised to come up for dinner. "My husband is a Vor. His life will always be in danger. If he has a child, that child's life will also be in danger. I can't help but wonder... maybe this is fate's way of preventing us from making a huge mistake and bringing a child into our messy lives."

"Nonsense," Fatima snapped as soon as the words had left Shaun's mouth. "Regardless of how you have a child, deliberate or not, you're still taking responsibility for it. You chose this life, now you need to embrace it."

Fatima pushed herself up off the couch and headed for the kitchen, patting Shaun's head along the way. She returned, handing Shaun her wineglass, then went back to the stove to stir the stew and start the jasmine rice.

Shaun sat cross-legged on the couch, sipped her wine and thought about what her mother had said to her.

Fatima was right. It was time to stop resisting the life she had finally accepted as hers. She needed to take the next step and embrace it. She could never condone the violence, but she accepted that it was part of being with Jozef.

If there was one thing she'd learned over the past few years, it was that life was messy. There were no simple answers. She could hate aspects of Jozef's profession, but she couldn't hate the man. In fact, she loved him beyond reason, and she wanted to have a baby. His baby.

She looked at her mother.

"Come to a decision?" Fatima asked, filling a pot with water.

"I'm going to get in touch with the gynecologist tomorrow, see if she has anything yet."

They continued to talk until supper time. Shaun described the rest of her trip to Russia and listened while Fatima filled Shaun in on Saskia's studies. Saskia was spending more and more time with Fatima. Shaun suspected her mother was becoming a surrogate for Saskia's parents. It was a sad thought, but hopefully Saskia might finally get what she needed from a parental figure.

Jozef knocked once before letting himself into the apartment. He beelined for Fatima, his nose twitching in anticipation.

Something smells amazing. My mother-in-law is the best cook I know.

He bent to kiss her cheek.

"Flatterer." Fatima waved him away, but a smile stretched her lips. "Go sit with your wife. Supper will be ready soon."

Jozef settled onto the couch next to Shaun, leaning over

to press a lingering kiss to her lips, while pulling her wineglass away.

He took a long sip before returning the glass to her and settling back against the couch cushions.

Shaun couldn't take her eyes off him. Her husband. The man she would spend the rest of her life with. He was breathtakingly beautiful in a hard, ruthless sort of way. She was becoming used to the deadly air about him. He would never hurt her. She was inside his bubble, safe at his side.

His eyes had drifted shut and his breathing slowed. His long dark eyelashes cast shadows over his cheeks, giving him an innocent look while his starkly painted tattoos peeked from beneath the collar of his shirt.

Though he had full command of the Czech Republic underworld, it was a full-time job. He didn't get enough sleep and was often called away in the night to put out a fire.

"Supper," Fatima called to them.

They helped her carry the dishes and food to the table, then sat together.

Jozef tapped the table and waved his hand across the spread of dishes. *Thank you for inviting us here to share your supper. These meals are some of my favourite. I will treasure them as I treasure you.*

Fatima blushed.

"You are a flatterer," Shaun laughed.

You're just jealous I'm not flattering you.

He dished himself up a heaping plate while Shaun and Fatima laughed.

CHAPTER FORTY-FOUR

Nikolay had a bad feeling. He'd had it for months, but when no one accused him of betraying Jozef, he'd shoved the feeling aside. They didn't know. He was safe.

Then why did he feel like the sword of Damocles was hanging over his head, awaiting the right moment to drop?

"Saskia."

He'd been standing in the shadows outside her suite, waiting for her to appear. She was coming down the hall toward him, her blue headphones wrapped around her neck, her wild brown hair a messy halo around her head. She wore tight ripped jeans, a black hoodie and running shoes. It hit him that she was really quite beautiful in her own way.

He'd never found her particularly attractive when they'd dated. She was too wild and headstrong, and he preferred his women compliant. Submissive. Not words one could use in association with Saskia Koba.

Yet, in this moment, with the light of the sun behind her, she looked ethereal. He felt a moment of loss, but quickly shook it away. His survival might depend on what he said. If he married Saskia, which was his plan, then he could insinuate himself in the family once more.

He thought he'd gotten away with Halil's murder, but gradually over the past few months he'd come to suspect that something wasn't right. Jozef had been coming up with excuses not to send him on missions with the other men. At first, the excuses sounded legitimate, and Nikolay hadn't worried.

Jozef had appealed to Nikolay's vanity, and like an idiot, he'd fallen for it. Jozef had told him that as a Koba heir, he was to be protected. He'd been flattered and allowed a temporary replacement on the team without complaint. But the more he thought about it, the more he realized Jozef's reason for not sending him on missions was bullshit.

Jozef had always been Krystoff's heir, yet he'd done the most dangerous work out of all of them. No one had ever used Nikolay's distant familial connection as a reason to keep him safe.

Gradually, over the past months, Nikolay was forced to conclude that since the night of the club attack, he'd been given fewer and fewer responsibilities. He was no longer privy to important information, and he was kept out of team meetings.

What he didn't understand was, if they knew about his involvement with Halil's death, why hadn't they already come after him? If they knew he was the betrayer, then he should be dead. Shouldn't he?

Saskia did what she did every time she saw him on the estate. She ignored him. She turned her back on him and dug her keys from her purse, while pretending he wasn't standing three feet away from her. It brought his predator to the surface.

He wanted her more than ever. Weird, considering she'd

always been a means to an end. Then again, she'd done most of the chasing. While not sexually experienced before meeting him, she was sexually assertive. She knew what she wanted, and she knew how to ask for it. He didn't like that in a woman. Now that she seemed indifferent to him, he wanted to chase her.

"Don't ignore me, kitten." He deliberately used his pet name for her, knowing he would get a response.

She turned her head to stare at him, fire in her eyes and a sneering twist to her lips. "Kitten?"

He sidled closer, reaching out to tuck a strand of hair behind her ear. "Yeah, I used to call you kitten, right? You act like a kitten. You have claws, but you're really sweet and cuddly."

He expected a response, was even goading her into one. He wanted to get physical, because once he got his hands on her, he could seduce her. She wouldn't be able to resist.

She growled, knocked his arm away and tried to bring her knee up between his legs. He wasn't expecting her to go for the boys, but he wasn't an elite team member for nothing. He easily knocked her leg aside.

He gripped her by the neck and swung her around. He knew exactly where each camera was in the corridor and where they were pointed. He dragged her into a blind spot before slamming her into a wall and knocking the breath from her.

Pleasure sizzled through his veins.

It had been a long time since he'd gotten to play rough, and he'd always wanted to try with this mouthy bitch. It was an added rush that he was doing it under the nose of her beloved cousin. Saskia wouldn't say a word. She was stubborn and prideful. She would never ask someone else to fight her battles.

Nikolay bent his knees, bringing himself to her eye level

and pinning her against the wall with his body. He pressed his erection against her and brushed his mouth against hers.

She turned her head to the side and glared blankly down the hall.

"You know you still have feelings, baby."

"Fuck you and your babies and kittens," she spat.

He bit her lip, hard enough to draw blood.

She gasped and he thrust his tongue into her mouth. He expected her negative reaction and gripped her jaw to stop her from biting him.

"Let her go, asshole."

Nikolay stopped kissing Saskia. He turned his head and found himself looking down the barrel of a gun. He lifted his gaze to meet the jewel bright stare of Ayaan.

"Get lost, bitch," he snapped.

She shoved the gun hard into the back of his head. "Is that any way to talk to your replacement?"

"You're Halil's replacement, not mine." Nikolay had come to hate this woman over the past several months. She'd taken every opportunity to get under his skin while they trained. Now he knew why. She and Saskia had become friends. He should've known. Bitches stuck together.

"Then why am I always being given your place on the team?" Ayaan smiled coldly at him.

Nikolay let Saskia go and reached for his gun, intent on taking the African bitch down a few pegs, but his holster was empty. When he looked down, he discovered the barrel of his own gun pressed against his stomach.

"A little slow on the draw, *kitten*," Saskia said sweetly, sliding along the wall and stepping away from him.

Both women held guns on him.

Helpless rage rushed through him and he nearly did something stupid that would've definitely gotten him shot.

"Give me the gun," he said through gritted teeth, staring hard at his former girlfriend.

She removed the clip, then the bullets from the clip. She threw the handful of bullets down the hall in one direction and the gun in the other. She pocketed the clip. "Go fetch."

Saskia bent to pick up the key she'd dropped on the floor when Nikolay had surprised her. Ayaan wrapped an arm around Saskia as she straightened. Together they backed away from him. Saskia turned to unlock her apartment door while Ayaan held her gun on him. Together they entered the suite and slammed the door shut. He heard the locks engaging on the other side.

If he'd had a working gun, he would have emptied the entire thing through the door.

He stalked down the hall toward his gun, bending to pick it up before continuing on. He didn't bother going after the bullets, without a clip they were useless.

He stood in the middle of the hall, in full view of the cameras.

It was time to go.

Not just away from Saskia or the mansion, but away from Prague. Maybe even out of the country, if he could manage it.

He rushed out the back door and strode toward the barracks where he'd parked his car. No one stopped him, no one said anything to him. They'd become used to his dark moods since Halil's death. No one would think it was suspicious if he left. They would assume he was doing something for Jozef or Havel.

He unlocked his car, climbed inside and drove around the estate toward the front gates. He didn't breathe easy again until he was on the highway.

Something was going on with the Koba family, and he wasn't going to wait around to find out what it was.

He drove straight home and took the stairs to his apartment two at a time. Unlocking his door, he immediately went to his bedroom.

He pulled his duffel bag from a loose panel in the top of his closet. It already contained guns, cash and passports. His go bag. He added several T-shirts, a few jeans, socks and underwear. He could go shopping when he was safely ensconced in his Argentinian safe house.

He reached for the zip on his bag, but a sound had him turning around.

His shocked exclamation rang through the apartment.

He was seeing a ghost.

"Nikolay."

The man standing in the doorway of his bedroom was dead.

Nikolay knew, because he'd put a bullet in his skull.

"H... Halil?"

Halil stepped from the shadowy doorway, allowing the harsh bedroom light to fall on him. He was thinner, lankier, haggard, as though he'd lost most of his muscle tone. His eyes were brittle and hard; the carefree sparkle that used to be there was gone.

Nikolay slid his hand toward his bag where his gun was resting.

Halil lifted his arm, the metal of his gun glinting in the soft light.

Nikolay might still have gone for his own gun, but two men followed Halil into the room, each armed and ready to shoot. Jozef stood on one side of Halil while Cooper took the other side.

Nikolay fucking hated Cooper. He should have shot him when he had the chance. He'd hesitated because he hadn't wanted to shoot the other man in the back, which would have raised suspicions.

It was looking like his careful planning had been for nothing. He hadn't gotten away with anything. Instead, these men had played him for over six months, like he was the mouse to their cat trio.

"What took you so long?" Nikolay tried to sound brave.

His mind was racing. He wasn't going to get out of this, not with three of the most experienced combat mercenaries he knew pointing weapons at him. Nikolay was good too. He wouldn't have been part of Jozef's team if he wasn't, but he couldn't take on these three by himself. He'd needed Krystoff and his army at his back.

"Knew from the start you were shady as shit," Cooper drawled. "You were the only one who went down that hallway after I set the explosives. Yet, somehow, the explosives didn't go off and Koba and his men got inside the building. It had to be you."

"My question still stands. What took you so long?" Nikolay snarled, narrowing his eyes at Cooper. Fucking smug American.

"Gunshot wounds take time to heal." This was from Halil. His voice was level, resigned, no censure. "I was in a medically induced coma for three weeks after the shooting, then it took months to relearn how to function again."

Nikolay swung his gaze back to Halil. Regret rose. It always did. Shooting his best friend was the one thing he regretted in his life of crime.

"I'm sorry."

Halil's lip lifted in a sneer, giving away emotion for the first time. "Words, Nikolay. They mean about as much as your honour."

Nikolay flinched, but straightened his spine. If he was going to die, then he was going to say his piece. He fixed a glare on Jozef.

"It should have been me. I wanted the mantle of leadership, but I was passed over for the cripple. The man without a voice who everyone treats with kid gloves because he has a good party trick. Well, fuck you and your sign language. If I'd been in charge, the Koba organization would've been on top of the world years ago. Krystoff would have been King of the Bratva, and I would have been his loyal prince. Instead, you're left with the ashes of a great man and a back seat to the Bratva."

Is that what you think? Jozef signed, gun still in hand. It should have looked awkward, but it didn't. The move was menacing.

Nikolay lifted his chin and stared at the three men. "What are you going to do?"

"We're going for a walk," Halil told him. "Just you and me."

Hope lit a small fire in Nikolay's chest. If it was just him and Halil, maybe he could talk to the younger man or overpower him. He looked as though he'd lost muscle tone in his recovery. He wouldn't be a match for Nikolay's bulk.

Silence reigned heavily in the room.

"Let's go."

Halil gestured toward the door.

The drive wasn't long. They took Nikolay to the same cemetery that housed the Koba crypt.

"You gonna be okay alone with him?" Cooper asked, looking back at Halil who sat with Nikolay in the back seat of the SUV. Jozef had driven.

Halil nodded. "Yes, this is what I want."

"Have fun then." Cooper turned forward in his seat.

Halil led Nikolay through the cemetery. It was spring and the flowers were blooming. The graveyard smelled sweet, like freshly cut grass and incense. It was strangely calming as they walked.

"I really am sorry," Nikolay said, losing his belligerence in the face of his imminent death.

Halil nodded, the glow of streetlamps illuminating him. "I know. You'd have to be an unfeeling monster to put a bullet in your best friend and not regret it. You may be a lot of things, but I never pegged you for a monster."

Relief flooded Nikolay. "Do you forgive me?"

Halil didn't answer, he pointed.

Nikolay squinted in the dim lighting. They were at the back of the cemetery where the oldest graves were. He could make out a mound of fresh soil. As they got closer, he saw an open grave.

"Inside." Halil waved his gun at the grave.

Nikolay stopped and stared into the darkness beyond the cemetery. He had three choices. He could get in the grave. He could refuse. Or he could run. All options would end in his death. Halil was an excellent shot.

If this was it, he wasn't going to fuck up his own death like he'd fucked up everything else.

He crouched down and sat on the edge of the grave before pushing himself inside. Something crunched under his booted feet. Rotten wood and bones, he suspected. They'd excavated an old grave. They would kill him and cover his body with the soil. They'd pay the cemetery caretaker to look the other way until grass grew over the grave and it looked the same as every other.

"Will you tell my mother?" Nikolay asked.

"No." Halil's voice held no inflection. "You never gave a shit about her. As far as she knows, you're already dead."

It was true, but now that he'd reached the end of his life, he felt the desire to be close to his mother, even if it meant she learned about his death, maybe mourned a little.

"Please."

"Goodbye, Niko."

The bullets were muffled by a silencer, but they seemed to roar with fire and brimstone as they struck his body. One, two, three, four, maybe more. He lost count as he collapsed into the grave. None in the head. No quick merciful death.

He'd turned his best friend into a cruel man.

While he lay bleeding out, Halil stood sentinel, silently watching over Nikolay as the minutes passed. When his dying breath rattled in a chest full of blood, he watched as the man who'd once been a brother to him disappeared into the shadows.

CHAPTER FORTY-FIVE

Jozef didn't know what to do. It was a strange sensation for him. He always knew what to do, but this time he was out of his element. He crouched next to Shaun's chair, holding her hands in his as she sobbed. He hated every tear that crawled down her face.

He was usually the one to cause her tears, but this time, it wasn't him. It was the doctor who'd disappeared discreetly from the room.

They were in the fertility clinic where Shaun had gotten her referral. They'd been called to the clinic for the results of their first round of testing.

Her tears dripped onto his hands where they were clasping hers. He bowed his own head, blinking back his own tears. Her heart was breaking, and he couldn't do anything about it. He couldn't kill the thing without hurting the woman he loved more than anyone or anything in the world.

He couldn't kill PCOS. Polycystic ovary syndrome.

Shaun was infertile and the diagnosis was destroying her. He would have to take good care of her. While she'd broken down, the doctor had discussed the complications of Shaun's condition. She could develop diabetes or heart problems. He wanted to make damn sure she would be okay in the long run.

The doctor had recommended they think about a hysterectomy. Jozef knew Shaun wasn't ready for that so he wouldn't mention it. Not until he'd healed her heart from this traumatic news.

He gently pulled his hands from hers and reached up to cup her face, soaking his hands in her tears.

She blinked rapidly so she could see him.

He dropped his hands so he could sign, *I will give you the world to make up for this hurt.*

"I don't want the world," she whispered. "Just you... and a baby."

I know, my love, and I am sorrier than you can know. If I could make you pregnant, I would. Remember our first day together?

"When you took me from the hospital?"

Yes, that day, he signed. *I took you because I wanted you. I kept you alive because I felt our connection, and I kept you with me because I could no longer imagine a life without you. Two years later and I still feel that way. Stronger even. You have my heart.*

He took her hand and pressed it against his chest, to his beating heart. He signed over top of her hand. *We will get through this together.*

She smiled even as she sobbed. She leaned forward, falling off the chair into his lap and wrapped her arms around his neck. "I only want you."

He rocked her against his body, feeling every part of her. He ached over the news of her diagnosis. He'd never held a baby in his life, didn't know what he was missing. But he would always want what Shaun wanted. She was the queen to his servant, the goddess to his slave, the sun to his darkness. She was everything to him.

"Please take me home."

He lifted her in his arms, picking her purse up from the floor where she'd dropped it.

He walked out of the exam room and out of the clinic with her held securely in his arms. Havel and Cooper walked with them outside the clinic, silently providing backup while Jozef and Shaun mourned something that would never be.

CHAPTER FORTY-SIX

"Krystoff..."

He moved closer to the bed.

Dasha squinted against the harsh glaring light, but he still looked like nothing more than a shadow, frustratingly insubstantial. She knew it was him, though. She knew his shape, his scent, his touch...

She'd poisoned him. More than once. She hadn't regretted it at the time, but she regretted it now. She worshipped him. She shouldn't have manipulated his love.

Soon she would be with him again, and she would have to explain her actions and hope he could forgive her.

Dasha had poisoned her first victim when she was five years old.

Miss Anya.

She'd hated her nursemaid. The woman was sour, dour, and no fun at all. She insisted Dasha wear dresses and always have her hair brushed. She was never allowed out if the weather was bad, and she was always made to complete her studies. If she didn't learn her letters, then she would get a sharp smack across the knuckles.

Dasha had overheard her mother talking about poisoning the pests that sometimes got into the horse barn. She'd snuck into the barn that night, found the bag with the skull and crossbones, and scooped some into her nursemaid's morning coffee.

Miss Anya hit the floor within minutes of drinking her tea, convulsing, vomiting, foaming. She died almost instantly. Too soon. Dasha had wanted the woman to suffer. It was Dasha's first lesson in poisoning. Too much would bring suspicion.

Her parents had suspected Dasha but had thought it was an accident. They'd quietly gotten rid of the body and watched their daughter more carefully.

Dasha decided that she needed to practice so she could get the reaction she wanted. She practiced on everyone. Her tutors, maids, the house staff, the stable staff. Even her parents.

This time, she was more careful. She used smaller amounts, tried different poisons. As she got older and learned how to read, she researched. She perfected her skills and used them to her advantage. If she didn't feel like riding, she poisoned the stable master. Just enough that he would be forced to spend the day in bed.

She realized at a young age that she was very smart, but she also suspected something was wrong with her. She had no qualms about maiming or murdering the people closest to her. Her only desire was for more. More of everything. She wanted more shoes, more outfits, purses, horses, money, prestige, attention. And she didn't care how she got it.

The second person she actively tried to kill was her sister. She'd planned the event, knew exactly how it would go. What she hadn't realized was that Vasha had watched her over the years. As soon as Vasha started feeling ill, she'd told their father and was rushed to the hospital where she was saved.

Dasha had been removed from the house and forced to go to boarding school. Later, she was married to the powerful mobster who'd courted her. She could still remember her parents' relief when she was no longer their problem.

Her proclivities continued.

She started perfecting the chemistry of her poisonings. She knew exactly what dose to give her husband when she didn't want him to leave for business meetings. She poisoned her daughters when she wanted them to stay home with her and cuddle in bed. She poisoned her lovers when she was finished with them, killing them.

Dasha lay curled on her side in her prison cell, her arms wrapped around a stomach that heaved with wave after wave of nausea and pain.

"I'm dying," she whispered to Krystoff.

He nodded, but didn't come closer.

She felt hot all over, but she was shivering too. The pain was unbelievable. Her body ached from head to toe, but especially her stomach and bowels.

She had all the symptoms she'd seen in others. Of course, her symptoms, especially in the early stages, could have mimicked the flu, but Dasha knew better. The cramping sealed her diagnosis.

Jozef was serving up a dish of poetic justice, and she had to admire him for the effort.

For five long days of slow poisoning, she forced herself to go through the motions of living. She got up with the other inmates, forced herself to eat, drink, walk around the yard, and sleep. She wanted to sleep so badly that by the time she was allowed in her cell, she collapsed on her bed, cradling her stomach. Occasionally she would have to rush to the toilet, vomit and diarrhea stinking up her small cell.

Now, she was too weak to pretend.

Her thoughts were becoming fragmented. She couldn't

concentrate. Could only lay still until she was forced to rise and join her fellow inmates in their daily ritual.

Yesterday... maybe... a female guard had stuck her head in and asked Dasha, her voice laced with concern, if she needed medical attention. Dasha had refused and had gone to bed. She couldn't be sure what Jozef's endgame was, but she suspected it wouldn't be poison. This was the first step in a larger plan for her, all designed to torture before death.

Even her placement in the Czech women's prison system was unusual. She'd been apprehended by Interpol. She should have been extradited to the country where they would lay charges against her. She wasn't sure where they'd intended for her to go, but she knew Jozef had pulled strings to keep her close.

She'd failed in her mission to take out the doctor, but she was at peace with it. Jozef had simply been better, and as his adoptive mother, she was proud of his cunning. She wished better for him than the spineless woman he'd attached himself to, but Dasha couldn't do anything about that now. She had no doubt she would soon join Krystoff in the family crypt.

She frowned at the wall opposite of where she was lying on her cot. She hoped Jozef would inter her ashes alongside her husband's urn. Perhaps she should write him a letter? Beg him to allow her final wishes. She didn't think he was spiteful enough to deny her a simple death wish.

She didn't know for sure, though. Shaun had turned him into a beast. He was as vicious as ever, but his protective instincts had focused on one person, his hostage. The woman who should've died but didn't. So many times, she should've died.

Jozef should've put a bullet in her the first day he met her. Then later, Krystoff should have rectified the situation, killed the girl himself. Instead, he'd allowed Jozef to keep her, allowed his attachment to grow. Dasha had paid the members of her hometown mafia, the Kiev boys, to come take care of the situation. Jozef had taken care of them instead, murdering them all in the dark alley where they'd grabbed Shaun. Dasha had paid Giselle to cause a scene at the club, hoping to drive Shaun from the building. Her plan had worked until Jozef caught up with his precious woman. Dasha had been forced to resort to her old fallback of poison. Again, the girl had escaped. She always escaped.

Maybe it was their fate to end this way. Shaun had replaced Dasha in the mansion and Jozef had replaced Krystoff. The next generation of Koba.

Dasha let out a scream of pain as her guts twisted, causing her to seize in agony. She clutched her stomach and turned her face into the pillow. It wouldn't be long now until the prison guards would be forced to do something. Once they transferred her, she would be dead.

"Stay with me, Krysto..."

CHAPTER FORTY-SEVEN

Your mother is here, Jozef signed, crouching next to the bed.

Shaun looked at him, tears bright in her eyes. She hadn't stopped crying in almost two days. She tried to tell herself to snap out of it, to stop feeling sorry for herself. But she couldn't. Of everything that had happened to her in the past few years, this felt the worst. It was the final straw. She couldn't take anymore.

"I don't want to see her."

Jozef frowned, thunderclouds growing in his eyes.

You turned her away yesterday, which we allowed since you need time to heal, but you will not turn her away today. You need your mother, and you will see her.

He was the epitome of patience when it came to Shaun and her feelings, but he wasn't going to allow Shaun to push her mother away. She could already see it on his face. He thought she needed her mother, and he wouldn't take no for an answer.

She pushed herself up on the bed, feeling dizzy and nauseous. She hadn't left the bed since coming home from the fertility clinic. She'd refused to eat or... she lifted her T-shirt and sniffed... shower.

Jozef watched her, his deep blue eyes a combination of impatience and concern. She got it. He wanted to make things better for her, but he couldn't fix this.

She knew she was being selfish. He was just as involved in her prognosis as she was. He must have feelings about being a father... yet she couldn't bring herself to ask. Not yet. She didn't think she could handle his grief as well as her own.

Despite that, it was time to get out of bed and start living again.

"I'll take a shower and meet her in the breakfast room." Shaun loved that room. At this time of day, it would be filled with sunlight and would have a clear view of the back of the estate.

Jozef took her hands and helped her to her feet, holding her steady as a wave of dizziness hit her.

"I'm okay," she whispered, then stepped against him, burying her face in his chest and wrapping her arms around his waist. "I'm sorry I've been so miserable."

He gave her a long, hard hug that made her feel a hundred times better, then took her face in his hands and tipped it up. He shook his head and kissed her before taking her hand and leading her into the washroom.

He turned the shower on for her, adjusting the temperature the way she liked it, hot enough to burn a few layers of skin off. Turning back to her, he hooked his fingers in the hem of her T-shirt and lifted it.

She raised her arms as he pulled it over her head. She blushed in embarrassment as her scent hit her. Two days in bed did not a bed of roses make. He slid her sweatpants and underwear down her legs, using a hand on each calf to help her lift her feet.

He was babying her, and she loved it. She needed it.

There was no sexual energy coming from him, as there usually was when she got naked in front of him. Neither did his actions feel clinical. They felt natural, like a husband caring for his distraught wife.

Tears formed in her eyes, but this time they weren't tears of pain. They were tears of joy. This was all she needed; all she'd ever needed. The type of unconditional love a good man could provide.

They were raised into completely different families, and had Jozef not marked her that fateful day, they likely would never have met. Their lives would have taken different directions. Now that she saw what life could be with Jozef, she wasn't willing to give it up. She would do whatever it took to protect him and their life together and knew that he would do the same.

She took a long shower, shaving her legs and armpits, and washing her hair. She felt a million times better as she stepped out of the streaming water and into the towel Jozef held open for her.

He patted her dry and then pushed her from the washroom, gently tapping her bare ass as she went.

She pulled a summery dress from the closet and wedge sandals. She added a blue leather jacket. She looked in the mirror and used her fingers to fluff her hair so it would dry in a halo instead of flat against her head. She was ready to face her mother.

Jozef was standing behind her, watching.

She will make you feel better, he signed in the mirror. *I think she brought cookies, although they might be gone now. Some of the guys were sniffing around her, looking for treats. They're worse than F-I-T-Z-Y.*

She laughed and signed back, *I'm ready to feel better now.*

His next sign was slow and deliberate. He lifted his left hand and pointed his thumb and index finger in the shape of an L, then lifted his little finger, leaving middle and ring fingers down. He pointed his hand at her, then released the sign, crossed his arms over his chest and thumped his fist over his heart.

It was his special sign for her, the one he used at their wedding. His way of telling her he loved her in every way possible, beyond reason, beyond life into eternity.

She copied his sign, her eyes never leaving his in the mirror, then she turned around and walked into his open arms.

CHAPTER FORTY-EIGHT

Dasha woke with a start, the clicking of heels on the tiles of the hospital floor reminding her of muffled gunshots. She took several deep breaths, trying to calm her pounding heart. Slowly, painfully, she sat up, reaching for the water on her nightstand.

The process was made awkward by her other hand being cuffed to the bed. She'd been transferred the day before. She'd waited as long as she could manage before finally giving away her condition. She'd been in so much pain, the poison twisting her guts; the fever raging through her that she'd raved with hallucinations. Screamed obscenities at the prison staff as they strapped her to a gurney and moved her.

She took long sips of water, pulling it through the paper straw. It felt like heaven against a throat raw from days of vomiting. Her hand shook as she set the water down.

Collapsing against the pillows, she forced herself to stay awake, to keep alert. She was here for a reason. Someone had poisoned her. Not someone, Jozef. He'd gotten to one of the guards or an inmate and ordered them to slowly poison

Dasha over the course of days, to weaken her to where she would need to be transferred.

He was coming for her.

Jozef's justice.

Dasha's eyes fluttered shut and she knew it was a matter of minutes and she'd be out again. Fear and satisfaction warred within her. She knew what was coming and she was afraid. She didn't want to die. But she wouldn't run from it either. She'd made her bed, now she would lie in it. She was satisfied with the life she'd led, the decisions she'd made.

Did she have regrets?

Sure, she had plenty. She regretted never getting another shot at killing her sister. She regretted not finding a way to remove Shaun and keep her family together. She regretted not being able to see her daughters one more time before the end.

She regretted Jozef.

She should have done more for him.

He was the son who should have been hers.

Perhaps if she'd fully accepted him as hers, this day might not have come. She'd wanted to call him son, but she'd always hesitated. Perhaps it was his lack of voice, not his fault, but still a disfigurement. He was less than perfect. Or perhaps, it was because she hadn't given birth to him. She loved him, but not as if he was one of hers. She'd pretended, but the feelings were never there.

Then, maybe she didn't have what it took to be a mother. She'd never felt maternal toward her own children. Leeza was Vasiliy's and for that, she would never be perfect. She would always have his weaknesses and none of Krystoff's strengths. She was beautiful, more beautiful than Dasha, which had also strained their relationship.

Saskia... she was the full blood child of Krystoff and

Dasha. Yet, of the three children, she was the least perfect. And Dasha loved her best.

It hurt that she wouldn't see her youngest before she died. She wondered if Saskia would miss her. Just a little.

She wasn't sure how long she slept, but probably only a few hours. This time the tap of shoes was inside her room, rather than the hall.

She opened her eyes and rolled her head toward the doorway, blinking against the harsh glare of the fluorescent lights in the hallway. Other than the shadow walking steadily toward her bed, the hospital corridor was quiet. Had he paid the guard to look the other way? Or had he killed the woman?

Not Dasha's problem anymore.

"Jozef," she whispered.

He didn't answer.

He couldn't answer.

She'd done that to him.

"It was me, you know," she whispered, trying to make out his stark features in the dim light filtering from the hallway. She could make out some of the tattoos on his neck. Her eyes dropped to his hands; he wasn't holding his gun. He intended to let her talk before he killed her. "I stabbed you in the throat. Took your voice and your parents."

He stepped closer until she could see his face.

He signed, *confession?*

"I suppose I just want you to know. Weren't you ever curious?"

He didn't say anything.

"I paid some local guys to break in and kill them. I went too, I needed to see their bodies, make sure the job got done." His eyes gave nothing away. "It was mafia politics, nothing personal. They were in the way. Your father wanted to rule with your uncle. It was a matter of time before Gregor wanted more, threatened everything we'd built."

Everything they built, not you. You've been trying to bring the family down from the start. It was you who should have died that night, not them.

"Maybe," she said. "Your mother was certainly suspicious. She never really warmed up to me, never took any of the food I offered her unless we were eating from the same dish. She knew. But it didn't save her."

Now she saw a flash of fire in his eyes.

Satisfaction hit her like a drug. She was a cruel bitch. Even as she was dying, about to be finished, she wanted to hurt those around her. Even the ones she loved. She didn't know why she was wired this way, and now it didn't matter.

"I was going to kill you too," she admitted. "But I didn't have the heart. You looked too much like my Kristo. I'd already begun to love him then, and looking at you was like looking at our future. Perhaps, if I'd given birth to a boy, I might have taken you out along the way."

She shifted in the bed, uncomfortable.

"I didn't have a boy and you were the only son I've ever known."

You were no mother to me, he signed. *You were barely a mother to your own children.*

"You don't know what it takes to make a parent. Wait until you have children. You'll see. It's not always easy to overcome our own nature and love children the way we're told we should."

Whatever makes you feel better, but I would argue a sociopathic serial killer could never make a good parent.

She laughed, surprising herself. It felt weird to smile in her last few minutes of life.

"Touché."

She pushed herself up in the bed, her arms shaking. Jozef slid his hands under her armpits and helped her, gently laying her back against the pillows before releasing her. It was the cruelest thing he could have done, and tears sprang to her eyes. He hadn't touched her since Shaun's poisoning, yet here he was, touching her as though he cared.

"Do you love me, Jozef?"

Yes. He answered without hesitation. *I believed you loved me, too. You kept me close after my parents died, you protected me. You kept me with your girls. I hate you for what you've done to our family, but I still love you.*

"I love you, too," she admitted. When he shook his head, silently denying her words, she added, "I still have feelings. I may be a... what did you call me... a sociopathic serial killer, but I can still feel love. You were the son I always wanted and never had."

He stared down at her. His face was set in stony lines, but his eyes were brittle. They shone with unshed tears. Tears for her.

It moved her. She felt responding tears pool in her eyes and trickle down her face.

"Sit with me." She patted the bed next to her.

He sat and she reached for him. He took her hand, holding it up against his chest.

The ache in Dasha's throat grew.

She pictured him as a child. His serious little face, his sharp chin, his dark hair flopping in his eyes. He was a beautiful child and he'd turned into a beautiful man.

"I'm proud of you," she whispered. "You're everything I could have wanted in a son."

The words were meant to stab him in the heart, to make his decision to kill her just as painful for him as it was going to be for her. But they stabbed at her as well, cutting deep.

Perhaps if she'd fully let him into her heart when he was a child in desperate need of love, this moment could have been avoided. Then, perhaps not. He'd have eventually learned of her part in the death of his parents. Secrets had a way of coming into the light eventually.

Close your eyes, he signed and reached beneath his coat, pulling his gun from its holster.

He wasn't wearing gloves. This was personal. His hand, his kill. She looked at the tattoos on the back of his gun hand, the spiderweb. She was the spider, patiently waiting for each victim to come along. Now she would be the victim, caught by another predator.

He was the same as her, only he was better.

Her eyes drifted shut and she thought of Krystoff, finding comfort in his image. She imagined him wrapping his arms around her and whispering in her ear that he loved her no matter what, despite everything.

She felt the press of the gun against her chest, over her heart.

Then intense fire.

The pain was incredible, but brief.

She felt the muzzle against her forehead.

Then nothing.

CHAPTER FORTY-NINE

Saskia loved everything about school. She loved the books, she loved her laptop, she loved taking notes, she even loved exams. When Jozef deemed it safe enough for her to return to the University, she'd immediately registered for her winter classes. It took some cajoling to get into a few of them, given her late attendance, but she managed a full course load.

Saskia loved university and opted to spend more time on campus than off. She ate in the cafeteria, she studied all over the place, wherever she could find a sunny nook. She spent time in the library almost every day, soaking in the atmosphere.

It was the university that made her return to Prague bearable. The shining goal of finishing her linguistics degree.

As a child she had grown up with tutors, only attending classes with other students in her two years of boarding school. That had been different from the university. The students were similar age and background, and class sizes were limited to a handful of students.

Saskia found she loved learning in large lecture halls with

dozens of other students. It gave her a sense of competition and comradery. She would occasionally eat lunch with one of her new friends, usually people who took classes with her. She hadn't stretched her wings much in the friend direction. Her security detail wasn't easy to work with and they preferred she kept to herself, minimizing her exposure to potential risks.

Saskia was currently holed up at the back of the library on the third floor. She was sitting at a table in the corner, so she was surrounded by windows and light. She loved the feel of the sunshine falling across her shoulders and spilling onto her books as she studied.

It was June. She was taking summer classes to make up for missed time.

She wore her noise cancelling headphones and had Metallica's Fade to Black blasting. She learned better with music.

She was so absorbed in her book that, at first, she didn't notice the man striding through the stacks toward her, a predator zeroing in on his prey. It wasn't until a shadow fell across her books that she realized someone was standing next to her, too close.

Her heart picked up as she stared down at the shadow across her notebook while reaching for her gun with the other. It was tucked in the front flap of her backpack, which she kept zipped.

Damn it, she couldn't reach it. She must've kicked her backpack away.

Finally, she turned her head and looked up.

Her breath caught and her heart began hammering a painful tattoo in her chest. The most terrifying man she'd ever seen was standing over her, his inscrutable dark eyes on her face. His skin was as dark as his dark brown, almost black gaze. His hands were loose at his sides, each roughly the size of her head. He was huge, his body filled with the bulk of muscle. He wore a uniform. Khaki pants, with a khaki jacket. There were medals pinned to his chest.

She didn't know who he was, but she had no doubt he knew who she was. He was there for her and, if the air of deadly menace he exuded was correct, he was there to kill her.

The track she was listening to switched to Rituál, a song by a Czech metal band, Master's Hammer. The intense, heavy metal intro was enough to send her strange confrontation with the assassin into the next level. She dove for her backpack, quickly unzipping her bag and pulling her pistol from its holster.

As she turned in her seat to point the gun, the stranger dropped to one knee next to her chair. She stared at him, her breath coming out in a gasp that sounded explosive in her earphones. Even crouched, he was taller than she was.

He ignored the gun pointed at his heart. He studied her with an intensity that made her skin feel first cold, then hot all over. His gaze went from unreadable to interested. He liked what he saw. She could tell.

Her heart pounded for an entirely different reason as her body reacted viscerally to the massive stranger. She didn't know why. Her logical brain thought he was the most terrifying human being she'd ever met, and she would bet every silly doll in their original packages she owned that this man was connected with the mafia.

Which meant it wasn't a coincidence his running into her in the library. He knew she'd be here, and he deliberately sought her out.

Where were her guards? Dead?

Was she about to die?

He lifted a hand and touched her head, his fingers wrapping around her earphone.

She thought he was going to lift it away from her ear so he

could speak to her, but he didn't. He caressed it, as though he was caressing skin. And despite that he didn't actually touch her a sizzle of awareness ran through her.

He leaned forward and for a crazy moment she thought he was going to kiss her full on the lips. She tightened her finger on the trigger. He pressed his lips to her forehead.

Without a word, he stood and left, striding away from her and giving her a full view of his truly massive form. He had to be damn near seven feet tall. She'd never seen anyone like him in person.

Long after he'd disappeared around the book racks, she sat frozen, her gun hand still up, her finger still on the trigger. Slowly, she lowered her hand and flipped the safety back on.

"What the fuck was that?" she whispered, though her music was too loud for her to hear her own voice.

She shoved her gun back into her bag, packed up her laptop and ran through the stacks, determined to see the man again and to find out what the fuck had happened to her guards. She really hoped they weren't dead; she'd just broken them in.

Radik's heart was pounding. It was actually pounding.

It never beat faster than normal. He'd survived gun battles without flinching. Watched explosions take out strongholds without breaking a sweat. Yet, one small girl set his heart beating in a way he'd never experienced. Perhaps he was getting old. He should get it checked.

But he knew better. He was in perfect health.

It was her, Saskia Koba.

She'd caused his heart to speed up. She'd caused him to hesitate, to pull back. To change his plans.

He'd planned on taking the girl. Now, today, from the

library. He was going to take her out from under the nose of her cousin, the way Koba had stolen his sister.

But something had stopped him. Not something. Someone. Saskia. The strange little mobster girl who was studying to become a translator.

He wanted to take her. Badly. And that was what stopped him.

He was confused by his reaction. It was instant, and he didn't enjoy having feelings he didn't understand. He'd spent years eradicating his feelings as he was forced to commit unspeakable atrocities in the name of his country.

Then he realized why he couldn't take her. She was an innocent, and he hadn't been prepared for that. She'd pulled a gun on him, but she hadn't shot him. She'd stared at him as though seeing a monster, and he saw himself through her eyes.

He couldn't be the monster who destroyed her world. Not yet. He would come back for her. Give her time to grow up, to finish her education and reach for her dreams.

He would take her when she was ready for him.

As he passed his men in the hallway leading to the elevator bank, he jerked his head. They'd relieved Koba's men of their guns. Not their fault. They'd been ambushed. Hadn't time to react to men used to moving stealthily through the bush before they were surrounded.

Radik's men fell into step behind him, and the trio waited until the elevator dinged the arrival of the car that would take them to the ground floor. They got on and Radik turned just as Saskia came running around the corner, her shoes screeching as she turned on the spot and sprinted for the elevator.

He got a full view of her in person and, again, his heart stuttered in his chest.

She wore jeans that were torn at both knees, a baggy

black T-shirt under a short jean jacket and red high-top runners. Her chestnut brown hair was spiked on top and pinned back at the sides. Her ridiculously huge earphones were still on.

One of her bodyguards grabbed her as she tried to pass them and pressed her back against the wall, covering her with his body.

Radik nodded. If the man hadn't done that, he'd have gotten off the elevator and put a bullet in him. He was pleased the men were competent, if a little slow. He knew Koba would quickly whip them into shape.

The elevator doors began to close and Radik sought the small, compact woman struggling against her bodyguard. She froze as their eyes met, and he could tell her heart was beating as hard as his. The doors closed, blocking his view of her.

He would find her again when the time was right.

CHAPTER FIFTY

Jozef sat in the window of his hut, looking out at the incredible cerulean blue of the ocean beyond. When Shaun had found out that Jozef had never spent time near the ocean, except briefly when he was on mission, she'd insisted they choose an oceanside setting for their honeymoon.

It had been four months since Jozef had murdered his aunt, and he still thought about that moment. Her confessions, her reaction to his being there. He felt intense anger when he thought of her killing his parents and her attacks on Shaun, but time had given him a better perspective. She'd grown up in the mafia. She'd been highly intelligent and motivated. Like Jozef, like his uncle, like the best in the business.

Perhaps if she'd been born a man, given her own organization to play god with, she might have channeled her abilities into better use.

Her death made him think long and hard about himself. He wasn't much different. He killed too. She used death and destruction to manipulate while he used it to make money and further his goals.

It was through skill, force of will and chance that he'd made it onto the winning team, while she'd lost the game. The game was mafia, the prize was life, money and power. The loser died.

His gaze drifted from the ocean to the woman sprawled naked across the bed.

Shaun had kicked the covers off during the night, the hot Filipino night giving her skin a beautiful sheen. Her face was turned away from him so he could only see her mop of messy hair, her fragile neck, the delicious curve of her back, an ass that made his hands itch with the need to fill and squeeze, to long curvy legs. One was straight, while the other was bent.

She was his saving grace.

Her love for him made him want to be better, made him more thoughtful, more careful.

If she asked him to quit the Bratva tomorrow, he thought he might.

He would do almost anything for this woman. The weapons, the money, the power. None of it meant anything if he didn't have her. She was his prize in a lifetime of death and destruction.

Though he was certain she would prefer he quit being part of the mafia, he was also certain she understood the dangers involved. No one left the mafia. Not alive, anyway. If they wanted to leave, they would have to leave everything. Their families, their lives. They would have to go on the run, looking over their shoulders until the day the Bratva caught up with them.

So, instead of asking him to quit, Shaun adapted. And she did it beautifully. She did it by integrating herself into the organization as much as he was, while still keeping her hands clean.

She was the Bratva angel, the doctor who saved lives.

She'd saved the life of Ivan Siberia's great grandson by

referring him to a top cardiologist, giving the old man three more months with his pride and joy before dying in his bed at 99. Now, word had gotten out that Shaun could solve almost any medical problem and members of the Bratva were flying her all over the place.

She was doctor to the Bratva now.

At first, Jozef had been concerned. What happened if she couldn't fix someone? Would she be sacrificed? Jozef had stepped in, negotiating an ironclad contract with Ivan before he died, signed by both Alexei Ivanov and Yuri Antonvich. Shaun could choose her patients and she would be allowed safe passage no matter where she went, who she saw, or the outcome of the treatment. Jozef and his men would act as her bodyguards.

So far, she'd treated two Bratva wives, one very stubborn Bratva elder who suffered from sleep apnea and a child with a broken leg. Though Shaun was specialized as a neurologist, she always seemed to either know the treatment or know who could help. The gifts of thanks Shaun had been given were absurdly over the top. She'd been given a yacht, which she hadn't known what to do with. It was still docked near St. Petersburg.

She continued to work at the hospital in Prague, working closely with her doctor friend. The two women were updating the neurology department, using a generous donation from Jozef to the hospital, earmarked for neurology. She was busy, but she was happy, and her happiness made Jozef content.

He was quite busy himself, though Shaun would always be his priority. He'd filled out two teams of mercenaries and sent them on frequent missions. Havel was head of the elite team, which also included Halil, who'd fully recovered, Terek, Ayaan, and Cooper. Jozef occasionally joined them for missions, but now that he was head of the Koba organization, he was forced to stay home more often than not. Shaun made an excellent consolation prize.

Havel and his team were on a mission now, which was what had Jozef up early. This one was personal and he didn't want to sleep through the call, confirming they had their target.

He stood and walked to the bed, careful to keep his tread light. Not that it would matter, Shaun slept like the dead. He was amazed by her ability to close her eyes and simply fall asleep no matter where she was and what was going on around her. Jozef had spent many pleasant hours watching her.

He set his phone on the table beside the bed, next to his gun.

He crawled onto the bed, a predator stalking his prey. He was going to eat her up.

She was twisted sideways on the bed, so he started at her feet, pressing his lips to the delicate arch. He grinned when she curled her toes in reaction but didn't wake up. He grazed his mouth against her ankle, then higher, across her smooth ebony legs, moving higher to her incredibly luscious ass. He lingered there, playing with the round globes, filling his hands as he'd longed to do earlier.

He worshipped her, running his fingers up her spine and across her shoulders. He wrapped his hand around the back of her neck and gently rolled her onto her back so he could start all over with the front of her body.

Her eyelashes fluttered but didn't lift. She tossed an arm over her head and tucked her face into the curve of her elbow.

Jozef took advantage of her sleepy sprawled position by touching, kissing, licking and biting every part of her until she was squirming and starting to wake up.

He paid close attention to her breasts, playing with her

turgid dark nipples before sucking the pert breast into his mouth. He loved that it was small enough to fit, loved the sensation of her wet little nipple against the top of his mouth. He used the edge of his teeth to drive her crazy.

Her eyes popped open as he separated her thighs and settled between her legs. She became fully aware at the first swipe of his tongue against her already engorged clitoris.

"Jozef!" she gasped, her hips surging upward involuntarily.

He gripped her, wrapping his hands around her hips and digging his fingers into her ass cheeks, holding her still for his feasting pleasure. He licked up every bit of cream she provided for him, then set about making more.

She cried out as her orgasm washed over her, her sweet voice telling him it was time to take his prize.

He climbed up her body, interlacing his fingers with hers and dragging her arms over her head. He took her lips in a fierce kiss as he surged inside her, stretching her, filling her. The warm walls of her pussy beckoned him home.

They stayed like that, unmoving as he allowed her to strangle his cock, milking him. They stared at each other, their silent language flowing between them, speaking louder than any words could.

He moved within her, at first slow, taking his time, building them both toward their crescendo, then faster, their hips slamming together, filling the room with their own private music. She came first, as it should be, her scream of pleasure the best thing he'd ever heard.

He followed her over the edge, dropping his head to hers, pressing his forehead against hers, gripping her hands tightly.

When they finished, they lay side by side, their bodies glistening as the bright morning sun crawled across the floor of the hut and onto the bed.

"Come on, I'm hungry."

Shaun began poking him to get his attention. He grabbed

her hands, rolled her onto her back and tickled until she cried out for mercy.

They showered together, signing about what they would do for the day.

They were on one of the islands of the Philippines. Jozef had men on the island with him, protecting their backs while they honeymooned, but they were ordered to keep their distance. So far, he hadn't caught sight of a single one of them, which meant they were earning their keep.

Shaun wanted to go on a catamaran tour of a neighbouring island, then eat at a beach barbecue the locals had told her about.

She'd fit right in once they arrived, absorbing the culture and learning some of the language.

Together they walked up the beach, purchasing some jasmine rice and meat wrapped in banana leaf. They booked their tour and while they waited for the boat, they ate their breakfast.

Later, Jozef relaxed on the beach, sitting in the sand, leaning back against a tree. He watched Shaun, crouched in the sand with a rapt audience of local children surrounding her. She was teaching them sign language while they made castles in the sand.

She adored children, and it looked like the feeling was mutual.

Jozef decided then and there that he would do whatever it took to make her a mother. They could adopt or find a surrogate. But she wouldn't go through her life without knowing the joy of children. She had so much love to give, and Jozef wanted to share that love.

He'd been a child in need once. Perhaps if he'd had a mother who cared, he might not have turned out to be a ruthless killer. Then again, fate liked to have her way. And if this was the life he was meant to have, he wouldn't complain.

His cell phone rang.

He answered, pressing it to his ear.

"We have Leeza and the boy."

Jozef grunted and hung up, his eyes still on Shaun. The final piece of their puzzle was in place. His cousin was coming back home where she belonged.

THE END

Thank you so much for reading Goodnight, Sinners. I've had such an amazing time building the Empire world that I've decided to write a trilogy for Havel and Leeza. Watch for the Gangster's Empire Series next year!

ALSO BY NIKITA SLATER

If you enjoyed this book, check out some other works by #1 International Bestselling Author, Nikita Slater. More titles are always in progress, so check back often to see what's new!

SINNER'S EMPIRE

Book 1 - Sin of Silence

Book 2 - A Silent Reckoning

Book 3 - Goodnight, Sinners - Coming Soon!

THE QUEENS SERIES

Book One – Scarred Queen

Book Two - Queen's Move

Book Three - Born a Queen

Book Four - The Red Queen (Coming 2021)

Alejandro's Prey (a novella)

The Queens 4 Book Box Set

FIRE & VICE SERIES

Book One – Prisoner of Fortune

Book Two – Fight or Flight

Book Three – King's Command

Book Four – Savage Vendetta

Savage Boss (a novella)

Book Five – Fear in Her Eyes

Book Six – Bound by Blood

Book Seven – In His Sights

Book Eight - Burning Beauty

Book Nine - Chasing Ecstasy (Coming soon!)

Fire & Vice 6 Book Box Set

THE DRIVEN HEARTS SERIES

Book One - Driven by Desire

Book Two - Thieving Hearts

Book Three - Capturing Victory

Novella - The Princess and Her Mercenary

Driven Hearts 4 Book Box Set

THE SANCTUARY SERIES

Book One - Sanctuary's Warlord

Book Two - Sanctuary on Fire

Book Three - The Last Sanctuary

Book Four - The Road to Wolfe

Book Five - Skye's Sanctuary (Coming soon!)

The Sanctuary Series 3 Book Box Set

LOVING THE BAD BOY SERIES

Loving Vincent

Loving Jared

Loving Rico (Coming Soon!)

STANDALONE BOOKS

The Assassin's Wife

Because You're Mine

Mine to Keep (a novella)

Luna & Andres

Kiss of the Cartel

Stalked

AFTER DARK

In collaboration with Jasmin Quinn

Collared: A Dark Captive Romance

Safeword: A Dark Romance

Chained: A Mafia Marriage Romance

Good Girl: A Captive BDSM Romance

Hostile Takeover: An Enemies to Lovers Romance

The After Dark Box Set

Visit ***nikitaslater.com*** for more information
and the latest updates!

Nikita Slater is the International Bestselling dark romance author of the Fire & Vice series, Angels & Assassins series, The Queens series and several standalone novels. Her favourite genre is mafia romance, the bloodier the better, though she loves to write about every subject under the sun. She lives on the beautiful Canadian prairies with her son and crazy awesome dog. She has an unholy affinity for books (especially erotic romance), wine, pets and anything chocolate. Despite some of the darker themes in her books (which are pure fun and fantasy), Nikita is a staunch feminist and advocate of equal rights for all races, genders and non-gender specific persons. When she isn't writing, dreaming about writing or talking about writing, she helps others discover a love of reading and writing through literacy and social work.